Charles Rogers, Charles Mackay

The Illustrated Book of Scottish Songs

From the 16th to the 19th Century

Charles Rogers, Charles Mackay

The Illustrated Book of Scottish Songs
From the 16th to the 19th Century

ISBN/EAN: 9783744774154

Printed in Europe, USA, Canada, Australia, Japan

Cover: Foto ©Andreas Hilbeck / pixelio.de

More available books at **www.hansebooks.com**

BOOK OF SCOTTISH SONGS

"Many a banner spread flutters above your head,
  Many a crest that is famous in story;
Mount and make ready, then, sons of the mountain glen—
  Fight for your queen and the old Scottish glory."

SIR WALTER SCOTT.

THE ILLUSTRATED

BOOK OF SCOTTISH SONGS

FROM THE 16TH TO THE 19TH CENTURY

EDITED BY

CHARLES MACKAY, LL.D.

NEW EDITION, CAREFULLY REVISED BY

CHARLES ROGERS, LL.D., F.S.A. Scot.

AUTHOR OF "FAMILIAR ILLUSTRATIONS OF SCOTTISH LIFE,"
EDITOR OF "THE MODERN SCOTTISH MINSTREL,"
ETC., ETC.

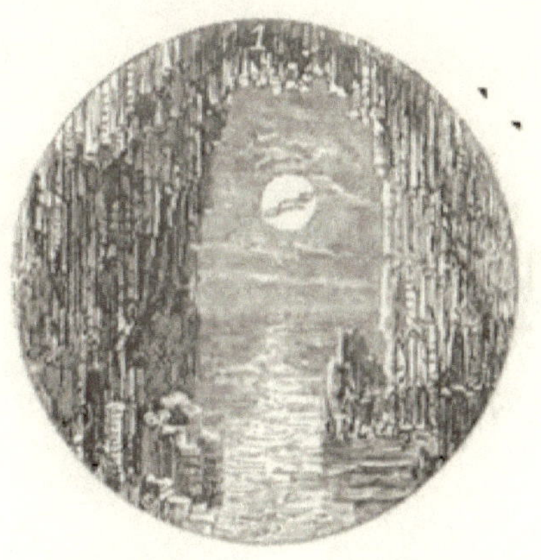

Nature herself, it seemed, would raise
A Minster to her Maker's praise."—SCOTT

LONDON

HOULSTON AND WRIGHT

65, PATERNOSTER ROW

MDCCCLXVII.

LONDON
PRINTED BY J. AND W. RIDER,
BARTHOLOMEW CLOSE.

ADVERTISEMENT TO THE NEW EDITION.

At the request of the Publishers, and in the absence
from this country of my accomplished friend, Dr. Charles
Mackay, I consented to examine this Work, preparatory
to its appearance in a new edition. I have carefully
performed what I undertook, and have made such corrections or additions in the editorial department as to
bring the work down to the present state of information
about Scottish Songs and Song-writers. That portion of
the Notes for which I am individually responsible I have
denoted by my initials.

Among the Song-writers whose names I have attached
to compositions hitherto designated anonymous, I would
especially refer to Sir Robert Aytoun, Caroline, Baroness
Nairn, and Mrs. Agnes Lyon. With the exception of a
few compositions scattered about in the older collections,
the English poems of Sir Robert Aytoun were understood
to have been lost. It was my good fortune to discover
a MS. of the long-lost poems when at a sale of books
in St. Andrews, near the poet's birthplace. The MS.
so discovered I proceeded to edit, along with Aytoun's
already known compositions, and although the performance
was accomplished so early as my seventeenth year, I have
no reason to withdraw from any of the deductions at which
I then arrived.

In editing "The Modern Scottish Minstrel," my friend
Mr. Robert Chambers introduced me to a respected gentle-
woman, the confidential friend of Lady Nairn, through
whom I obtained the use of the MSS. of that singularly

gifted lady, and full particulars of her ladyship's personal history. It was then (1855) I was enabled to make known that Lady Nairn was the writer of the popular version of the "Lass o' Gowrie," and that most of the other anonymous Songs which had become popular in Scotland since the era of Burns had proceeded from her pen.

Mrs. Agnes Lyon, a connection of my own, was wife of the Rev. Dr. James Lyon, minister of Glammis. It had long been reported in the family that she had composed the song, "Neil Gow's Farewell to Whisky," which had usually been attributed to the great violinist himself. The report proved true, and Mrs. Lyon's MSS., including "The Farewell" in her own handwriting, and authenticated as her own composition, were entrusted to my care by her daughter-in-law, to whom they had been specially bequeathed.

I cordially recommend the present Collection of Songs to my fellow-countrymen, and to all lovers of Scottish minstrelsy. The gifted compiler has done his part with his usual discrimination. There are Songs for all classes and for all moods. The swain will find this volume a delightful companion on the hill-side ; while it is admirably adapted for the boudoir and the drawing-room table. There are Songs inciting to virtue and to patriotism—Songs companionable in the hours of sorrow and sadness—and Songs brimful of joyousness for the hopeful and the merry-hearted.

CHARLES ROGERS.

2, Heath Terrace, Lewisham,
October, 1866.

I.—SONGS OF THE AFFECTIONS.

Note.—INDEX OF THE FIRST LINES WILL BE FOUND AT PAGE 317.

Page

II.—MILITARY AND PATRIOTIC SONGS.

III.—MORAL AND SATIRICAL SONGS.

IV.—CONVIVIAL SONGS.

V.—JACOBITE SONGS.

VI.—MISCELLANEOUS SONGS.

INTRODUCTION.

MOST writers upon the subject of Scottish song and music have hitherto drawn a marked distinction between England and Scotland. They have considered the people on the two sides of the Tweed to be quite distinct—each with a music and a literature as well as opinions of its own. While it has been impossible for any writer to deny that England possessed a literature exclusively of English growth, of which it might well be proud, and of the whole benefit of which Scotland has been the partaker, it has been very generally denied that England possessed any music worthy of the name. On the other hand, honours have been heaped upon Scotland, both for her literature and for her music, which, though by no means undeserved, ought to have been shared with England as the mother and source from which they were derived. It is possible that, in attempting to clear up some of the misconceptions which appear to exist upon this subject, we may run counter to the preconceived notions of many persons. But we shall not rob " the land of cakes" of any thing—not of a single melody out of the many hundreds of beautiful compositions that have given Scottish music a reputation as wide as the civilised world; we shall merely endeavour to show that English and Scottish music and song are of the same root and stock, that the birth-place of both was England, and that their separate growth and individuality have by no means effaced the strong family-likeness. All readers and singers will readily admit that the stores of Scottish song are not only extremely fertile, but that the Scottish mind has a tendency to develop its overflowing tenderness and earnest passionateness in lyrical strains of the simplest beauty, which no literature and no age of the world have surpassed. It is also beyond doubt that the Scottish lyra possesses, in addition to all the excellences which it can derive from the fervid and vigorous English language, a quaintness and a grace, an elegant simplicity, and an affectionate tenderness, which are peculiarly its own. But in acknowledging all this, and much more, it is not necessary to admit the claim of those who assert Scottish music to be a thing apart as well as transcendent, and who would deny England any share in its merits, or in the glory of having either originated it or developed it.

Nearly all the beautiful music and delicious snatches of song, commonly considered to be Scottish, belong to that section of Scotland known as the Lowlands, a country in which the people speak one of the many " Doric " dialects of the

Saxon-English language. On the English side of the Tweed these dialects, differing greatly from each other, are usually called broad Scotch, even by the people of Northumberland and Cumberland, who speak a very similar "Doric," and have a music as well as manners and language as much Scotch as English. If a line be drawn from Greenock on the Clyde north-east by Perth to Inverness, it will be found that by far the greater portion of the songs and melodies which are known as Scotch to Scotchmen and to the world, and of which Scotch-men speak and write with the highest pride and enthusiasm, have been produced to the south and east of it. North and west of that line is a country where, until of late years, and even now, the people speak a totally different language, and sing a music of a totally different character. North-west of that line is the land of the Gael—of the semi-barbarous and imperfect instrument the bagpipe, of pibroch tunes, of rude, wild melodies, very little known, and still less admired, and of a species of song which has rarely been considered worth the trouble of translation.

But on the south-east of the line, and all the way to the English Border, where the Saxon tongue prevails, and where the minds of the people have for ages had access to English literature, the land is vocal with sweet sounds. Every river, stream, and lake—every mountain-slope and summit—every pastoral valley—nay, almost every farmhouse, has been cele-brated in a song. The Highlander, who has no right or title to this music or song, is as proud of both as the Lowlander; and not unfrequently claims for his own wild melodies, and for his rude attempts at lyrical poetry in the native language of the Gael, a large portion of the admiration lavished upon com-positions of a totally different origin and character. The Low-landers, while they admit the claim of the Highlanders, take to themselves the little that is good in Celtic music and song, in order that with it they may swell the triumphs of a land that, not being geographically English, is considered to be Scotch. The English public, believing what it has been told, that England has not, and never had any music, join their loud voices to the chorus of acclamation, and make no attempt to claim any portion of the merit which belongs to the Scotch, not because they are Celts, but because, like the English, they are Saxon and Scandinavian.

It was recently remarked by a musical professor, who formed one of the numerous audience at a lecture on the writings and genius of Chaucer, that the allusions to music and singing in that writer were frequent; and that all, or nearly all, of his characters were represented as being able to sing or play. This fact also seems to have struck other persons. In the valuable and interesting introduction to a collection of national English airs, consisting of ancient song, ballad, and dance tunes, edited by Mr. W. Chappell, F.S.A., and published in 1840, we find the following passage:

"It were useless to quote all the numerous and respectful allusions made to the music of his time by Chaucer, 'the most illustrious ornament of the reign of Edward III., and of his successor Richard II.,' or by his friend and contemporary John Gower; a reference to their works *passim* will satisfactorily prove how highly the love of song was held in this country at the time. A few, however, of the more interesting ones will probably prove acceptable to the reader. In Chaucer's description of the Squire, he tells us not only that

> *'Singing* he was or *floyting* (fluting) all the day,'

but

> *'He coudè songès make,* and wel endite,
> Juste and eke dance, and wel pourtraie and write.'

Of his mendicant friar he says:

> ‘ And certainly he hadde a merry note,
> Wel coude *he singe, and plaien on the rote.*’*

Again:

> ‘ In his *harping*, when that he had *songe*,
> His eyen twinkled in his head aright,
> As don the starrès in a frosty night.’

The poor scholar Nicholas, in the ‘Miller’s Tale,’ was an excellent singer and performer on the psaltry; and we learn that the parish clerk in the same tale

> ‘ Could playen songès on a small ribible.’†

In the ‘Pardoner’s Tale’ we have perhaps the first mention of the lute: ‡

> ‘ Whereas with harpès, lutès, and giternes,
> They dance and play,’ &c.

That *organs* were very general in our abbeys and cathedrals is plain from the description of Chaunticlerc, in his ‘ Nonnes Prieste’s tale :’

> ‘ His vois was merrier than the mery *orgon*
> On massè days that in the churches gon.’

In the contention between ‘ The Cuckoo and the Nightingale,’ and ‘The Flower and the Leaf,’ there are many beautiful passages concerning music. In Gower, Lydgate, Spencer, *passim.* The elder poets only are mentioned here, to show how much the art of minstrelsy was beloved at an early period in this land.”

---

* The “ rote” is the “ lyra mendicorum” of Kircher, the “ veille” of the French, and the English hurdygurdy.

† “ Ribible” is, by Mr. Urry, in his glossary to Chaucer, from Speght, a former editor, rendered a fiddle or gittern. It seems that *rebeb* is a Moorish word, signifying an instrument with two strings, played on with a bow. The Moors brought it into Spain, whence it passed into Italy, and obtained the appellation of *ribeca ;* from whence the English *rebec*, which Phillips, and others after him, render a “ fiddle with three strings.”—*Sir J. Hawkins*, vol. ii. p. 86

‡ Vin. Galilei bears testimony that the lute was the invention of the English, and the best instruments of the kind were made by them; also that their music was worthy the excellence of their workmanship.—*Il Fronimo*, Venice, 1583.

It will appear that in the year 1405—at the time when Chaucer's poetry was the delight of the educated classes, and when music was so highly popular in England, that all ranks of society cultivated the art of singing, and when a gentleman's education was considered incomplete if he had not been taught music, and when in many public schools, like that of Winchester, part-singing was a part of the regular and compulsory course of study—a young Scotch boy was brought to England, and there educated in all the accomplishments of the more civilised country. This boy, then aged eleven years, was James Stuart, son of Robert III. King of Scotland. He was on his way to France to be educated, when the vessel in which he sailed was taken by an English squadron, in defiance, it was alleged, of a truce then subsisting between England and Scotland. The young prince was conveyed a prisoner to the Tower of London, where he was held captive for two years. At the end of that time he was consigned to Windsor Castle, where he was educated in a manner befitting his high rank; and where he remained, with more or less of personal freedom, until he attained the age of thirty. He manifested a strong taste for music and poetry, composed many songs, which are either lost, or, if extant, not known to be his, and wrote an English poem of great merit in imitation of the style of Chaucer, then the prevailing favourite. This poem, entitled " The King's Quair," or " The King's Book," celebrates his love for the beautiful Lady Jane, or Joanna Beaufort, an English lady, daughter of the Duke of Somerset, of whose charms he became enamoured, on seeing her from his turret-window, walking among her maidens in the garden of Windsor Castle. The prince afterwards married this lady; and being restored to his own country, ascended the throne under the title of James I. He introduced into Scotland the arts which he had cultivated with such success in England, especially music and poetry. The contemporary historians Fordun and Boece make honourable mention of him. Fordun says "he excelled in music, and not only in the vocal kind, but also in instrumental, which is the perfection of the art; in tabor and choir, in psalter and organ. Nature, apparently having calculated upon his requiring something more than the ordinary qualifications of men, had implanted in him a force and power of divine genius above all human estimation; and this genius showed itself most particularly in music. His touch upon the harp produced a sound so utterly sweet, and so truly delightful to the hearers, that he seemed to be born a second Orpheus, or, as it were, the prince and prelate of all harpers."

Ballenden, Arch-Dean of Murray, in his translation of Boece's History, is equally emphatic: "He was well learnt to fecht with the sword, to just, to tournay, to warsel, to sing and dance; he was an expert mediciner; richt crafty in playing baith of lute and harp, and sindry other instruments of musik; he was expert in gramar, oratory, and poetry, and made so flowand and sententious verses, appeared weel he was ane naturall and borne Poete."

But the most remarkable testimony to his merits, and to the influence which he exercised over the musical taste of his countrymen, is afforded in the *Pensieri Diversi* of Alessandro Tassoni, an Italian writer, who in the twenty-third chapter of his tenth book thus distinguishes the king: "Noi ancora possiamo connumerar tra nostri, Jacopo Rè di Scozia, che non pur cose sacre compose in canto, ma trova da se stesso *una nuova musica, lamentevole e mestà, differente da tutte l'altre.* Nel che poi è stato imitato da Carlo Gesualdo Principe di Venosa, che in questa nostra età ha illustrato anch' egli la musica con nuove mirabili invenzioni."　"We may reckon among us moderns James King of Scotland, who not only composed many pieces of sacred music, *but also of himself invented a new kind of music, plaintive and melancholy, different from all others,* in which he has been imitated by Carlo Gesualdo, Prince of Venosa, who, in our age, has improved music with many new and admirable inventions."

Among the list of song-tunes popular in Scotland at and after the time of James, we find that the names preserved to us show an English origin. In a humorous poem entitled "Cockelby's Sow," of which the earliest copy is a MS. dated in 1568, but from internal and other evidence supposed to have been composed at least a century earlier, occurs the following passage:

> "And his cousin Copyn Cull
> Led the dance and began,
> Play us *Jolly Lemmane.*
> Sum trottit *Tras and Trewass,*
> Sum balterit *The Bass,*
> Sum *Perdolly,* sum *Trolly lolly,*
> Sum *Cok craw thou all day*
> *Twysbank* and *Terway,*
> Sum *Lincolne,* sum *Lindsay,*
> Sum *Joly Lemman, dawis it not day,*
> Sum *Be yon woodsyd singis,*
> Sum *Lait last in evinnynis,*
> Sum *Joly Martene with a mok,*
> Sum *Lulalowe lute cok,*
> Sum movit *Most mak revell,*
> Sum *Symon sonis of Quhynfell,*
> Sum *Maister Peir de cougate,*
> Sum *Ourfate,* sum *Orliance,*
> Sum *Rusty Bully with a Sek.*"

Many of these songs are either lost altogether, or are extant under other names and known to be English. In the "Complaint of Scotland," published in 1549, there is still more remarkable evidence of the English origin and character of the songs then popular in Scotland. The author representing himself as weary with study, "walks out into the wholesome fields, to hear the songs of the shepherds," and gives a list of thirty-seven of these compositions. "Now I will rehearse," says he, "some of the sweet songs that I heard among them." Among others, he mentions, "Pastime with gude company," a song the composition of King Henry VIII.; "Still under the levis grene," and "Coll thou me the rashis grene," two songs acknowledged by later Scottish writers to be English; "King William's note,"—supposed to be the song sung by *Nicholas* in Chaucer's "Miller's Tale :"

> "And after that he sang *the King's note*,
> Full often bless'd was his mery throat."

"Trolly, lolly," of the English origin of which there needs no other proof than the title; "The frog came to the mill-door," better known to English readers at the present time under the title of "The frog he would a wooing go;" "The Percy and the Montgomery met," or the English ballad of "Otterbourne," printed in "Percy's Reliques," and six songs entitled, "Alone I weep in great distress," "Right sorely musing in my mind," "O mine heart, this is my song," "Grievous is my sorrow," "Alas, that seeming sweet face," and "In one mirthful morrow." These songs have been lost; but their music has been fortunately preserved in the work of Andro Hart, printed in Aberdeen about the commencement of the seventeenth century, and called "Ane Compendious Book of Godly and Spiritual Songs, collectit out of sundrie parts of the Scripture, with sundrie of other Ballats, chainged out of Profaine Songs, for the avoiding of Sinne and Harlotrie." In this work the tunes appear under their old titles, as given above, but with the "godly words" of the strange religious parodies which were made upon them. These six tunes, as well as *all* the other melodies in Hart's book, are acknowledged by all investigators to be English, and to have none of the marks by which songs in the Scottish manner are now distinguished.

Thus it would appear that the intercourse between England and Scotland, or the identical origin of the two nations, or the similarity of literary and musical taste and development at this time, were such, that they possessed many songs in common, as they do now. It is clear, moreover, from these and other circumstances already mentioned, that the influence exercised upon Scottish song and music by James I. was strong and lasting. He is recognised as the father of Scottish melody, and popular tradition ascribes to him the composition of many beautiful and well-known airs. Circumstances at a later period tended to develop the musical taste of the people, and to make it somewhat different from that of England, from which it sprung. Constant intercourse with France was probably not without some effect; and the career of James V., himself a composer and song-writer, as well as that of the beautiful, accomplished, and unfortunate Mary, tended to improve the musical taste of the country. Mary's two secretaries, Chatelar, a Frenchman, and Rizzio, an Italian, were both admitted to her favour and intimacy in consequence of their musical skill; and both, it is to be presumed, encouraged a love of music among the frequenters of the court, and influenced in a greater or less degree the musical taste of the people. To Chatelar are ascribed many tender melodies now considered Scottish, which are obviously of French parentage; and to Rizzio Scotland is probably indebted for more music than will ever be discovered to have come from Italy. Be this as it may, music flourished in this little-known and but half-civilised portion of the empire when it began to decay elsewhere; and not even the Reformation, which in England had the effect of consigning to oblivion or to popular hatred many ancient songs and tunes, could damp in Scotland the musical ardour of the people. Many Roman Catholic chants became the property of the secular Muse; and such airs as "John, come kiss me now," "Auld lang syne," "John Anderson my Jo," and "We're a' noddin," which belonged to the cathedral service of both countries, were appropriated to profane purposes and indecent parodies, and sung sometimes in ridicule of that Church from which they had been taken, and sometimes to words of the most objectionable character.

Scottish music was, however, but little known to the world until Allan Ramsay, in the year 1724, collected the songs of his country. His "Tea-Table Miscellany," however, gave no account of the sources from which he derived his materials, and fully one-half of the four volumes to which the work extended consisted of English songs, including the whole series of the "Beggar's Opera," then recently published and in the height of its popularity. But Allan Ramsay, though the most valuable of the early labourers in the field, was not the first. Towards the middle of the seventeenth century Scottish music began to be spoken of in England, and from that period to the reign of Queen Ann became so fashionable as to be imitated by English musicians. English song-writers, of the class of D'Urfey and others, also began to imitate the Scottish manner, and produced some very barbarous songs, as distasteful to Scotchmen as they were incomprehensible to Englishmen. But in Scotland itself at this time the current music was purely traditional and popular; and the first music-book printed north of the Tweed, the book of Andro Hart, of which we have already made mention, contained no Scottish melodies whatsoever, but tunes that were notoriously and avowedly English.

Nevertheless, the national music continued to flourish in

Scotland; and if not to decline in England, to be banished
almost entirely from the higher circles of the nobility and the
Court.   Scotland was peculiarly fortunate in this respect.   It
never became the fashion to deny the existence of her national
melodies, whether of her own or of English growth; and zealous
collectors appeared from time to time to preserve both her
songs and her music.   Allan Ramsay, who not only preserved
the ancient lyrics of his country, and improved them by many
masterly touches of his own, but enriched its literature by
many beautiful original compositions, which he adapted to the
old tunes, was followed, after a short interval, by David
Herd, an investigator of great industry, judgment, and taste.
To him Scotland owes the preservation of many admirable old
songs and ballads, abounding either with its characteristic tenderness, or with its no less characteristic humour.   Johnson's
" Musical Museum,"* the first number of which appeared in
1787, was an effort both to preserve and to improve the songs
and music of Scotland—an effort in which the publisher and
editor was admirably assisted by Robert Burns, a writer then
but little known, but whose fame is now as wide as the two
hemispheres, and penetrates as far as the influence of the English language and the pastures or farm-steadings of our colonies.
Burns wrote some songs for this work, and brought from
obscurity, by the easy light of his genius, a still greater
number, that in their old shape were either too uncouth or
too indecent for introduction into refined and moral company.
A greater than Johnson shortly afterwards appeared in the
person of the late George Thomson of Edinburgh.   Mr. Thomson availed himself of the same renowned and happy pen;

* The imprint of this volume states it to have been sold by " James Johnson,
Engraver, Bell's Wynd, Edinburgh;" and that it was sold " by T. Kay and Co., 332
Strand; and by Longman and Brodripp, 26 Cheapside, London." No. 332 Strand is
the present office of the *Morning Chronicle*.

and with this assistance, did more than any previous collector had done to give Scottish music the world-wide celebrity and favour which it now enjoys.

Burns created no new taste among his countrymen. He but developed, extended, and improved that which he found already existing; and hence his immediate and long-continued popularity. The Muse of Scotland is a pastoral fair one,—a beautiful bare-footed lassie, "with her loose robes" and "her yellow hair" floating in the wind; with blue eyes full of passion, romance, and tenderness; with a quaint, yet pleasing and highly melodious expression on her tongue; with a heart as prone to be fanatical in religion as romantic in affection; and above all, with a luxurious sense of physical enjoyment, and with a keen appreciation and taste for the humorous.

The beauty of Scottish song is its truth and simplicity. Burns, as well as his great forerunners, compeers, and successors, always appealed to the heart. Unlike the song-writers of England, whom, with few exceptions, they immeasurably excel, they never wasted their time in mere conceits and prettinesses. What they felt they said, and what they said they expressed in the pithy language of real emotion, not the less effective because expressed in a provincial dialect. Their tenderness is as manly as their independence; and their wit, if sometimes coarse, is always genial and genuine. Their pictures of rural life are full of charm and of a vivid reality. The landscape, with all its colours and sounds, exists in their lays.

It may be doubted whether the song-writers of any other people ever depicted youthful passion in all its varieties of joy and sorrow with more heart-felt fervour and irresistible fascination. These bards, many of them nameless, make no pretence to be refined; yet amidst their rudest snatches we often light upon the happiest thoughts, expressed in the happiest manner, and with refinement that no poets in any age have excelled. The stream of their song is a true Pactolus. There may be small flowers and weeds upon its banks; but it runs over golden sands, and abounds in treasures that may be had for the seeking, even when the current appears most turbid and least promising.

We may sum up its characteristics in one word,—earnestness. Scottish song is earnest in love and friendship, earnest in war, earnest in patriotism, and earnest even in drinking. Though the moralist might wish that, in the latter respect, the Scottish bards were not quite so emphatic, we must take the defects with the virtues, and be thankful that we have a literature with so few faults and so many beauties, and, above all, with so much heart in it, as they have given to us.

In a collection limited to one volume it is manifestly impossible that we could have included more than "the cream"— perhaps we might say, "the cream of the cream"—of such vast stores of songs as have been accumulating for the last three centuries. We think, however, that it will be found, even by those readers the best acquainted with the subject, that this volume contains all, or nearly all, the most celebrated, beautiful, and characteristic of the Scottish songs, whether pastoral, amatory, patriotic, convivial, or Jacobite ; and that the selections under each of these heads are as copious as is consistent with the design. We have been reluctantly compelled to omit the songs of living writers, not from any unwillingness on the part of the most distinguished among them to allow their compositions to appear in these pages, but from the utter impossibility of conveying in the small space to which we have restricted ourselves any thing like an adequate view of a department of modern literature so extensive and so varied. The name of these writers is indeed " legion ;" for the popular ear is so susceptible to the sweet sounds of the national melodies, and the dialect of Scotland lends itself so naturally and so easily to song, that the feelings of the illiterate, as well as of the educated, seem to flow more copiously into lyrical expression than is the case in other countries. Not only the scholar

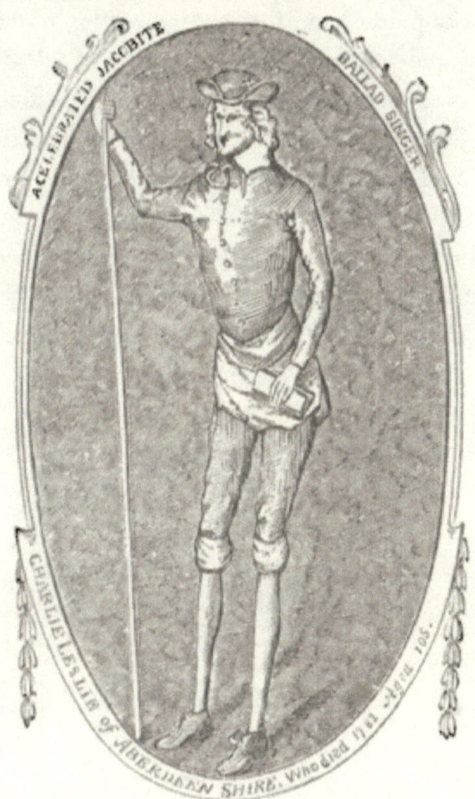

in his study, and the professed rhymers and authors, but the tradesman behind his counter, the weaver at the mill, the ploughman in the field, and the fisherman in his boat, have written or composed songs; and even the tramps and vagrants have been known in our days, as well as in those of Allan Ramsay and Robert Burns, to have been the authors of no contemptible emendations and new readings of the old ballads, as well as of original snatches of poetry adapted to the old tunes. The cities of Edinburgh and of Glasgow alone have produced within the last dozen years as many good Scottish songs as would fill three or four such volumes as that we now offer to the public, and the greater portion of which have been collected and published under the title of " Whistle Binkie." A few of the compositions of the late Alexander Rodger and Donald Carrick, the most distinguished contributors to that volume, will be found in our pages,—which, by the kind permission of the publisher, might have included many more, had not the limited space at our command imperatively forced us to exclude the multitude of living writers that would have had as much title to appear as any one whom we might have selected. "For," to use the words of Burns,

> " the great genius of the land
> Has many a light aerial band,
> Who all beneath his high command
>   Harmoniously,
> As arts or arms they understand,
>   Their labours ply.
>
> Some hint the lover's harmless wile,
> Some grace the maiden's artless smile,
> Some soothe the labourer's weary toil
>   For humble gains,
> And make his cottage scenes beguile
>   His care and pains."

O LUSTY MAY.

This song was first printed in the year 1508 by Chapman and Myllar, the
"fathers of Scottish typography."

O LUSTY May, with Flora queen,
Whose balmy drops from Phœbus sheene
  Prelucent beam before the day;
By thee Diana groweth green,
  Through gladness of this lusty May.

Then Aurora that is so bright,
To woful hearts she casts great light
  Right pleasantly before the day,
And show and sheds forth of that light,
  Through gladness of this lusty May.

Birds on their boughs of every sort
Send forth their notes, and make great mirth
  On banks that bloom and every brae,
And fare and flee ower every firth,
  Through gladness of this lusty May.

And lovers all that are in care,
To their ladies they do repair
 In fresh mornings before the day,
And are in mirth aye mair and mair,
 Through gladness of this lusty May.

Of every moneth in the year
To mirthful May there is no peer,
 Her glittering garments are so gay:
You lovers all, make merry cheer,
 Through gladness of this lusty May.

———◆———

I'LL NEVER LOVE THEE MORE.

Marquis of Montrose, born 1612, died May 21, 1650

My dear and only love, I pray
 That little world of thee
Be govern'd by no other sway
 But purest monarchy;
For if confusion have a part,
 Which virtuous souls abhor,
I'll call a synod in my heart,
 And never love thee more.

As Alexander I will reign,
 And I will reign alone;
My thoughts did evermore disdain
 A rival on my throne.
He either fears his fate too much,
 Or his deserts are small,
Who dares not put it to the touch
 To gain or lose it all.

But I will reign and govern still,
 And always give the law,
And have each subject at my will,
 And all to stand in awe:
But 'gainst my batteries if I find
 Thou storm or vex me sore,
As if thou set me as a blind,
 I'll never love thee more.

And in the empire of thy heart,
　Where I should solely be,
If others do pretend a part,
　Or dare to share with me;
Or committees if thou erect,
　Or go on such a score,
I'll smiling mock at thy neglect,
　And never love thee more.

But if no faithless action stain
　Thy love and constant word,
I'll make thee famous by my pen,
　And glorious by my sword;
I'll serve thee in such noble ways
　As ne'er was known before;
I'll deck and crown thy head with bays,
　And love thee evermore.

WERE NA MY HEART LICHT, I WAD DEE.

LADY GRIZZEL BAILLIE, born 1665, died 1746. From the "Orpheus
Caledonius," 1725.

THERE was anes a maid, and she loo'd na men:
She biggit her bonnie bower doun i' yon glen;
But now she cries dool and well-a-day!
Come doun the green gate, and come here away.

When bonnie young Jamie cam' ower the sea,
He said he saw naething sae lovely as me;
He hecht me baith rings an' mony braw things;
And were na my heart licht, I wad dee.

He had a wee titty that lo'ed na me,
Because I was twice as bonny as she;
She raised such a pother 'twixt him and his mother,
That were na my heart licht, I wad dee.

The day it was set and the bridal to be;
The wife took a dwam and lay doun to dee;
She main'd and she grain'd out o' dolour and pain,
Till he vow'd he never wad see me again.

His kin was for ane of a high degree,
Said, What had he to do wi' the like o' me?
Albeit I was bonnie, I was na for Johnnie;
And were na my heart licht, I wad dee.

They said I had neither cow nor calf,
Nor dribbles o' drink rins through the draff,
Nor pickles o' meal rins through the mill-ee;
And were na my heart licht, I wad dee.

His titty she was baith wylie an' slee,
She spied me as I cam ower the lea;
An' then she ran in an' made a loud din;
Believe your ain ee, an' ye trow na me.

His bonnet stood aye fou round on his brow,
His auld ane look'd aye as well as some's new;
But now he lets't wear ony gate it will hing,
And casts himself dowie upon the corn-bing.

And now he gaes daundrin' about the dykes,
And a' he dow do is to hund the tykes;
The live-lang nicht he ne'er steeks his ee;
And were na my heart licht, I wad dee.

Were I young for thee, as I hae been,
We should ha' been gallopin' down on yon green,
And linkin' it on yon lily-white lea;
And wow; gin I were but young for thee!

SHE ROSE AND LET ME IN.

FRANCIS SEMPLE.   From Watson's Collection, 1706.

THE night her silent sable wore,
    And gloomy were the skies;
Of glittering stars appear'd no more
    Than those in Nelly's eyes.
When to her father's door I came,
    Where I had often been,
I begg'd my fair and lovely dame
    To rise and let me in.

But she with accents all divine
    Did my fond suit reprove;
And while she chid my rash design,
    She but inflamed my love.
Her beauty oft had pleased before,
    While her bright eyes did roll;
But virtue had the very power
    To charm my very soul.

Then who would cruelly deceive,
    Or from such beauty part?
I loved her so, I could not leave
    The charmer of my heart.
My eager fondness I obey'd,
    Resolved she should be mine,
Till Hymen to my arms convey'd
    My treasure so divine.

Now, happy in my Nelly's love,
    Transporting is my joy;
No greater blessing can I prove,
    So blest a man am I:
For beauty may a while retain
    The conquer'd fluttering heart;
But virtue only is the chain
    Holds never to depart.

OLD LONG SYNE.

The following song was composed by Sir Robert Aytoun, Secretary to the Queens of James VI. and Charles I. He is supposed to have rendered it in its present form from an older version. Sir Robert Aytoun was born in 1570, and died in March, 1638. He was buried in Westminster Abbey, where a handsome monument has been erected to his memory. See "The Poems" of Sir Robert Aytoun, edited by Charles Rogers, from a MS. in his possession. Edinburgh, 1844, 8vo.—C. R.

PART FIRST.

SHOULD old acquaintance be forgot,
  And never thought upon,
The flames of love extinguish'd,
  And freely past and gone?
Is thy kind heart now grown so cold
  In that loving breast of thine,
That thou canst never once reflect
  On old long syne?

Where are thy protestations,
  Thy vows and oaths, my dear,
Thou mad'st to me and I to thee
  In register yet clear?
Is faith and truth so violate
  To th' immortal gods divine,
That thou canst never once reflect
  On old long syne?

Is't Cupid's fears, or frosty cares,
  That makes thy spirits decay?
Or is't some object of more worth
  That's stolen thy heart away?
Or some desert makes thee neglect
  Him so much once was thine,
That thou canst never once reflect
  On old long syne?

Is't worldly cares so desperate
  That makes thee to despair?
Is't that makes thee exasperate,
  And makes thee to forbear?
If thou of that were free as I,
  Thou surely should be mine;
If this were true, we should renew
  Kind old long syne.

But since that nothing can prevail,
  And all hope is in vain,
From these dejected eyes of mine
  Still showers of tears shall rain;
And though thou hast me now forgot,
  Yet I'll continue thine,
And ne'er forget for to reflect
  On old long syne.

If e'er I have a house, my dear,
  That truly is call'd mine,
And can afford but country cheer,
  Or aught that's good therein;
Though thou wert rebel to the king,
  And beat with wind and rain,
Assure thyself of welcome, love,
  For old long syne.

PART SECOND.

My soul is ravish'd with delight
  When you I think upon;
All griefs and sorrows take their flight,
  And hastily are gone;
The fair resemblance of your face
  So fills this breast of mine,
No fate nor force can it displace
  For old long syne.

Since thoughts of you do banish grief,
  When I'm from you removed,
And if in them I find relief
  When with sad cares I'm moved,
How doth your presence me affect
  With ecstasies divine,
Especially when I reflect
  On old long syne.

Since thou hast robb'd me of my heart,
  By those resistless powers
Which Madam Nature doth impart
  To those fair eyes of yours,

With honour it doth not consist
  To hold a slave in pyne ;
Pray let your rigour, then, desist,
  For old long syne.

'Tis not my freedom I do crave,
  By deprecating pains ;
Sure, liberty he would not have
  Who glories in his chains ;
But this I wish—the gods would move
  That noble soul of thine
To pity, if thou canst not love,
  For old long syne.

Allan Ramsay also wrote a song under this title. It appeared as follows in the
"Tea-Table Miscellany."

Should auld acquaintance be forgot,
  Though they return with scars?
These are the noble hero's lot,
  Obtain'd in glorious wars.
Welcome, my Varo, to my breast,
  Thy arms about me twine,
And make me once again as blest
  As I was lang syne.

Methinks around us on each bough
  A thousand Cupids play ;
Whilst through the groves I walk with you
  Each object makes me gay.
Since your return the sun and moon
  With brighter beams do shine ;
Streams murmur soft notes while they run
  As they did lang syne.

------◆------

SPEAK ON, SPEAK THUS.

ALLAN RAMSAY, born Oct. 15, 1686, died Jan 7, 1758. From the "Gentle Shepherd."
Air—"Wae's my heart that we should sunder."

SPEAK on, speak thus, and still my grief ;
  Hold up a heart that's sinkin' under
These fears that soon will want relief
  When Pate must from his Peggy sunder.

A gentler face and silk attire,
    A lady rich in beauty's blossom,
Alake, poor me will now conspire
    To steal thee from thy Peggy's bosom.

No more the shepherd who excell'd
    The rest, whose wit made them to wonder,
Shall now his Peggy's praises tell ;—
    Oh, I can die, but never sunder !
Ye meadows where we often stray'd,
    Ye banks where we were wont to wander,
Sweet-scented rocks round which we play'd.
    You'll lose your sweets when we're asunder.

Again, ah, shall I never creep
    Around the knowe, with silent duty,
Kindly to watch thee while asleep,
    And wonder at thy manly beauty ?
Hear, heaven, while solemnly I vow,
    Though thou shouldst prove a wand'ring lover,
Through life to thee I shall prove true,
    Nor be a wife to any other.

I'LL NEVER LEAVE THEE.

ALLAN RAMSAY. From the "Tea-Table Miscellany."

JOHNNY.

THOUGH for seven years and mair honour should reave me
To fields were cannons rair, thou needsna grieve thee ;
For deep in my spirit thy sweets are indented,
And love shall preserve aye what love has imprented.
Leave thee, leave thee ! I'll never leave thee,
Gang the warld as it will, dearest, believe me.

NELLY.

O Johnny, I'm jealous, whene'er ye discover
My sentiments yielding, ye'll turn a loose rover ;
An' nought in the world would vex my heart sairer,
If you prove inconstant, and fancy ane fairer.
Grieve me, grieve me, oh, it wad grieve me,
A' the long night and day, if you deceive me !

JOHNNY.

My Nelly, let never sic fancies oppress ye;
For while my blood's warm I'll kindly caress ye:
Your saft blooming beauties first kindled love's fire,
Your virtue and wit mak' it aye flame the higher.
Leave thee, leave thee! I'll never leave thee,
Gang the warld as it will, dearest, believe me,

NELLY.

Then, Johnny, I frankly this minute allow ye
To think me your mistress, for love gars me trow ye;
And gin ye prove false, to yoursel' be it said then,
Ye win but sma' honour to wrang a puir maiden.
Reave me, reave me, oh, it would reave me
Of my rest night and day, if you deceive me!

JOHNNY.

Bid ice-shogles hammer red gauds on the studdy,
And fair summer mornings nae mair appear ruddy;
Bid Briton's think ae gate, and when they obey thee,
But never till that time, believe I'll betray thee.
Leave thee, leave thee! I'll never leave thee;
The starns shall gae withershins ere I deceive thee.

----♦----

LOCHABER NO MORE.

ALLAN RAMSAY.

FAREWELL to Lochaber, farewell to my Jean,
Where heartsome wi' her I ha'e mony a day been;
To Lochaber no more, to Lochaber no more,
We'll maybe return to Lochaber no more!
These tears that I shed, they're a' for my dear,
And no for the dangers attending on weir;
Though borne on rough seas to a far bloody shore,
Maybe to return to Lochaber no more!

Though hurricanes rise, though rise every wind,
No tempest can equal the storm in my mind;
Though loudest of thunders on louder waves roar,
That's naething like leavin' my love on the shore.

To leave thee behind me my heart is sair pain'd ;
But by ease that's inglorious no fame can be gain'd ;
And beauty and love 's the reward of the brave,
And I maun deserve it before I can crave.

Then glory, my Jeanie, maun plead my excuse ;
Since honour commands me, how can I refuse ?
Without it, I ne'er can have merit for thee ;
And losing thy favour, I'd better not be.
I gae then, my lass, to win honour and fame ;
And if I should chance to come glorious hame,
I'll bring a heart to thee with love running o'er,
And then I'll leave thee and Lochaber no more.

The exquisite melody to which this song is sung has rendered it a general favourite.
Its effect upon the mind of Highlanders in a foreign land, or in emigration, is sometimes painful, and has been known to melt the roughest and rudest of men to tears.
The song itself, as a literary composition, is of little or no merit. It first appeared
in the " Tea-Table Miscellany," 1724. The air was originally entitled " King James's
march to Ireland."

BESSIE BELL AND MARY GRAY.

ALLAN RAMSAY.

O Bessie Bell and Mary Gray,
  They were twa bonnie lasses ;
They biggit a bower on yon burn-brae,
  And theekit it ower wi' rashes.

Bessie Bell I lo'ed yestreen,
   And thocht I ne'er could alter;
But Mary Gray's twa pawky een
   Gar'd a' my fancy falter.

Bessie's hair's like a lint-tap,
   She smiles like a May mornin',
When Phœbus starts from Thetis' lap,
   The hills with rays adornin'.
White is her neck, saft is her hand,
   Her waist and feet fu' genty;
With ilka grace she can command,—
   Her lips, oh, now, they're denty!

Mary's locks are like the craw,
   Her een like diamonds' glances;
She's aye sae clean, redd up, and braw,
   She kills whene'er she dances.
Blythe as a kid, wi' wit at will,
   She blooming, tight, and tall is,
And guides her airs sae gracefu' still,—
   O Jove! she's like thy Pallas.

Young Bessie Bell and Mary Gray,
   Ye unco sair oppress us;
Our fancies jee between ye twa,
   Ye are sic bonnie lasses.
Wae's me! for baith I canna get,
   To ane by law we're stentit;
Then I'll draw cuts, and tak my fate,
   And be wi' ane contentit.

The heroines of this well-known ballad were the daughters of two Perthshire gentlemen. Bessy Bell was the daughter of the Laird of Kinnaird and Mary Gray of the Laird of Lynedoch. A romantic attachment subsisted between them, and they retired together to a secluded spot called the "Burn Braes," in the neighbourhood of Lynedoch, to avoid the plague that then raged in Perth, Dundee, and other towns. They caught the infection, however, and both died. Tradition asserts that a young gentleman, in love with one of them, visited them in their solitude, and that it was from him they caught the contagion. The late gallant Lord Lynedoch, on whose estate the heroines lie buried, erected a kind of bower over their graves. The following is the original ballad on which Allan Ramsay's is founded. The melody to which it is sung was introduced by Gay into the "Beggars' Opera," to the words commencing:

"A curse attends that woman's love
Who always would be pleasing."

O Bessie Bell and Mary Gray,
  They were twa bonnie lasses;
They biggit a bower on yon burn-brae,
  And theekit it ower wi' rashes.
They theekit it ower wi' rashes green,
  They theekit it ower wi' heather;
But the pest came frae the burrow town,
  And slew them baith thegither.

They thought to lie in Methven kirkyard
  Amang their noble kin;
But they maun lie in Stronach Haugh
  To beek forenent the sun.
And Bessie Bell and Mary Gray,
  They were twa bonnie lasses;
They biggit a bower on yon burn-brae,
  And theekit it ower wi' rashes.

THE LAST TIME I CAM' O'ER THE MUIR.

ALLAN RAMSAY.

THE last time I cam' ower the muir,
  I left my love behind me:
Ye powers, what pains do I endure
  When soft ideas mind me!
Soon as the ruddy morn display'd
  The beaming day ensuing,
I met betimes my lovely maid
  In fit retreats for wooing.

We stray'd beside yon wand'ring stream,
  And talk'd with hearts o'erflowing,
Until the sun's last setting beam
  Was in the ocean glowing.
I pitied all beneath the skies,
  Even kings, when she was nigh me;
In raptures I beheld her eyes,
  Which could but ill deny me.

Should I be call'd where cannons roar,
   Where mortal steel may wound me,
Or cast upon some foreign shore,
   Where dangers may surround me;
Yet hopes again to see my love,
   To feast on glowing kisses,
Shall make my cares at distance move,
   In prospect of such blisses.

In all my soul there's not one place
   To let a rival enter;
Since she excels in ev'ry grace,
   In her my love shall centre.
Sooner the seas shall cease to flow,
   Their waves the Alps shall cover,
On Greenland ice shall roses grow,
   Before I cease to love her.

The neist time I gang ower the muir,
   She shall a lover find me;
And that my faith is firm and pure,
   Though I left her behind me;
Then Hymen's sacred bonds shall chain
   My heart to her fair bosom;
There, while my being does remain,
   My love more fresh shall blossom.

"The first lines of this song, and several others in it, are beautiful; but in my opinion—pardon me, revered shade of Ramsay!—the song is unworthy of the divine air."—BURNS.

PEGGIE AND PATIE.

ALLAN RAMSAY.

PEGGY.

WHEN first my dear laddie gae'd to the green hill,
And I at ewe-milking first sey'd my young skill,
To bear the milk-bowie nae pain was to me,
When I at the bughting forgather'd with thee.

PATIE.

When corn-riggs waved yellow, and blue heather-bells
Bloom'd brightly on moorland and sweet rising fells;
Nae burns, briar, or bracken, gave trouble to me,
If I found but the berries right ripen'd for thee.

PEGGY.

When thou ran, or wrestled, or putted the stane,
And cam aff the victor, my heart was aye fain;
Thy ilka sport manly gave pleasure to me,
For nane can put, wrestle, or run swift as thee.

PATIE.

Our Jenny sings saftly the " Cowden-Broom-Knowes,"
And Rosie lilts sweetly the " Milking the Ewes;"
There's few " Jenny Nettles" like Nancy can sing;
With " Through the wood, laddie," Bess gars our lugs ring

But when my dear Peggy sings, with better skill,
The " Boatman," " Tweedsdale," or the " Lass o' the Mill,"
'Tis many times sweeter and pleasing to me;
For though they sing nicely, they cannot like thee."

PEGGY.

How easy can lasses trow what they desire,
With praises sae kindly increasing love's fire!
Give me still this pleasure, my study shall be
To make myself better and sweeter for thee.

THE YELLOW-HAIR'D LADDIE.

ALLAN RAMSAY.

In April, when primroses paint the sweet plain,
And summer approaching rejoiceth the swain,
The yellow-hair'd laddie would oftentimes go
To woods and deep glens where the hawthorn-trees grow.

There under the shade of an old sacred thorn
With freedom he sung his loves ev'ning and morn:
He sung with so soft and enchanting a sound,
That silvans and fairies, unseen, danced around.

The shepherd thus sung: "Though young Maddie be fair,
Her beauty is dash'd by a scornfu' proud air;
But Susie was handsome, and sweetly could sing,—
Her breath's like the breezes perfumed i' the spring.

That Maddie, in all the gay bloom of her youth,
Like the moon, was inconstant, and never spoke truth;
But Susie was faithful, good-humoured and free,
And fair as the goddess that sprung from the sea.

That mamma's fine daughter, with all her great dower,
Was awkwardly airy, and frequently sour."
Then sighing, he wish'd, would but parents agree,
The witty sweet Susie his mistress might be.

Allan Ramsay founded this song upon a much older composition—of itself not devoid of merit, and free from the *concetti* of its more modern namesake. It was inserted in his "Tea-Table Miscellany," and is here appended.

The yellow-hair'd laddie sat down on yon brae,
Crying, "Milk the ewes, lassie; let nane o' them gae."
And aye as she milkit she merrily sang,
The yellow-hair'd laddie shall be my gudeman.

The weather is cauld and my cleadin' is thin,
The yowes are new-clipt and they winna bught in;
They winna bught in, although I should dee,
O yellow-hair'd laddie, be kind unto me!

The gudewife cries butt the house, "Jennie, come ben;
The cheese is to mak and the butter's to kirn."
Though butter and cheese and a' should gang sour,
I'll crack and I'll kiss with my love a half-hour.
It's ae lang half-hour, and we'll e'en mak it three,
For the yellow hair'd laddie my gudeman shall be.

DUNT, DUNT, DUNT, PITTIE, PATTIE.

Air—"The yellow-hair'd laddie." From the "Tea-Table Miscellany."

On Whitsunday morning
I went to the fair;
My yellow-hair'd laddie
Was selling his ware;
He gied a blythe blink
O' his bonny black ee,
And a dear blink and a fair blink
It was unto me.

I wist not what ail'd me
  When my laddie cam' in
The little wee sternies
  Flew aye frae my een;
And the sweat it dropp'd down
  From my very ee-bree;
For my heart aye ylay'd
  Dunt, dunt, dunt, pittie, pattie.

I wist not what ail'd me
  When I went to my bed;
I toss'd and I tumbled,
  And sleep frae me fled.
Now it's sleeping and waking
  He's aye in my ee;
And my heart aye plays
  Dunt, dunt, dunt, pittie, pattie.

MARY SCOTT, THE FLOWER OF YARROW.

ALLAN RAMSAY. From the "Tea-Table Miscellany."

HAPPY's the love which meets return,
When in soft flames souls equal burn;
But words are wanting to discover
The torments of a hopeless lover.
Ye registers of heaven, relate,
If looking o'er the rolls of fate,
Did you there see me mark'd to marrow
Mary Scott, the flower of Yarrow?

Ah, no! her form's too heavenly fair,
Her love the gods above must share;
While mortals with despair explore her,
And at a distance due adore her.
O lovely maid! my doubts beguile,
Revive and bless me with a smile;
Alas! if not you'll soon debar a
Sighing swain the banks of Yarrow.

Be hush'd ye fears; I'll not despair;
My Mary's tender as she's fair;
Then I'll go tell her all my anguish;
She is too good to let me languish:
With success crowned, I'll not envy
The folks who dwell above the sky;
When Mary Scott becomes my marrow,
We'll make a paradise on Yarrow.

The heroine of this song is supposed to have been Mary, daughter of Philip Scott of Dryhope, in Selkirkshire. She was married to Scott of Harden, the notorious border-reiver, or freebooter. A different and possibly an earlier version of this song has been discovered by Mr. Peter Buchan. We copy it from a manuscript volume of the Songs of the North of Scotland collected by that gentleman.

Oh, Mary's red, and Mary's white,
And Mary she's the king's delight;
The king's delight and the prince's marrow,
Mary Scott, the flower of Yarrow.

When I look east, my heart grows sair;
But when I look west, it's mair and mair;
And when I look to the banks of Yarrow,
There I mind my winsome marrow.

Now she's gone to Edinburgh town,
To buy braw ribbons to tie her gown;
She's bought them broad, and laid them narrow,—
Mary Scott is the flower of Yarrow.

BONNIE CHIRSTY.

ALLAN RAMSAY. From the "Tea-Table Miscellany."

" How sweetly smells the simmer green,
      Sweet taste the peach and cherry;
Painting and order please our een,
      And claret makes us merry!
But finest colours, fruits and flowers,
      And wine, though I be thirsty,
Lose a' their charms and weaker powers,
      Compar'd wi' those of Chirsty.

When wand'ring o'er the flow'ry park,
      No natural beauty wanting;
How lightsome is't to hear the lark,
      And birds in concert chanting!

But if my Chirsty tunes her voice,
   I'm rapt in admiration;
My thoughts wi' ecstasies rejoice,
   And drap the haill creation.

Whene'er she smiles a kindly glance,
   I take the happy omen,
And aften mint to make advance,
   Hoping she'll prove a woman.
But, dubious of my ain desert,
   My sentiments I smother;
Wi' secret sighs I vex my heart,
   For fear she love another."

Thus sang blate Edie by a burn,
   His Chirsty did o'erhear him;
She doughtna let her lover mourn,
   But, ere he wist, drew near him.
She spak' her favour wi' a look,
   Which left nae room to doubt her:
He wisely this white minute took,
   And flang his arms about her.

" My Chirsty! witness, bonny stream,
   Sic joys frae tears arising;
I wish this may na be a dream,—
   Oh, love the maist surprising!"
Time was too precious now for tauk,
   This point of a' his wishes;
He wadna wi' set speeches bauk,
   But wair'd it a' on kisses.

The heroine of this song was Miss Christina Dundas, daughter of Sir James Dundas of Arniston, and wife of Sir Charles Erskine of Alva, Lord Justice Clerk of Scotland in 1763. The song is the first in the "Tea-Table Miscellany," from which it has been conjectured that it was an especial favourite of its author.

THE LASS O' PATIE'S MILL.

ALLAN RAMSAY.

THE lass o' Patie's mill,
   Sae bonnie, blythe, and gay,
In spite of a' my skill
   She stole my heart away.
When teddin out the hay
   Bare-headed on the green,
Love 'mid her locks did play,
   And wanton'd in her een.

Without the help of art,
   Like flowers that grace the wild,
She did her sweets impart
   Whene'er she spake or smiled:
Her looks they were so mild,
   Free from affected pride,
She me to love beguiled;
   I wish'd her for my bride.

Oh, had I a' the wealth
   Hopetoun's high mountains fill,
Insured lang life and health,
   And pleasure at my will;

I'd promise and fulfil
That nane but bonnie she,
The lass o' Patie's Mill,
Should share the same wi' me.

Patie's or Patrick's Mill is supposed to have been on the south bank of the Irwine, near Newmills, in Ayrshire.

"'The Lass o' Patie's Mill,'" says Burns, " is one of Ramsay's best songs.   In Sir J. Sinclair's statistical volumes are two claims, one, I think, from Aberdeenshire, and the other from Ayrshire, for the honour of this song.   The following anecdote, which I had from the present Sir William Cunningham of Robertland, who had it of the late John Earl of Loudon, I can, on such authorities, believe : Allan Ramsay was residing at Loudon Castle with the then earl, father to Earl John ; and one afternoon, riding or walking out together, his lordship and Allan pa 'd a sweet romantic spot on Irwine water, still called 'Patie's Mill,' where a bonr. lassie was 'tedding hay bare-headed on the green.' My lord observed to Allan that it would be a fine theme for a song. Ramsay took the hint, and lingering behind he composed the first sketch of it, which he produced at dinner."

THE WAUKIN' O' THE FAULD.

ALLAN RAMSAY.

My Peggy is a young thing
Just enter'd in her teens,
Fair as the day, and sweet as May,
Fair as the day, and always gay :
My Peggy is a young thing,
And I'm nae very auld,
And weel I like to meet her at
The waukin' o' the fauld.

My Peggy speaks sae sweetly
Whene'er we meet alane ;
I wish nae mair to lay my care,
I wish na mair o' a' that's rare :
My Peggy speaks sae sweetly—
To a' the lave I'm cauld ;
But she gars a' my spirits glow
At waukin' o' the fauld.

My Peggy smiles sae kindly
Whene'er I whisper love,
That I look doun on a' the toun,
That I look doun upon a croun :

My Peggy smiles sae kindly,
  It maks me blyth and bauld;
And naething gies me sic delight
  At waukin' o' the fauld.

My Peggy sings sae saftly
  When on my pipe I play;
By a' the rest it is confest,
By a' the rest, that she sings best:
  My Peggy sings sae saftly,
    And in her sangs are tauld
  With innocence the wale o' sense,
    At waukin' o' the fauld.

This song, which is sung to a beautiful and characteristic melody, describes a custom of the olden time. The "watching of the fold" was a duty that devolved upon the shepherds, to prevent the lambs when weaned from getting back to their dams. Upon these occasions the shepherd was allowed, by the universal custom of the pastoral districts, to have the girl of his choice to bear him company.

------◆------

THE COLLIER'S BONNIE LASSIE.

ALLAN RAMSAY.

THE collier has a daughter,
  And, oh, she's wondrous bonnie;
A laird he was that sought her,
  Rich baith in lands and money.
The tutors watch'd the motion
  Of this young honest lover;
But love is like the ocean,
  Wha can its depths discover?

He had the art to please ye,
  And was by a' respected;
His airs sat round him easy,
  Genteel but unaffected.
The collier's bonnie lassie,
  Fair as the new-blown lilie,
Aye sweet and never saucy,
  Secured the heart o' Willie.

He loved beyond expression
  The charms that were about her,
And panted for possession—
  His life was dull without her.
After mature resolving,
  Close to his breast he held her;
In saftest flames dissolving,
  He tenderly thus tell'd her:

"My bonnie collier's daughter,
  Let naething discompose ye;
It's no your scanty tocher
  Shall ever gar me lose ye;
For I have gear in plenty,
  And love says it's my duty
To ware what heaven has lent me
  Upon your wit and beauty."

This song was founded by Ramsay upon an older one with the same title, of which the following is a specimen:

The collier has a daughter,
  And, oh, she's wondrous bonnie;
A laird he was that sought her,
  Rich baith in lands and money.
She wadna hae a laird,
  Nor wad she be a lady;
But she would hae a collier,
  The colour o' her daddie.

OWER BOGIE.

ALLAN RAMSAY.

I will awa' wi' my love,
  I will awa' wi' her,
Though a' my kin had sworn and said,
  I'll ower Bogie wi' her.
If I can get but her consent,
  I dinna care a strae;
Though ilka ane be discontent,
  Awa' wi' her I'll gae.

For now she's mistress o' my heart,
  And worthy o' my hand;
And weel I wat we shanna part
  For siller or for land.
Let rakes delight to swear and drink,
  And beaux admire fine lace;
But my chief pleasure is to blink
  On Betty's bonnie face.

There a' the beauties do combine
  Of colour, treats, and air;
The saul that sparkles in her een
  Makes her a jewel rare.
Her flowin' wit gives shining life
  To a' her other charms;
How blest I'll be when she's my wife,
  And lock'd up in my arms!

There blythely will I rant and sing,
  While o'er her sweets I'll range;
I'll cry, Your humble servant, king,
  Shame fa' them that wad change!
A kiss of Betty and a smile,
  A'beit ye wad lay down
The right ye hae to Britain's isle,
  And offer me your crown.

To go "ower Bogie" is a phrase that expresses in Aberdeenshire the same idea as that of running to Gretna Green does in England. It is also used to express a marriage performed by a magistrate instead of a clergyman. The first four lines of this song were borrowed by Ramsay from an older song unworthy of preservation. Mr. Peter Buchan has collected, upon the same subject, the following fragments of song:

Bonnie lassie, come my road,
  And gangna through the Boggie o';
Bonnie lassie, come my road,
  Yours is wondrous scroggy o'.
The Boggie water's wide an' deep,
Gin ye gang in, ye'll wet your feet;
Sae, bonnie lassie, come my road,
  And gangna through the Boggie 'o.

Your road and my road
  Lie na baith thegither o';
I'll gang up the water-side,
  And ye'll gang down the river 'o.

> Bonnie lassie, come my road,
>   And gangna through the Boggie o';
> Bonnie lassie, come my road,
>   To gangna through the Boggie o'.

The second fragment is as follows :

> As I came by Strathboggie's yetts,
>   Strathboggie's trees were green,
> There I heard the drums to beat,
>   I'll ower Boggie wi' him ;
> I'll ower Boggie wi' my love,
>   I'll ower Boggie wi' him :
> He says he's crossing Gawdie side ;
>   I'll awa' wi' him.

THIS IS NO MINE AIN HOUSE.

ALLAN RAMSAY.   Air—"This is no my ain house."

THIS is no mine ain house,
  I ken by the rigging o't ;
Since with my love I've changed vows,
  I dinna like the bigging o't.
For now that I'm young Robbie's bride,
And mistress of his fire-side,
Mine ain house I'll like to guide,
  And please me with the rigging o't.

Then fareweel to my father's house,
  I gang whare love invites me ;
The strictest duty this allows,
  When love with honour meets me.
When Hymen moulds us into ane,
My Robbie's nearer than my kin ;
And to refuse him were a sin,
  Sae lang's he kindly treats me.

When I'm in my ain house,
  True love shall be at hand aye,
To make me still a prudent spouse,
  And let my man command aye ;
Avoiding ilka cause of strife,
The common pest of married life,
That makes ane wearied of his wife,
  And breaks the kindly band aye.

"I consider the melody 'This is no my ain house,' perhaps better known as 'This is no my ain lassie,' to be one of the most beautiful that Scotland has produced. It has always had for me an inexpressible charm."—H. R. BISHOP.

THE HIGHLAND LADDIE.

ALLAN RAMSAY.   From the "Tea-Table Miscellany."

THE Lawland lads think they are fine,
  But, oh, they're vain and idly gaudy;
How much unlike the gracefu' mien
  And manly looks of my Highland laddie!
    O my bonnie Highland laddie,
    My handsome, charming Highland laddie;
    May Heaven still guard, and love reward,
    The Lawland lass and her Highland laddie!

If I were free at will to choose
  To be the wealthiest Lawland lady,
I'd tak' young Donald without trews,
  Wi' bonnet blue and belted plaidie.
    O my bonnie, &c.

The brawest beau in burrows town,
  In a' his airs wi' art made ready,
Compared to him he's but a clown,
  He's finer far in's tartan plaidie.
    O my bonnie, &c.

O'er benty hill wi' him I'll run,
  And leave my Lawland kin and daddie;
Frae winter's cauld and summer's sun
  He'll screen me wi' his Highland plaidie.
    O my bonnie, &c.

A painted room and silken bed
  May please a Lawland laird and lady;
But I can kiss and be as glad
  Behind a bush in's Highland plaidie.
    O my bonnie, &c.

Few compliments between us pass;
  I ca' him my dear Highland laddie,
And he ca's me his Lawland lass,
  Syne rows me in beneath his plaidie.
    O my bonnie, &c.

Nae greater joy I'll e'er pretend
  Than that his love prove true and steady,
Like mine to him, which ne'er shall end
  While Heaven preserves my Highland laddie.
    O my bonnie, &c.

OWER THE MUIR TO MAGGY.

ALLAN RAMSAY. From the "Tea-Table Miscellany."

I'LL ower the muir to Maggy;
  Her wit and sweetness call me,
There to my fair I'll show my mind,
  Whatever may befall me.
If she love mirth, I'll learn to sing;
  Or likes the Nine to follow,
I'll lay my lugs in Pindus' spring,
  And invocate Apollo.

If she admire a martial mind,
  I'll sheath my limbs in armour;
If to the softer dance inclined,
  With gayest airs I'll charm her;
If she love grandeur, day and night
  I'll plot my nation's glory,
Find favour in my prince's sight,
  And shine in future story.

Beauty can wonders work with ease,
  Where wit is corresponding,
And bravest men know best to please
  With complaisance abounding.
My bonny Maggy's love can turn
  Me to what shape she pleases,
If in her breast the flame shall burn
  Which in my bosom bleezes.

AN' THOU WERE MY AIN THING.

An' thou were my ain thing,
  I would lo'e thee, I would lo'e thee;
An' thou were my ain thing,
  How dearly would I lo'e thee!

I would clasp thee in my arms,
I'd secure thee from all harms;
For above mortal thou hast charms:
  How dearly do I lo'e thee!
    An' thou were, &c.

Of race divine thou needs must be,
Since nothing earthly equals thee,
So I must still presumptuous be,
  To show how much I lo'e thee.
    An' thou were, &c.

The gods one thing peculiar have,
To ruin none whom they can save;
Oh, for their sake support a slave
  Who only lives to lo'e thee.
    An' thou were, &c.

To merit I no claim can make,
But that I lo'e; and for your sake
What man can more I'll undertake.
  So dearly do I lo'e thee.
    An' thou were, &c.

My passion, constant as the sun,
Flames stronger still, will ne'er have done
Till fates my thread of life have spun,
  Which breathing out I'll lo'e thee.
    An' thou were, &c.

Like bees that suck the morning dew
Frae flowers of sweetest scent and hue,
Sae wad I dwell upo' thy mou',
  And gar the gods envy me.
    An' thou were, &c.

Sae lang's I had the use of light,
I'd on thy beauties feast my sight,
Syne in saft whispers through the night
  I'd tell how much I loo'd thee.
    An' thou were, &c.

How fair and ruddy is my Jean,
She moves a goddess o'er the green!
Were I a king, thou should be queen,
  Nane but mysel' aboon thee.
    An' thou were, &c.

I'd grasp thee to this breast of mine,
Whilst thou, like ivy or the vine,
Around my stronger limbs should twine,
  Form'd hardy to defend thee.
    An' thou were, &c.

Time's on the wing, and will not stay;
In shining youth let's make our hay,
Since love admits of nae delay,
  Oh, let nae scorn undo thee.
    An' thou were, &c.

While love does at his altar stand,
Ha'e there's my heart, gi'e me thy hand,
And with ilk smile thou shalt command
  The will of him wha loves thee.
    An' thou were, &c.

This song appears in Allan Ramsay's "Tea-Table Miscellany," with the signature X., indicating that he did not know who the author was. The air is very beautiful, and is traced to as early a period as 1627, but is supposed to be much older. The last six stanzas were written by Allan Ramsay, and appended to the original song.

BARBARA ALLAN.

ANONYMOUS. From the "Tea-Table Miscellany."

IT was in and about the Martinmas time,
  When the green leaves were a-fallin',
That Sir John Graham, in the west countrie,
  Fell in love wi' Barbara Allan.

He sent his man down through the town
   To the place where she was dwallin'.
Oh, haste and come to my master dear,
   Gin ye be Barbara Allan.

Oh, hooly, hooly, rase she up
   To the place where he was lyin',
And when she drew the curtain by,
   Young man, I think ye're dyin'.

It's oh I'm sick, I'm very very sick,
   And it's a' for Barbara Allan.
Oh, the better for me ye'se never be,
   Though your heart's blude were a-spillin'.

Oh, dinna ye mind, young man, she said,
   When ye was in the tavern a-drinkin',
That ye made the healths gae round and round,
   And slichtit Barbara Allan?

He turn'd his face unto the wa',
   And death was with him dealin':
Adieu, adieu, my dear friends a',
   And be kind to Barbara Allan.

And slowly, slowly rose she up,
   And slowly, slowly left him,
And sighin' said, she could not stay,
   Since death of life had reft him.

She hadna gane a mile but twa,
   When she heard the deid-bell ringin',
And every jow that the deid-bell gied,
   It cried, Woe to Barbara Allan.

Oh, mother, mother, mak' my bed,
   And mak' it saft and narrow;
Since my love died for me to-day,
   I'll die for him to-morrow.

A version of this celebrated old song has been inserted in Percy's "Reliques of
Ancient English Poetry;" but it seems to be generally acknowledged that the Scottish is the original, upon which the English has been founded, without being improved. The author of the song is unknown. The world is indebted to Allan Ramsay
for its preservation.

CROMLET'S LILT.

ANONYMOUS. From the "Tea-Table Miscellany." 1724.

SINCE all thy vows, false maid,
  Are blown to air,
And my poor heart betray'd
  To sad despair;
Into some wilderness
My grief I will express,
And thy hard-heartedness,
  O cruel fair!

Have I not graven our loves
  On every tree
In yonder spreading grove,
  Though false thou be?
Was not a solemn oath
Plighted betwixt us both,
Thou thy faith, I my troth,
  Constant to be?

Some gloomy place I'll find,
  Some doleful shade,
Where neither sun nor wind
  E'er entrance had.
Into that hollow cave
There will I sigh and rave,
Because thou dost behave
  So faithlessly.

Wild fruit shall be my meat,
  I'll drink the spring;
Cold earth shall be my seat;
  For covering
I'll have the starry sky
My head to canopy,
Until my soul on high
  Shall spread its wing.

I'll have no funeral fire,
    No tears nor sighs;
No grave do I require,
    Nor obsequies;
The courteous redbreast, he
    With leaves will cover me,
And sing my elegy
    With doleful voice.

And when a ghost I am,
    I'll visit thee,
O thou deceitful dame,
    Whose cruelty
Has kill'd the kindest heart
That e'er felt Cupid's dart,
And never can desert
    From loving thee!

Burns, in his notes to "Johnson's Museum," says: "The following interesting account of this plaintive dirge was communicated to Mr. Riddel by Alexander Fraser Tytler, Esq., of Woodhouselee: 'In the latter end of the sixteenth century the Chisholms were proprietors of the estate of Cromleck (now possessed by the Drummonds). The eldest son of that family was very much attached to a daughter of Stirling of Ardoch, commonly known by the name of fair Helen of Ardoch. At that time the opportunities of meeting betwixt the sexes were more rare, consequently more sought after than now; and the Scottish ladies, far from priding themselves on extensive literature, were thought sufficiently book-learned if they could make out the Scriptures in their mother-tongue. Writing was entirely out of the line of female education: at that period the most of our young men of family sought a fortune, or found a grave, in France. Cromleck, when he went abroad to the war, was obliged to leave the management of his correspondence with his mistress to a lay brother of the monastery of Dumblain, in the immediate neighbourhood of Cromleck, and near Ardoch. This man, unfortunately, was deeply sensible of Helen's charms. He artfully prepossessed her with stories to the disadvantage of Cromleck, and by the misinterpreting or keeping up the letters and messages intrusted to his care, he entirely irritated both. All connexion was broken off betwixt them: Helen was inconsolable; and Cromleck has left behind him, in the ballad called 'Cromlet's Lilt,' a proof of the elegance of his genius, as well as the steadiness of his love. When the artful monk thought time had sufficiently softened Helen's sorrow, he proposed himself as a lover: Helen was obdurate; but at last, overcome by the persuasions of her brother, with whom she lived, and who, having a family of thirty-one children, was probably very well pleased to get her off his hands, she submitted rather than consented to the ceremony. But there her compliance ended; and, when forcibly put into bed, she started quite frantic from it, screaming out, that, after three gentle taps on the wainscot, at the bed-head, she heard Cromleck's voice, crying, 'Helen, Helen, mind me!' Cromleck soon after coming home, the treachery of the confidant was discovered, her marriage disannulled, and Helen became Lady Cromleck."

This song is usually sung to the fine old melody claimed by the Irish and the Scotch, and known to the one as "Aileen Aroon," and to the other as "Robin Adair."

THROUGH THE WOOD, LADDIE.

From the "Tea-Table Miscellany," 1724.
Air—"Through the wood."

O Sandy, why leav'st thou thy Nelly to mourn?
Thy presence could ease me;
When naething could please me;
Now dowie I sigh on the bank o' the burn
Or through the wood, laddie, until thou return.

Though woods now are bonnie, and mornings are clear,
While lav'rocks are singing,
And primroses springing;
Yet nane o' them pleases my eye or my ear,
When through the wood, laddie, ye dinna appear.

That I am forsaken, some spare na to tell;
I'm fash'd wi' their scornin',
Baith e'enin' an' mornin';
Their jeering gaes aft to my heart wi' a knell,
When through the wood, laddie, I wander mysel.

Then stay, my dear Sandy, nae langer away;
But quick as an arrow
Haste, haste to thy marrow,
Wha's living in languor till that happy day,
When through the wood, laddie, thegither we'll gae!

OH, WALY, WALY UP THE BANK.

Anonymous. From the "Tea-Table Miscellany," 1724.

Oh, waly, waly up the bank,
And waly, waly down the brae,
And waly, waly yon burn-side,
Where I and my love wont to gae!
I lean'd my back unto an aik,
And thoucht it was a trusty tree;
But first it bow'd, and syne it brak:
Sae my true-love did lichtlie me.

D

Oh, waly, waly, but love be bonnie
    A little time while it is new ;
But when it's auld it waxes cauld,
    And fades away like the morning dew.
Oh, wherefore should I busk my heid,
    Or wherefore should I kame my hair ?
For my true-love has me forsook,
    And says he'll never love me mair.

Now Arthur's Seat shall be my bed,
    The sheets shall ne'er be press'd by me,
St. Anton's Well shall be my drink,
    Since my true-love has forsaken me.
Martinmas wind, when wilt thou blaw,
    And shake the green leaves aff the tree ?
O gentle death, when wilt thou come ?
    For of my life I am wearie.

'Tis not the frost that freezes fell,
    Nor blawing snaw's inclemencie ;
'Tis not sic cauld that makes me cry ;
    But my love's heart grown cauld to me.
When we came in by Glasgow toun,
    We were a comely sicht to see ;
My love was clad in the black velvet,
    And I mysel' in cramasie.

But had I wist before I kiss'd
    That love had been sae ill to win,
I'd lock'd my heart in a case of gowd,
    And pinn'd it wi' a siller pin.
And it's oh ! if my young babe were born,
    And set upon the nurse's knee,
And I mysel' were dead and gone,
    And the green grass growin' ower me !

Nothing is known with certainty as to the authorship of this exquisite song—one of the most affecting of the many that Scotland can boast. It has been supposed to refer to an incident in the life of the Lady Barbara Erskine, wife of the second Marquis of Douglas ; but the allusions are evidently to the deeper woes of one not a wife —who "loved not wisely, but too well."

WILL YE GAE TO THE EWE-BUGHTS, MARION?

From the "Tea-Table Miscellany," 1724.

WILL ye gae to the ewe-bughts, Marion,
  And wear-in the sheep wi' me?
The sun shines sweet, my Marion,
  But nae half sae sweet as thee.

Oh, Marion's a bonnie lass,
  And the blythe blink's in her ee;
And fain wad I marry Marion,
  Gin Marion wad marry me.

There's gowd in your garters, Marion,
  And silk on your white hause-bane;
Fu' fain wad I kiss my Marion
  At e'en when I come hame.

There's braw lads in Earnslaw, Marion,
  Wha gape and glower wi' their ee,
At kirk when they see my Marion;
  But nane o' them lo'es like me.

I've nine milk-ewes, my Marion,
  A cow and a brawny quey;
I'll gi'e them a' to my Marion
  Just on her bridal-day.

And ye'se get a green sey apron,
  And waistcoat o' London broun;
And wow but ye'se be vap'rin'
  Whene'er ye gang to the toun.

I'm young and stout, my Marion;
  Nane dances like me on the green;
And gin ye forsake me, Marion,
  I'll e'en gae draw up wi' Jean.

Sae put on your pearlins, Marion,
  And kirtle o' cramasie;
And as sune as the sun's down, Marion,
  I will come west and see ye.

This song is signed by Allan Ramsay with a Q., signifying that it was an old
song with additions and amendments by himself. The air is old and very beautiful.
" Your remarks on the ' Ewe-Bughts' are just," says Burns in a letter to Thomson;

"still it has obtained a place among our more classical Scottish songs; and what with many beauties in its composition, and more prejudices in its favour, you will not find it easy to supplant it."

MAXWELTON BANKS.

MAXWELTON banks are bonnie,
  Where early fa's the dew;
Where me and Annie Laurie
  Made up the promise true;
Made up the promise true,
  And never forget will I;
And for bonnie Annie Laurie
  I'll lay me doun and die.

She's backit like the peacock,
  She breistit like the swan,
She's jimp about the middle,
  Her waist ye weel micht span;
Her waist ye weel micht span,
  And she has a rolling eye;
And for bonnie Annie Laurie
  I'll lay me doun and die.

"These two verses," as we are informed by Mr. Robert Chambers, "were written by a Mr. Douglas of Fingland, upon Anne, one of the four daughters of Sir Robert Laurie, first baronet of Maxwelton, by his second wife, who was a daughter of Riddell of Minto. As Sir Robert was created a baronet in the year 1685, it is probable that the verses were composed about the end of the seventeenth or the beginning of the eighteenth century. It is painful to record, that, notwithstanding the ardent and chivalrous affection displayed by Mr. Douglas in his poem, he did not obtain the heroine for a wife: she was married to Mr. Ferguson of Craigdarroch."

The first four lines of the second stanza are taken from the old and indecent ballad of "John Anderson my Jo." "John Anderson," as it was sung before it was rendered presentable by Robert Burns, appeared in a very scarce volume of English songs, with the music, entitled "The Convivial Songster," published in 1782.

ANNIE LAURIE.

MAXWELTON braes are bonnie,
  Where early fa's the dew;
And it's there that Annie Laurie
  Gied me her promise true;

Gied me her promise true,
    Which ne'er forgot will be;
And for bonnie Annie Laurie
    I'd lay me doun and dee.

Her brow is like the snaw-drift,
    Her neck is like the swan,
Her face it is the fairest
    That e'er the sun shone on;
That e'er the sun shone on,
    And dark blue is her ee;
And for bonnie Annie Laurie
    I'd lay me doun and dee.

Like dew on the gowan lying,
    Is the fa' o' her fairy feet;
And like winds in summer sighing,
    Her voice is low and sweet;
Her voice is low and sweet,
    And she's a' the world to me;
And for bonnie Annie Laurie
    I'd lay me doun and dee.

This song, which is a modern version of the preceding, was the favourite of the
British soldiers in their weary encampment before Sebastopol in 1854—5.

THE BUSH ABOON TRAQUAIR.

ROBERT CRAWFORD. From the "Tea-Table Miscellany." 1724. Traquair is on the
bank of the water or river of Quair, in Peebleshire.

HEAR me, ye nymphs and ev'ry swain,
    I'll tell how Peggy grieves me;
Though thus I languish and complain,
    Alas! she ne'er believes me.
My vows and sighs, like silent air,
    Unheeded, never move her;
The bonnie bush aboon Traquair,
    'Twas there I first did love her.

That day she smiled, and made me glad,
    No maid seem'd ever kinder;
I thought myself the luckiest lad,
    So sweetly there to find her.

I tried to soothe my amorous flame
  In words that I thought tender :
If more there pass'd, I'm not to blame ;
  I meant not to offend her.

Yet now she scornful flies the plain,
  The fields we then frequented ;
If e'er we meet, she shows disdain,
  She looks as ne'er acquainted.
The bonnie bush bloom'd fair in May,
  Its sweets I'll aye remember ;
But now her frowns make it decay,
  It fades as in December.

Ye rural pow'rs, who hear my strains,
  Why thus should Peggy grieve me ?
Oh, make her partner in my pains,
  Then let her smiles relieve me.
If not, my love will turn despair,
  My passion no more tender ;
I'll leave the bush aboon Traquair,
  To lonely wilds I'll wander.

DOUN THE BURN, DAVIE.

ROBERT CRAWFORD.

WHEN trees did bud and fields were green,
  And broom bloom'd fair to see ;
When Mary was complete fifteen,
  And love laugh'd in her ee,
Blythe Davie's blinks her heart did move
  To speak her mind thus free :
Gang doun the burn, Davie love,
  An' I will follow thee.

Now Davie did each lad surpass
  That dwelt on this burnside ;
And Mary was the bonniest lass,
  Just meet to be a bride :
Her cheeks were rosie, red and white ;
  Her een were bonnie blue ;
Her looks were like the morning bright,
  Her lips like dropping dew.

As doun the burn they took their way
  An' through the flowery dale,
His cheek to hers he aft did lay,
  An' love was aye the tale.
With, " Mary, when shall we return,
  Sic pleasures to renew ?"
Quoth Mary, " Love, I like the burn,
  An' aye will follow you."

This song first appeared in Ramsay's "Tea-Table Miscellany." The last stanza was added by Burns, who was informed by the tradition of his neighbourhood, that the air was the composition of one David Maigh, keeper of the bloodhounds to the Laird of Riddell in Roxburghshire.

ONE DAY I HEARD MARY SAY.

ROBERT CRAWFORD.   From the " Tea-Table Miscellany."

ONE day I heard Mary say, How shall I leave thee ?
Stay, dearest Adonis, stay ; why wilt thou grieve me?
Alas ! my fond heart would break, if thou should leave me ;
I'll live and die for thy sake, yet never leave thee !

Say, lovely Adonis, say, has Mary deceived thee ?
Did e'er her young heart betray, love, that has grieved thee ?
My constant mind ne'er shall stray ; thou may believe me :
I'll love thee, lad, night and day, and never leave thee !

Adonis, my charming youth, what can relieve thee ?
Can Mary thy anguish soothe ? this breast shall receive thee.
My passion can ne'er decay, never deceive thee ;
Delight shall drive pain away, pleasure revive thee.

But leave thee, leave thee, lad, how shall I leave thee ?
Oh ! that thought makes me sad : I'll never leave thee !
Where would my Adonis fly ? Why does he grieve me ?
Alas ! my poor heart will die, if I should leave thee.

" 'One day I heard Mary say' is a fine song," says Burns to Thomson ; " but for consistency's sake, alter the name of Adonis. Were there ever such banns published as a purpose of marriage between *Adonis* and Mary ?"

MY DEARIE, IF THOU DEE.

ROBERT CRAWFORD.   From the " Tea-Table Miscellany," 1724.

LOVE never more shall give me pain,
  My fancy's fixed on thee;
Nor ever maid my heart shall gain,
  My Peggie, if thou dee.
Thy beauties did such pleasure give,
  Thy love's so true to me;
Without thee I shall never live,
  My dearie, if thou dee.

If fate shall tear thee from my breast,
  How shall I lonely stray!
In dreary dreams the night I'll waste,
  In sighs the silent day.
I ne'er can so much virtue find,
  Nor such perfection see:
Then I'll renounce all womankind,
  My Peggie, after thee.

No new-blown beauty fires my heart
  With Cupid's raving rage;
But thine, which can such sweets impart,
  Must all the world engage.
'Twas this that, like the morning sun,
  Gave joy and life to me;
And when its destined day is done,
  With Peggy let me dee.

Ye powers that smile on virtuous love,
  And in such pleasures share;
Ye who its faithful flames approve,
  With pity view the fair;
Restore my Peggie's wonted charms,
  Those charms so dear to me;
Oh, never rob them from those arms—
  I'm lost if Peggy dee.

The beautiful air to which this song is sung has been traced back in MS. to
the year 1692; but is probably much older.

JOHN HAY'S BONNIE LASSIE.

From the "Tea-Table Miscellany."

By smooth-winding Tay a swain was reclining,
Aft cried he, Oh, hey! maun I still live pining
Mysel' thus away, and daurna discover
To my bonny Hay that I am her lover!

Nae mair it will hide, the flame waxes stranger;
If she's not my bride, my days are nae langer;
Then I'll take a heart, and try at a venture,—
Maybe, ere we part, my vows may content her.

She's fresh as the spring, and sweet as Aurora,
When birds mount and sing, bidding day a good morrow;
The sward of the mead enamell'd with daisies
Looks wither'd and dead when twined of her graces.

But if she appears where verdure invites her,
The fountains run clear, and the flowers smell the sweeter;
'Tis heaven to be by when her wit is a-flowing;
Her smiles and bright eyes set my spirits a-glowing.

The mair that I gaze, the deeper I'm wounded,
Struck dumb with amaze, my mind is confounded;
I'm all in a fire, dear maid, to caress ye;
For a' my desire is John Hay's bonnie lassie.

Mr. Chambers states that there is a tradition in Roxburghshire that this song was written by a carpenter or joiner in honour of a daughter of John Hay, first Marquis of Tweeddale.

--------◆--------

JOHN HAY'S BONNIE MARY.

From Peter Buchan's manuscript collection of ancient and traditional Scottish songs.

As I gaed down an' farther down,
  An' down into a cellar,
There I saw the bonniest lass
  Was writing a letter.
She was writing an' inditing,
  And losing her colour,
But ilka kiss of her mou'
  Cost me a dollar.

Cost me a dollar,
    An' a glass o' canary ;
An, oh, for a kiss
    Of John Hay's bonnie Mary !
John Hay, hoch, hey,
    John Hay's bonnie Mary ;
What wad I gie
    For John Hay's bonnie Mary !

Her father was handsome,
    Her mother was tall ;
But as for their daughter,
    She's the flower o' them all.
She's handsome and sprightly,
    Genteel but not saucy ;
I wad gang the warld
    Wi' John Hay's bonnie lassie.

------♦------

THY FATAL SHAFTS.

Tobias Smollett, the novelist, born 1721, died 1774.

Thy fatal shafts unerring move,
I bow before thine altar, Love !
I feel thy soft resistless flame
Glide swift through all my vital frame.

For while I gaze my bosom glows,
My blood in tides impetuous flows ;
Hope, fear, and joy alternate roll,
And floods of transport 'whelm my soul.

My falt'ring tongue attempts in vain
In soothing murmurs to complain ;
My tongue some secret magic ties,
My murmurs sink in broken sighs.

Condemn'd to nurse eternal care,
And ever drop the silent tear ;
Unheard I mourn, unknown I sigh,
Unfriended live, unpitied die !

ABSENCE.

Dr. Thomas Blacklock, "the blind poet," born 1721, died 1791.

Ye rivers so limpid and clear,
  Who reflect, as in cadence you flow,
All the beauties that vary the year,
  All the flow'rs on your margins that grow;
How blest on your banks could I dwell,
  Were Marg'ret the pleasure to share,
And teach your sweet echoes to tell
  With what fondness I doat on the fair!

Ye harvests, that wave in the breeze
  As far as the view can extend;
Ye mountains, umbrageous with trees,
  Whose tops so majestic ascend;
Your landscape what joy to survey,
  Were Marg'ret with me to admire;
Then the harvest would glitter how gay,
  How majestic the mountains aspire!

In pensive regret whilst I rove,
  The fragrance of flow'rs to inhale;
Or catch, as it swells from the grove,
  The music that floats on the gale:
Alas, the delusion how vain!
  Nor odours nor harmony please
A heart agonising with pain,
  Which tries every posture for ease.

If anxious to flatter my woes,
  Or the languor of absence to cheer,
Her breath I would catch in the rose,
  Or her voice in the nightingale hear;
To cheat my despair of its prey,
  What object her charms can assume!
How harsh is the nightingale's lay!
  How insipid the rose's perfume!

Ye zephyrs that visit my fair,
  Ye sunbeams around her that play,
Does her sympathy dwell on my care?
  Does she number the hours of my stay?
First perish ambition and wealth,
  First perish all else that is dear,
Ere one sigh should escape her by stealth,
  Ere my absence should cost her one tear.

When, when shall her beauties once more
  This desolate bosom surprise?
Ye fates, the blest moments restore
  When I bask'd in the beams of her eyes;
When with sweet emulation of heart,
  Our kindness we struggled to show;
But the more that we strove to impart,
  We felt it more ardently glow.

BENEATH A GREEN SHADE.

Dr. Thomas Blacklock.

Beneath a green shade a lovely young swain
Ae evening reclined to discover his pain ;
So sad yet so sweetly he warbled his woe,
The winds ceased to breathe, and the fountain to flow ;
Rude winds wi' compassion could hear him complain,
Yet Chloe, less gentle, was deaf to his strain.

How happy, he cried, my moments once flew,
Ere Chloe's bright charms first flash'd in my view !
Those eyes then wi' pleasure the dawn could survey,
Nor smiled the fair morning mair cheerful than they.
Now scenes of distress please only my sight ;
I'm tortured in pleasure, and languish in light.

Through changes in vain relief I pursue,
All, all but conspire my griefs to renew ;
From sunshine to zephyrs and shades we repair—
To sunshine we fly from too piercing an air ;
But love's ardent fire burns always the same,
No winter can cool it, no summer inflame.

But see the pale moon, all clouded, retires ;
The breezes grow cool, not Strephon's desires ;
I fly from the dangers of tempest and wind,
Yet nourish the madness that preys on my mind.
Ah, wretch ! how can life be worthy thy care ?
To lengthen its moments but lengthens despair.

MY SHEEP I NEGLECTED.

Sir Gilbert Elliot of Minto, born 1722, died 1777, first Earl of Minto.
Printed in Yair's "Charmer," 1749, and in Herd's Collection.
Air—"My apron, dearie."

My sheep I neglected—I lost my sheep-hook,
And all the gay haunts of my youth I forsook ;
No more for Amynta fresh garlands I wove ;
For ambition, I said, would soon cure me of love.

Oh, what had my youth with ambition to do?
Why left I Amynta? why broke I my vow?
Oh, give me my sheep, and my sheep-hook restore,
And I'll wander from love and Amynta no more.

Through regions remote in vain do I rove,
And bid the wide ocean secure me from love:
Oh, fool, to imagine that aught could subdue
A love so well founded, a passion so true!
          Oh, what, &c.

Alas! 'tis too late at thy fate to repine;
Poor shepherd, Amynta can never be thine:
Thy tears are all fruitless, thy wishes are vain;
The moments neglected return not again.
          Oh, what, &c.

———◆———

AH, THE POOR SHEPHERD'S MOURNFUL FATE!

WILLIAM HAMILTON of Bangour.   From the " Tea-Table Miscellany," 1724.

Ah, the poor shepherd's mournful fate,
    When doom'd to love and doom'd to languish,
To bear the scornful fair one's hate,
    Nor dare disclose his anguish!
Yet eager looks and dying sighs
    My secret soul discover,
While rapture trembling through mine eyes
    Reveals how much I love her.
The tender glance, the reddening cheek
    O'erspread with rising blushes,
A thousand various ways they speak,
    A thousand various wishes.

For, oh, that form so heavenly fair,
  Those languid eyes so sweetly smiling;
That artless blush and modest air,
  So fatally beguiling;
Thy every look and every grace,
  So charm whene'er I view thee,—
Till death o'ertake me in the chase,
  Still will my hopes pursue thee.
Then, when my tedious hours are past,
  Be this last blessing given,
Low at thy feet to breathe my last,
  And die in sight of heaven.

MY MOTHER BIDS ME BIND MY HAIR.

Mrs. John Hunter, wife of the celebrated surgeon, born 1742, died 1821.

The Music by Sir H. R. Bishop.

My mother bids me bind my hair
  With bands of rosy hue,
Tie up my sleeves with ribands rare,
  And lace my bodice blue.

For why, she cries, sit still and weep,
  While others dance and play?
Alas! I scarce can go or creep
  While Lubin is away.

'Tis sad to think the days are gone
  When those we love were near:
I sit upon this mossy stone,
  And sigh when none can hear.

And while I spin my flaxen thread,
  And sing my simple lay,
The village seems asleep, or dead,
  Now Lubin is away.

ROY'S WIFE OF ALDIVALLOCH.

MRS. GRANT of Carron, born 1745, died 1814.

ROY's wife of Aldivalloch,
   Roy's wife of Aldivalloch,
Wat ye how she cheated me
   As I cam o'er the braes of Balloch ?

She vow'd, she swore she wad be mine,
   She said she lo'ed me best o' onie;
But ah ! the faithless, fickle quean,
   She's ta'en the carle, and left her Johnnie.
     Roy's wife, &c.

O she was a cantie quean,
   Weel could she dance the Highland walloch;
How happy I, had she been mine,
   Or I'd been Roy of Aldivalloch !
     Roy's wife, &c.

Her hair sae fair, her een sae clear,
   Her wee bit mou' sae sweet and bonnie;
To me she ever will be dear,
   Though she's for ever left her Johnnie.
     Roy's wife, &c.

The *Inverness Courier* says :—"A friend who has been examining the parish register in Cabrach, Banffshire, says he has lighted on the veritable Roy of Aldivalloch and his once fickle wife, so famous in Scottish song. On 21st February, 1727, John Roy, lawful son to Thomas Roy in Aldivalloch, was married to Isabel, daughter of Alister Stewart, sometime resident in Cabrach. They had been previously "contracted" on the 28th January. The Braes of Balloch are in the neighbourhood of Aldivalloch; and the song was written by a lady of the district. Allan Cunningham says :—'Mr. Oromek, an anxious inquirer into all matters illustrative of Northern song, ascribes 'Roy's Wife of Aldivalloch ' to Mrs. Murray, of Bath; while George Thomson and all other editors of Scottish song impute it to Mrs. Grant, of Carron. I am not aware that the authorship has been settled.' Our old friend was not so zealous a literary antiquary as his son, Mr. Peter Cunningham. There is no doubt as to the authorship of the song. It was written by a lady named Grant, a native of Aberlour, who was married first to her cousin, Mr. Grant of Carron, near Elchies, and, on his death, to a physician—Dr. Murray, of Bath. The dates of this lady's birth and death are said to have been 1745 and 1814—consequently, she was long after the period of John Roy mentioned in the parish register. Perhaps there was some popular tradition as to the courtship and the rustic dame's inconstancy, or Mrs. Grant may have taken up the burden of some older forgotten ballad. Many of our best songs were modelled on rude fragmentary lyrics that had floated down through generations, emblaming some piece of local history, or celebrating some fine river, hill, or landscape."

In corroboration of the idea of the accomplished writer of the "Inverness Courier," whose fine taste and accuracy are well known, the following may be cited. It appears in Mr. Peter Buchan's manuscript collection of songs taken down from the mouths of the peasantry in the North of Scotland, and is probably the original on which Mrs. Grant founded her own and vastly superior version. It may be objected that Mr. Buchan's version is later than Mrs. Grant's, or a parody upon it. On this point it is impossible to speak with certainty :—

> Davie Gordon in Kirktown
>   And Tibbie Stewart o' Aldivalloch,
> Sae merrily's they play'd the loon
>   As they sat in the braes o' Balloch.
>   Roy's wife o' Aldivalloch,
>   Roy's wife o' Aldivalloch;
>   She's gien her puir auld man the glaiks
>   Coming through the braes o' Balloch.
>
> Auld Roy spied them's he passed by,
>   An, oh, he gae an unco walloch;
> And after them he soon did hie,
>   And chas'd them through the braes o' Balloch.
>   Roy's wife, &c.
>
> Silly body, Aldivalloch;
>   Puir body, Aldivalloch;
> He lost his hose and baith his sheen
>   Coming through the braes o' Balloch.
>   Roy's wife, &c.
>
> He drew a stick when he came near,
>   And sware he'd gie the lad a thrashin';
> Than he lap and vow'd and sware,
>   He was in sic an awfu' passion.
>   Roy's wife, &c.
>
> But Davie soon did rin awa,
>   He wudna bide to banter wi' him;
> Syne Roy Tibbie's back did claw,
>   An' hame she ran like birds a-flying.
>   Roy's wife, &c.
>
> Now Tibbie's promised there for life
>   To meet nae ither man in Balloch,
> But be a gude an' kindly wife,
>   And gang nae mair to Aldivalloch.
>   Roy's wife, &c.

MY BOY TAMMY.

HECTOR MACNEIL.   Born 1746, died July 15, 1818.

WHAR ha'e ye been a' day,
      My boy Tammy?—
I've been by burn and flow'ry brae,
Meadow green and mountain grey,
Courting o' this young thing,
      Just come frae her mammy.

And whar gat ye that young thing,
      My boy Tammy?—
I got her down in yonder howe,
Smiling on a bonnie knowe,
Herding ae wee lamb and ewe
      For her poor mammy.

What said ye to the bonnie bairn,
      My boy Tammy?—
I praised her een sae lovely blue,
Her dimpled cheek and cherry mou'
I pree'd it aft, as ye may trow,—
      She said she'd tell her mammy

I held her to my beating heart,
    My young, my smiling lammie;
I hae a house, it cost me dear,
I've walth o'plenishen and gear;
Ye'se get it a', were't ten times mair,
    Gin ye will leave your mammy.

The smile ga'ed aff her bonny face—
    I mauna leave my mammy;
She's gien me meet, she's gien me claise,
She's been my comfort a' my days;
My father's death brought monny waes:
    I canna leave my mammy.

We'll tak her hame and mak her fain,
    My ain kind-hearted lammie;
We'll gie her meet, we'll gie her claise,
We'll be her comfort a' her days.
The wee thing gies her hand and says,
    There, gang and ask my mammy.

Has she been to the kirk wi' thee,
    My boy Tammy?—
She has been to the kirk wi' me,
And the tear was in her ee:
For, oh, she's but a young thing,
    Just come frae her mammy!

SAW YE MY WEE THING?

HECTOR MACNEIL. 'Air—"Bonnie Dundee."

"Saw ye my wee thing? saw ye my ain thing?
    Saw ye my true-love down on yon lea?
Cross'd she the meadow yestreen at the gloamin?
    Sought she the burnie whar flow'rs the haw-tree?
Her hair it is lint-white, her skin it is milk-white;
    Dark is the blue o' her saft-rolling ee;
Red, red her ripe lips, and sweeter than roses;
    Whar could my wee thing wander frae me?"

" I saw nae your wee thing, I saw nae your ain thing,
   Na saw I your true-love down on yon lea;
But I met my bonnie thing late in the gloamin
   Down by the burnie whar flow'rs the haw-tree.
Her hair it was lint-white, her skin it was milk-white;
   Dark is the blue o' her saft-rolling ee;
Red were her ripe lips, and sweeter than roses;
   Sweet were the kisses that she gae to me!"

" It was na my wee thing, it was na my ain thing,
   It was na my true-love ye met by the tree:
Proud is her lael heart, and modest her nature;
   She never lo'ed onie till ance she lo'ed me.
Her name it is Mary; she's frae Castle-Cary;
   Aft has she sat, when a bairn, on my knee;
Fair as your face is, war't fifty times fairer,
   Young braggart, she ne'er would gie kisses to thee!"

" It was then your Mary; she's frae Castle-Cary;
   It was then your true-love I met by the tree;
Proud as her heart is, and modest her nature,
   Sweet were the kisses that she ga'e to me."
Sair gloom'd his dark brow—blood-red his cheek grew—
   Wild flash'd the fire frae his red-rolling ee:
" Ye'se rue sair this morning your boasts and your scorning:
   Defend ye, fause traitor! fu' loudly ye lee!"

" Awa wi' beguiling!" cried the youth, smiling;
   Aff went the bonnet, the lint-white locks flee;
The belted plaid fa'ing, her white bosom shawing,
   Fair stood the loved maid wi' the dark-rolling ee!
" Is it my wee thing? is it mine ain thing?
   Is it my true-love here that I see?"—
" Oh, Jamie, forgive me; your heart's constant to me;
   I'll never mair wander, dear laddie, frae thee!"

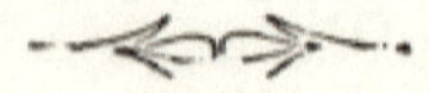

COME UNDER MY PLAIDIE.

HECTOR MACNEIL.   Air—"Johnnie McGill."

"COME under my plaidie, the night's gaun to fa';
   Come in frae the cauld blast, the drift, and the snaw:
   Come under my plaidie, and sit down beside me;
   There's room in't, dear lassie, believe me, for twa.
   Come under my plaidie, and sit down beside me;
   I'll hap ye frae every cauld blast that can blaw:
   Come under my plaidie, and sit down beside me;
   There's room in't, dear lassie, believe me, for twa."

"Gae 'wa wi' yere plaidie, auld Donald, gae 'wa;
   I fear na the cauld blast, the drift, nor the snaw:
   Gae 'wa wi' yere plaidie, I'll no sit beside ye;
   Ye micht be my gutcher; auld Donald, gae 'wa.
   I'm gaun to meet Johnnie—he's young and he's bonnie;
   He's been at Meg's bridal, fou trig and fou braw;
   Nane dances sae lichtly, sae gracefu', sae tichtly,
   His cheek's like the new rose, his brow's like the snaw."

"Dear Marion, let that flee stick fast to the wa';
   Your Jock's but a gowk, and has naething ava;
   The haill o' his pack he has now on his back;
   He's thretty, and I am but three-score and twa.
   Be frank now and kindly—I'll busk ye aye finely;
   To kirk or to market there few gang sae braw;
   A bien house to 'bide in, a chaise for to ride in,
   And flunkies to 'tend ye as aft as ye ca'."

"My father aye tell'd me, my mither and a',
   Ye'd make a gude husband, and keep me aye braw;
   It's true I lo'e Johnnie, he's young and he's bonnie;
   But, wae's me, I ken he has naething ava!
   I hae little tocher—ye've made a gude offer;
   I'm now mair than twenty—my time is but sma'!
   Sae gi'e me your plaidie, I'll creep in beside ye;
   I thocht ye'd been aulder than three-score and twa!"

She crap in ayont him, beside the stane wa',
Whare Johnnie was listenin', and heard her tell a':
The day was appointed;—his proud heart it dunted,
And strak 'gainst his side as if burstin' in twa.
He wander'd hame weary, the nicht it was dreary,
And thowless he tint his gate 'mang the deep snaw:
The howlet was screeming; while Johnnie cried, " Women
Wad marry auld Nick if he'd keep them aye braw!

Oh, the deil's in the lassies! they gang now sae braw;
They'll lie down wi' auld men o' threescore and twa;
The haill o' their marriage is gowd and a carriage;
Plain love is the cauldest blast now that can blaw.
Auld dotards, be wary, tak' tent when ye marry;
Young wives wi' their coaches, they'll whip and they'll ca',
Till they meet wi' some Johnnie that's youthfu' and bonnie,
And they'll gie ye horns on ilk haffit to claw."

DINNA THINK, BONNIE LASSIE.

HECTOR MACNEIL. The last verse was added by John Hamilton. On account of
this addition the song was not included by Macneil in his " Poetical Works."—C. R.

OH, dinna think, bonnie lassie, I'm gaun to leave thee;
Dinna think, bonnie lassie, I'm gaun to leave thee;
Dinna think, bonnie lassie, I'm gaun to leave thee;
I'll tak' a stick into my hand, and come again and see thee.

Far's the gate ye ha'e to gang, dark's the night and eerie;
Far's the gate ye ha'e to gang, dark's the night and eerie;
Far's the gate ye ha'e to gang, dark's the night and eerie;
Oh, stay this night wi' your love, and dinna gang and leave me.

It's but a night and hauf a day that I'll leave my dearie;
But a night and hauf a day that I'll leave my dearie;
But a night and hauf a day that I'll leave my dearie;
Whene'er the sun gaes west the loch, I'll come again and see thee.

Dinna gang, my bonnie lad, dinna gang and leave me;
Dinna gang, my bonnie lad, dinna gang and leave me;
When a' the lave are sound asleep, I am dull and eerie;
And a' the lee-lang night I'm sad wi' thinking on my dearie.

Oh, dinna think, bonnie lassie, I'm gaun to leave thee;
Dinna think, bonnie lassie, I'm gaun to leave thee;
Dinna think, bonnie lassie, I'm gaun to leave thee;
Whene'er the sun gaes out o' sight, I'll come again and see thee.

Waves are rising o'er the sea, winds blaw loud and fear me;
Waves are rising o'er the sea, winds blaw loud and fear me;
While the winds and waves do roar I am wae and drearie;
And gin ye lo'e me as ye say, ye winna gang and leave me.

Oh, never mair, bonnie lassie, will I gang and leave thee;
Never mair, bonnie lassie, will I gang and leave thee;
Never mair, bonnie lassie, will I gang and leave thee;
E'en let the world gang as it will, I'll stay at hame and cheer thee.

Frae his hand he coost his stick—I winna gang and leave thee;
Threw his plaid into the neuk—Never can I grieve thee;
Drew off his boots, and flang them by; cried, My lass, be cheerie;
I'll kiss the tear frae aff thy cheek, and never leave my dearie.

------♦------

OH, HOW COULD I VENTURE?

DR. WEBSTER.   First printed in the "Scots Magazine," 1747.

OH, how could I venture to love one like thee,
And you not despise a poor conquest like me;
On lords, thy admirers, could look wi' disdain,
And knew I was naething, yet pitied my pain!
You said, while they teased you with nonsense and dress,
When real the passion, the vanity's less;
You saw through that silence which others despise,
And while beaux were a talking, read love in my eyes.

Oh, how shall I fauld thee, and kiss a' thy charms,
Till, fainting wi' pleasure, I die in your arms;
Through all the wild transports of ecstasy tost,
Till, sinking together, together we're lost!
Oh, where is the maid that like thee ne'er can cloy,
Whose wit can enliven each dull pause of joy;
And when the short raptures are all at an end,
From beautiful mistress turn sensible friend?

In vain do I praise thee, or strive to reveal
(Too nice for expression) what only we feel:
In a' that ye do, in each look and each mien,
The **Graces** in waiting adorn you unseen.
When I see you, I love you; when hearing, adore;
I wonder and think you a woman no more:
Till, mad wi' admiring, I canna contain,
And kissing your lips, you turn woman again.

With thee in my bosom, how can I despair?
I'll gaze on thy beauties, and look awa' care;
I'll ask thy advice, when with troubles opprest,
Which never displeases, but always is best.
In all that I write I'll thy judgment require;
Thy wit shall correct what thy charms did inspire.
I'll kiss thee and press thee till youth is all o'er,
And then live in friendship when passion's no more.

I HAE LAID A HERRING IN SAUT.

JAMES TYTLER.   Born 1747, died 1805.

I HAE laid a herring in saut—
   Lass, gin ye lo'e me, tell me now;
I hae brew'd a forpit o' maut,
   An' I canna come ilka day to woo.
I hae a calf that will soon be a cow—
   Lass, gin ye lo'e me, tell me now;
I hae a stook, and I'll soon hae a mowe,
   . An' I canna come ilka day to woo.

I hae a house upon yon moor—
   Lass, gin ye lo'e me, tell me now;
Three sparrows may dance upon the moor,
   An' I canna come ilka day to woo.
I hae a but and I hae a ben—
   Lass, gin ye lo'e me, tell me now;
A penny to keep and a penny to spen',
   An' I canna come ilka day to woo.

I hae a hen wi' a happitie leg—
  Lass, gin ye lo'e me, tell me now;
That ilka day lays me an egg,
  An' I canna come ilka day to woo.
I hae a cheese upon my shelf—
  Lass, gin ye lo'e me, tell me now;
An' soon wi' mites 'twill rin itself,
  An' I canna come ilka day to woo.

The following, which is another version of the above, appeared in Herd's Collection, 1776:—

I hae a herrin' in saut—
  Bonnie lassie, gin ye'll tak' me, tell me now;
An' I hae brewn three pickles o' maut,
  An' I canna come ilka day to woo—
    To woo, to woo, to lilt and to woo;
    An' I canna come ilka day to woo.

I hae a wee calf that wad fain be a cow—
  Bonnie lassie, gin ye'll tak' me, tell me now;
I hae a wee gryce that wad fain be a sow,
  An' I canna come ilka day to woo—
    To woo, to woo, to lilt and to woo;
    An' I canna come ilka day to woo.

WHILE FREQUENT ON TWEED.

Rev. John Logan, born 1748, died 1788.

While frequent on Tweed and on Tay,
  Their harps all the Muses have strung,
Should a river more limpid than they,
  The wood-fringed Esk, flow unsung?
While Nelly and Nancy inspire
  The poet with pastoral strains:
Why silent the voice of the lyre
  On Mary, the pride of the plains?

Oh, nature's most beautiful bloom
  May flourish unseen and unknown;
And the shadows of solitude gloom
  A form that might shine on a throne.
Through the wilderness blossoms the rose,
  In sweetness retired from the sight;
And Philomel warbles her woes
  Alone to the ear of the night.

How often the beauty is hid
 Amid shades that her triumphs deny!
How often the hero forbid
 From the path that conducts to the sky!
A Helen has pined in the grove,
 A Homer has wanted his name,
Unseen in the circle of love,
 Unknown to the temple of fame.

Yet let us walk forth to the stream,
 Where poet ne'er wander'd before;
Enamour'd of Mary's sweet name,
 How the echoes will spread to the shore!
If the voice of the Muse be divine,
 Thy beauties shall live in my lay;
While reflecting the forest so fine,
 Sweet Esk o'er the valleys shall stray.

THE BRAES OF YARROW.

Rev. John Logan.

Thy braes were bonnie, Yarrow stream,
 When first on them I met my lover;
Thy braes how dreary, Yarrow stream,
 When now thy waves his body cover!
For ever, now, O Yarrow stream!
 Thou art to me a stream of sorrow;
For ever on thy banks shall I
 Behold my love, the flower of Yarrow!

He promised me a milk-white steed,
 To bear me to his father's bowers;
He promised me a little page,
 To squire me to his father's towers;
He promised me a wedding-ring—
 The wedding-day was fixed to-morrow:
Now he is wedded to his grave,
 Alas, his watery grave in Yarrow!

Sweet were his words when last we met;
　My passion I as freely told him:
Clasp'd in his arms, I little thought
　That I should never more behold him.
Scarce was he gone, I saw his ghost;
　It vanish'd with a shriek of sorrow:
Thrice did the water-wraith ascend;
　And gave a doleful groan through Yarrow.

His mother from the window look'd,
　With all the longing of a mother;
His little sister weeping walk'd
　The greenwood path to meet her brother:
They sought him east, they sought him west,
　They sought him all the forest thorough;
They only saw the cloud of night,
　They only heard the roar of Yarrow.

No longer from thy window look;
　Thou hast no son, thou tender mother!
No longer walk, thou lovely maid;
　Alas, thou hast no more a brother!
No longer seek him east or west,
　No longer search the forest thorough;
For wandering in the night so dark,
　He fell a lifeless corpse in Yarrow.

The tear shall never leave my cheek,
　No other youth shall be my marrow;
I'll seek thy body in the stream,
　And then with thee I'll sleep in Yarrow.
The tear did never leave her cheek,
　No other youth became her marrow;
She found his body in the stream,
　And now with him she sleeps in Yarrow.

This beautiful song was founded upon the well-known story made immortal in
the ballads of Scotland, both old and new. There are several versions—the story
being the same in each, but in none of them told so exquisitely as by Mr. William
Hamilton of Bangour, in his ballad commencing, "Busk ye, busk ye, my bonnie,
bonnie bride!" and rendered still more famous than it formerly was by the fine poem
of Wordsworth, "Yarrow Unvisited."

THE FLOWERS OF THE FOREST.

FIRST VERSION.

JANE ELLIOT, about the year 1750.

I'VE heard the lilting at our yowe-milking,
  Lasses a lilting before the dawn of day;
But now they are moaning on ilka green loaning—
  The Flowers of the Forest are a' wede away.

At bughts in the morning nae blythe lads are scorning,
  The lassies are lonely and dowie and wae;
Nae-daffin', nae gabbin', but sighing and sabbing,
  Ilk ane lifts her leglen and hies her away.

In hairst at the shearing nae youths now are jeering,
  The bandsters are lyart and runkled and grey;
At fair or at preaching, nae wooing, nae fleeching—
  The Flowers of the Forest are a' wede away.

At e'en at the glooming nae swankies are roaming
  'Bout stacks wi' the lasses at bogle to play;
But ilk ane sits dreary, lamenting her dearie—
  The Flowers of the Forest are a' wede away.

Dule and wae for the order sent our lads to the border!
  The English for ance by guile won the day;
The Flowers of the Forest that focht aye the foremost,
  The prime o' our land, are cauld in the clay.

We hear nae mair lilting at our yowe-milking,
  Women and bairns are heartless and wae;
Sighing and moaning on ilka green loaning—
  The Flowers of the Forest are a' wede away.

The "Flowers of the Forest" were the young men of the districts of Selkirkshire and Peebleshire, anciently known as "The Forest." The song is founded by the authoress upon an older composition of the same name, deploring the loss of the Scotch at Flodden Field.

THE FLOWERS OF THE FOREST.

SECOND VERSION.

Mrs. Cockburn, born about the year 1710, died 1794.

I've seen the smiling
Of fortune beguiling;
I've felt all its favours, and found its decay :
Sweet was its blessing,
Kind its caressing ;
But now 'tis fled—fled far away.

I've seen the forest
Adorn'd the foremost
With flowers of the fairest, most pleasant and gay ;
Sae bonnie was their blooming,
Their scent the air perfuming;
But now they are wither'd and weeded away.

I've seen the morning
With gold the hills adorning,
And loud tempest storming before the mid-day ;
I've seen Tweed's silver streams
Shining in the sunny beams
Grow drumly and dark as he row'd on his way.

O fickle Fortune,
Why this cruel sporting ;
Oh, why still perplex us, poor sons of a day ?
Nae mair your smiles can cheer me,
Nae mair your frowns can fear me ;
For the Flowers of the Forest are a' wede away.

This song is an imitation, but not a good one, of Miss Elliot's, and appear'd originally in Herd's Collection in 1776.

MARY'S DREAM.

John Lowe, born 1750, died about the year 1800.

The moon had climb'd the highest hill
  Which rises o'er the source of Dee,
And from the eastern summit shed
  Her silver light on tower and tree,
When Mary laid her down to sleep,
  Her thoughts on Sandy far at sea;
When soft and low a voice was heard,
  Saying, "Mary, weep no more for me!"

She from her pillow gently raised
  Her head, to ask who there might be,
And saw young Sandy shivering stand,
  With visage pale and hollow ee;
"O Mary dear, cold is my clay,
  It lies beneath a stormy sea;
Far, far from thee I sleep in death;
  So, Mary, weep no more for me!

Three stormy nights and stormy days
  We toss'd upon the raging main,
And long we strove our bark to save;
  But all our striving was in vain.
Even then, when horror chill'd my blood,
  My heart was fill'd with love for thee:
The storm is past, and I at rest;
  So, Mary, weep no more for me!

O maiden dear, thyself prepare;
  We soon shall meet upon that shore
Where love is free from doubt and care,
  And thou and I shall part no more!"
Loud crow'd the cock, the shadow fled,
  No more of Sandy could she see;
But soft the passing spirit said,
  "Sweet Mary, weep no more for me!"

LOGIE O' BUCHAN.

GEORGE HALKET, died 1756.

O LOGIE o' Buchan, O Logie the laird!
They ha'e ta'en awa' Jamie, that delved in the yard,
Wha play'd on the pipe and the viol sae sma',
They ha'e ta'en awa' Jamie, the flower o' them a'.
  He said, Think na lang, lassie, though I gang awa';
  He said, Think na lang, lassie, though I gang awa';
  For simmer is coming, cauld winter's awa',
  And I'll come back and see thee in spite of them a'.

Though Sandy has ousen, has gear, and has kye,
A house and a hadden, and siller forbye;
Yet I'd tak' mine ain lad wi' his staff in his hand,
Before I'd ha'e him wi' the houses and land.
  He said, Think na lang, &c.

My daddie looks sulky, my minnie looks sour,
They frown upon Jamie because he is poor:
Though I lo'e them as weel as a daughter should do,
They're na haef sae dear to me, Jamie, as you.
  He said, Think na lang, &c.

I sit on my creepie, I spin at my wheel,
And think on the laddie that lo'ed me sae weel;
He had but a saxpence, he brak' it in twa,
And gi'ed me the haef o't when he gade awa'.
    Then haste ye back, Jamie, and bide na awa';
    Then haste ye back, Jamie, and bide na awa';
    The simmer is coming, cauld winter's awa',
    And ye'll come back and see me in spite o' them a'.

Mr. Peter Buchan states that this song was written by a schoolmaster at Rathen in Aberdeenshire, of the name of George Halket, who died in 1756. Mr. Halket was a Jacobite, and wrote some squibs after the "Forty-five," which gave such offence to the Duke of Cumberland, that he offered a reward of 100*l.* for the author's head. The poet, however, escaped the danger, and died peaceably in his bed. The hero of the piece was a James Robertson, gardener at Logie.

LOW DOUN I' THE BRUME.

JAMES CARNEGIE. From "The Lark," a collection of Scottish Songs, 1765.

My daddie is a cankert carle,
    He'll no twine wi' his gear;
My minnie she's a scaulding' wife,
    Hauds a' the house asteer.
      But let them say, or let them do,
        It's a' ane to me;
      For he's low doun, he's in the brume,
        That's waitin' on me:
      Waitin' on me, my love,
        He's waitin' on me:
      For he's low doun, he's in the brume,
        That's waitin' on me.

My auntie Kate sits at her wheel,
    And sair she lightlies me;
But weel ken I it's a' envy,
    For ne'er a joe has she.
      But let them say, &c.

My cousin Kate was sair beguiled
  Wi' Johnnie o' the Glen;
And aye sinsyne she cries, Beware
  O' fause deluding men!
    But let them say, &c.

Gleed Sandy he cam' wast yestreen,
  And speir'd when I saw Pate;
And aye sinsyne the necbors round
  They jeer me air and late.
    But let them say, &c.

WHEN I UPON THY BOSOM LEAN.

JOHN LAPRAIK. 1780.

WHEN I upon thy bosom lean,
  And fondly clasp thee a' my ain,
I glory in the sacred ties
  That made us ane wha ance were twain.
A mutual flame inspires us baith,
  The tender look, the meltin' kiss:
Even years shall ne'er destroy our love,
  But only gie us change o' bliss.

Hae I a wish? it's a' for thee!
  I ken thy wish is me to please;
Our moments pass sae smooth away,
  That numbers on us look and gaze;
Weel pleased they see our happy days,
  Nor envy's sel' finds aught to blame;
And aye when weary cares arise,
  Thy bosom still shall be my hame.

I'll lay me there and tak my rest;
  And if that aught disturb my dear,
I'll bid her laugh her cares away,
  And beg her not to drop a tear.

F

Hae I a joy? it's a' **her ain**!
United still her heart **and mine**;
They're like the woodbine round the tree,
That's twined till death shall them disjoin.

The author of **this beautiful song was the friend and** correspondent of Robert Burns.   In his "Epistle to **J.** Lapraik, an old Scottish bard," dated April 1st, 1785. Burns pays his predecessor the following fine compliment:

There was ae sang amang the rest,
Aboon them a' it pleased me best,
That some kind husband had addrest
    To some sweet wife:
It **thirl'd** the heart-strings through the breast
    A' to the life.

I've scarce heard sught described **sae weel,**
What gen'rous, manly bosoms feel;
Thought I, 'Can this be Pope, or Steele,
    Or Beattie's wark?'
They told me 'twas an odd kind chiel
    About Muirkirk.

It pat me fidgin fain to hear't,
And sae about him there I spiert;
Then a' that ken't him round declared
    He had ingine,
That nane excell'd **it, few** cam near't,
    It was sae **fine.**

That set him to a pint **of** ale,
An' either douce or **merry** tale,
Or rhymes an' sangs **he'd** made **himsel',**
    Or witty catches,
'Tween Inverness and Teviotdale
    He had few matches.

Then up I gat an' swoor an aith,
Though I should pawn my pleugh an' graith,
Or die a cadger pownie's death
    At some dyke-back,
A pint and gill I'd gie them baith
    To hear your crack.

"Lapraik," says Burns, "was **a very** worthy facetious old fellow, late of Dalfram, near Muirkirk, which little property **he** was obliged to sell in consequence of some connexion as security for some **persons** concerned in that villanous bubble, 'the Ayr Bank.'   He has often told me that he composed this song one day when his **wife** had **been fretting over** their misfortunes."   Lapraik died in 1807.

'TWAS WITHIN A MILE OF EDINBURGH.

This song was composed by Thomas D'Urfey. It originally appeared in a collection
entitled " Wit and Mirth," 1698.—C. R.

'Twas within a mile of Edinburgh town,
   In the rosy time of the year;
Sweet flowers bloom'd, and the grass was down,
   And each shepherd woo'd his dear.
     Bonnie Jockie, blythe and gay,
     Kiss'd sweet Jenny making hay :
The lassie blush'd, and frowning cried, " Na, na, it winna do ;
I canna, canna, winna, winna, maunna buckle to."

Jockie was a wag that never would wed,
   Though long he had follow'd the lass :
Contented she earn'd and eat her brown bread,
   And merrily turn'd up the grass.
     Bonnie Jockie, blythe and free,
     Won her heart right merrily :
Yet still she blush'd, and frowning cried, " Na, na, it winna do ;
I canna, canna, winna, winna, maunna buckle to."

But when he vow'd he would make her his bride,
   Though his flocks and herds were not few,
She gave him her hand, and a kiss beside,
   And vow'd she'd for ever be true.

Bonnie Jockie, blythe and free,
Won her heart right merrily:
At church she no more frowning cried, " Na, na, it winna do;
I canna, canna, winna, winna, maunna buckle to."

Modernised from a song by Thomas D'Urfey. The air to which the song is now usually sung is of more recent origin than the words, having been the composition of Mr. Hook, father of the late Theodore Hook the novelist. Mr. Hook, besides composing many beautiful English melodies, wrote several in imitation of the Scottish manner, many of which are still popular.

THOU ART GANE AWA' FRAE ME, MARY.

ANONYMOUS.   From "Johnson's Museum," 1787.   To the tune of " Haud awa'
frae me, Donald."

THOU art gane awa', thou art gane awa',
    Thou art gane awa' frae me, Mary;
Nor friends nor I could make thee stay—
    Thou hast cheated them and me, Mary.
Until this hour I never thought
    That aught could alter thee, Mary;
Thou art still the mistress of my heart,
    Think what you will of me, Mary.

Whate'er he said or might pretend
    That stole the heart of thine, Mary,
True love, I'm sure, was ne'er his end,
    Or nae sic love as mine, Mary.
I spoke sincere, nor flatter'd much,
    Had no unworthy thoughts, Mary;
Ambition, wealth, nor naething such:
    No, I loved only thee, Mary.

Though you've been false, yet while I live
    I'll lo'e nae maid but thee, Mary;
Let friends forget, as I forgive,
    Thy wrongs to them and me, Mary.
So then, farewell! of this be sure,
    Since you've been false to me, Mary,
For all the world I'd not endure
    Half what I've done for thee, Mary.

THE TEARS I SHED MUST EVER FALL.

Mrs. Dugald Stewart, wife of the philosopher. From "Johnson's
Museum," 1792.

The tears I shed must ever fall,—
 I mourn not for an absent swain;
For thoughts may past delights recall,
 And parted lovers meet again.
I weep not for the silent dead,—
 Their toils are past, their sorrows o'er;
And those they loved their steps shall tread,
 And death shall join to part no more.

Though boundless oceans roll'd between,
 If certain that his death is near,
A conscious transport glads each scene,
 Soft is the sigh and sweet the tear.
E'en when by death's cold hand removed,
 We mourn the tenant of the tomb;
To think that e'en in death he loved,
 Can gild the horrors of the gloom.

But bitter, bitter are the tears
 Of her who slighted love bewails;
No hope her dreary prospect cheers,
 No pleasing melancholy hails.
Hers are the pangs of wounded pride,
 Of blasted hope, of wither'd joy;
The flattering veil is rent aside,
 The flame of love burns to destroy.

In vain does memory renew
 The hours once tinged in transport's dye;
The sad reverse soon starts to view,
 And turns the past to agony.
E'en time itself despairs to cure
 Those pangs to every feeling due:
Ungenerous youth, thy boast how poor,
 To win a heart and break it too!

No cold approach, no alter'd mien,
    Just what would make suspicion start;
No pause the dire extremes between,—
    He made me blest—and broke my heart. *
From hope, the wretched's anchor, torn;
    Neglected and neglecting all,
Friendless, forsaken, and forlorn,
    The tears I shed must ever fall.

THE BOATIE ROWS.

John Ewen, merchant, Aberdeen, born 1741, died 1821.—C. R.

Oh, weel may the boatie row,
    And better may she speed;
And liesome may the boatie row
    That wins the bairns' bread.
The boatie rows, the boatie rows,
    The boatie rows indeed;
And weel may the boatie row
    That wins the bairns' bread.

I coost my line in Largo Bay,
    And fishes I caught nine;
'Twas three to boil, and three to fry,
    And three to bait the line.

* The first four lines of the last stanza are by Burns.—C. R.

The boatie rows, the boatie rows,
  The boatie rows indeed;
And happy be the lot o' a'
  Wha wishes her to speed.

Oh, weel may the boatie row,
  That fills a heavy creel,
And cleeds us a' frae tap to tae,
  And buys our parritch meal.
The boatie rows, the boatie rows,
  The boatie rows indeed;
And happy be the lot o' a'
  That wish the boatie speed.

When Jamie vow'd he wad be mine,
  And wan frae me my heart,
Oh, muckle lighter grew my creel—
  He swore we'd never part.
The boatie rows, the boatie rows,
  The boatie rows fu' weel;
And muckle lighter is the load
  When love bears up the creel.

My kurtch I put upo' my head,
  And dress'd mysel' fu' braw;
I trow my heart was dowf and wae,
  When Jamie gaed awa'.
But weel may the boatie row,
  And lucky be her part,
And lightsome be the lassie's care
  That yields an honest heart.

When Sawnie, Jock, and Janetie,
  Are up and gotten lear,
They'll help to gar the boatie row,
  And lighten a' our care.
The boatie rows, the boatie rows,
  The boatie rows fu' weel;
And lightsome be her heart that bears
  The murlain and the creel!

And when wi' age we're worn down,
  And hirpling round the door,
They'll row to keep us dry and warm,
  As we did them before.
Then weel may the boatie row
  That wins the bairns' bread,
And happy be the lot o' a'
  That with the boatie speed!

The author of this song, Mr. John Ewen, ironmonger in Aberdeen, died on the 21st October, 1821, in his eightieth year. He bequeathed his fortune of £16,000 to found and endow an hospital for children at Montrose, of which place he was a native. In this settlement he entirely overlooked his daughter, who married, as he thought imprudently. An action was raised for the reduction of the will; it was carried in the House of Lords.—C. R.

LIZZY LINDSAY.

From "Johnson's Museum," 1787. Air—"The Ewe-Bughts."

"WILL ye gang to the Highlands, Lizzy Lindsay?
  Will ye gang to the Highlands wi' me?
Will ye gang to the Highlands, Lizzy Lindsay,
  My bride and my darling to be?"

"To gang to the Highlands wi' you, sir,
  I dinna ken how that may be;
For I ken nae the land that ye live in,
  Nor ken I the lad I'm gaun wi'."

"O Lizzy lass, ye maun ken little,
  If sae that ye dinna ken me;
For my name is Lord Roland MacDonald,
  A chieftain o' high degree."

She has kilted her coats o' green satin,
  She has kilted them up to the knee,
And she's aff wi' Lord Roland MacDonald,
  His bride and his darling to be.

There is another and more modern version of this song by Mr. Robert Gilfillan, which appears in some collections of Scottish songs.

AULD ROBIN GRAY.*

Lady Anne Lindsay.

Young Jamie lo'ed me weel, and he sought me for his bride,
But saving a crown he had naething else beside;
To mak that crown a pound, my Jamie gaed to sea,
And the crown and the pound were baith for me.
He hadna been gane a week but only twa,
When my mither she fell sick, and the cow was stown awa',
My father brak his arm, and my Jamie at the sea,
And auld Robin Gray cam' a-courting to me.

My father cou'dna work, and my mither cou'dna spin;
I toil'd baith day and night, but their bread I cou'dna win;
Auld Rob maintain'd them baith, and wi' tears in his ee
Said, Jeanie, for their sakes, oh, will you marry me?
My heart it said nay; I look'd for Jamie back;
But the wind it blew high, and the ship it proved a wreck;
The ship it proved a wreck,—why didna Jeanie die?
And why do I live to say, Oh, waes me!

My father urged me sair; my mither didna speak,
But she look'd in my face till my heart was like to break;
So they gied him my hand, though my heart was at the sea,
And auld Robin Gray is gudeman to me.
I hadna been a wife a week but only four,
When sitting sae mournfully ae day at the door,
I saw my Jamie's wraith, for I cou'dna think it he,
Until he said, Jeanie, I'm come to marry thee.

* "This pathetic ballad, of which the authorship was long a mystery, was written
by Lady Anne Lindsay, daughter of the Earl of Balcarras, and afterwards Lady Barnard. It appears to have been composed at the commencement of the year 1772,
when the author was yet a young girl. It was published anonymously, and acquired
great popularity. No one, however, came forward to lay claim to the laurels lavished
upon it; and a literary controversy sprung up to decide the authorship. Many conjectured that it was as old as the days of David Rizzio, if not composed by that unfortunate minstrel himself; while others considered it of a much later date. The real
author was, however, suspected; and ultimately, when she was an old woman, Sir
Walter Scott received a letter from Lady Anne herself, openly avowing that she had
written it. She stated that she had been long suspected by her more intimate friends,
and often questioned with respect to the mysterious ballad, but that she had always
managed to keep her secret to herself without a direct and absolute denial. She was
induced to write the song by a desire to see an old plaintive Scottish air (" The bridegroom grat when the sun gaed down "), which was a favourite with her, fitted with

Oh, sair did we greet, and muckle did we say
We took but ae kiss, and tore ourselves away:
I wish I were dead, but I'm nae like to die;
And why do I live to say, Oh, waes me!
I gang like a ghaist, I carena to spin,
I darena think on Jamie, for that wad be a sin;
But I'll do my best a gude wife to be,
For auld Robin Gray is a kind man to me.

———◆———

THERE'S NAE LUCK ABOUT THE HOUSE.

WILLIAM JULIUS MICKLE.   From Herd's Collection, 1776.

BUT are ye sure the news is true?
  And are ye sure he's weel?
Is this a time to think o' wark?
  Ye jauds, fling by your wheel!
Is this a time to think o' wark,
  When Colin's at the door?
Rax down my cloak—I'll to the quay,
  And see him come ashore.
    For there's nae luck about the house,
     There's nae luck at a';
    There's nae luck about the house,
     When our gudeman's awa'.

words more suitable to its character than the ribald verses which had always hitherto, for want of better, been sung to it. It struck her that some tale of virtuous distress in humble life would be most suitable to the plaintive character of her favourite air; and she accordingly set about such an attempt, taking the name of "Auld Robin Gray" from an ancient herd at Balcarras. When she had written two or three of the verses, she called to her junior sister (afterwards Lady Hardwicke), who was the only person near her, and thus addressed her: "I have been writing a ballad, my dear; I am oppressing my heroine with many misfortunes; I have already sent her Jamie to sea, and broken her father's arm, and made her mother fall sick, and given her Auld Robin Gray for her lover; but I wish to load her with a fifth sorrow within the four lines—poor thing! Help me to one." "Steal the cow, Sister Anne," said the little Elizabeth. "The cow," adds Lady Anne in her letter, "was immediately lifted by me, and the song completed."

Lady Anne Barnard died in a vigorous old age about two years after her confession to Sir Walter Scott. The air to which the song is now usually sung is the composition of an English amateur, the Rev. William Leeves, rector of Wrington, who died in 1828, at the age of eighty.

And gie to me my bigonet,
  My bishop satin gown,
For I maun tell the baillie's wife
  That Colin's come to town.
My Turkey slippers I'll put on,
  My stockins pearl-blue—
It's a' to pleasure our gudeman,
  For he's baith leal and true.
          For there's nae luck, &c.

Rise up and mak a clean fireside,
  Put on the muckle pat;
Gie little Kate her cotton gown,
  And Jock his Sunday's coat.
Mak their shoon as black as slaes,
  Their stockins white as snaw;
It's a' to pleasure our gudeman—
  He likes to see them braw.
          For there's nae luck, &c.

There are twa hens into the crib
  Hae fed this month or mair;
Mak haste and thraw their necks about,
  That Colin weel may fare.
And spread the table neat and clean,
  Gar ilka thing look braw,
For wha can tell how Colin fared
  When he was far awa'?
          For there's nae luck, &c.

Sae sweet his voice, sae smooth his tongue,
  His breath's like cauler air;
His very foot has music in't,
  As he comes up the stair.
And will I see his face again,
  And will I hear him speak?
I'm downright dizzy wi' the thought,
  In troth I'm like to greet.
          For there's nae luck, &c.

The cauld blasts o' the winter wind
  That thirlèd through my heart,
They're a' blawn bye, I hae him safe,
  Till death we'll never part.

But what puts parting in my head ?
    It may be far awa',
The present moment is our ain,
    The neist we never saw.
                 For there's nae luck, &c.

Since Colin's weel, I'm weel content,
    I hae nae mair to crave ;
Could I but live, to mak him blest,
    I'm blest aboon the lave.
And will I see his face again ?
    And will I hear him speak ?
I'm downright dizzy wi' the thought,
    In troth I'm like to greet.
                 For there's nae luck, &c.

"This," says Burns, "is positively the finest love-ballad in the Scotch, or perhaps in any other language ;"—a verdict in which every lover of poetry and every feeling heart will agree. There is some doubt as to the authorship, which has been claimed on behalf of several persons ; but the claim of William Julius Mickle appears preferable to that of any other person.

TO MARY IN HEAVEN.*

ROBERT BURNS, born 25th January, 1759, died July 21st, 1796.
Air—"Miss Forbes' farewell to Banff."

THOU lingering star, with less'ning ray
    That lov'st to greet the early morn,
Again thou usher'st in the day
    My Mary from my soul was torn.

O Mary, dear departed shade !
    Where is thy place of blissful rest ?
Seest thou thy lover lowly laid,
    Hear'st thou the groans that rend his breast ?

* "The song of 'Highland Mary' was written," says Burns, "on one of the most interesting passages of my youthful days." The object of this passion died early in life, and the impression left on the mind of Burns seems to have been deep and lasting. Several years afterwards, when he was removed to Nithsdale, he gave vent to the sensibility of his recollections in these impassioned lines ("To Mary in Heaven").—DR. CURRIE.

ROBERT BURNS.

That sacred hour can I forget,
    Can I forget the hallow'd grove
Where by the winding Ayr we met,
    To live one day of parting love?

Eternity will not efface
    Those records dear of transports past;
Thy image at our last embrace—
    Ah, little thought we 'twas our last!

Ayr gurgling kiss'd his pebbled shore,
    O'erhung with wild woods thick'ning green;
The fragrant birch and hawthorn hoar
    Twined am'rous round the raptured scene.

The flowers sprang wanton to be press'd,
    The birds sang love on ev'ry spray,
Till soon, too soon the glowing west
    Proclaim'd the speed of wingèd day.

Still o'er these scenes my mem'ry wakes,
    And fondly broods with miser care;
Time but the impression deeper makes,
    As streams their channels deeper wear.

My Mary, dear departed shade !
　Where is thy place of blissful rest ?
Seest thou thy lover lowly laid,
　Hear'st thou the groans that rend his breast ?

WILL YE GO TO THE INDIES, MY MARY ?

BURNS.

WILL ye go to the Indies, my Mary,
　And leave auld Scotia's shore ?
Will ye go to the Indies, my Mary,
　Across the Atlantic's roar ?

Oh, sweet grow the lime and the orange,
　And the apple on the pine :
But a' the charms o' the Indies
　Can never equal thine.

I hae sworn by the heavens to my Mary,
　I hae sworn by the heavens to be true ;
And sae may the heavens forget me
　When I forget my vow.

Oh, plight me your faith, my Mary,
　And plight me your lily-white hand ;
Oh, plight me your faith, my Mary,
　Before I leave Scotia's strand.

We hae plighted our troth, my Mary,
　In mutual affection to join ;
And curst be the hour that shall part us,
　The hour and the moment o' time !

"In my very early years, when I was thinking of going to the West Indies, I took the following farewell of a dear girl. It is quite trifling, and has nothing of the merit of ' Ewe-Bughts ;' but it will fill up this page. You must know that my earlier love-songs were the breathing of ardent passion; and though it might have been easy in after-times to have given them a polish, yet that polish to me, whose they were, and who perhaps alone cared for them, would have defaced the legend of my heart, which was so faithfully inscribed on them. Their uncouth simplicity was, as they say of wines, their *race*."— BURNS *to Thomson*.

Mr. Thomson did not think sufficiently well of this song to insert it in his collection.

THE SOLDIER'S RETURN.

BURNS.   Air—"The mill, mill O."

WHEN wild war's deadly blast was blawn,
  And gentle peace returning,
Wi' mony a sweet babe fatherless,
  And mony a widow mourning,
I left the lines and tented field,
  Where lang I'd been a lodger,
My humble knapsack a' my wealth,
  A poor but honest sodger.

A leal light heart was in my breast,
  My hand unstain'd wi' plunder;
And for fair Scotia, hame again,
  I cheerily did wander.
I thought upon the banks o' Coil,
  I thought upon my Nancy,
I thought upon the witching smile
  That pleased my youthful fancy.

At length I reached the bonnie glen
  Where early life I sported;
I passed the mill and trysting thorn
  Where Nancy aft I courted;
Wha spied I but my ain dear maid,
  Down by her mother's dwelling!—
I turn'd me round to hide the flood
  That in my een was swelling.

Wi' alter'd voice quoth I, "Sweet lass,
  Sweet as yon hawthorn's blossom,
Oh, happy, happy may he be
  That's dearest to thy bosom!
My purse is light, I've far to gang,
  And fain wad be thy lodger;
I've served my king and country lang,—
  Take pity on a sodger."

Sae wistfully she gazed on me,
  And lovelier was than ever:
Quo' she, " A sodger ance I lo'ed,
  Forget him shall I never:
Our humble cot and hamely fare
  Ye freely shall partake it;
That gallant badge, the dear cockade,
  Ye're welcome for the sake o't!"

She gazed—she redden'd like a rose,*
  Syne pale like ony lily;
She sank within my arms, and cried,
  " Art thou my ain dear Willie ?"
" By Him who made yon sun and sky,
  By whom true love's regarded,
I am the man; and thus may still
  True lovers be rewarded.

The wars are o'er, and I'm come hame,
  And find thee still true-hearted;
Though poor in gear, we're rich in love,
  And mair we'se ne'er be parted."
Quo' she, " My grandsire left me gowd,
  A mailin plenish'd fairly;
And come, my faithful sodger lad,
  Thou'rt welcome to it dearly!"

For gold the merchant ploughs the main
  The farmer ploughs the manor;
But glory is the sodger's prize,
  The sodger's wealth is honour.
The brave poor sodger ne'er despise,
  Nor count him as a stranger;
Remember he's his country's stay
  In day and hour of danger.

---

* Mr. Thomson having written to Burns that he should get Mr. (afterwards Sir William) Allan to paint him a picture from this song, the poet wrote to him: " As to the point of time for the expression in your proposed print of my ' Sodger's Return,' it must certainly be at ' She gazed, she redden'd like a rose.' The interesting dubiety and suspense taking possession of her countenance, and the gushing fondness, with a mixture of roguish playfulness in his, strike me as things of which a master will make a great deal."

OH, GIN MY LOVE WERE YON RED ROSE.

In Witherspoon's Collection of Scots Songs.

"Do you know," says Burns, in a letter to Mr. Thomson, "the beautiful little fragment in Witherspoon's collection of Scots Songs, called, 'Oh, gin my love!' The thought it contains is inexpressibly beautiful, and quite, so far as I know, original. It is too short for a song, else I would forswear you altogether, unless you gave it a place. I have often tried to eke a stanza to it, but in vain."

Oh, gin my love were yon red rose
　　That grows upon the castle wa',
And I mysel' a drap o' dew,
　　Into her bonnie breast to fa'!

Oh, there, beyond expression blest,
　　I'd feast on beauty a' the night;
Seal'd on her silk-saft faulds to rest,
　　Till fley'd awa' by Phœbus' light.

"After balancing myself for a few minutes on the hind legs of my elbow-chair, I produced the following. That they are far inferior to the foregoing I frankly confess; but if worthy of insertion at all, they might be first in place, as every poet, who knows anything of his trade, will husband his best thoughts for a concluding stroke."

Oh, were my love yon lilac fair,
　　Wi' purple blossoms to the spring;
And I a bird to shelter there,
　　When wearied on my little wing;

How I wad mourn when it was torn
　　By autumn wild and winter rude!
But I wad sing on wanton wing
　　When youthfu' May its bloom renew'd.

A third stanza, written by a Mr. Richardson, appears in some collections; but it is scarcely worthy of association with these two. The air is Highland, and was formerly known as "Lord Balgonie's favourite."

OH, MY LOVE IS LIKE A RED, RED ROSE.

Anonymous.—Revised by Burns for " Johnson's Musical Museum."

Oh, my love is like a red, red rose
  That's newly sprung in June;
Oh, my love is like a melody
  That's sweetly play'd in tune.
As fair art thou, my bonnie lass,
  Sae deep in love am I;
And I will love thee still, my dear,
  Till a' the seas gang dry.

Till a' the seas gang dry, my dear,
  And the rocks melt wi' the sun;
Oh, I will love thee still, my dear,
  While the sands o' life shall run.
And fare thee weel, my only love,
  And fare thee weel awhile!
And I will come again, my love,
  Though it were ten thousand mile.

OH, POORTITH CAULD.

Burns.   Air—"I had a horse, I had nae mair."

Oh, poortith cauld and restless love,
  Ye wreck my peace between ye;
Yet poortith a' I could forgive,
  An' 'twere na for my Jeanie.
    Oh, why should fate sic pleasure have,
      Life's dearest bands untwining?
    Or why sae sweet a flower as love
      Depend on fortune's shining?

This warld's wealth when I think on,
  It's pride and a' the lave o't;
Fie, fie, on silly coward man,
  That he should be the slave o't!
         Oh, why, &c.

Her een sae bonnie blue betray
  How she repays my passion ;
But prudence is her o'erword aye,
  She talks o' rank and fashion.
                    Oh, why, &c.

Oh, wha can prudence think upon,
  And sic a lassie by him ?
Oh, wha can prudence think upon,
  And sae in love as I am ?
                    Oh, why, &c.

How blest the humble cottar's fate !
  He woos his simple dearie ;
The silly bogles wealth and state
  Can never make him eerie.
                    Oh, why, &c

MY AIN KIND DEARIE O.

Burns.   Air—"The Lea-Rig."

When o'er the hill the eastern star
  Tells bughtin-time is near, my jo,
And owsen frae the furrow'd field
  Return sae dowf and weary O ;
Down by the burn where scented birks
  Wi' dew are hanging clear, my jo,
I'll meet thee on the lea-rig,
  My ain kind dearie O.

In mirkest glen at midnicht hour
  I'd rove and ne'er be eerie O,
If through that glen I gaed to thee,
  My ain kind dearie O.
Although the night were ne'er sae wild,
  An' I were ne'er sae wearie O,
I'd meet thee on the lea-rig,
  My ain kind dearie O.

The hunter lo'es the morning sun,
　　To rouse the mountain deer, my jo;
At noon the fisher seeks the glen,
　　Along the burn to steer, my jo:
Gie me the hour o' gloamin' grey;
　　It maks my heart sae cheery O,
To meet thee on the lea-rig,
　　My ain kind dearie O.

Burns, in sending this song to George Thomson, which he had founded upon an olden composition with the same title, says, "Who shall rise up, and say, ' Go to! I will make a better' (then an old song)? For instance, on reading over the ' Lea-rig,' I immediately set trying my hand upon it, and after all, I could make nothing more of it than the following, which, Heaven knows, is poor enough!"

THE BANKS OF AYR.

Burns.　Air—"Roslin Castle."

The gloomy night is gath'ring fast,
Loud roars the wild inconstant blast;
Yon murky cloud is foul with rain,
I see it driving o'er the plain:
The hunter now has left the moor,
The scatter'd coveys meet secure;
While here I wander, prest with care,
Along the lonely banks of Ayr.

The Autumn mourns her rip'ning corn
By early Winter's ravage torn,
Across her placid azure sky
She sees the scowling tempest fly :
Chill runs my blood to hear it rave,
I think upon the stormy wave,
Where many a danger I must dare,
Far from the bonnie banks of Ayr.

'Tis not the surging billows' roar,
'Tis not that fatal, deadly shore ;
Though death in ev'ry shape appear,
The wretched have no more to fear :
But round my heart the ties are bound,
That heart transpierced with many a wound ;
These bleed afresh, those ties I tear,
To leave the bonnie banks of Ayr.

Farewell, old Coila's hills and dales,
Her heathy moors and winding vales ;
The scenes where wretched fancy roves,
Pursuing past, unhappy loves !
Farewell, my friends ! farewell, my foes !
My peace with these, my love with those -
The bursting tears my heart declare,
Farewell the bonnie banks of Ayr !

---♦---

AGAIN REJOICING NATURE SEES.

Burns.   Air—"I wish my love were in a myre."

AGAIN rejoicing Nature sees
   Her robe assume its vernal hue,
Her leafy locks wave in the breeze,
   All freshly steep'd in morning dew.

      And maun I still on Menie doat,
         And fear the scorn that's in her ee ?
      For it's jet, jet black, and it's like a hawk,
         And it winna let a bodie be.

In vain to me the cowslips blaw;
  In vain to me the vi'lets spring;
In vain to me in glen or shaw
  The mavis and the lint-white sing.
        And maun I still, &c.

The merry ploughboy cheers his team;
  Wi' joy the tentie seedman stauks;
But life to me's a weary dream,
  A dream of ane that never wauks.
        And maun I still, &c.

The wanton coot the water skims;
  Amang the reeds the ducklings cry;
The stately swan majestic swims;
  And everything is blest but I.
        And maun I still, &c.

The shepherd steeks his faulding slaps,
  And o'er the moorland whistles shrill;
Wi' wild, unequal, wandering step,
  I meet him on the dewy hill.
        And maun I still, &c.

And when the lark, 'tween light and dark,
  Blythe waukens by the daisie's side,
And mounts and sings on fluttering wings,
  A woe-worn ghaist I hameward glide.
        And maun I still, &c.

Come, Winter, with thine angry howl,
  And raging bend the naked tree;
Thy gloom will soothe my cheerless soul,
  When nature all is sad like me!

    And maun I still on Menie doat,
      And bear the scorn that's in her ee?
    For it's jet, jet black, and it's like a hawk,
    And it winna let a bodie be.

The chorus of this song is the composition of a gentleman in Edinburgh, a friend
of Robert Burns. 'Menie' is a term of endearment for Marianne. "We cannot,"
says Dr. Currie, "presume to alter any of the poems of our bard, and more especially
those printed under his own direction; yet it is to be regretted that this chorus,
which is not his own composition, should be attached to these fine stanzas, as it per-
petually interrupts the train of sentiment which they excite." Mr. George Thomson,
in printing the music, with Burns's poetry, omitted the chorus and the fourth
stanza.

THE BIRKS OF ABERFELDY.

BURNS.

BONNIE lassie, will ye go, will ye go, will ye go;
Bonnie lassie, will ye go to the birks of Aberfeldy?

Now simmer blinks on flowery braes,
And o'er the crystal streamlets plays;
Come, let us spend the lichtsome days
        In the birks of Aberfeldy.

While o'er their head the hazels hing,
The little birdies blythely sing,
Or lichtly flit on wanton wing,
        In the birks of Aberfeldy.

The braes ascend like lofty wa's,
The foamin' stream deep-roaring fa's,
O'erhung wi' fragrant spreading shaws,
        The birks of Aberfeldy.

The hoary cliffs are crown'd wi' flowers,
White ower the lin the burnie pours,
And risin weets wi' misty showers
        The birks of Aberfeldy.

Let Fortune's gifts at random flee,
They ne'er shall draw a wish frae me,
Supremely blest wi' love and thee,
        In the birks of Aberfeldy.

This song was written for "Johnson's Musical Museum," to the air of "The birks of Aberfeldy." From the original song Burns borrowed nothing but the chorus. The air is to be found, with some variations, in Playford's "Dancing Master," 1657.

CA' THE YOWES TO THE KNOWES.*

BURNS.

Ca' the yowes to the knowes,
Ca' them where the heather grows,
Ca' them where the burnie rows,
    My bonnie dearie.

Hark the mavis' evening sang,
Sounding Cluden's woods amang;
Then a-faulding let us gang,
    My bonnie dearie.

We'll gang doun by Cluden side,
Through the hàzels spreading wide
O'er the waves that sweetly glide,
    My bonnie dearie.

Yonder Cluden's silent towers,
Where, at moonshine midnight hours,
O'er the dewy budding flowers
    The fairies dance sae cheerie.

Ghaist nor bogle shalt thou fear;
Thou'rt to love and heaven sae dear,
Nocht of ill may come thee near,
    My bonnie dearie.

Fair and lovely as thou art,
Thou hast stown my very heart;
I can die, but canna part,
    My bonnie dearie.

* Burns says of this song, in a letter to Thomson, "I am flattered at your adopting 'Ca' the yowes to the knowes,' as it was owing to me that it ever saw the light. About seven years ago I was well acquainted with a worthy little fellow of a clergyman, a Mr. Clunie, who sang it charmingly; and, at my request, Mr. Clarke took it down from his singing. When I gave it to Johnson, I added some stanzas to the song, and mended others; but still it will not do for you. In a solitary stroll which I took to-day, I tried my hand on a few pastoral lines, following up the idea of the chorus, which I would preserve. Here it is, with all its crudities and imperfections on its head." Mr. Thomson, in reply, calls the song "a precious *morceau;*" and adds, "I am perfectly astonished and charmed with the endless variety of your fancy."

The original song upon which Burns founded his version is attributed to Isabell or Tibbie Pagan, who died in the neighbourhood of Muirkirk, Ayrshire, in 1821. aged eighty. Some account of her appears in the "Ayrshire Contemporaries of Burns," Edinburgh, 1840. The following version is the original, as revised by Burns for "Johnson's Musical Museum." The last verse is by Burns himself.

Ca' the yowes to the knowes,
Ca' them whare the heather grows,
Ca' them whare the burnie rows,
   My bonnie dearie.

As I gaed down the water-side,
There I met my shepherd lad,
He row'd me sweetly in his plaid,
  And ca'd me his dearie.
    Ca' the yowes, &c.

Will ye gang down the water-side,
And see the waves sae sweetly glide
Beneath the hazels spreading wide,
  The moon it shines fu' clearly.
    Ca' the yowes, &c.

I was bred up at nae sic school,
My shepherd lad, to play the fool,
And a' the day to sit in dool,
  And naebody to see me.
    Ca' the yowes, &c.

Ye shall get gowns and ribbons meet,
Cauf-leather shoon upon your feet,
And in my arms ye'se lie and sleep,
  And ye shall be my dearie.
    Ca' the yowes, &c.

If ye'll but stand to what ye've said,
I'se gang with you, my shepherd lad,
And ye may row me in your plaid,
  And I shall be your dearie.
    Ca' the yowes, &c.

While waters wimple to the sea,
While day blinks in the lift sae hie,
Till clay-cauld death shall blin' my ee,
  Ye aye shall be my dearie.
    Ca' the yowes, &c.

GALA WATER.

BURNS.

THERE's braw, braw lads on Yarrow braes,
  That wander through the blooming heather;
But Yarrow braes nor Ettrick shaws
  Can match the lads o' Gala water.

But there is ane, a secret ane,
  Abune them a' I lo'e him better;
And I'll be his, and he'll be mine,
  The bonnie lad o' Gala water.

Although his daddie was nae laird,
  And though I hae nae mickle tocher;
Yet rich in kindest, truest love,
  We'll tent our flocks on Gala water.

It ne'er was wealth, it ne'er was wealth,
  That coft contentment, peace, or pleasure;
The bands and bliss o' mutual love,
  Oh, that's the chiefest warld's treasure!

The old tune to which this is sung is very beautiful. Its exact date is unknown. Mr. Stenhouse, to whom the public are indebted for many valuable particulars relating to Scottish music, says it was harmonised by Haydn, for Whyte's collection. On the MS. of the music, which he (Mr. Stenhouse) had seen, Haydn expressed his opinion of the melody in the best English he was master of, in the following emphatic sentence: "This one Dr. Haydn favourite song." The words of the old song are lost, with the exception of the following stanzas :—

> Braw, braw lads of Gala water,
>   Braw, braw lads of Gala water;
> I'll kilt my coats aboon my knee,
>   And follow my love through the water.
>
> O'er yon bank and o'er yon brae,
>   O'er yon moss amang the heather,
> I'll kilt my coats aboon my knee,
>   And follow my love through the water.

MY NANNIE'S AWA.

Burns.   Air—"There'll never be peace until Jamie comes hame."

Now in her green mantle blythe Nature arrays,
And listens the lambkins that bleat ower the braes,
While birds warble welcome in ilka green shaw;
But to me it's delightless—my Nannie's awa.

The snaw-drap and primrose our woodlands adorn,
And violets bathe in the weet o' the morn;
They pain my sad bosom, sae sweetly they blaw;
They mind me o' Nannie—and Nannie's awa.

Thou laverock that springs frae the dews of the lawn,
The shepherd to warn of the grey-breaking dawn;
And thou mellow mavis that hails the night-fa',
Give over for pity—my Nannie's awa.

Come, Autumn, sae pensive in yellow and grey,
And soothe me wi' tidings o' nature's decay;
The dark dreary winter and wild driving snaw
Alane can delight me—my Nannie's awa.

The germ of "Nannie's Awa" is to be found in one of Clarinda's letters (*see* Correspondence, &c., page 185), written thirty-five days after they became acquainted. They were about to part, and she says:—"You'll hardly write me once a month, and other objects will weaken your affection for Clarinda; yet I cannot believe so. Oh! let the scenes of nature remind you of Clarinda! In winter, remember the dark shades of her fate; in summer, the warmth, the cordial warmth of her friendship; in autumn, her glowing wishes to bestow plenty on all; and let spring animate you with hope that your poor friend may yet live to surmount the wintry blast of life, and revive to taste a spring-time of happiness!" This passage, so beautifully descriptive, in the letter of his fair correspondent, was not overlooked by Burns. He says in reply:—"There is one fine passage in your last charming letter—Thomson nor Shenstone never exceeded it, nor often came up to it. I shall certainly steal it, and set it in some future production, and get immortal fame by it. 'Tis where you bid the scenes of nature remind me of Clarinda." The poet was as good as his word. Some months after Clarinda had left this country, Burns, reverting to the passage we have quoted from her letter, made it his own by stamping it in immortal verse, bewailing the absence of Clarinda in a strain of rural imagery that has seldom or never been surpassed."—Cursory Remarks on Scottish Song, by Captain Charles Gray, R.M.

WANDERING WILLIE.

BURNS. Air—"Wandering Willie."

HERE awa, there awa, wandering Willie,
　　Here awa, there awa, haud awa hame;
Come to my bosom, my ain only dearie,
　　Tell me thou bringst me my Willie the same.

Winter-winds blew loud and cauld at our parting,
　　Fears for my Willie brought tears in my ee;
Welcome now simmer, and welcome my Willie,—
　　As simmer to nature, so Willie to me.

Rest, ye wild storms, in the caves o' your slumbers;
　　How your dread howlings a lover alarms!
Blow soft, ye breezes, roll gently, ye billows,
　　And waft my dear laddie ance mair to my arms.

But oh, if he's faithless, and minds not his Nannie,
　　Flow still between us, thou dark heaving main;
May I never see it, may I never trow it;
　　While dying I think that my Willie's my ain!

This song was altered by Mr. Erskine and Mr. George Thomson. Burns, with
his usual sound judgment, adopted some of these alterations, and rejected others.

MY NANNIE O.

BURNS.

BEHIND yon hills where Lugar flows
　　Mang moors an' mosses many O,
The wintry sun the day has closed,
　　And I'll awa to Nannie O.

The westlan wind blaws loud an' shrill,
　　The night's baith mirk and rainy O;
But I'll get my plaid an' out I'll steal,
　　An' ower the hills to Nannie O.

My Nannie's charming, sweet, an' young
    Nae artfu' wiles to win ye O;
May ill befa' the flatt'ring tongue
    That wad beguile my Nannie O.

Her face is fair, her heart is true,
    As spotless as she's bonnie O;
The opening gowan wet wi' dew
    Nae purer is than Nannie O.

A country lad is my degree,
    An' few there be that ken me O;
But what care I how few they be?
    I'm welcome aye to Nannie O.

My riches a' 's my penny-fee,
    An' I maun guide it cannie O;
But warl's gear ne'er troubles me,
    My thoughts are o' my Nannie O.

Our auld gudeman delights to view
    His sheep an' kye thrive bonnie O;
But I'm as blithe that hauds his pleugh,
    An' hae nae care but Nannie O.

Come weel, come wae, I care na by,
    I'll take what Heaven will sen' me O;
Nae ither care in life have I
    But live an' love my Nannie O.

Burns founded this song upon a pre-existing one of a similar title. The name of the river which it celebrated was the Stinchar.

"In the printed copy of 'My Nannie O,'" he says, in a letter to Thomson, "the name of the river is horridly prosaic. I will alter it to 'Behind yon hills where Lugar flows.' Girvan is the name of the river that suits the idea of the stanza best, but Lugar is the most agreeeble modulation of syllables." The heroine of this song, written when the poet was very young, was Agnes Fleming, daughter of a small farmer in the parish of Tarbolton, Ayrshire. Allan Ramsay wrote a song to the same exquisite melody, but it is in no respect equal to the song of Burns. The air is exceedingly beautiful, and is believed to be old. It cannot, however, be traced further back than the "Orpheus Caledonians," 1725.

THE DAY RETURNS, MY BOSOM BURNS.

Burns.   Air—"Seventh of November."

THE day returns, my bosom burns,
  The blissful day we twa did meet;
Though winter wild in tempest toil'd,
  Ne'er summer sun was half sae sweet.
Than a' the pride that loads the tide,
  And crosses o'er the sultry line;
Than kingly robes, than crowns and globes,
  Heaven gave me more—it made thee mine.

While day and night can bring delight,
  Or nature aught of pleasure give;
While joys above my mind can move,
  For thee, and thee alone, I live!
When that grim foe of life below
  Comes in between to make us part;
The iron hand that breaks our band,
  It breaks my bliss—it breaks my heart.

The air was the composition of Robert Riddell, Esq., of Glenriddell, in honour
of whose marriage Burns wrote the song. The seventh of November was Mr.
Riddell's wedding day.

YE BANKS AND BRAES O' BONNIE DOON.*

BURNS.

YE banks and braes o' bonnie Doon,
　　How can ye bloom sae fresh and fair!
How can ye chant, ye little birds,
　　And I sae weary fou o' care!
Ye'll break my heart, ye little birds,
　　That wanton through the flowery thorn;
Ye mind me o' departed joys,
　　Departed never to return.

* "There is an air," says Burns, in a letter to Mr. Thomson, "called 'The Caledonian Hunt's delight,' to which I wrote a song that you will find in Johnson. 'Ye banks and braes o' bonnie Doon,' might, I think, find a place among your hundred, as Lear says of his nights. Do you know the history of the air? It is curious enough. A good many years ago, Mr. James Miller, writer in your good town, a gentleman whom possibly you know, was in company with our friend Clarke; and talking of Scottish music, Miller expressed an ardent ambition to be able to compose a Scots air. Mr. Clarke, partly by way of joke, told him to keep to the black keys of the harpsicord, and preserve some kind of rhythm, and he would infallibly compose a Scots air. Certain it is that in a few days Mr. Miller produced the rudiments of an air, which Mr. Clarke, with some touches and corrections, fashioned into the tune in question. Ritson, you know, has the same story of the *black keys;* but this account which I have just given you, Mr. Clarke informed me of several years ago. Now, to show you how difficult it is to trace the origin of our airs, I have heard it repeatedly asserted that this was an Irish air; nay, I met with an Irish gentleman who affirmed that he had heard it in Ireland among the old women; while, on the other hand, a countess informed me that the first person who introduced the air into this country was a baronet's lady of her acquaintance, who took down the notes from an itinerant piper in the Isle of Man. How difficult, then, to ascertain the truth respecting our poesy and music!"

Aft hae I roved by bonnie Doon,
  To see the rose and woodbine twine;
While ilka bird sang o' its luve,
  And fondly sae did I o' mine.
Wi' lightsome heart I pu'd a rose,
  The sweetest on its thorny tree;
But my fawse lover stole my rose,
  And left the thorn behind wi' me.

LASSIE WI' THE LINT-WHITE LOCKS.

BURNS. Air—"Rothiemurchus's rant."*

LASSIE wi' the lint-white locks,
  Bonnie lassie, artless lassie,
Wilt thou wi' me tent the flocks,
  Wilt thou be my dearie O?

Now Nature cleeds the flowery lea,
And a' is young and sweet like thee;
Oh, wilt thou share its joys wi' me,
  And say thou'lt be my dearie O?
    Lassie wi', &c.

And when the welcome summer shower
Has cheer'd ilk drooping little flower,
We'll to the breathing woodbine bower,
  At sultry noon, my dearie O.
    Lassie wi', &c.

When Cynthia lights wi' silver ray
The weary shearers' hameward way,
Through yellow waving fields we'll stray,
  And talk o' love, my dearie O.
    Lassie wi', &c.

* "The air of 'Rothiemurchus's rant,'" says Burns, "puts me in raptures. Unless I be pleased with a tune, I can never put verses to it. This piece," he adds, in a letter to Mr. Thomson, "has at least the merit of being a regular pastoral; the vernal morning, the summer noon, the autumnal evening, and the winter night, are regularly rounded. If you like it, well; if not, I will insert it in the Museum." Mr. Thomson replied, "Your verses for the 'Rothiemurchus' are so sweetly pastoral that I have sung myself into raptures with them."

And when the howling wintry blast
Disturbs my lassie's midnight rest,
Enclaspèd to my faithfu' breast,
   I'll comfort thee, my dearie O.
     Lassie wi', &c.

THE WOODLARK.

BURNS. Air—"Loch Erroch side."

OH, stay, sweet-warbling woodlark, stay,
Nor quit for me the trembling spray ;
A helpless lover courts thy lay,
   Thy soothing fond complaining.

Again, again that tender part,
That I may catch thy melting art ;
For surely that wad touch her heart,
   Wha kills me wi' disdaining.

Say, was thy little mate unkind,
And heard thee as the careless wind ?
Oh, nocht but love and sorrow join'd
   Sic notes o' woe could wauken.

Thou tells o' never-ending care,
O' speechless grief and dark despair ;
For pity's sake, sweet bird, nae mair,
   Or my poor heart is broken.

"Let me know at your very first leisure," says Burns to Thomson, "how you like this song." Thomson replied, "I cannot express the feeling of admiration with which I read your pathetic ' Woodlark.'"

HIGHLAND MARY.

BURNS. Air—"Katharine Ogie."

YE banks and braes and streams around
   The castle o' Montgomery,
Green be your woods, and fair your flowers,
   Your waters never drumlie.

There Simmer first unfald her robes,
  And there the langest tarry ;
For there I took the last farcweel
  O' my sweet Highland Mary.

How sweetly bloom'd the gay green birk,
  How rich the hawthorn's blossom,
As underneath their fragrant shade
  I clasp'd her to my bosom !
The golden hours on angel wings
  Flew o'er me and my dearie;
For dear to me as light and life
  Was my sweet Highland Mary.

Wi' mony a vow and lock'd embrace,
  Our parting was fu' tender ;
And pledging aft to meet again,
  We tore oursels asunder !
But, oh, fell death's untimely frost,
  That nipt my flower sae early !
Now green's the sod and cauld's the clay
  That wraps my Highland Mary !

Oh, pale, pale now those rosy lips
  I aft hae kiss'd sae fondly ;
And closed for aye the sparkling glance
  That dwelt on me sae kindly ;
And mould'ring now in silent dust
  That heart that lo'ed me dearly ;
But still within my bosom's core
  Shall live my Highland Mary.

"'Highland Mary,'" says the Hon. A. Erskine, in a letter to Mr. George Thomson, "is most enchantingly pathetic." Burns says of it himself, in a letter to Mr. Thomson : "The foregoing song pleases myself; I think it is in my happiest manner; you will see at first glance that it suits the air. The subject of the song is one of the most interesting passages of my youthful days [see note to "Mary in Heaven," p. 92]; and I own that I should be much flattered to see the verses set to an air which would insure celebrity. Perhaps, after all, 'tis the still-growing prejudice of my heart that throws a borrowed lustre over the merits of the composition."

I GAED A WAEFU' GATE YESTREEN.

BURNS. Air—" The blaithrie o't."

I GAED a waefu' gate yestreen,
  A gate, I fear, I'll dearly rue;
I gat my death frae twa sweet een,
  Twa lovely een o' bonnie blue.
'Twas not her golden ringlets bright,
  Her lips like roses wet wi' dew,
Her heaving bosom lily-white—
  It was her een sae bonnie blue.

She talk'd, she smil'd, my heart she wiled,
  She charm'd my soul I wistna how;
And aye the stound, the deadly wound,
  Cam' frae her een sae bonnie blue.
But spare to speak, and spare to speed,
  She'll aiblins listen to my vow;
Should she refuse, I'll lay me dead
  To her twa een sae bonnie blue.

MY WIFE'S A WINSOME WEE THING.

BURNS. Air—" My wife's a wanton wee thing."

SHE is a winsome wee thing,
She is a handsome wee thing,
She is a bonnie wee thing,
This sweet wee wife o' mine.

I never saw a fairer,
I never lo'ed a dearer,
And niest my heart I'll wear her,
For fear my jewel tine.

She is a winsome wee thing,
She is a handsome wee thing,
She is a bonnie wee thing,
This sweet wee wife o' mine.

The warld's wrack we share o't,
The warstle and the care o't;
Wi' her I'll blithely bear it,
And think my lot divine.

"There is a peculiar rhythmus," says Burns, in a letter to Thomson, " in many of
our airs, and a necessity of adapting syllables to the emphasis, or what I would call
the *feature-notes* of the tune, that cramp the poet, and lay him under most insuperable
difficulties. For instance, in the air, ' My wife's a winsome wee thing,' if a few
lines smooth and pretty can be adapted to it, it is all you can expect. The following
were made extempore to it; and though, on further study, I might give you something more profound, yet it might not suit the light-horse gallop of the air so well as
this random clink."

MY HEART IS SAIR, I DARENA TELL.

BURNS.   Air—"The Highland watch's farewell."

My heart is sair, I darena tell,
    My heart is sair for somebody;
I could wake a winter night
    For the sake o' somebody.
        Och-hon for somebody!
        Och-hey for somebody!
I could range the world around
    For the sake o' somebody.

Ye powers that smile on virtuous love,
    Oh, sweetly smile on somebody;
Frae ilka danger keep him free,
    And send me safe my somebody.
        Och-hon for somebody!
        Och-hey for somebody!
I wad do—what wad I not?
    For the sake o' somebody!

Altered and much improved from an older song of the same title.

HERE'S A HEALTH TO ANE I LO'E DEAR.

BURNS.   Air—" Here's a health to them that's awa' hinney."

HERE'S a health to ane I lo'e dear,
Here's a health to ane I lo'e dear;
Thou art sweet as the smile when fond lovers meet,
And soft as their parting tear—Jessy!

Although thou maun never be mine,
 Although even hope is denied;
'Tis sweeter for thee despairing
 Than aught in the world beside—Jessy!
  Here's a health, &c.

I mourn through the gay, gaudy day,
 As, hopeless, I muse on thy charms;
But welcome the dream o' sweet slumber,
 For then I am lockt in thy arms—Jessy!
  Here's a health, &c.

I guess by the dear angel smile,
 I guess by the love-rolling ee;
But why urge the tender confession
 'Gainst fortune's fell cruel decree—Jessy!
  Here's a health, &c.

" I once mentioned to you," says Burns, in a letter to Thomson, " an air which I
have long admired, ' Here's a health to them that's awa', hinney,' but I forget if you
took any notice of it. I have just been trying to suit it with verses, and I beg leave
to recommend the air to your attention once more." A great critic has affirmed that
the sentiment in the lines commencing, " Although thou maun never be mine," is
unparalleled in modern or ancient poetry for its beauty and depth of feeling. It
appears, however, to have been borrowed by Burns from Dryden's song, " Oh, how
sweet is young desire;" in which occur the lines :

Pains of love are sweeter far
Than all other pleasures are.

AE FOND KISS, AND THEN WE SEVER.

BURNS.

AE fond kiss, and then we sever;
Ae farewell, alas, for ever!
Deep in heart-wrung tears I'll pledge thee,
Warring sighs and groans I'll wage thee.

Who shall say that fortune grieves him
While the star of hope she leaves him ?
Me, nae cheerfu' twinkle lights me;
Dark despair around benights me.

I'll ne'er blame my partial fancy,
Naething could resist my Nancy;
But to see her was to love her,
Love but her, and love for ever.
Had we never loved sae kindly,
Had we never loved sae blindly,
Never met, or never parted,
We had ne'er been broken-hearted.

Fare thee weel, thou first and fairest;
Fare thee weel, thou best and dearest;
Thine be ilka joy and treasure,
Peace, enjoyment, love, and pleasure.
Ae fond kiss, and then we sever;
Ae fareweel, alas, for ever !
Deep in heart-wrung tears I pledge thee,
Warring sighs and groans I'll wage thee.

OF A' THE AIRTS THE WIND CAN BLAW.

Burns.   Air—" Miss Admiral Gordon's strathspey."

Of a' the airts the wind can blaw,
   I dearly like the west,
For there the bonnie lassie lives,
   The lassie I lo'e best;
There wild woods grow, and rivers flow,
   And mony a hill between;
But day and night my fancy's flight
   Is ever wi' my Jean.

I see her in the dewy flowers,
   I see her sweet and fair;
I hear her in the tunefu' birds,
   I hear her charm the air:

> There's not a bonnie flower that springs
>   By fountain, shaw, or green,
> There's not a bonnie bird that sings,
>   But minds me o' my Jean.

This song was written in celebration of the charms of Jean Armour, afterwards the poet's wife. In some editions there are four stanzas, but the two we have quoted are those usually sung, and were the only ones published by the poet himself. The beautiful melody was composed by a "native genius" of the name of Marshall, butler to the Duke of Gordon.

JOHN ANDERSON MY JO.

Burns.

> John Anderson my jo, John,
>   When we were first acquent,
> Your locks were like the raven,
>   Your bonnie brow was brent;
> But now your brow is bald, John,
>   Your locks are like the snaw;
> But blessings on your frosty pow,
>   John Anderson my jo.

John Anderson my jo, John,
    We clamb the hill thegither;
And mony a canty day, John,
    We've had wi' ane anither.
Now we maun totter down, John,
    But hand in hand we'll go,
And sleep thegither at the foot,
    John Anderson my jo.

In the first volume of a collection, entitled "Poetry, Original and Selected," printed in penny numbers by Brash and Reid, booksellers of Glasgow, between the years 1795 and 1798, this song is given as follows:

John Anderson my jo, John, I wonder what you mean,
To rise so soon in the morning, and sit up so late at e'en;
Ye'll blear out a' your een, John, and why should you do so?
Gang sooner to your bed at e'en, John Anderson my jo.

John Anderson my jo, John, when Nature first began
To try her canny hand, John, her masterwork was ma' ;
And you amang them a', John, sae trig frae tap to toe,
She proved to be nae journey-work, John Anderson my jo.

John Anderson my jo, John, ye were my first conceit,
And ye maunna think it strange, John, though I ca' ye trim and neat;
Though some folk think ye're auld, John, I never think ye so,
But I think ye're a' the same to me, John Anderson my jo.

John Anderson my jo, John, we've seen our bairns' bairns;
And yet, my dear John Anderson, I'm happy in your arms;
And sae are ye in mine, John,—I'm sure ye'll ne'er say no,
Though the days are gane that we have seen, John Anderson my jo.

John Anderson my jo, John, what pleasure does it gie
To see sae mony sprouts, John, spring up 'tween you and me!
And ilka lad and lass, John, in our footsteps to go,
Makes perfect heaven here on earth, John Anderson my jo.

John Anderson my jo, John, when we were first acquent,
Your locks were like the raven, your bonnie brow was brent;
But now your head's turn'd bauld, John, your locks are like the snaw,
Yet blessings on your frosty pow, John Anderson my jo.

John Anderson my jo, John, frae year to year we've pass'd,
And soon that year maun come, John, will bring us to our last;
But let na' that affright us, John, our hearts were ne'er our foe,
While in innocent delight we lived, John Anderson my jo.

John Anderson my jo, John, we clamb the hill thegither.
And mony a canty day, John, we've had wi' ane anither;
Now we maun totter down, John, but hand in hand we'll go,
And we'll sleep thegither at the foot, John Anderson my jo.

"The stanza," says Dr. Currie, "with which this song, inserted by Brash and Reid, begins, is the chorus of the old song under this title; and though perfectly suitable to that wicked but witty ballad, it has no accordance with the strain of delicate and tender sentiment of this improved song. In regard to the five other additional stanzas, though they are in the spirit of the two that are unquestionably our bard's, yet every reader of discernment will see they are by an inferior hand; and the real author of them ought neither to have given them, nor suffered them to be given to the world, as the production of Burns. If there were no other mark of their spurious origin, the latter half of the third line in the seventh stanza,—'our hearts were ne'er our foe,'—would be proof sufficient. Many are the instances in which our bard has adopted defective rhymes; but a single instance cannot be produced in which, to preserve the rhyme, he has given a feeble thought in false grammar. These additional stanzas are not, however, without merit, and they may serve to prolong the pleasure which every person of taste must feel from listening to a most happy union of beautiful music with moral sentiments that are singularly interesting."

The following three stanzas were published by Brash and Reid, but not quoted by Dr. Currie. The idea is the same as that expressed by Burns, but has not the masterly expression he gave to it.

> John Anderson my jo, John,
>   Our siller ne'er was rife,
> And yet we ne'er saw poverty
>   Sin' we were man and wife:
> We've aye haen bit and brat, John,
>   Great blessings here below,
> And that helps to keep peace at hame,
>   John Anderson my jo.
>
> John Anderson my jo, John,
>   The world lo'es us baith;
> We ne'er spak' ill o' neibours, John,
>   Nor did them ony skaith;
> To live in peace and quietness
>   Was a' our care, ye know;
> And I'm sure they'll greet when we are dead,
>   John Anderson my jo.
>
> John Anderson my jo, John,
>   And when the time is come,
> That we, like ither auld folk, John,
>   Maun sink into the tomb;
> A motto we will hae, my John,
>   To let the world know
> We happy lived, contented died,
>   John Anderson my jo.

SAE FLAXEN WERE HER RINGLETS.

BURNS.   Air—"Onagh's waterfall."

Sae flaxen were her ringlets,
    Her eyebrows of a darker hue
Bewitchingly o'erarching
    Twa laughing een o' bonnie blue.
Her smiling sae wyling
    Wad make a wretch forget his woe;
What pleasure, what treasure,
    Unto these rosy lips to grow!

Such was my Chloris' bonnie face
  When first her bonnie face I saw ;
And aye my Chloris' dearest charm,—
  She says she lo'es me best of a'.

Like harmony her motion ;
  Her pretty ancle is a spy
Betraying fair proportion
  Wad make a saint forget the sky.
Sae warming, sae charming,
  Her faultless form and gracefu' air ;
Ilk feature—auld Nature
  Declared that she could do nae mair.
Hers are the willing chains o' love,
  By conquering beauty's sovereign law ;
And aye my Chloris' dearest charm,—
  She says she lo'es me best of a'.

Let others love the city,
  And gaudy show at sunny noon ;
Gie me the lonely valley,
  The dewy eve, and rising moon
Fair beaming, and streaming
  Her silver light the boughs amang ;
While falling, recalling,
  The amorous thrush concludes his sang ;
There, dearest Chloris, wilt thou rove
  By whimpling burn and leafy shaw,
And hear my vows o' truth and love,
  And say thou lo'e me best of a' ?

Burns's songs were not all adapted to Scottish, but some few of them to Irish and
to English melodies. " Do you know," he says, in a letter to Thomson, " a black-
guard Irish song called ' Onagh's waterfall?' The air is charming, and I have often
regretted the want of decent verses to it. It is too much, at least for my humble
rustic Muse, to expect that every effort of hers shall have merit ; still I think that it
is better to have mediocre verses to a favourite air than none at all."

DINNA ASK ME GIN I LUVE THEE.

From the " Minstrelsy of the North of Scotland," collected by Peter Buchan.

Dinna ask me gin I luve thee,
  Deed I darena tell ;
Dinna ask me gin I luve thee,
  Ask it o' yoursel'.

When ye come to yon town end—
Full mony a lass ye'll see—
Dinna, dinna look at them,
For fear ye mindna me.
Dinna ask me, &c.

Oh, dinna look at me sa aft,
Sae well as ye may trow;
For when ye look at me sae aft,
I canna look at you.
Dinna ask me, &c.

Little ken ye but mony ane
Will say they fancy thee;
But only keep you, mind, to them
That fancy nane but thee.
Dinna ask me, &c.

DELVIN SIDE.

From a manuscript collection of the " Northern Scottish Minstrelsy,"
by Peter Buchan.

WILL ye gae, my bonny May;
Will ye gae, my bonny bridie;
Will ye gae, my bonny May,
An' breast the braes o' Delvin sidie?

Where got ye that bonny May;
Where got ye that bonny bridie?
I got her down by Buchan's how,
An' brought her up to Delvin sidie.

Can ye play me Delvin side;
Can ye play me Delvin diddle?
Oh, play me up sweet Delvin side,
Or else I swear I'll brak your fiddle.

I can play ye Delvin side,
I can play ye Delvin diddle,
I can play ye Delvin side;
My bowstring's sweet, an' sweet's my fiddle.

This composition is of no merit, but is given, with others from Mr. Buchan's
collection, as a specimen of the songs that continue to be popular among the peasantry,
notwithstanding all that was done by Burns and others to introduce a higher style
and better taste among them.

THE EVENING STAR.

DR. JOHN LEYDEN, died 1811.

How sweet thy modest light to view,
   Fair star! to love and lovers dear;
While trembling on the falling dew,
   Like beauty shining through the tear;

Or hanging o'er that mirror-stream
   To mark each image trembling there,
Thou seem'st to smile with softer gleam
   To see thy lovely face so fair.

Though, blazing o'er the arch of night,
   The moon thy timid beams outshine
As far as thine each starry light—
   Her rays can never vie with thine.

Thine are the soft enchanting hours
   When twilight lingers on the plain,
And whispers to the closing flow'rs,
   That soon the sun will rise again.

Thine is the breeze that, murmuring bland
   As music, wafts the lover's sigh;
And bids the yielding heart expand
   In love's delicious ecstasy.

Fair star! though I be doomed to prove
   That rapture's tears are mixed with pain
Ah! still I feel 'tis sweet to love,—
   But sweeter to be loved again.

WHERE SHALL THE LOVER REST?

Sir Walter Scott, born 1771, died 1832. From " Marmion."

Where shall the lover rest,
  Whom the fates sever
From his true maiden's breast,
  Parted for ever?
Where through groves deep and high
  Sounds the far billow,
Where early violets die
  Under the willow.
      Eleu loro.
  Soft shall be his pillow.

There, through the summer day,
  Cool streams are laving;
There, while the tempests sway,
  Scarce are boughs waving;
There thy rest shalt thou take,
  Parted for ever,
Never again to wake,
  Never, oh, never!
      Eleu loro.
  Never, oh, never!

Where shall the traitor rest,
  He the deceiver,
Who could win maiden's breast,
  Ruin, and leave her?
In the lost battle,
  Borne down by the flying,
Where mingles war's rattle
  With groans of the dying.
      Eleu loro.
  There shall he be lying.

Her wing shall the eagle flap
  O'er the false-hearted;
His warm blood the wolf shall lap
  Ere life be parted;
Shame and dishonour sit
  By his grave ever;
Blessing shall hallow it—
  Never, oh, never!
      Eleu loro.
  Never, oh, never!

THE CAPTIVE HUNTSMAN.

SIR WALTER SCOTT.   From the " Lady of the Lake."

My hawk is tired of perch and hood,
My idle greyhound loathes his food,
My horse is weary of his stall,
And I am sick of captive thrall.
I wish I were as I have been,
Hunting the hart in forests green,
With bended bow and bloodhound free,
For that's the life is meet for me.

I hate to learn the ebb of time
From yon dull steeple's drowsy chime,

Or mark it as the sunbeams crawl
Inch after inch along the wall.
The lark was wont my matin ring,
The sable rook my vespers sing;
These towers, although a king's they be,
Have not a hall of joy for me.

No more at dawning morn I rise,
And sun myself in Ellen's eyes,
Drive the fleet deer the forest through,
And homeward wend with evening dew;
A blythesome welcome blythely meet,
And lay my trophies at her feet,
While fled the eve on wing of glee—
That life is lost to love and me.

HE IS GONE ON THE MOUNTAIN.

Sir Walter Scott.   From the " Lady of the Lake."

He is gone on the mountain,
   He is lost to the forest,
Like a summer-dried fountain,
   When our need was the sorest.
The font, re-appearing,
   From the rain-drops shall borrow;
But to us comes no cheering,
   To Duncan no morrow!

The hand of the reaper
   Takes the ears that are hoary;
But the voice of the weeper
   Wails manhood in glory.
The autumn winds rushing
   Waft the leaves that are searest;
But our flower was in flushing
   When blighting was nearest.

Fleet foot on the correi,
  Sage counsel in cumber,
Red hand in the foray,
  How sound is thy slumber!
Like the dew on the mountain,
  Like the foam on the river,
Like the bubble on the fountain,
  Thou art gone, and for ever!

JOCK O' HAZELDEAN.

SIR WALTER SCOTT. Modernised from the ancient ballad of "Jock o' Hazelgreen."

"WHY weep ye by the tide, ladye—
  Why weep ye by the tide?
I'll wed ye to my youngest son,
  And ye shall be his bride;
And ye shall be his bride, ladye,
  Sae comely to be seen:"
But aye she loot the tears down fa'
  For Jock o' Hazeldean.

"Now let this wilful grief be done,
  And dry that cheek so pale;
Young Frank is chief of Errington,
  And lord of Langley dale;
His step is first in peaceful ha',
  His sword in battle keen:"
But aye she loot the tears down fa'
  For Jock o' Hazeldean.

"A chain o' gold ye sall not lack,
  Nor braid to bind your hair,
Nor mettled hound, nor managed hawk,
  Nor palfrey fresh and fair;
And you, the foremost o' them a',
  Shall ride our forest queen:"
But aye she loot the tears down fa'
  For Jock o' Hazeldean.

The kirk was deck'd at morning-tide,
  The tapers glimmer'd fair;
The priest and bridegroom wait the bride,
  And dame and knight were there:
They sought her baith by bower and ha';
  The ladye was not seen!
She's o'er the Border and awa'
  Wi' Jock o' Hazeldean.

A WEARY LOT IS THINE, FAIR MAID.

SIR WALTER SCOTT.   From "Rokeby."

A WEARY lot is thine, fair maid,
  A weary lot is thine;
To pull the thorn thy brow to braid,
  And press the rue for wine.
A lightsome eye, a soldier's mien,
  A feather of the blue,
A doublet of the Lincoln green,—
    No more of me you knew, my love;
    No more of me you knew.

This morn is merry June, I trow,
  The rose is budding fain;
But it shall bloom in winter snow
  Ere we two meet again.—
He turned his charger as he spake
  Upon the river shore;
He gave his bridle-reins a shake,
    Said, Adieu for evermore, my love;
    And adieu for evermore.

BLYTHE AND CHEERIE.

Jamws Hogg, the " Ettrick Shepherd," born Jan. 25, 1772, died Nov. 21, 1835.
Air—"Andro and his cutty gun."

On Ettrick clear there grows a brier,
  An' monie a bonnie bloomin' shaw;
But Peggy's grown the fairest flower
  The braes o' Ettrick ever saw.
Her cheek is like the woodland rose,
  Her ee the violet set wi' dew;
The lily's fair without compare,
  Yet in her bosom tines its hue.

Had I her hame at my wee house,
  That stands aneath yon mountain high,
To help me wi' the kye an' ewes,
  An' in my arms at e'ening lie;
Oh, sae blythe, an', oh, sae cheerie,
  Oh, sae happy we wad be!
The lammie to the ewe is dear,
  But Peggy's dearer far to me.

WHEN THE KYE COME HAME.

JAMES HOGG.   Air—"The blaithrie o't."

COME, all ye jolly shepherds
    That whistle through the glen,
I'll tell ye of a secret
    That courtiers dinna ken.
What is the greatest bliss
    That the tongue o' man can name?
'Tis to woo a bonnie lassie
    When the kye come hame.
        When the kye come hame,
            When the kye come hame;
        'Tween the gloamin' and the mirk,
            When the kye come hame.

'Tis not beneath the burgonet,
    Nor yet beneath the crown,
'Tis not on couch of velvet,
    Nor yet on bed of down;
'Tis beneath the spreading birch,
    In the dell without a name,
Wi' a bonnie, bonnie lassie
    When the kye come hame.

There the blackbird bigs his nest
    For the mate he loves to see,
And up upon the tapmost bough,
    Oh, a happy bird is he!
Then he pours his melting ditty,
    And love 'tis a' the theme,
And he'll woo his bonnie lassie
    When the kye come hame.

When the bluart bears a pearl,
    And the daisy turns a pea,
And the bonnie lucken gowan
    Has fauldit up his ee,

Then the laverock frae the blue lift
  Draps down, and thinks nae shame
To woo his bonnie lassie
  When the kye come hame.

Then the eye shines sae bright,
  The haill soul to beguile,
There's love in every whisper,
  And joy in every smile.
Oh, who would choose a crown,
  Wi' its perils and its fame,
And miss a bonnie lassie
  When the kye come hame?

See yonder pawky shepherd
  That lingers on the hill—
His yowes are in the fauld,
  And his lambs are lying still;
Yet he downa gang to rest,
  For his heart is in a flame
To meet his bonnie lassie
  When the kye come hame.

Awa' wi' fame and fortune—
  What comfort can they gi'e ?—
And a' the arts that prey
  On man's life and libertie.
Gi'e me the highest joy
  That the heart o' man can frame,
My bonnie, bonnie lassie,
  When the kye come hame.

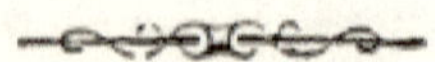

GLOOMY WINTER'S NOW AWA'.

ROBERT TANNAHILL, born June 3, 1774, died May 17, 1810.

GLOOMY winter's now awa',
Saft the westling breezes blaw,
'Mang the birks of Stanley shaw
  The mavis sings fu' cheery O;
Sweet the crawflow'r's early bell
Decks Gleniffer's dewy dell,
Blooming like thy bonnie sel',
  My young, my artless dearie O.
Come, my lassie, let us stray
O'er Glenkilloch's sunny brae,
Blythely spend the gowden day
  'Midst joys that never weary O.

Tow'ring o'er the Newton woods,
Lav'rocks fan the snaw-white clouds,
Siller saughs with downy buds
  Adorn the banks sae briery O.
Round the sylvan fairy nooks
Feath'ry breckans fringe the rocks,
'Neath the brae the burnie jouks,
  And ilka thing is cheery O.
Trees may bud and birds may sing,
Flow'rs may bloom and verdure spring,
Joy to me they canna bring,
  Unless wi' thee, my dearie O.

THE LASS O' ARRANTEENIE.

ROBERT TANNAHILL. This poet, a weaver in Paisley—an amiable but most
unfortunate man—wrote upon many imaginary fair ones, and associated their names
with places he had never seen. Arranteenie is a place unknown, but is supposed to
have been intended for Ardentinny, a lovely spot on the shore of Loch Long, in
Argyleshire.

FAR lone amang the Highland hills,
  'Midst nature's wildest grandeur,
By rocky dens and woody glens,
  With weary steps I wander.
The langsome way, the darksome day,
  The mountain mist sae rainy,
Are nought to me when gaun to thee,
  Sweet lass o' Arranteenie.

Yon mossy rose-bud down the how
  Just opening fresh and bonny,
It blinks beneath the hazel bough,
  And 's scarcely seen by ony.
Sae sweet amidst her native hills
  Obscurely blooms my Jeanie,
Mair fair and gay than rosy May,
  The flower o' Arranteenie.

Now from the mountain's lofty brow
  I view the distant ocean;
There avarice guides the bounding prow,
  Ambition courts promotion.
Let Fortune pour her golden store,
  Her laurell'd favours many,
Give me but this, my soul's first wish,
  The lass o' Arranteenie.

JESSIE, THE FLOWER O' DUMBLANE.

ROBERT TANNAHILL. The music by R. A. SMITH. One of the most popular
of the modern Scotch melodies.

THE sun has gane down o'er the lofty Benlomond,
  And left the red clouds to preside o'er the scene,
While lanely I stray in the calm summer gloaming,
  To muse on sweet Jessie, the flow'r o' Dumblane.

How sweet is the brier wi' its soft faulding blossom,
 And sweet is the birk wi' its mantle o' green;
Yet sweeter and fairer, and dear to this bosom,
 Is lovely young Jessie, the flow'r o' Dumblane.

She's modest as 'ony, and blythe as she's bonny,
 For guileless simplicity marks her its ain;
And far be the villain, divested of feeling,
 Wha'd blight in its bloom the sweet flow'r o' Dumblane.
Sing on, thou sweet mavis, thy hymn to the e'ening,
 Thou'rt dear to the echoes of Calderwood glen;
Sae dear to this bosom, sae artless and winning,
 Is charming young Jessie, the flow'r o' Dumblane.

How lost were my days till I met wi' my Jessie,
 The sports of the city seemed foolish and vain;
I ne'er saw a nymph I could ca' my dear lassie,
 Till charm'd with young Jessie, the flow'r o' Dumblane.
Though mine were the station o' loftiest grandeur,
 Amidst its profusion I'd languish in pain,
And reckon as naething the height o' its splendour,
 If wanting young Jessie, the flow'r o' Dumblane.

OH, ARE YE SLEEPING, MAGGIE?

Robert Tannahill. Air—"Sleepy Maggie."

  Oh, are ye sleeping, Maggie,
  Oh, are ye sleeping, Maggie?
  Let me in, for loud the linn
  Is roaring o'er the warlock craigie.

  Mirk and rainy is the night,
   No a starn in a' the carry;
  Lightnings gleam athwart the lift,
   And winds drive wi' winter's fury.
    Oh, are ye sleeping, Maggie, &c.

Fearful soughs the boortree bank,
  The rifted wood roars wild and dreary;
Loud the iron yate goes clank,
  And cry of howlets makes me eerie.
        Oh, are ye sleeping, Maggie, &c.

Aboon my breath I darna speak,
  For fear I rouse your waukrife daddie;
Cauld's the blast upon my cheek,—
  Oh, rise, rise, my bonnie ladye!
        Oh, are ye sleeping, Maggie, &c.

She opt the door, she let him in,
  He cuist aside his dreeping plaidie.
" Blaw your warst, ye rain and win',
  Since, Maggie, now I'm in aside ye."

Now since ye're waking, Maggie,
Now since ye're waking, Maggie;
What care I for the howlet's cry,
For boortree bank, or warlock craigie?

LOUDON'S BONNIE WOODS AND BRAES.

ROBERT TANNAHILL.

" LOUDON's bonnie woods and braes,
  I maun leave them a', lassie;
Wha can thole when Britain's faes
  Would gi'e to Britons law, lassie?
Wha wad shun the field o' danger;
Wha to fame would live a stranger?
Now when freedom bids avenge her,
  Wha should shun her ca', lassie?
Loudon's bonnie woods and braes
Hae seen our happy bridal days,
And gentle hope shall soothe thy waes,
  When I am far awa', lassie."

" Hark, the swelling bugle rings,
   Yielding joy to thee, laddie;
But the dolefu' bugle brings
   Waefu' thochts to me, laddie.
Lanely I may climb the mountain,
Lanely stray beside the fountain,
Still the weary moments counting,
   Far frae love and thee, laddie.
Ower the gory fields o' war,
Where vengeance drives his crimson car,
Thou may fa' frae me afar,
   And nane to close thy ee, laddie."

" Oh, resume thy wonted smile,
   Oh, suppress thy fears, lassie;
Glorious honour crowns the toil
   That the soldier shares, lassie.
Heaven will shield thy faithful lover
Till the vengeful strife is over;
Then we'll meet nae mair to sever,
   Till the day we dee, lassie.
'Midst our bonnie woods and braes
We'll spend our peaceful, happy days,
As blythe's yon lichtsome lamb that plays
   On Loudon's flowery lea, lassie.

------------◆------------

WHAT AILS THIS HEART O' MINE?

Susanna Blamire.
Air—" Sir James Baird's favourite," or " My dearie, an' thou dee."

What ails this heart o' mine?
   What ails this watery ee?
What gars me a' turn cauld as death
   When I take leave o' thee?
When thou art far awa',
   Thou'lt dearer grow to me;
But change o' place and change o' folk
   May gar thy fancy jee.

When I gae out at e'en,
　Or walk at morning air,
Ilk rustling bush will seem to say,
　I used to meet thee there.
Then I'll sit down and cry,
　And live aneath the tree,
And when a leaf fa's i' my lap,
　I'll ca't a word frae thee.

I'll hie me to the bower
　That thou wi' roses tied,
And where wi' mony a blushing bud
　I strove mysel' to hide.
I'll doat on ilka spot
　Where I hae been wi' thee,
And ca' to mind some kindly word
　By ilka burn and tree.

Wi' sic thoughts i' my mind,
　Time through the world may gae,
And find my heart in twenty years
　The same as 'tis to-day,
'Tis thoughts that bind the soul,
　And keep friends i' the ee ;
And gin I think I see thee aye,
　What can part thee and me ?

------♦------

THE WAEFU' HEART.

Susanna Blamire.　Published 1788.

Gin livin' worth could win my heart,
　You would not speak in vain ;
But in the darksome grave it's laid,
　Never to rise again.
My waefu' heart lies low wi' his,
　Whose heart was only mine ;
Oh, what a heart was that to lose !
　But I maun no repine.

Yet, oh, gin Heaven in mercy soon
　Would grant the boon I crave,
And take this life, now naething worth,
　Sin' Jamie's in his grave !
And see, his gentle spirit comes,
　To show me on my way;
Surprised, nae doubt, I still am here,
　Sair wondering at my stay.

I come, I come, my Jamie dear,
　And, oh, wi' what guid will
I follow wheresoe'er ye lead,
　Ye canna lead to ill.——
She said, and soon a deadly pale
　Her faded cheek possess'd;
Her waefu' heart forgot to beat,
　Her sorrows sunk to rest.

This excellent song is erroneously stated, in the notes to the collection of melodies published in Glasgow in 1841, under the title of "The Garland of Scotia," to be the production of one Jeanie Ferguson.

* * *

AND YE SHALL WALK IN SILK ATTIRE.

SUSANNA BLAMIRE.　From the "Musical Museum," 1790.
Air—"The siller crown."

AND ye shall walk in silk attire,
　And siller hae to spare,
Gin ye'll consent to be his bride,
　Nor think o' Donald mair.
Oh, wha wad buy a silken goun
　Wi' a pure broken heart?
Or what's to me a siller crown,
　Gin frae my love I part?

The mind whase every wish is pure
　Far dearer is to me;
And ere I'm forced to break my faith,
　I'll lay me down and dee:

For I hae pledged my virgin troth
   Brave Donald's fate to share,
And he has gi'en to me his heart,
   Wi' a' its virtues rare.

His gentle manners wan my heart,
   He gratefu' took the gift ;
Could I but think to see it back,
   It wad be waur than theft.
For langest life can ne'er repay
   The love he bears to me ;
And ere I'm forced to break my troth,
   I'll lay me down and dee.

I WINNA GANG BACK TO MY MAMMY AGAIN.

RICHARD GALL, born 1776, died 1801.

I WINNA gang back to my mammy again,
I'll never gae back to my mammy again ;
I've held by her apron these aught years an' ten,
But I'll never gang back to my mammy again.
    I've held by her apron, &c.

Young Johnnie cam' down i' the gloamin' to woo,
Wi' plaidie sae bonnie an' bonnet sae blue :
" Oh, come awa', lassie, ne'er let mammy ken ;"
An' I flew wi' my laddie o'er meadow an' glen.
    Oh, come awa', lassie, &c.

He ca'd me his dawtie, his dearie, his dow,
An' press'd hame his words wi' a smack o' my mou';
While I fell on his bosom, heart-flichter'd an' fain,
An' sigh'd out, " O Johnnie, I'll aye be your ain !"
    While I fell on his bosom, &c.

Some lasses will talk to the lads wi' their ee,
Yet hanker to tell what their hearts really dree ;
Wi' Johnnie I stood upon nae stappin'-stane,
Sae I'll never gang back to my mammy again.
    Wi' Johnnie I stood, &c.

For mony lang year sin' I play'd on the lea,
My mammy was kind as a mither could be ;
I've held by her apron these aught years an' ten,
But I'll never gang back to my mammy again.
    I've held by her apron, &c.

FAREWELL TO AYRSHIRE.

RICHARD GALL.

SCENES of woe and scenes of pleasure,
  Scenes that former thoughts renew,
Scenes of woe and scenes of pleasure,
  Now a sad and last adieu !
Bonnie Doon, sae sweet at gloamin',
  Fare thee weel before I gang ;
Bonnie Doon, whare, early roaming,
  First I weaved the rustic sang.

Bowers, adieu ! whare love decoying
  First enthrall'd this heart o' mine ;
There the saftest sweets enjoying,
  Sweets that memory ne'er shall tine.
Friends, sae near my bosom ever,
  Ye hae render'd moments dear ;
But, alas, when forced to sever,
  Then the stroke, oh, how severe !

Friends, that parting tear, reserve it,
  Though 'tis doubly dear to me ;
Could I think I did deserve it,
  How much happier would I be !

Scenes of woe and scenes of pleasure,
Scenes that former thoughts renew,
Scenes of woe and scenes of pleasure,
Now a sad and last adieu!

The following particulars regarding this song are given by Mr. Starke in the life of the author in the " Biographica Scotica," Edinburgh, 1805 : " One of Mr. Gall's songs in particular, the original manuscript of which I have by me, has acquired a high degree of praise, from its having been printed among the works of Burns, and generally thought the production of that poet. The reverse, indeed, was only known to a few of Mr. Gall's friends, to whom he communicated the verses before they were published. The fame of Burns stands in no need of the aid of others to support it; and to render back the song in question to its true author, is but an act of distributive justice due alike to both these departed poets, whose ears are now equally insensible to the incense of flattery or the slanders of malevolence. At the time when the 'Scots Musical Museum' was published at Edinburgh by Mr. Johnson, several of Burns's songs made their appearance in that publication. Mr. Gall wrote the song entitled 'A Farewell to Ayrshire,' prefixed Burns's name to it, and sent it anonymously to the publisher of that work. From thence it has been copied into the later editions of the works of Burns. In publishing the song in this manner, Mr. Gall probably thought that it might, under the sanction of a name known to the world, acquire some notice, while in other circumstances its fate might have been 'to waste its sweetness on the desert air.'" Neither Mr. Gall nor his biographer seem to have reflected upon the dishonesty of the proceeding towards the public, and of the gross unfairness towards the greater poet, whose name was used.

LOGAN BRAES.

JOHN MAYNE,* author of the "Siller Gun." First printed in the "Star"
newspaper, 1789. Air—"Logan water."

" BY Logan's streams, that rin sae deep,
Fu' aft wi' glee I've herded sheep—
Herded sheep, or gather'd slaes,
Wi' my dear lad on Logan braes.
But wae's my heart! thae days are gane,
And I wi' grief may herd alane ;
While my dear lad maun face his faes
Far, far frae me an' Logan braes.

Nae mair at Logan kirk will he
Atween the preachings meet wi' me—
Meet wi' me, or when its mirk
Convoy me hame frae Logan kirk.

* John Mayne, formerly editor of the "Star" newspaper, died in the year 1836.

I weel may sing thae days are gane—
Frae kirk an' fair I come alane;
While my dear lad maun face his faes
Far, far frae me an' Logan braes.

At e'en, when hope amaist is gone,
I dauner out, or sit alane—
Sit alane beneath the tree
Where aft he kept his tryst wi' me.
Oh, could I see thae days again,
My lover skaithless an' my ain !
Beloved by frien's, revered by faes,
We'd live in bliss on Logan braes."

While for her love she thus did sigh,
She saw a sodger passing by—
Passing by wi' scarlet claes,
While sair she grat on Logan braes.
Says he, " What gars thee greet sae sair,
What fills thy heart sae fu' o' care ?
Thae sporting lambs hae blythesome days,
An' playfu' skip on Logan braes."

" What can I do but weep and mourn ?
I fear my lad will ne'er return—
Ne'er return to ease my waes,
Will ne'er come home to Logan braes."
Wi' that he clasp'd her in his arms,
And said, " I'm free from war's alarms ;
I now hae conquered a' my faes,—
We'll happy live on Logan braes."

Then straight to Logan kirk they went,
And join'd their hands wi' one consent—
Wi' one consent to end their days
An' live in bliss on Logan braes.
An' now she sings, " Thae days are gane,
When I wi' grief did herd alane,
While my dear lad did fight his faes
Far, far frae me an' Logan braes."

THERE'S KAMES O' HINNIE 'TWEEN MY LUVE'S LIPS.

ALLAN CUNNINGHAM, born 1784, died 1842. From "Cromek's Remains of Nithsdale and Galloway Song."

THERE'S kames o' hinnie 'tween my luve's lips,
    And gowd amang her hair;
Her breists are lapt in a holy veil,
    Nae mortal een keek there.
What lips daur kiss, or what hand daur touch,
    Or what arm o' luve daur span,
The hinnie lips, the creamy lufe,
    Or the waist o' Lady Ann?

She kisses the lips o' her bonnie red rose,
    Wat wi' the blobs o' dew;
But nae gentle lip nor semple lip
    Maun touch her ladie mou'.
But a broider'd belt, wi' a buckle o' gowd,
    Her jimpy waist maun span;
Oh, she's an armfu' fit for heaven—
    My bonnie Lady Ann.

Her bower casement is latticed wi' flowers
    Tied up wi' siller thread,
And comely sits she in the midst,
    Men's longing een to feed.
She waves the ringlets frae her cheek
    Wi' her milky, milky hand;
And her every look beams wi' grace divine,
    My bonnie Lady Ann.

The mornin' clud is tasselt wi' gowd,
    Like my luve's broider'd cap;
And on the mantle that my luve wears
    Is mony a gowden drap.
Her bonnie ee-bree's a holy arch,
    Cast by nae earthly han';
And the breath o' heaven is atween the lips
    O' my bonnie Lady Ann.

I wonderin' gaze on her stately steps,
    And I beet a hopeless flame;
To my luve, alas! she mauna stoop,
    It wad stain her honour'd name.

My een are bauld, they dwall on a place
  Where I daurna mint my han';
But I water and tend and kiss the flowers
  O' my bonnie Lady Ann.

I am but her father's gardener lad,
  And puir, puir is my fa';
My auld mither gets my wee wee fee,
  Wi' fatherless bairnies twa.
My lady comes, my lady gaes
  Wi' a fu' and kindly han';
Oh, their blessin' maun mix wi' my luve,
  And fa' on Lady Ann!

THE SPRING OF THE YEAR.

ALLAN CUNNINGHAM.   From "Cromek's Remains."

GONE were but the winter cold,
  And gone were but the snaw,
I could sleep in the wild woods,
  Where primroses blaw.

Cold's the snaw at my head,
  And cold at my feet;
And the finger of death's at my een,
  Closing them to sleep.

Let none tell my father,
  Or my mother sae dear—
I'll meet them both in heaven
  At the spring of the year.

OUR LADYE'S BLESSED WELL.

ALLAN CUNNINGHAM.

THE moon is gleaming far and near,
  The stars are streaming free;
And cold comes down the evening dew
  On my sweet babe and me.

K

There is a time for holy song,
　An hour for charm and spell,
And now's the time to bathe my babe
　In our blessed Ladye's well.

Oh, thou wert born as fair a babe
　As light e'er shone aboon,
And fairer than the gowan is,
　Born in the April moon;
First like the lily pale ye grew,
　Syne like the violet wan;
As in the sunshine dies the dew,
　So faded my fair Ann.

Was it a breath of evil wind
　That harm'd thee, lovely child?
Or was't the fairy's charmèd touch
　That all thy bloom defiled?
I've watched thee in the mirk midnight,
　And watch'd thee in the day,
And sung our Ladye's sacred song,
　To keep the elves away.

The moon is sitting on the hill,
　The night is in its prime,
The owl doth chase the bearded bat,
　The mark of witching time;
And o'er the seven sister-stars
　A silver cloud is drawn,
And pure the blessed water is
　To bathe thee, gentle Ann.

On a fair sea thy father sails
　Among the spicy isles:
He thinks on thee, he thinks on me,
　And as he thinks he smiles;
And sings, while he his white sail trims,
　And severs swift the sea,
About his Anna's sunny locks,
　And of her bright blue ee.

O blessed fountain, give her back
  The brightness of her brow!
O blessed water, bid her cheeks
  Like summer roses glow!
'Tis a small gift, thou blessed well,
  To a thing divine as thee;
But kingdoms to a mother's heart,
  Fu' dear is Ann to me.

———◆———

THOU HAST SWORN BY THY GOD, MY JEANIE.

ALLAN CUNNINGHAM. From " Cromek's Remains."

THOU hast sworn by thy God, my Jeanie,
  By that pretty white hand o' thine,
And by a' the lowing stars in heaven,
  That thou wad aye be mine;
And I hae sworn by my God, my Jeanie,
  And by that kind heart o' thine,
By a' the stars sown thick ower heaven,
  That thou wad aye be mine.

Then foul fa' the hands that loose sic bands,
  And the heart that wad part sic love;
But there's nae hand can loose my band
  But the finger o' God above.
Though the wee, wee cot maun be my bield,
  And my claithing e'er sae mean,
I wad lap me up rich i' the faulds o' luve,
  Heaven's armfu' o' my Jean.

Her white arm wad be a pillow for me,
  Fu' safter than the down,
And Luve wad winnow ower us his kind, kind wings,
  And sweetly I'll sleep, an' soun'.
Come here to me, thou lass o' my luve,
  Come here and kneel wi' me;
The morn is fu' o' the presence o' God,
  And I canna pray but thee.

The morn-wind is sweet 'mang the beds o' new flowers,
  The wee birds sing kindlie an' hie;
Our gudeman leans owre his kale-yard dyke,
  And a blythe auld bodie is he.
The Beuk maun be taen whan the carle comes hame
  Wi' the holie psalmodie,
And thou maun speak o' me to thy God,
  And I will speak o' thee.

THE LASS O' GOWRIE.

Carolina, Baroness Nairn, born 1766, died 1845. Air—"Loch-Erroch side."—C. R.

'Twas on a summer's afternoon,
A wee afore the sun gaed down,
A lassie wi' a braw new gown
  Cam' ower the hills to Gowrie.
The rose-bud, washed in summer's shower,
Bloom'd fresh within the sunny bower;
But Kitty was the fairest flower
  That e'er was seen in Gowrie.

To see her cousin she cam' there,
And oh, the scene was passing fair!
For what in Scotland can compare
  Wi' the Carse o' Gowrie?

The sun was setting on the Tay,
The blue hills melting into gray,
The mavis' and the blackbird's lay
  Were sweetly heard in Gowrie.

Oh lang the lassie I had woo'd!
An' truth and constancy had vow'd;
But cam' no speed wi' her I lo'ed;
  Until she saw fair Gowrie.
I pointed to my faither's ha',
Yon bonnie bield ayont the shaw,
Sae lown that there nae blast could blaw,
  Wad she no bide in Gowrie.

Her faither was baith glad and wae;
Her mither she wad naething say;
The bairnies thocht they wad get play
  If Kitty gaed to Gowrie.
She whiles did smile, she whiles did greet,
The blush and tear were on her cheek:
She naething said, and hung her head;
  But now she's Leddy Gowrie.

There are several versions of this popular song. One of these, composed by William Reid, of Glasgow (1764—1831), begins,—

    "When Katie was scarce out nineteen."

Another version is in the first two stanzas nearly the same with those of Lady Nairn's composition. It thus proceeds:—

    "I praised her beauty loud an' lang,
      Then round her waist my arms I flang,
      And said, 'My dearie, will ye gang
        To see the Carse o' Gowrie?'" &c.

Mr. Lyle, in his "Ancient Ballads and Songs" (London, 1827, 12mo., p. 139), presents an additional version, beginning,—

    "A wee bit north frae yon green wood."   C. R.

KELVIN GROVE.

THOMAS LYLE. Born 1792, died 1859.—C. R.

LET us haste to Kelvin grove, bonnie lassie O;
Through its mazes let us rove, bonnie lassie O,
  Where the rose in all her pride
  Paints the hollow dingle's side,
Where the midnight fairies glide, bonnie lassie O.

Let us wander by the mill, bonnie lassie O ;
To the cove beside the rill, bonnie lassie O,
    Where the glens rebound the call
    Of the roaring waters' fall,
Through the mountain's rocky hall, bonnie lassie O.

Oh, Kelvin banks are fair, bonnie lassie O,
When in simmer we are there, bonnie lassie O ;
    There the May-pink's crimson plume
    Throws a soft but sweet perfume
Round the yellow banks of broom, bonnie lassie O.

Though I dare not call thee mine, bonnie lassie O,
As the smile of fortune's thine, bonnie lassie O ;
    Yet with fortune on my side,
    I could stay thy father's pride,
And win thee for my bride, bonnie lassie O.

But the frowns of fortune lower, bonnie lassie O,
On thy lover at this hour, bonnie lassie O ;
    Ere yon golden orb of day
    Wake the warblers on the spray,
From this land I must away, bonnie lassie O.

Then farewell to Kelvin grove, bonnie lassie O,
And adieu to all I love, bonnie lassie O ;
    To the river winding clear,
    To the fragrant-scented brier,
Even to thee, of all most dear, bonnie lassie O.

When upon a foreign shore, bonnie lassie O,
Should I fall midst battle's roar, bonnie lassie O,
    Then, Helen, shouldst thou hear
    Of thy lover on his bier,
'o his memory shed a tear, bonnie lassie O.

The author of this celebrated song is Thomas Lyle, surgeon in Glasgow. The music was arranged by R. A. Smith, composer of " Jessie, the flower o' Dumblane," from the old Scottish melody, " Bonnie lassie O."

Kelvin Grove is situated about two miles west from Glasgow, but bids fair to be included within the bounds of that rapidly increasing city.

BEHAVE YOURSEL' BEFORE FOLK.

ALEXANDER RODGER, born 1784, died 1846. Air—" Good morrow to your nightcap."

BEHAVE yoursel' before folk ;
Behave yoursel' before folk ;
And dinna be sae rude to me,
As kiss me sae before folk.

It wadna gi'e me meikle pain,
Gin we were seen and heard by nane,
To tak' a kiss, or grant you ane ;
  But, guidsake ! no before folk.
    Behave yoursel' before folk,
    Behave yoursel' before folk ;
  Whate'er ye do when out o' view,
    Be cautious aye before folk.

Consider, lad, how folks will crack,
And what a great affair they'll mak'
O' naething but a simple smack
  That's gi'en or ta'en before folk.
    Behave yoursel' before folk,
    Behave yoursel' before folk ;
  Nor gi'e the tongue o' auld or young
    Occasion to come o'er folk.

It's no through hatred o' a kiss
That I sae plainly tell you this;
But, losh ! I tak' it sair amiss
  To be sae teased before folk.
    Behave yoursel' before folk,
    Behave yoursel' before folk ;
  When we're our lane, you may tak' ane.
    But fient a ane before folk.

I'm sure wi' you I've been as free
As ony modest lass should be ;
But yet it doesna do to see
  Sic freedom used before folk.

> Behave yoursel' before folk,
> Behave yoursel' before folk ;
> I'll ne'er submit again to it—
> So mind you that—before folk.

> Ye tell me that my face is fair ;
> It may be sae, I dinna care ;
> But ne'er again gar't blush sae sair
> As ye hae done before folk.
> Behave yoursel' before folk,
> Behave yoursel' before folk ;
> Nor heat my cheeks wi' your mad freaks,
> But aye be douce before folk.

> Ye tell me that my lips are sweet ;
> Sic tales I doubt are a' deceit ;
> At ony rate, it's hardly meet
> To pree their sweets before folk.
> Behave yoursel' before folk,
> Behave yoursel' before folk ;
> Gin that's the case there's time and place,
> But surely no before folk.

> But gin you really do insist
> That I should suffer to be kiss'd,
> Gae get a license frae the priest,
> And mak' me yours before folk.
> Behave yoursel' before folk,
> Behave yoursel' before folk ;
> And when we're ane baith flesh and bane,
> Ye may tak' ten before folk.

From " Whistle Binkie, or the Piper of the Party ; a Collection of Songs for the Social Circle"—a very interesting series of modern songs, edited by Alexander Rodger, and published by David Robertson of Glasgow, between the years 1832 and 1846. This work, from which we have copied, with the kind permission of the late Mr. Robertson, the admirable songs of Rodger and others, contains some hundreds of songs, mostly original, which present, in the words of the preface to the collected edition published in 1846, " a remarkable instance of the universality of that peculiar talent for song-writing for which the natives of Scotland have always been distinguished.

ANSWER TO "BEHAVE YOURSEL' BEFORE FOLK."

ALEXANDER RODGER. From " Whistle Binkie."

CAN I behave, can I behave,
Can I behave before folk,
When wily elf, your sleeky self,
Gars me gang gyte before folk?

In a' ye do, in a' ye say,
Ye've sic a pawkie coaxing way,
That my poor wits ye lead astray,
An' ding me doilt before folk.
Can I behave, can I behave,
Can I behave before folk;
While ye ensnare, can I forbear
A kissing ye before folk?

Can I behold that dimpling cheek,
Whar love 'mang sunny smiles might beek,
Yet howlet-like my eelids steek,
And shun sic light before folk?
Can I behave, can I behave,
Can I behave before folk,
When ilka smile becomes a wile,
Enticing me before folk?

That lip, like Eve's forbidden fruit,
Sweet, plump, an' ripe, sae tempts me t'ot,
That I maun pree't, though I should rue't,
Ay twenty times before folk !
Can I behave, can I behave,
Can I behave before folk,
When temptingly it offers me
So rich a treat before folk?

That gowden hair sae sunny bright,
That shapely neck o' snowy white;
That tongue, e'en when it tries to flyte,
Provokes me till't before folk!

Can I behave, can I behave,
Can I behave before folk,
When ilka charm, young, fresh, and warm,
Cries, " Kiss me now !" before folk ?

An', oh, that pawkie, rowin ee,
Sae roguishly it blinks on me,
I canna, for my soul, let be
Frae kissing you before folk !
Can I behave, can I behave,
Can I behave before folk,
When ilka glint conveys a hint
To tak a smack before folk ?

Ye own that were we baith our lane,
Ye wadna grudge to grant me ane ;
Weel, gin there be no harm in't then,
What harm is in't before folk ?
Can I behave, can I behave,
Can I behave before folk ?
Sly hypocrite, an anchorite
Could scarce desist before folk !

But after a' that has been said,
Since ye are willing to be wed,
We'll hae a " blythesome bridal" made,
When ye'll be mine before folk.
Then I'll behave, then I'll behave,
Then I'll behave before folk ;
For whereas then ye'll aft get ten,
It winna be before folk.

--------•--------

JEANIE MORRISON.

WILLIAM MOTHERWELL, born 1797, died 1835.

I'VE wander'd east, I've wander'd west,
Through mony a weary way !
But never, never can forget
The luve o' life's young day.

The fire that's blawn on Beltane e'en
  May weel be black gin Yule;
But blacker fa' awaits the heart
  Where first fond love grows cule.

O dear, dear Jeanie Morrison,
  The thochts o' bygane years
Still fling their shadows ower my path,
  And blind my een wi' tears!
They blind my een wi' saut, saut tears,
  And sair and sick I pine,
As memory idly summons up
  The blythe blinks o' langsyne.

'Twas then we luvit ilk ither weel,
  'Twas then we twa did part;
Sweet time—sad time! twa bairns at schule,
  Twa bairns, and but ae heart!
'Twas then we sat on ae laigh bink,
  To leir ilk ither lear;
And tones, and looks, and smiles were shed,
  Remember'd evermair.

I wonder, Jeanie, aften yet,
  When sitting on that bink,
Cheek touchin' cheek, loof lock'd in loof,
  What our wee heads could think!
When baith bent doun ower ae braid page,
  Wi' ae buik on our knee,
Thy lips were on thy lesson, but
  My lesson was in thee.

Oh, mind ye how we hung our heads,
  How cheeks brent red wi' shame,
Whene'er the schule-weans laughin' said,
  We cleek'd thegither hame?
And mind ye o' the Saturdays
  (The schule then skail't at noon),
When we ran aff to speel the braes—
  The broomy braes o' June?

My head rins round and round about,
  My heart flows like a sea,
As ane by ane the thochts rush back
  O' schule-time and o' thee.
O mornin' life! O mornin' luve!
  O lichtsome days and lang,
When hinnied hopes around our hearts,
  Like simmer blossoms, sprang!

Oh, mind ye, luve, how aft we left
  The deavin' dinsome toun,
To wander by the green burnside,
  And hear its water croon?
The simmer leaves hung ower our heads,
  The flowers burst round our feet,
And in the gloamin' o' the wud
  The throssil whusslit sweet.

The throssil whusslit in the wud,
  The burn sung to the trees,
And we, with Nature's heart in tune,
  Concerted harmonies;
And on the knowe abune the burn
  For hours thegither sat
In the silentness o' joy, till baith
  Wi' very gladness grat.

Aye, aye, dear Jeanie Morrison,
  Tears trinkled down your cheek,
Like dew-beads on a rose, yet nane
  Had ony power to speak!
That was a time, a blessed time,
  When hearts were fresh and young,
When freely gush'd all feelings forth,
  Unsyllabled—unsung!

I marvel, Jeanie Morrison,
  Gin I hae been to thee
As closely twined wi' earliest thochts
  As ye hae been to me!

Oh, tell me gin their music fills
  Thine ear as it does mine ;
Oh, say gin e'er your heart grows grit
  Wi' dreamings o' langsyne !

I've wander'd east, I've wander'd west,
  I've borne a weary lot ;
But in my wanderings far or near
  Ye never were forgot.
The fount that first burst frae this heart
  Still travels on its way,
And channels deeper as it rins
  The life of luve's young day.

O dear, dear Jeanie Morrison,
  Since we were sinder'd young,
I've never seen your face, nor heard
  The music o' your tongue ;
But I could hug all wretchedness,
  And happy could I die,
Did I but ken your heart still dream'd
  O' bygane days and me !

MY HEID IS LIKE TO REND, WILLIE.

WILLIAM MOTHERWELL.

MY heid is like to rend, Willie,
  My heart is like to break ;
I'm wearin' aff my feet, Willie,
  I'm dyin' for your sake !
Oh, lay your cheek to mine, Willie,
  Your hand on my briest-bane !
Oh, say ye'll think on me, Willie,
  When I am deid and gane !

It's vain to comfort me, Willie,
  Sair grief maun hae its will ;
But let me rest upon your briest,
  To sab and greet my fill.

Let me sit on your knee, Willie,
 Let me shed by your hair,
And look into the face, Willie,
 I never shall see mair!

I'm sittin' on your knee, Willie,
 For the last time in my life,
A puir heart-broken thing, Willie—
 A mither, yet nae wife.
Ay, press your hand upon my heart,
 And press it mair and mair,
Or it will burst the silken twine,
 Sae strang is its despair!

Oh, wae's me for the hour, Willie,
 When we thegither met!
Oh, wae's me for the time, Willie,
 That our first tryst was set!
Oh, wae's me for the loanin' green
 Where we were wont to gae,
And wae's me for the destinie
 That gart me luve thee sae!

Oh, dinna mind my words, Willie,
 I downa seek to blame;
But, oh, it's hard to live, Willie,
 And dree a world's shame!
Het tears are haillin' ower your cheek,
 And haillin' ower your chin;
Why weep ye sae for worthlessness,
 For sorrow and for sin?

I'm weary o' this world, Willie,
 And sick wi' a' I see;
I canna live as I hae lived,
 Or be as I should be.
But fauld unto your heart, Willie,
 The heart that still is thine;
And kiss ance mair the white, white cheek
 Ye said was red langsyne.

A stoun' gaes through my heid, Willie,
 A sair stoun' through my heart;
Oh, haud me up, and let me kiss
 Thy brow ere we twa part.

Anither, and anither yet—
  How fast my life-strings break!
Fareweel! fareweel! through yon kirkyard
  Tread lichtly for my sake.

The lavrock in the lift, Willie,
  That lilts far ower our heid,
Will sing the morn as merrilie
  Abune the clay-cauld deid;
And this green turf we're sittin' on,
  Wi' dew-draps shimmerin' sheen,
Will hap the heart that luvit thee
  As warld has seldom seen.

But, oh, remember me, Willie,
  On land where'er ye bo!
And, oh, think on the leal, leal heart
  That ne'er luvit ane but thee!
And, oh, think on the cauld, cauld mools
  That file my yellow hair,
That kiss the cheek, that kiss the chin,
  Ye never sall kiss mair!

MAY-MORN SONG.

Motherwell. From " Whistle Binkie."

The grass is wet with shining dews,
  Their silver bells hang on each tree;
While opening flower and bursting bud
  Breathe incense forth unceasingly
The mavis pipes in greenwood shaw,
  The throstle glads the spreading thorn,
And cheerily the blythesome lark
  Salutes the rosy face of morn.
     'Tis early prime;
       And hark, hark, hark,
     His merry chime
       Chirrups the lark.
   Chirrup, chirrup! he heralds in
  The jolly sun with matin hymn.

Come, come, my love, and May-dews shake
  In pailfuls from each drooping bough,
They'll give fresh lustre to the bloom
  That breaks upon thy young cheek now.
O'er hill and dale, o'er waste and wood,
  Aurora's smiles are streaming free;
With earth it seems brave holiday,
  In heaven it looks high jubilee:
      And it is right, love;
        For mark, love, mark,
     How, bathed in light,
       Chirrups the lark.
Chirrup, chirrup! he upward flies,
Like holy thoughts to cloudless skies.

They lack all heart who cannot feel
  The voice of heaven within them thrill
In summer morn, when, mounting high,
  This merry minstrel sings his fill.
Now let us seek yon bosky dell,
  Where brightest wildflowers choose to be,
And where its clear stream murmurs on,
  Meet type of our love's purity.
      No witness there;
        And o'er us, hark,
     High in the air
       Chirrups the lark.
Chirrup, chirrup! away soars he,
Bearing to heaven my vows to thee.

MARY'S GANE.

John Donald Carrick, born 1787, died 1835. From " Whistle Binkie."
Air—" Coming o'er the craigs o' Kyle."

Oh, wae's my heart, now Mary's gane,
  An' we nae mair shall meet thegither,
To sit an' crack at gloamin' hour,
  By yon auld grey stane amang the heather:

Trysting-stane amang the heather,
Trysting-stane amang the heather;
How bless'd were we at gloamin' hour,
By yon auld grey stane amang the heather!

Her father's laird, sae gair on gear,
He set their mailin to anither;
Sae they've selt their kye, and ower the sea
They've gane and left their native heather:
Left their native blooming heather,
Left their native blooming heather;
They've selt their kye, and ower the sea
They've gane and left their native heather.

Her parting look bespake a heart
Whase rising grief she couldna smother,
As she waved a last farewell to me
And Scotland's braes and blooming heather:
Scotland's braes and blooming heather,
Scotland's braes and blooming heather;
'Twas sair against the lassie's will
To lea' her native blooming heather.

A burning curse licht on the heads
O' worthless lairds colleagued thegither
To drive auld Scotland's hardy clans
Frae their native hills and blooming heather:
Native glens and blooming heather,
Native glens and blooming heather;
To drive auld Scotland's hardy clans
Frae their native hills and blooming heather.

I'll sell the cot my granny left,
Its plenishing an' a' thegither,
An' I'll seek her out 'mang foreign wilds,
Wha used to meet me amang the heather:
Used to meet me amang the heather,
Used to meet me amang the heather;
I'll seek her out 'mang foreign wilds,
Wha used to meet me amang the heather.

L

O POVERTY.

ALEXANDER HUME, born 1809, died 1851.—C. R.

ELIZA was a bonnie lass, an', oh, she lo'ed me weel,
Sic love as canna find a tongue, but only hearts can feel;
But I was poor, her father doure, he wadna look on me:
O poverty! O poverty! that love should bow to thee.

I went unto her mother, an' I argued an' I fleech'd,
I spak' o' love an' honesty, an' mair an' mair beseech'd;
But she was deaf to a' my grief, she wadna look on me:
O poverty! O poverty! that love should bow to thee.

I neist went to her brother, an' I told him a' my pain—
Oh, he was wae, he tried to say, but it was a' in vain;
Though he was weel in love himsel', nae feeling he'd for me:
O poverty! O poverty! that love should bow to thee.

O wealth! it makes the fool a sage, the knave an honest man,
An' canker'd grey locks young again, gin he hae gear an' lau';
To age maun beauty ope her arms, though wi' a tearful ee:
O poverty! O poverty! that love should bow to thee.

But wait a wee; oh, love is slee, and winna be said nay,
It breaks a' chains except its ain, but it maun hae its way;—
Auld age was blind, the priest was kind—now happy as can be:
O poverty! O poverty! we're wed in spite of thee.

------◆------

HELEN OF KIRKCONNELL.

Modernised version of the older song.

I WISH I were where Helen lies—
Night and day on me she cries;
Oh, that I were where Helen lies,
   On fair Kirkconnell lea!

O Helen, fair beyond compare!
I'll make a garland of thy hair,
Shall bind my heart for evermair,
   Until the day I die.

Cursed be the heart that thought the thought,
And cursed the hand that fired the shot,
When in my arms burd Helen dropt,
   And died for sake o' me.

Oh, think nae but my heart was sair
When my love fell and spak' nae mair;
I laid her down wi' meikle care
   On fair Kirkconnell lea.

I laid her down, my sword did draw,
Stern was our strife in Kirtle-shaw;
I hew'd him down in pieces sma',
   For her that died for me.

Oh, that I were where Helen lies;
Night and day on me she cries,
Out of my bed she bids me rise,
   "Oh, come, my love, to me!"

O Helen fair, O Helen chaste!
Were I with thee I would be blest,
Where thou liest low and tak'st thy rest
   On fair Kirkconnell lea.

I wish I were where Helen lies—
Night and day on me she cries;
I'm sick of all beneath the skies,
   Since my love died for me.

LUCY'S FLITTIN'.

WILLIAM LAIDLAW, died 1846. Mr. Laidlaw was the steward, amanuensis,
and tried and trusted friend of Sir Walter Scott.

'TWAS when the wan leaf frae the birk-tree was fa'in',
   And Martinmas dowie had wound up the year,
That Lucy row'd up her wee kist wi' her a' in't,
   And left her auld maister and neebours sae dear:
For Lucy had served in the glen a' the simmer;
   She cam' there afore the flower bloom'd on the pea;
An orphan was she, and they had been kind till her—
   Sure that was the thing brocht the tear to her ee.

She gaed by the stable where Jamie was stannin';
  Richt sair was his kind heart the flittin' to see:
Fare ye weel, Lucy! quo' Jamie, and ran in,
  The gatherin' tears trickled fast frae his ee.
As down the burn-side she gaed slow wi' the flittin',
  Fare ye weel, Lucy! was ilka bird's sang;
She heard the craw sayin't high on the tree sittin',
  And robin was chirpin't the brown leaves amang.

Oh, what is't that pits my puir heart in a flutter?
  And what gars the tears come sae fast to my ee?
If I wasna ettled to be ony better,
  Then what gars me wish ony better to be?
I'm just like a lammie that loses its mither;
  Nae mither or friend the puir lammie can see;
I fear I hae tint my puir heart a'thegither,—
  Nae wonder the tears fa' sae fast frae my ee.

Wi' the rest o' my claes I hae row'd up the ribbon,
  The bonnie blue ribbon that Jamie ga'e me;
Yestreen, when he ga'e me't, and saw I was sabbin',
  I'll never forget the wae blink o' his ee.
Though now he said naething but, Fare ye weel, Lucy!
  It made me I neither could speak, hear, nor see:
He could nae say mair but just, Fare ye weel, Lucy!
  Yet that I will mind till the day that I dee.

The lamb likes the gowan wi' dew when its droukit,
  The hare likes the brake and the braird on the lea;
But Lucy likes Jamie: she turn'd and she lookit,
  She thocht the dear place she wad never mair see.
Ah, weel may young Jamie gang dowie and cheerless,
  And weel may he greet on the bank o' the burn;
For bonnie sweet Lucy, sae gentle and peerless,
  Lies cauld in her grave, and will never return!

MY AIN FIRESIDE.

Elizabeth Hamilton, authoress of the "Cottagers of Glenburnie."

I hae seen great anes, and sat in great ha's
Mang lords and fine ladies a' cover'd wi' braws;
At feasts made for princes wi' princes I've been,
Whare the grand shine o' splendour has dazzled my een;
But a sight sae delightfu' I trow I ne'er spied
As the bonnie blythe blink o' my ain fireside!
My ain fireside, my ain fireside,
Oh, cheery's the blink o' my ain fireside!
 My ain fireside, my ain fireside,
 Oh, there's nought to compare wi' ane's ain fireside!

Ance mair, Gude be thanket, round my ain heartsome ingle
Wi' the friends o' my youth I cordially mingle;
Nae forms to compel me to seem wae or glad,
I may laugh when I'm merry, and sigh when I'm sad.
Nae falsehood to dread, and nae malice to fear,
But truth to delight me, and friendship to cheer:
Of a' roads to happiness ever were tried,
There's nane half so sure as ane's ain fireside.
 My ain fireside, my ain fireside,
 Oh, there's nought to compare wi' ane's ain fireside!

When I draw in my stool on my cosey hearthstane,
My heart loups sae light I scarce ken't for my ain;
Care's down on the wind—it is clean out of sight,
Past troubles they seem but as dreams of the night.
I hear but kend voices, kend faces I see,
And mark saft affection glent fond frae ilk ee;
Nae fleetchings o' flattery, nae boastings of pride,
'Tis heart speaks to heart at ane's ain fireside.
 My ain fireside, my ain fireside,
 Oh, there's nought to compare wi' ane's ain fireside!

OUR AIN FIRESIDE.

From Peter Buchan's manuscript collection of ancient Scottish songs.

My country, o'er thy mountains wild
  Though stormy clouds may ride,
There's mony a noble generous heart
  Sits round thy fireside.
      Her ain fireside, my friends,
        Her ain fireside;
      May ne'er a tyrant's ruthless arm
        Rule o'er her fireside.

How cheery round the ingle-cheek
  To hear cauld winter chide;
While nappy ale an' hearty tale
  Gae round the fireside!
      Our ain fireside, my friends,
        Our ain fireside;
      I'm glad to see ye a' set round
        A social fireside.

The poison'd shafts that malice throws
  O'er harmless pastime slide,
While honest worth an' cheerfu' mirth
  Sit round the fireside.
      Our ain fireside, my friends,
        Our ain fireside;
      The warmest glow o' friendship's flame
        Shall heat the fireside.

On human worth by length of purse
  Let worldly slaves decide;
The heart to share the world's care
  Aye heats the fireside.
      Our ain fireside, my friends,
        Our ain fireside;
      The sterling value o' the heart
        Aye gilds the fireside.

Through rocks and sands to distant lands
  The sailor wanders wide,
In hopes to shield his crazy eild
  By couthy fireside.
      The couthy fireside, my friends,
        The couthy fireside ;
      Heaven send the lyart pow o' age
        A couthy fireside.

'Tis Heaven that nerves the soldier's arm
  The battle's heat to bide ;
He boldly dares the fiercest foe
  To shield his fireside.
      His ain fireside, my friends,
        His country's fireside ;
      Would ye but warm a coward's heart,
        Insult his fireside.

Gi'e luxury her painted domes,
  Her palaces gi'e pride ;
But be my lot a snug warm cot
  And canty fireside.
      A canty fireside, my friends,
        A canty fireside ;
      Be aye my lot a snug warm cot
        And canty fireside.

When bairnies brattlin round our knees
  On chairs and stoolies ride,
What joy heaves up a parent's heart
  To see his fireside!
      To see his fireside, my friends,
        His ain fireside ;
      May Heaven protect the rising sprouts
        Around his fireside.

Misfortune dour, wi' cauldrife stour,
  A neighbour may betide ;
'Twill edge a bit and lit him sit
  Just next the fireside.
      Our ain fireside, my friends,
        Our ain fireside ;
      May ne'er a cauld nor hungry heart
        Gae by your fireside.

And, oh, may He whose powerful arm
The steps o' mortals guides,
Wi' health and wealth and length o' days
Bless a' our firesides!
Our ain firesides, my friends,
Our ain firesides;
The choicest blessings Heaven bestows
Bless a' our firesides.

THE MAKING O' THE HAY.

ROBERT NICOLL.

ACROSS the riggs we'll wander
The new-mawn hay amang,
And hear the blackbird in the wood,
And gi'e it sang for sang;—
We'll gi'e it sang for sang, we will,
For ilka heart is gay,
As lads and lasses trip alang
At making o' the hay!

It is sae sweetly scented,
   It seems a maiden's breath;
Aboon the sun has wither'd it,
   But there is green beneath;—
   But there is caller green beneath,
Come, lasses, foot away!
   The heart is dowie can be cauld
At making o' the hay!

Step lightly o'er, gang saftly by,
   Mak' rig and furrow clean,
And coil it up in fragrant heaps,—
   We maun hae done at e'en;—
   We maun hae done at gloaming e'en;
And when the clouds grow grey,
   Ilk lad may kiss his bonnie lass
Amang the new-made hay!

THE BONNIE ROWAN BUSH.

ROBERT NICOLL.

THE bonnie rowan bush
   In yon lane glen,
Where the burnie clear doth gush
   In yon lane glen;
My head is white and auld,
An' my bluid is thin an' cauld;
But I lo'e the bonnie rowan bush
   In yon lane glen.

My Jeanie first I met
   In yon lane glen,
When the grass wi' dew was wet
   In yon lane glen;
The moon was shinin' sweet,
An' our hearts wi' love did beat,
By the bonnie, bonnie rowan bush
   In yon lane glen.

Oh, she promised to be mine
　　In yon lane glen !
Her heart she did resign
　　In yon lane glen :
An' monie a happy day
Did o'er us pass away
Beside the bonnie rowan bush
　　In yon lane glen.

Sax bonnie bairns had we
　　In yon lane glen,
Lads an' lasses young an' spree
　　In yon lane glen ;
An' a blither family
Than ours there cou'dna be,
Beside the bonnie rowan bush
　　In yon lane glen.

Now my auld wife's gane awa'
　　Frae yon lane glen ;
An' though simmer sweet doth fa'
　　In yon lane glen,
To me its beauty's gane,
For, alake, I sit alane
Beside the bonnie rowan bush
　　In yon lane glen !

IN THE GARB OF OLD GAUL.

Sir Harry Erskine, Bart., died 1765.
Air—"The Highland or 42nd regiment's march," composed by General Reid.

In the garb of old Gaul, with the fire of old Rome,
From the heath-cover'd mountains of Scotia we come,
Where the Romans endeavour'd our country to gain;
But our ancestors fought, and they fought not in vain.
  Such is our love of liberty, our country, and our laws,
  That, like our ancestors of old, we'll stand in freedom's cause:
  We'll bravely fight, like heroes bold, for honour and applause,
  And defy the French, with all their arts, to alter our laws.

No effeminate customs our sinews unbrace,
No luxurious tables enervate our race;
Our loud-sounding pipe breathes the true martial strain,
And our hearts still the old Scottish valour retain.
        Such is our love, &c.

We're tall as the oak on the mount of the vale,
And swift as the roe which the hound doth assail;
As the full moon in autumn our shields do appear;
E'en Minerva would dread to encounter our spear.
        Such is our love, &c.

As a storm in the ocean when Boreas blows,
So are we enraged when we rush on our foes,
We sons of the mountains, tremendous as rocks,
Dash the force of our foes with our thundering strokes.
        Such is our love, &c.

Quebec and Cape Breton, the pride of old France,
In their numbers fondly boasted till we did advance;
But when our claymores they saw us produce,
Their courage did fail, and they sued for a truce.
        Such is our love, &c.

In our realm may the fury of faction long cease,
May our councils be wise, and our commerce increase;
And in Scotia's cold climate may each of us find
That our friends still prove true, and our beauties prove kind.
  Then we'll defend our liberty, our country, and our laws,
  And teach our late posterity to fight in freedom's cause
  That they, like their ancestors bold, for honour and applause,
  May defy the French, with all their arts, to alter our laws.

SCOTS WHA HAE WI' WALLACE BLED.

Scots, wha hae wi' Wallace bled ;
Scots, wham Bruce has aften led ;
Welcome to your gory bed,
   Or to victory !

Now's the day and now's the hour ;
See the front o' battle lour :
See approach proud Edward's power—
   Chains and slavery !

Wha will be a traitor knave ?
Wha can fill a coward's grave ?
Wha sae base as be a slave ?
   Let him turn and flee !

Wha for Scotland's king and law
Freedom's sword will strongly draw,
Freeman stand or freeman fa'?
   Let him on wi' me !

By oppression's woes and pains,
By your sons in servile chains,
We will drain our dearest veins,
    But they shall be free!

Lay the proud usurpers low,
Tyrants fall in every foe;
Liberty's in every blow;
    Let us do or die!

"This noble strain," says Dr. Currie, "was conceived by the poet during a storm among the wilds of Glen Ken, in Galloway." Burns himself says, in a letter to Mr. Thomson, dated Sept. 1793, in which he enclosed it, "I borrowed the last stanza from the common stall edition of Wallace:

'A false usurper sinks in every foe,
    And liberty returns with every blow.'

A stanza worthy of Homer." In another letter he says: "I do not know whether the old air of 'Hey tuttie taittie' may rank among this number; but well I know that, with Fraser's hautboy, it has often filled my eyes with tears. There is a tradition which I have met with in many places of Scotland, that it was Robert Bruce's march at the battle of Bannockburn. This thought, in my solitary wanderings, warmed me to a pitch of enthusiasm on the theme of liberty and independence, which I threw into a kind of Scottish ode, fitted to the air, that one might suppose to be the gallant royal Scot's address to his heroic followers on that eventful morning.

"So may God ever defend the cause of truth and liberty, as he did that day! Amen.

"P.S. I showed the air to Urbani, who was highly pleased with it, and begged me to make soft verses for it; but I had no idea of giving myself any trouble upon the subject, till the accidental recollection of that glorious struggle for freedom, associated with the glowing ideas of some other struggles of the same nature, not quite so ancient, roused my rhyming mania."

In answer to this letter, Thomson writes the following: "I believe it is generally allowed that the greatest modesty is the sure attendant of the greatest merit. While you are sending me verses that even Shakspeare might be proud to own, you speak of them as if they were ordinary productions! Your heroic ode is to me the noblest composition of the kind in the Scottish language. I happened to dine yesterday with a party of your friends, to whom I read it. They were all charmed with it, entreated me to find a suitable air for it, and reprobated the idea of giving it a tune so totally devoid of interest or grandeur as 'Hey tuttie taittie.' Assuredly your partiality for this tune must arise from association; for I never heard any person—and I have conversed again and again with the greatest enthusiasts for Scottish airs—I say I never heard any one speak of it as worthy of notice."

In some versions of this song, the concluding line of each stanza is lengthened to seven feet. In the first stanza the line is, "Or to *glorious* victory;" in the second, "*Edward*, chains, and slavery!" in the third, "*Traitor, coward*, turn and flee!" in the fourth, "*Caledonian!* on wi' me!" in the fifth, "But they shall be, *shall* be free!" and in the sixth, "*Forward!* Let us do or die!" But these elongations mar the music and weaken the poetry.

The old song of "Hey tuttie taittie" has been preserved by Mr. Peter Buchan; the chorus will suffice as a specimen:

Hey tuttie taittie,
Hey talerettie;
Hey, my bonnie Mary,
She's aye roarin' fu'.

FAREWELL, THOU FAIR DAY.

Burns. Air—"My lodging is on the cold ground."

Farewell, thou fair day, thou green earth, and ye skies,
    Now gay with the bright setting sun!
Farewell, loves and friendships, ye dear tender ties!
    Our race of existence is run.
Thou grim king of terrors, thou life's gloomy foe,
    Go frighten the coward and slave!
Go teach them to tremble, fell tyrant! but know
    No terrors hast thou to the brave.

Thou strik'st the dull peasant, he sinks in the dark,
    Nor saves e'en the wreck of a name;
Thou strik'st the young hero, a glorious mark,
    He falls in the blaze of his fame.
In the field of proud honour, our swords in our hands,
    Our king and our country to save;
While victory shines on life's last ebbing sands,
    Oh, who would not die with the brave!

This song, written by Burns to a Highland air called "Oran an oig," is now usually adapted to the English melody of "My lodging is on the cold ground," an air also claimed by the late Thomas Moore as Irish, and for which he wrote the beautiful song, "Believe me, if all those endearing young charms." The original song of "The mad shepherdess," whose lodging was on the cold ground, was sung in Davenant's comedy of "The Rivals," produced in London in 1688. "As this song," says Mr. Chappell, in his valuable collection of "Ancient English Airs," "has been published by Moore in his 'Irish Melodies,' the editor wishes to state it as the opinion of Mr. Bunting, who has devoted his life to the collection of Irish music; of Mr. Wade, who has also made it a particular study; of Mr. Edward Taylor, the Gresham lecturer; of Dr. Crotch, Mr. Ayrton, and many other eminent musical antiquaries, that from internal evidence of the tune itself, it is *not* Irish, but English; nor indeed has he hitherto met with any difference of opinion amongst musicians upon the subject. About the time that it was printed in 'Moore's *Irish* Melodies,' it was also published (in Dublin) in 'Clifton's *British* Melodies.'"

The late Sir Henry R. Bishop often asserted his positive belief that neither the Scotch nor the Irish had any true claim to this fine melody, which he held to be unmistakably English.

DOES HAUGHTY GAUL INVASION THREAT?

Burns. April 1795.

Does haughty Gaul invasion threat?
    Then let the loons beware, sir;
There's wooden walls upon our seas,
    And volunteers on shore, sir.

The Nith shall run to Corsincon,
  And Criffel sink in Solway,
Ere we permit a foreign foe
  On British ground to rally.

Oh, let us not, like snarling curs,
  In wrangling be divided,
Till slap come in an unco loon,
  And wi' a rung decide it.
Be Britain still to Britain true,
  Among ourselves united;
For never but by British hands
  Must British wrongs be righted.

The kettle o' the kirk and state,
  Perhaps a clout may fail in't;
But de'il a foreign tinkler loon
  Shall ever ca' a nail in't.
Our fathers' blood the kettle bought,
  And who would dare to spoil it?
By Heaven, the sacrilegious dog
  Shall fuel be to boil it!

The wretch that would a tyrant own,
  And the wretch, his true-born brother,
Who'd set the mob aboon the throne—
  May they be damn'd together!
Who will not sing "God save the king!"
  Shall hing as high's the steeple;
But while we sing "God save the king!"
  We'll ne'er forget the people.

This song was written by Burns to the English air of "Push about the jorum."
The Scotch melody of "The barrin' of our door" was afterwards found for it.

LAND OF MY FATHERS.

Dr. John Leyden.   The music by R. A. Smith.

Land of my fathers! though no mangrove here
O'er thy blue streams her flexile branches rear,
Nor scaly palm her finger'd scions shoot,
Nor luscious guava wave her yellow fruit,

Nor golden apples glimmer from the tree;
Land of dark heaths and mountains, thou art free!
Free as his lord the peasant treads the plain,
And heaps his harvest on the groaning wain.

Proud of his laws, tenacious of his right,
And vain of Scotia's old unconquer'd might:
Dear native valleys, may ye long retain
The chartered freedom of the mountain swain
Long, mid your sounding glades, in union sweet,
May rural innocence and beauty meet;
And still be duly heard, at twilight calm,
From every cot the peasant's chanted psalm!

Then, Jedworth, though thy ancient choirs shall fade,
And time lay bare each lofty colonnade,
From the damp roof the massy sculptures die,
And in their vaults thy rifted arches lie;
Still in these vales shall angel harps prolong,
By Jed's pure stream, a sweeter ev'ning song
Than long processions once, with mystic zeal,
Pour'd to the harp and solemn organ's peal.

PIBROCH OF DONUIL DHU.

SIR WALTER SCOTT.

Written for Mr. Thomson's Collection, on the return of the Highland regiment from Waterloo.

PIBROCH of Donuil Dhu,
   Pibroch of Donuil,
Wake thy wild voice anew,
   Summon Clan Conuil:
Come away, come away,
   Hark to the summons;
Come in your war array,
   Gentles and commons!

Come from deep glen and
　　From mountain so rocky;
The war-pipe and pennon
　　Are at Inverlochy.
Come every hill-plaid,
　　And true heart that wears one;
Come every steel blade,
　　And strong hand that bears one!

Leave the deer, leave the steer,
　　Leave nets and barges;
Come with your fighting gear,
　　Broadswords and targes.
Leave untended the herd,
　　The flock without shelter;
Leave the corpse uninterr'd,
　　The bride at the altar.

Come as the winds come
　　When forests are rended;
Come as the waves come
　　When navies are stranded.
Faster come, faster come,
　　Faster and faster,
Chief, vassal, page, and groom,
　　Tenant and master.

Fast they come, fast they come;
　　See how they gather;
Wide waves the eagle plume
　　Blended with heather.
Cast your plaids, draw your blades,
　　Forward each man set:
Pibroch of Donuil Dhu,
　　Now for the onset!

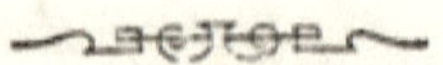

BLUE BONNETS OVER THE BORDER.

Sir Walter Scott.

March, march, Ettrick and Teviotdale!
  Why, my lads, dinna ye march forward in order?
March, march, Eskdale and Liddesdale;
  All the blue bonnets are over the Border.
Many a banner spread flutters above your head,
  Many a crest that is famous in story;
Mount and make ready, then, sons of the mountain glen
  Fight for your queen and the old Scottish glory.

Come from the hills where your hirsels are grazing;
  Come from the glen of the buck and the roe;
Come to the crag where the beacon is blazing;
  Come with the buckler, the lance, and the bow.
Trumpets are sounding, war-steeds are bounding;
  Stand to your arms and march in good order;
England shall many a day tell of the bloody fray,
  When the blue bonnets came over the Border.

The above spirited song, by Sir Walter Scott, was founded upon "General Leslie's march to Longmarston Moor," which appeared in Allan Ramsay's "Tea-Table Miscellany," where it is marked as ancient, and as one of which Ramsay neither knew the age nor the author. The old song is of little or no merit, but is inserted here as a curiosity, and as showing out of what rude materials Scott constructed the modern song, which has since become so celebrated.

GENERAL LESLIE'S MARCH TO LONGMARSTON MOOR.

March, march, why the deil dinna ye march?
  Stand to your arms, my lads; fight in good order.
Front about, ye musketeers all,
  Till ye come to the English Border.
    Stand till't and fight like men,
    True gospel to maintain;
The Parliament's blythe to see us a-coming.
    When to the kirk we come,
    We'll purge it ilka room
Frae Popish relics and a' sic innovation,
    That a' the world may see
    There's nane in the right but we
Of the auld Scottish nation.

    Jenny shall wear the hood,
    Jockie the sark of God;
And the kist fu' o' whistles that maks sic a cleiro,
    Our pipers braw
    Shall hae them a'.
    Whate'er come on it,
    Busk up your plaids, my lads,
    Cock up your bonnets.

OH, WHERE, TELL ME WHERE?

Mrs. Grant of Laggan; born 1755, died 1838. Air—"The blue-bells of Scotland."

Oh, where, tell me where is your Highland laddie gone?
Oh, where, tell me where is your Highland laddie gone?
He's gone with streaming banners where noble deeds are done,
And my sad heart will tremble till he come safely home.

Oh, where, tell me where did your Highland laddie stay?
Oh, where, tell me where did your Highland laddie stay?
He dwelt beneath the holly-trees beside the rapid Spey,
And many a blessing follow'd him the day he went away.

Oh, what, tell me what does your Highland laddie wear?
Oh, what, tell me what does your Highland laddie wear?
A bonnet with a lofty plume, the gallant badge of war,
And a plaid across the manly breast that yet shall wear a star.

Suppose, ah, suppose, that some cruel, cruel wound
Should pierce your Highland laddie, and all your hopes confound.
The pipe would play a cheering march, the banners round him fly,
The spirit of a Highland chief would lighten in his eye.

But I will hope to see him yet in Scotland's bonnie bounds,
But I will hope to see him yet in Scotland's bonnie bounds.
His native land of liberty shall nurse his glorious wounds,
While wide through all our Highland hills his warlike name re-
 sounds.

This song, founded on a more ancient one with the same title, was written for
the collection of Mr. George Thomson after the death of Burns. The subject was
the departure for the Continent, with his regiment, of the Marquis of Huntly in 1799.

------◆------

THE BATTLE OF VITTORIA.

WILLIAM GLEN.   Air—" Whistle o'er the lave o't."

SING, a' ye bards, wi' loud acclaim,
High glory gi'e to gallant Grahame,
Heap laurels on our marshal's fame,
 Wha conquer'd at Vittoria.
Triumphant freedom smiled on Spain,
An' raised her stately form again,
Whan the British Lion shook his mane
 On the mountains o' Vittoria.

Let blust'rin' Suchet crously crack,
Let Joseph rin the coward's track,
And Jourdan wish his baton back
 He left upon Vittoria ;
If e'er they meet their worthy king,
Let them dance roun' him in a ring,
An' some Scottish piper play the spring
 He blew them at Vittoria.

Gi'e truth an' honour to the Dane,
Gi'e German's monarch heart and brain ;
But aye in sic a cause as Spain,
 Gi'e Britons a Vittoria.

The English Rose was ne'er sae red,
The Shamrock waved whare glory led,
And the Scottish Thistle raised its head
    An' smiled upon Vittoria.

Loud was the battle's stormy swell,
Whare thousands fought and mony fell;
But the Glasgow heroes bore the bell
    At the battle of Vittoria.
The Paris maids may ban them a',
Their lads are maistly wede awa,
An' cauld an' pale as wreaths o' snaw
    They lie upon Vittoria.

Wi' quakin' heart and tremblin' knees,
The Eagle standard-bearer flees,
While the "meteor-flag" floats to the breeze,
    An' wantons on Vittoria.
Britannia's glory there was shown
By the undaunted Wellington,
An' the tyrant trembled on his throne,
    Whan hearin' o' Vittoria.

Peace to the spirits o' the brave,
Let a' their trophies for them wave,
An' green be our Cadogan's grave
    Upon thy field, Vittoria!
There let eternal laurels bloom,
While maidens mourn his early doom,
An' deck his lowly honour'd tomb
    Wi' roses on Vittoria.

Ye Caledonian war-pipes, play;
Barossa heard your Highlan' lay,
An' the gallant Scot show'd there that day
    A prelude to Vittoria.
Shout to the heroes—swell ilk voice
To them wha made poor Spain rejoice;
Shout Wellington an' Lynedoch, boys,
    Barossa an' Vittoria!

BACK AGAIN.

ANONYMOUS.   About the year 1801.

WHEN Abercromby, gallant Scot,
  Made Britain's faes to tack again,
To fight by him it was my lot;
  But now I'm safe come back again.

The cannons didna Donald fleg,—
  I'd like to hear them crack again;
My fears were for my bonnie Meg,
  Lest I should ne'er come back again.

Our leader fell,—so died the brave,
  We'll never see his like again;
I was denied a sodger's grave,
  For I am safe come back again.

It's true they've ta'en frae me a leg;
  But wha for that would mak' a maen?
Cheer up your heart, my bonnie Meg,
  I've brought a leal heart back again.

And though the wound it carried smart,
  And twitch'd me sair wi' rackin' pain,
Wi' honour's scars I wadna part,
  Nor yet my leg take back again.

Cheer up your heart since I am here,
  Wi' smiles your cheek gae deck again;
Cheer up, my lass, an' dinna fear,
  Your Donald's safe come back again.

Though mony a rattlin' blast has blawn,
  There's plenty in the stack again;
My wee lock siller's a' your ain
  Now sin' I'm safe come back again.

Now may the wars for ever cease,
  Your heart nae mair to rack again;
And may we live in love and peace,
  Sin' Donald's safe come back again.

But should my country call me forth,
  Her freedom to protect again,
Claymore in hand I'd leave the North,
  If I should ne'er come back again.

CALEDONIA.

James Hogg.

Caledonia! thou land of the mountain and rock,
    Of the ocean, the mist, and the wind;
Thou land of the torrent, the pine, and the oak,
    Of the roebuck, the hart, and the hind;
Though bare are thy cliffs, and though barren thy glens,
    Though bleak thy dun islands appear,
Yet kind are the hearts and undaunted the clans
    That roam on these mountains so drear.

A foe from abroad, or a tyrant at home,
    Could never thy ardour restrain;
The marshall'd array of imperial Rome
    Essay'd thy proud spirit in vain!
Firm seat of religion, of valour, of truth,
    Of genius unshackled and free,
The Muses have left all the vales of the south,
    My loved Caledonia, for thee!

Sweet land of the bay and the wild-winding deeps,
    Where loveliness slumbers at even,
While far in the depth of the blue water sleeps
    A calm little motionless heaven!

Thou land of the valley, the moor, and the hill,
Of the storm and the proud rolling wave—
Yes, thou art the land of fair liberty still,
And the land of my forefather's grave!

THE THISTLE OF SCOTLAND.

Air—"The Black Joke."

LET them boast of the country gave Patrick his fame,
Of the land of the ocean and Anglian name,
  With the red-blushing roses and shamrock so green :
Far dearer to me are the hills of the North,
The land of blue mountains, the birth-place of worth ;
Those mountains where Freedom has fix'd her abode,
Those wide-spreading glens where no slave ever trode,
  Where blooms the red heather and thistle so green.

Though rich be the soil where blossoms the rose,
And barren the mountains and cover'd with snows
  Where blooms the red heather and thistle so green ;
Yet for friendship sincere, and for loyalty true,
And for courage so bold which no foe could subdue,
Unmatch'd is our country, unrivall'd our swains,
And lovely and true are the nymphs on our plains,
  Where rises the thistle, the thistle so green.

Far-famed are our sires in the battles of yore,
And many the cairnies that rise on our shore
   O'er the foes of the land of the thistle so green ;
And many a cairnie shall rise on our strand,
Should the torrent of war ever burst on our land.
Let foe come on foe, as wave comes on wave,
We'll give them a welcome, we'll give them a grave
   Beneath the red heather and thistle so green.

Oh dear to our souls as the blessings of heaven,
Is the freedom we boast, is the land that we live in,
   The land of red heather and thistle so green :
For that land and that freedom our fathers have bled,
And we swear by the blood that our fathers have shed,
No foot of a foe shall e'er tread on their grave ;
But the thistle shall bloom on the bed of the brave,
   The thistle of Scotland, the thistle so green.

This song was inserted in Hogg's "Jacobite Relics." The Shepherd states, in
introducing it: "This is a modern song, and the only one that is in the volume, to
my knowledge. It had no right to be here, for it is a national, not a Jacobite song ;
but I insert it out of a whim, to vary the theme a little. It is an excellent song,
though professedly an imitation, and when tolerably sung, never misses of having
a good effect among a company of Scots people. It has been published as mine in
several collections ; I wish it were ; but I am told that it was written by Mr. Suther-
land, land surveyor, a gentleman of whom I know nothing, save that he is the author
of some other popular songs." As nothing else has been discovered of Mr Suther-
land, the song is supposed to have been written by Hogg himself.

MY AIN COUNTRIE.

ALLAN CUNNINGHAM.

THE sun rises bright in France,
   And fair sets he ;
But he has tint the blythe blink he had
   In my ain countrie.
Oh, gladness comes to many,
   But sorrow comes to me,
As I look o'er the wide ocean
   To my ain countrie.

Oh, it's not my ain ruin,
    That saddens aye my ee,
But the love I left in Galloway,
    Wi' bonnie bairnies three;
My hamely hearth burnt bonnie,
    And smiled my fair Marie:
I've left my heart behind me
    In my ain countrie.

The bud comes back to summer,
    And the blossom to the tree;
But I win back—oh, never,
    To my ain countrie.
I'm leal to the high Heaven,
    Which will be leal to me;
And there I'll meet ye a' sune
    Frae my ain countrie.

———◆———

HAME, HAME, HAME!

ALLAN CUNNINGHAM.   From Cromek's " Remains of Nithsdale and Galloway
Song."

HAME, hame, hame! oh, hame fain wad I be!
Oh, hame, hame, hame, to my ain countrie!
When the flower is i' the bud, and the leaf is on the tree,
The lark shall sing me hame to my ain countrie.
    Hame, hame, hame! oh, hame fain wad I be!
    Oh, hame, hame, hame, to my ain countrie!

The green leaf o' loyaltie's beginning now to fa';
The bonnie white rose it is withering an' a';
But we'll water't wi' the bluid of usurping tyrannic,
And fresh it shll blaw in my ain countrie.
    Hame, hame, hame! oh, hame fain wad I be!
    Oh, hame, hame, hame, to my ain countrie!

Oh, there's nocht now frae ruin my countrie can save,
But the keys o' kind Heaven, to open the grave,
That a' the noble martyrs who died for loyaltie
May rise again and fight for their ain countrie.
    Hame, hame, hame! oh, hame fain wad I be!
    Oh, hame, hame, hame, to my ain countrie!

The great now are gane wha attempted to save,
The green grass is growing abune their grave;
Yet the sun through the mirk seems to promise to me,
I'll shine on ye yet in your ain countrie.
   Hame, hame, hame! oh, hame fain wad I be!
   Oh, hame, hame, hame, to my ain countrie!

FAREWELL TO BONNIE TEVIOTDALE.

THOMAS PRINGLE, born 1789, died 1834.

OUR native land, our native vale,
   A long, a last adieu;
Farewell to bonnie Teviotdale,
   And Cheviot's mountains blue!

Farewell, ye hills of glorious deeds,
   Ye streams renown'd in song;
Farewell, ye braes and blossom'd meads
   Our hearts have loved so long!

Farewell the blythesome broomy knowes
   Where thyme and harebells grow;
Farewell the hoary haunted hows
   O'erhung with birk and sloe!

The mossy cave and mouldering tower
   That skirt our native dell,
The martyr's grave and lover's bower
   We bid a sad farewell!

Home of our love, our father's home,
   Land of the brave and free,
The sail is flapping on the foam
   That bears us far from thee!

We seek a wild and distant shore
  Beyond the western main ;
We leave thee to return no more,
  Nor view thy cliffs again !

Our native land, our native vale,
  A long, a last adieu ;
Farewell to bonnie Teviotdale,
  And Scotland's mountains blue.

TAK' YOUR AULD CLOAK ABOUT YE.

ANONYMOUS.

In winter, when the rain rain'd cauld,
    And frost and snaw on ilka hill,
And Boreas wi' his blasts sae bauld
    Was threat'ning a' our kye to kill;
Then Bell my wife, wha lo'es nae strife,
    She said to me richt hastilie,
Get up, gudeman, save Crummie's life,
    And tak' your auld cloak about ye.

My Crummie is a usefu' cow,
  And she is come of a good kin ;
Aft has she wet the bairnie's mou',
  And I am laith that she should tyne :
Get up, gudeman, it is fu' time,
  The sun shines frae the lift sae hie ;
Sloth never made a gracious end,—
  Gae, tak' your auld cloak about ye.

My cloak was ance a gude grey cloak,
  When it was fitting for my wear ;
But now it's scantly worth a groat,
  For I hae worn't this thretty year :
Let's spend the gear that we hae won,
  We little ken the day we'll dee ;
Then I'll be proud, since I hae sworn
  To hae a new cloak about me.

In days when our king Robert rang,
  His trews they cost but half-a-croun,
He said they were a great ower dear,
  And ca'd the tailor thief and loon.
He was the king that wore the croun,
  And thou the man of laigh degree :
It's pride puts a' the country doun,
  Sae tak' your auld cloak about ye.

Ilka land has its ain lauch,
  Ilk kind o' corn has its ain hool ;
I think the warld has a' gane wrang,
  When ilka wife her man wad rule.
Do ye no see Rob, Jock, and Hab,
  As they are girded gallantlie,
While I sit huyklin i' the ase ?—
  I'll hae a new cloak about me.

Gudeman, I wat it's thretty year
  Sin' we did ane anither ken,
And we hae had atween us twa
  Of lads and bonnie lasses ten ;
Now they are women grown and men,
  I wish and pray weel may they be :
If you would prove a good husband,
  E'en tak' your auld cloak about ye.

Bell my wife she lo'es nae strife,
  But she would guide me if she can;
And to maintain an easy life,
  I aft maun yield, though I'm gudeman.
Nocht's to be gain'd at woman's hand,
  Unless ye gi'e her a' the plea:
Then I'll leave aff where I began,
  And tak' my auld cloak about me.

This is one of the most ancient Scottish songs extant. That it was known to Shakspeare in its English garb is evident from his having quoted the antepenultimate stanza in the second act of "Othello." The English version appears in Percy's "Reliques." It differs from the Scottish in some respects, but not materially; and Percy evidently inclines to admit that the Scottish is the original version. The Scottish version appears to have been first published in a complete form by Allan Ramsay, in the "Tea-Table Miscellany."

WIDOW, ARE YE WAUKIN?

ALLAN RAMSAY. From the "Tea-Table Miscellany."

"OH, wha's that at my chamber-door?"
  "Fair widow, are ye waukin?"
"Auld carle, your suit give o'er,
  Your love lies a' in talking.
Gi'e me a lad that's young and tight,
  Sweet like an April meadow;
'Tis sic as he can bless the sight
  And bosom of a widow."

"O widow, wilt thou let me in?
  I'm pawky, wise, and thrifty,
And come of a right gentle kin—
  I'm little mair than fifty."
"Daft carle, ye may dicht your mouth;
  What signifies how pawky
Or gentle-born ye be, bot youth,
  In love you're but a gawky."

"Then, widow, let these guineas speak,
  That powerfully plead clinkan;
And if they fail, my mouth I'll steek,
  And nae mair love will think on.'

" These court indeed, I maun confess;
   I think they make you young, sir,
And ten times better can express
   Affection than your tongue, sir."

HOW, WANTON WIDOW!

" How, wanton widow,
   Are ye waukin yet?
Hey, wanton widow,
   Are ye waukin yet?"
Quoth the widow to the man,
   " Ye may come in an' see."
Quoth the man to the widow,
   " Will ye marry me?"

Quoth the widow to the man,
   " I maun think awhile;
Ye hae spoken o'er rash,
   For me first to tell;
But if ye be kindly,
   We yet may agree."
Quoth the man to the widow,
   " Ye maun marry me."

This song, somewhat similar in character to the one preceding, has been recovered
from tradition, and preserved in the manuscript copy of the ancient songs of the
north of Scotland collected by the late Peter Buchan.

JOCKEY FOU, JENNY FAIN.

From the "Tea-Table Miscellany," 1724.   Air—"Jockey fou."

JOCKEY fou, Jenny fain,
Jenny was na ill to gain;
She was couthie, he was kind,
And thus the wooer tell'd his mind:

Jenny, I'll nae mair be nice,
Gi'e me love at ony price;
I winna prig for red or white—
Love alane can gi'e delyte.

Others seek they kenna what,
In looks, in carriage, and a' that;
Gi'e me love for her I court—
Love in love makes a' the sport.

Let love sparkle in her ee,
Let her love nae man but me;
That's the tocher-gude I prize,
There the lover's treasure lies.

Colours mingled unco fine,
Common notions lang sinsyne,
Never can engage my love,
Until my fancy first approve.

Allan Ramsay inserted this song in his " Miscellany " with the signature Q, to
signify that it was old, with additions by himself.   The air is also very ancient.

------◆------

MY WIFE HAS TA'EN THE GEE.

Anonymous.   From Herd's Collection, 1776.

A friend o' mine cam' here yestreen,
    An' he wad hae me doun
To drink a bottle o' ale wi' him
    In the neist burrows toun.
But oh, indeed, it was, sir,
    Sae far the waur for me;
For lang or e'er that I cam' hame
    My wife had ta'en the gee.

We sat sae late and drank sae stout,
    The truth I tell to you,
That lang or e'er the midnight cam',
    We a' were roarin' fou.
My wife sits at the fireside,
    And the tear blinds aye her ee;
The ne'er a bed wad she gang to,
    But sit and tak' the gee.

In the mornin' sune, when I cam' doun,
  The ne'er a word she spake,
But mony a sad and sour look,
  And aye her head she'd shake.
"My dear," quo' I, "what aileth thee,
  To look sae sour on me ?
I'll never do the like again,
  If you'll ne'er tak' the gee."

When that she heard, she ran, she flang
  Her arms about my neck,
And twenty kisses in a crack
  And, poor wee thing, she grat
"If you'll ne'er do the like again,
  But bide at hame wi' me,
I'll lay my life, I'll be the wife
  That never taks the gee."

----------◆----------

THE MILLER.

Sir John Clerk, of Pennycuick, Bart.; born about the year 1680, died 1755.
From the "Charmer," Edinburgh, 1751.

MERRY may the maid be
  That marries the miller,
For foul day and fair day
  He's aye bringing till her ;
He's aye a penny in his purse
  For dinner and for supper ;
And gin she please, a good fat cheese,
  And lumps of yellow butter.

When Jamie first did woo me,
  I spier'd what was his calling :
Fair maid, says he, oh, come and see ;
  Ye're welcome to my dwelling.
Though I was shy, yet I could spy
  The truth of what he told me,
And that his house was warm and couth,
  And room in it to hold me.

Behind the door a bag of meal,
   And in the kist was plenty
Of good hard cakes his mither bakes,
   And bannocks were na scunty ;
A good fat sow, a sleeky cow
   Was standin' in the byre ;
Whilst lazy puss, with mealy mous,
   Was playing at the fire.

Good signs are these, my mither says,
   And bids me tak' the miller ;
For foul day and fair day
   He's aye bringing till her :
For meal and malt she does na want,
   Nor ony thing that's dainty ;
And now and then a keckling hen
   To lay her eggs in plenty.

In winter, when the wind and rain
   Blaws o'er the house and byre,
He sits beside a clean hearthstane
   Before a rousing fire ;
With nut-brown ale he tells his tale,
   Which rows him o'er fu' nappy :
Who'd be a king—a petty thing,
   When a miller lives so happy ?

This song originally appeared in the "Charmer" without the concluding stanza.
It was afterwards added by the author, at that time one of the Scottish judges.

ARGYLL IS MY NAME.

JOHN Duke of Argyll and Greenwich, born 1680, died 1743.

ARGYLL is my name, and you may think it strange
To live at a court, yet never to change ;
A' falsehood and flattery I do disdain,
In my secret thoughts nae guile does remain.
My king and my country's foes I have faced,
In city or battle I ne'er was disgraced ;
I do every thing for my country's weal,
And feast upon bannocks o' barley meal.

Adieu to the courtie of London town,
For to my ain countrie I will gang down;
At the sight of Kirkaldy ance again,
I'll cock up my bonnet and march amain.
Oh, the muckle deil tak' a' your noise and strife
I'm fully resolved for a country life,
Where a' the braw lasses, wha ken me weel,
Will feed me wi' bannocks o' barley meal.

I will quickly lay down my sword and my gun,
And put my blue bonnet and my plaidie on;
With my silk-tartan hose and leather-heel'd shoon.
And then I will look like a sprightly loon.
And when I'm sae dress'd frae tap to tae,
To meet my dear Maggie I vow I will gae,
Wi' target and hanger hung down to my heel,
And I'll feast upon bannocks o' barley meal.

I'll buy a rich garment to gi'e to my dear,
A ribbon o' green for Maggie to wear;
And mony thing brawer than that, I declare,
Gin she will gang wi' me to Paisley fair.
And when we are married, I'll keep her a cow,
And Maggie will milk when I gae to plow;
We'll live a' the winter on beef and lang kail,
And feast upon bannocks o' barley meal.

Gin Maggie should chance to bring me a son,
He'll fight for his king as his daddy has done;
He'll hie him to Flanders some breeding to learn,
And then hame to Scotland and get him a farm.
And there we will live by our industry,
And wha'll be sae happy as Maggie and me?
We'll a' grow as fat as a Norway seal,
Wi' our feasting on bannocks o' barley meal.

Then fare ye weel, citizens, noisy men,
Wha jolt in your coaches to Drury-lane;
Ye bucks o' Bear-garden, I bid you adieu,
For drinking and swearing, I leave it to you.
I'm fairly resolved for a country life,
And nae langer will live in hurry and strife;

I'll aff to the Highlands as hard's I can reel,
And whang at the bannocks o' barley meal.

This song is generally attributed to the celebrated Duke of Argyll, but the state-
ment does not appear to rest on sufficient authority. There is no doubt, however,
that it was written of, if not by him.

GIN YE MEET A BONNIE LASSIE.

ALLAN RAMSAY.   Air— "Fie, gar rub her ower wi' strae."

GIN ye meet a bonnie lassie,
 Gi'e her a kiss and let her gae ;
But if ye meet a dirty hizzie,
 Fie, gar rub her ower wi' strae.
Be sure ye dinna quit the grip
 Of ilka joy when ye are young,
Before auld age your vitals nip,
 And lay ye twa-fauld ower a rung.

Sweet youth's a blythe and heartsome time :
 Then, lads and lasses, while it's May,
Gae pou the gowan in its prime,
 Before it wither and decay.
Watch the saft minutes o' delight,
 When Jenny speaks below her breath,
And kisses, layin' a' the wyte
 On you if she kep ony skaith.

Haith, ye're ill-bred, she'll smilin' say,
 Ye'll worry me, ye greedy rook.
Syne frae your arms she'll rin away,
 And hide hersel' in some dark neuk.
Her lauch will lead ye to the place
 Where lies the happiness ye want ;
And plainly tell ye to your face,
 Nineteen nay-says are hauf a grant.

Now to her heavin' bosom cling,
 And sweitly tuilyie for a kiss ;
Frae her fair finger whup a ring,
 As taiken o' a future bliss.

These benisons, I'm very sure,
   Are of kind heaven's indulgent grant;
Then, surly carles, wheesht, forbear
   To plague us wi' your whinin' cant!

From the "Tea-Table Miscellany," 1724. "Connected with this song," says Chambers, "which few readers will need to be informed is a paraphrase, and a very happy one, of the celebrated 'Vides ut alta' of Horace, the following anecdote may be told. In a large mixed company, which had assembled one night in the house of a citizen of Edinburgh, where Robert Burns happened to be present, somebody sung 'Gin ye meet a bonnie lassie,' with excellent effect, insomuch as to throw all present into a sort of rapture. The only exception lay with a stiff pedantic old schoolmaster, who, in all the consciousness of superior critical acumen, and determined to be pleased with nothing which was not strictly classical, sat erect in his chair, with a countenance full of disdain, and rigidly abstained from expressing the slightest symptom of satisfaction. 'What ails you at the sang, Mr. —— ?' inquired an honest citizen of the name of Boag, who had been particularly delighted with it. 'Oh, nothing!' answered the man of learning; 'only the whole of it is stolen from Horace.' 'Houts, man!' replied Boag, 'Horace has rather stolen from the auld sang.' This ludicrous observation was met with absolute shouts of laughter, the whole of which was at the expense of the discomfited critic; and Burns was pleased to express his hearty thanks to the citizen for having set the matter to rights. He seems, from a passage in Cromek's 'Relics,' to have made use of the observation as his own."

MY JO JANET.

From the "Tea-Table Miscellany."

Air—"The keekin' glass," or "My jo Janet."

SWEET sir, for your courtesie,
   When ye come by the Bass, then,
For the love ye bear to me,
   Buy me a keekin' glass, then.
"Keek into the draw-well,
   Janet, Janet;
There ye'll see your bonnie sel',
   My jo Janet."

Keekin' in the draw-well clear,
   What if I fa' in, sir?
Then a' my kin' will say and swear
   I droun'd mysel' for sin, sir.
"Haud the better by the brae,
   Janet, Janet;
Haud the better by the brae,
   My jo Janet."

Gude sir, for your courtesie,
  Comin' through Aberdeen, then
For the love ye bear to me,
  Buy me a pair o' sheen, then.
" Clout the auld—the new are dear,
    Janet, Janet;
Ae pair may serve ye hauf a year,
    My jo Janet."

But what if, dancin' on the green
  And skippin' like a maukin,
They should see my clouted sheen,
  Of me they will be taukin'.
" Dance aye laigh and late at e'en,
    Janet, Janet;
Syne their fauts will no be seen,
    My jo Janet."

Kind sir, for your courtesie,
  When ye gae to the cross, then,
For the love ye bear to me,
  Buy me a pacin' horse, then.
" Pace upon your spinnin' wheel,
    Janet, Janet;
Pace upon your spinnin' wheel,
    My jo Janet."

There is another stanza, which is generally omitted, and not without reason.

AULD ROB MORRIS.

Air—"Jock's the laird's brither."

MOTHER.

AULD Rob Morris, that wons in yon glen,
He's the king o' guid fallows, and wale o' auld men ;
He has fourscore o' black sheep, and fourscore too ;
Auld Rob Morris is the man ye maun lo'e.

DAUGHTER.

Haud your tongue, mother, and let that abee ;
For his eild and my eild can never agree :
They'll never agree, and that will be seen,
For he is fourscore, and I'm but fifteen.

MOTHER.

Haud your tongue, dochter, and lay by your pride,
For he is the bridegroom, and ye'se be the bride ;
He shall lie by your side, and kiss you too ;
Auld Rob Morris is the man ye maun lo'e

DAUGHTER.

Auld Rob Morris, I ken him fu' weel,
His back sticks out like ony peat-creel ;
He's out-shinn'd, in-knee'd, and ringle-eyed too;
Auld Rob Morris is the man I'll ne'er lo'e.

MOTHER.

Though auld Rob Morris be an elderly man,
Yet his auld brass will buy you a new pan ;
Then, dochter, ye should na be sae ill to shoe,
For auld Rob Morris is the man ye maun lo'e.

DAUGHTER.

But auld Rob Morris I never will hae,
His back is so stiff and his beard is grown gray ;
I had rather die than live wi' him a year,
Sae mair o' Rob Morris I never will hear.

This song appears in the "Tea-Table Miscellany" with the signature of Q.
Burns has written a love song with the same title, in which he has preserved the
first two lines, and some other portions of the above.

THE BLAITHRIE O'T.

From the "Charmer," 1749, but known to be much older.

WHEN I think on this warld's pelf,
And the little wee share I hae o't to myself,
And how the lass that wants it is by the lads forgot ;—
May the shame fa' the gear and the blaithrie o't!

Jockie was the laddie that held the pleugh,
But now he's got gowd and gear enough ;
He thinks nae mair o' me that wears the plaiden coat ;—
May the shame fa' the gear and the blaithrie o't!

Jenny was the lassie that muck'd the byre,
But now she is clad in her silken attire ;
And Jockie says he lo'es her, and swears he's me forgot ;—
May the shame fa' the gear and the blaithrie o't!

But all this shall never daunton me,
Sae lang as I keep my fancy free ;
For the lad that's sae inconstant he is not worth a groat ;—
May the shame fa' the gear and the blaithrie o't!

SECOND VERSION.

WHEN I think on this warld's pelf,
And how little o't I hae to myself,
I sich and look down on my threadbare coat ;—
Yet the shame tak' the gear and the baigrie o't!

Johnnie was the lad that held the pleuch,
But now he has gowd and gear eneuch ;
I mind weel the day when he was na worth a groat ;—
And the shame fa' the gear and the baigrie o't!

Jenny was the lassie that muckit the byre,
But now she goes in her silken attire ;
And she was a lass wha wore a plaiden coat ;—
Oh, the shame fa' the gear and the baigrie o't!

Yet a' this shall never daunton me,
Sae lang as I keep my fancy free;
While I've but a penny to pay the t'other pot,
May the shame fa' the gear and the baigrie o't!

THIRD VERSION.

O WILLY, weel I mind, I lent you my hand
To sing you a song which you did me command;
But my memory's so bad, I had almost forgot
That you call'd it the gear and the blaithrie o't.

I'll not sing about confusion, delusion, or pride,
I'll sing about a laddie was for a virtuous bride;
For virtue is an ornament that time will never rot,
And preferable to gear and the blaithrie o't.

Though my lassie hae nae scarlets or silks to put on,
We envy not the greatest that sits upon the throne;
I wad rather hae my lassie, though she cam' in her smock,
Than a princess wi' the gear and the blaithrie o't.

Though we hae nae horses or menzie at command,
We will toil on our foot, and we'll work wi' our hand;
And when wearied without rest, we'll find it sweet in any spot,
And we'll value not the gear and the blaithrie o't.

If we hae ony babies, we'll count them as lent;
Hae we less, hae we mair, we will aye be content;
For they say they hae mair pleasure that wins but a groat,
Than the miser wi' his gear and the blaithrie o't.

I'll not meddle wi' th' affairs o' the kirk or the queen;
They're nae matters for a sang,—let them sink, let them swim;
On your kirk I'll ne'er encroach, but I'll hold it still remote,
Sae tak' this for the gear and the blaithrie o't.

"The above is a set of this song," says Burns, "which was the earliest song I remember to have got by heart. When a child, an old woman sung it to me, and I picked it up every word at first hearing."

UP IN THE MORNIN' EARLY.*

CAULD blaws the wind frae east to west,
  The drift is driving sairly;
Sae loud and shrill's I hear the blast,
  I'm sure it's winter fairly.
      Up in the mornin's no for me,
        Up in the mornin' early;
      When a' the hills are cover'd wi' snaw,
        I'm sure it's winter fairly.

The birds sit chittering in the thorn,
  A' day they fare but sparely;
And lang's the night frae e'en to morn—
  I'm sure it's winter fairly.
      Up in the mornin's no for me,
        Up in the mornin' early;
      When a' the hills are cover'd wi' snaw,
        I'm sure it's winter fairly.

---

* The chorus of this song is old, and with the melody forms one of the earliest specimens of Scottish poetry and music. The rest of the song is founded by Burns upon the original lyric, of which it is a striking improvement. A convivial song with the same title, but in no other respect resembling it, appears in another part of this collection.

CAULD blaws the wind frae north to south,
  The drift is drifting sairly;
The sheep are cowrin' i' the heuch;
  Oh, sirs, it's winter fairly!
Now up in the mornin's no for me,
  Up in the mornin' early;
I'd rather gae supperless to my bed
  Than rise in the mornin' early.

Loud roars the blast amang the woods,
  And tirls the branches barely;
On hill and house hear how it thuds;
  The frost is nipping sairly.
Now up in the mornin's no for me,
  Up in the mornin' early;
To sit a' nicht wad better agree
  Than rise in the mornin' early.

The sun peeps owre yon southland hills
  Like ony timorous carlie,
Just blinks a wee, then sinks again;
  And that we find severely.
Now up in the mornin's no for me,
  Up in the mornin' early;
When snaw blaws in at the chimley-cheek,
  Wha'd rise in the mornin' early?

Nae linties lilt on hedge or bush,—
  Poor things, they suffer sairly;
In cauldrife quarters a' the nicht,
  A' day they feed but sparely.
Now up in the mornin's no for me,
  Up in the mornin' early;
A pennyless purse I wad rather dree
  Than rise in the mornin' early.

A cosie house and canty wife
  Aye keep a body cheerly;
And pantries stow'd wi' meat and drink,
  They answer unco rarely.

But up in the mornin'—na, na, na !
  Up in the mornin' early;
The gowans maun glent on bank and brae,
  When I rise in the mornin' early.

COMING THROUGH THE RYE.

ANONYMOUS. Old version, as altered by Burns.

Air—"Coming through the rye."

COMING through the rye, poor body,
  Coming through the rye,
She draiglet a' her petticoatie
  Coming through the rye.
    Oh, Jenny's a' wat, poor body,
      Jenny's seldom dry;
    She draiglet a' her petticoatie
      Coming through the rye.

Gin a body meet a body
  Coming through the rye ;
Gin a body kiss a body,
  Need a body cry ?
Gin a body meet a body
  Coming through the glen ;
Gin a body kiss a body,
  Need the warld ken ?
    Oh, Jenny's a' wat, poor body,
      Jenny's seldom dry ;
    She draiglet a' her petticoatie
      Coming through the rye.

NEW STAGE VERSION.

GIN a body meet a body
  Comin' through the rye,
Gin a body kiss a body,
  Need a body cry ?

Every lassie has her laddie,
　　Ne'er a ane hae I ;
Yet a' the lads they smile at me
　　When comin' through the rye.
Amang the train there is a swain
　　I dearly lo'e mysel' ;
But whaur his hame, or what his name,
　　I dinna care to tell.

Gin a body meet a body
　　Comin' frae the town,
Gin a body greet a body,
　　Need a body frown ?
Every lassie has her laddie,
　　Ne'er a ane hae I ;
Yet a' the lads they smile at me
　　When comin' through the rye.
Amang the train there is a swain
　　I dearly lo'e mysel' ;
But whaur his hame, or what his name,
　　I dinna care to tell.

BIDE YE YET.

ANONYMOUS. From Herd's Collection, 1769. Air—"The wayward wife."

GIN I had a wee house an' a canty wee fire,
An' a bonnie wee wifie to praise and admire,
Wi' a bonnie wee yardie aside a wee burn,
Fareweel to the bodies that yaumer and mourn.
　　Sae bide ye yet, an' bide ye yet ;
　　Ye little ken what's to betide ye yet ;
　　Some bonnie wee body may fa' to my lot,
　　An I'll aye be canty wi' thinkin' o't.

When I gang a-field, an' come hame at e'en,
I'll get my wee wifie fu' neat an' fu' clean,
Wi' a bonnie wee bairnie upon her knee,
That'll cry papa or daddy to me.
　　Sae bide ye yet, &c.

An' if there should ever happen to be
A difference atween my wee wifie an' me,
In hearty good humour, although she be teased,
I'll kiss her an' clap her until she be pleased.
    Sae bide ye yet, &c.

THE BRISK YOUNG LAD.

ANONYMOUS.   Herd's Collection, 1776.   Air - "Bung your eye in the morning."

THERE cam' a young man to my daddie's door,
My daddie's door, my daddie's door;
There cam' a young man to my daddie's door,
  Cam' seeking me to woo.
    And wow, but he was a braw young lad,
    A brisk young lad, and a braw young lad;
    And wow, but he was a braw young lad,
      Cam' seeking me to woo.

But I was baking when he came,
When he came, when he came;
I took him in and gied him a scone,
  To thowe his frozen mou'.

I set him in aside the bink;
I ga'e him bread and ale to drink;
But ne'er a blythe styme wad he blink
  Until his wame was fu'.

Gae, get you gone, you cauldrife wooer,
Ye sour-looking, cauldrife wooer!
I straightway show'd him to the door,
  Saying, Come nae mair to woo.

There lay a deuk-dub before the door,
Before the door, before the door;
There lay a deuk-dub before the door,
  And there fell he, I trow.

Out cam' the gudeman, and high he shouted;
Out cam' the gudewife, and laigh she louted;
And a' the toun-neebors were gather'd about it;
  And there lay he, I trow.

Then out cam' I, and sneer'd and smiled:
Ye cam' to woo, but ye're a' beguiled;
Ye've fa'en i' the dirt, and ye're a' befiled:
  We'll hae nae mair o' you.

The chorus is repeated at the end of every stanza. The music of this old song is quaint, characteristic, and peculiarly Scottish.

TIBBIE FOWLER.

From Herd's Collection, 1776. Air—"Tibbie Fowler."

TIBBIE Fowler o' the glen,
  There's ower many wooin' at her;
Tibbie Fowler o' the glen,
  There's ower many wooin' at her.

Wooin' at her, pu'in' at her,
  Courtin' her, and canna get her;
Filthy elf! it's for her pelf
  That a' the lads are wooin' at her.

Ten cam' east, and ten cam' west,
  Ten cam' rowin' o'er the water;
Twa cam' down the lang dyke-side:
  There's twa-and-thirty wooin' at her!

There's seven but and seven ben,
  Seven i' the pantry wi' her;
Twenty head about the door:
  There's ane-and-forty wooin' at her!

She's got pendles in her lugs—
  Cockle-shells wad set her better!
High-heel'd shoon and siller tags;
  An' a' the lads are wooin' at her!

Be a lassie e'er sae black,
 Gin she hae the penny siller,
Set her up on Tintock tap,
 The wind will blaw a man till her.

Be a lassie e'er sae fair,
 An' she want the penny siller,
A flie may fell her i' the air,
 Before a man be even'd till her.

The first two stanzas of this song appeared in Herd's Collection. The song itself
is mentioned by Allan Ramsay in the "Tea-Table Miscellany." The authorship
has been claimed for the Rev. Dr Strachan, minister of Carnwater; but he appears
to have simply remodelled, and perhaps improved, the old song spoken of by Ramsay.

OUR GUDEMAN CAM' HAME AT E'EN.

ANONYMOUS. Herd's Collection, 1776. Air—"Our gudeman."

OUR gudeman cam' hame at e'en,
 And hame cam' he;
And there he saw a saddle-horse
 Where nae horse should be.
Oh, how cam' this horse here?
 How can this be?
How cam' this horse here
 Without the leave o' me?
  A horse! quo' she;
  Ay, a horse, quo' he.
Ye auld blind dotard carle,
 And blinder mat ye be!
It's but a bonnie milk-cow
 My mither sent to me.
  A milk-cow! quo' he;
  Ay, a milk-cow, quo' she.
Far hae I ridden,
 And muckle hae I seen;
But a saddle on a milk-cow
 Saw I never nane.

Our gudeman cam' hame at e'en,
 And hame cam' he;

He spied a pair o' jack-boots
  Where nae boots should be.
What's this now, gudewife?
  What's this I see?
How cam' thae boots here
  Without the leave o' me?
    Boots! quo' she;
    Ay, boots, quo' he.
Ye auld blind dotard carle,
  And blinder mat ye be!
It's but a pair o' water-stoups
  The cooper sent to me.
    Water-stoups! quo' he;
    Ay, water-stoups, quo' she,
Far hae I ridden,
  And muckle hae I seen;
But siller spurs on water-stoups
  Saw I never nane.

Our gudeman cam' hame at e'en,
  And hame cam' he;
And there he saw a siller sword
  Where nae sword should be.
What's this now, gudewife?
  What's this I see?
Oh, how cam' this sword here
  Without the leave o' me?
    A sword! quo' she;
    Ay, a sword, quo' he.
Ye auld blind dotard carle,
  And blinder mat ye be!
It's but a parridge-spurtle
  My minnie sent to me.
    A parridge-spurtle, quo' he;
    Ay, a parridge-spurtle, quo' she.
Weel, far hae I ridden,
  And muckle hae I seen;
But siller-handed parridge-spurtles
  Saw I never nane.

Our gudeman cam' hame at e'en,
  And hame cam' he;

And there he spied a powder'd wig
　　Where nae wig should be.
What's this now, gudewife?
　　What's this I see?
How cam' this wig here
　　Without the leave o' me?
　　　A wig! quo' she;
　　　Ay, a wig, quo' he.
Ye auld blind dotard carle,
　　And blinder mat ye be!
'Tis naething but a clocken-hen
　　My minnie sent to me.
　　　A clocken-hen! quo' he;
　　　Ay, a clocken-hen, quo' she.
Far hae I ridden,
　　And muckle hae I seen;
But powder on a clocken-hen
　　Saw I never nane.

Our gudeman cam' hame at e'en,
　　And hame cam' he;
And there he saw a muckle coat
　　Where nae coat should be.
How cam' this coat here?
　　How can this be?
How cam' this coat here?
　　Without the leave o' me?
　　　A coat! quo' she;
　　　Ay, a coat, quo' he.
Ye auld blind dotard carle,
　　And blinder mat ye be!
It's but a pair o' blankets
　　My minnie sent to me.
　　　Blankets! quo' he;
　　　Ay, blankets, quo' she.
Far hae I ridden,
　　And muckle hae I seen;
But buttons upon blankets
　　Saw I never nane.

Ben gaed our gudeman
　　And ben gaed he;

And there he spied a sturdy man
  Where nae man should be.
How cam' this man here?
  How can this be?
How cam' this man here
  Without the leave o' me?
    A man! quo' she;
    Ay, a man, quo' he.
Puir blind body,
  And blinder mat ye be!
It's but a new milkin' maid
  My mither sent to me.
    A maid! quo he;
    Ay, a maid, quo' she.
Far hae I ridden,
  And muckle hae I seen;
But lang-bearded maidens
  Saw I never nane.

This excellent old song has been claimed as English, but its whole character is evidently Scottish. Johnson, the editor of the "Musical Museum," recovered the air, which had been lost, from the singing of a barber in Edinburgh, and printed it for the first time in his collection. There is another version with a denouement more suitable to the delicacy of the present age than that commonly sung, and in which the following stanza concludes the story:—

Oh, hame cam' our gudeman at e'en,
  An' ben ga'ed he;
An' he saw a muckle man
  Where nae man should be
What's this now, gudewife?
  Wha's this I see?
An' how cam' this man here
  Without the leave o' me?
    A man! quo' she;
    Ay, a man, quo' he.
Oh, hooly, hooly, our gudeman!
  An' dinna anger'd be;
It's just our cousin Mackintosh
  Come frae the North Countrie.
    Cousin Mackintosh! quo' he;
    Ay, Cousin Mackintosh, quo' she
Oh, ye'll hae us a' hang'd, gudewife,
  I've een eneuch to see;
Ye're hidin' rebels in the house
  Without the leave o' me.

THE BARRING O' THE DOOR.

From Herd's Collection. The song is sung to an English tune called " An old
woman clothed in grey."

It fell about the Martinmas time,
  And a gay time it was than,
When our gudewife got puddings to mak',
  And she boiled them in the pan.

The wind sae cauld blew east and north,
  It blew into the floor;
Quoth our gudeman to our gudewife,
  " Gae out and bar the door."

" My hand is in my hussy'f skap,
  Gudeman, as ye may see;
An' it shou'd nae be barred this hundred year,
  It's no be barr'd for me."

They made a paction 'tween them twa,
  They made it firm and sure,
That whae'er should speak the foremost word
  Shou'd get up and bar the door.

Then by there came twa gentlemen
  At twelve o'clock at night,
And they could neither see house nor hall,
  Nor coal nor candle light.

Now whether is this a rich man's house,
  Or whether is it a poor?
But never a word wad ane o' them speak,
  For barring o' the door.

And first they ate the white puddings,
  And then they ate the black;
Though muckle thought the gudewife to hersel',
  Yet ne'er a word she spak'.

Then said the one unto the other,
    " Here, man, tak' ye my knife ;
Do ye tak' aff the auld man's beard,
    And I'll kiss the gudewife."

" But there's nae water in the house,
    And what shall we do than ?"
" What ails ye at the puddin' broo
    That boils into the pan ?"

Oh, up then started our gudeman,
    And an angry man was he :
" Will ye kiss my wife before my een,
    And scaud me wi' puddin' bree ?"

Then up and started our gudewife,
    Gied three skips on the floor :
" Gudeman, ye've spoken the foremost word,—
    Get up and bar the door."

This song was first printed by David Herd, who wrote it down from a traditionary version. It is generally sung with the following lines as a chorus :

    " Oh, the barring of our door,
        Weel, weel, weel ;
    And the barring of our door, weel."

THE DUSTY MILLER.

From " Johnson's Museum," 1782.

HEY, the dusty miller
    And his dusty coat ;
He will win a shilling
    Ere he spend a groat.
Dusty was the coat,
    Dusty was the colour ;
Dusty was the kiss
    That I gat frae the miller.

Hey, the dusty miller,
  And his dusty sack;
Leeze me on the calling
  Fills the dusty peck,—
Fills the dusty peck,
  Brings the dusty siller
I wad gi'e my coatie
  For the dusty miller.

FAIRLY SHOT OF HER.

From " Johnson's Museum "

Oh, gin I were fairly shot o' her,
Fairly, fairly, fairly shot o' her!
Oh, gin I were fairly shot o' her!
If she were dead, I wad dance on the top o' her.

Till we were married I couldna see licht till her;
For a month after a' thing aye gaed richt wi' her;
But these ten years I hae pray'd for a wright to her—
Oh. gin I were fairly shot o' her!

Nane o' her relations or friends could stay wi' her;
The neebours and bairns are a' fain to flee frae her;
And I my ain sel' am forced to gi'e way till her—
Oh, gin I were fairly shot o' her!

She gangs aye sae braw, she's sae muckle pride in her;
There's no a gudewife in the haill country-side like till her;
Wi' dress and wi' drink, the deil wadna bide wi' her—
Oh, gin I were fairly shot o' her!

If the time were but come that to the kirk-gate wi' her,
And into the yird I'd mak' mysel' quit o' her,
I'd then be as blythe as first when I met wi' her—
Oh, gin I were fairly shot o' her!

This is a modern version of an old song, and is said to have been written by one
John Anderson, at that time apprentice to Johnson the engraver, and publisher of
the " Museum," where the song first appeared.

MAGGIE LAUDER.

Anonymous, but attributed to FRANCIS SEMPLE.

WHA wadna be in love
    Wi' bonnie Maggie Lauder?
A piper met her gaun to Fife,
    And speir'd what was't they ca'd her.
Right scornfully she answer'd him,
    Begone, you hallanshaker!
Jog on your gate, you bladderskate!
    My name is Maggie Lauder.

Maggie, quo' he, and by my bags,
    I'm fidgin' fain to see thee;
Sit down by me, my bonnie bird,
    In troth I winna steer thee;
For I'm a piper to my trade,
    My name is Rob the Ranter;
The lasses loup as they were daft
    When I blaw up my chanter.

Piper, quo' Meg, hae ye your bags,
    Or is your drone in order?
If ye be Rob, I've heard of you,—
    Live you upo' the Border?

The lasses a', baith far and near,
　Hae heard o' Rob the Ranter ;
I'll shake my foot with right gude will,
　Gif you'll blaw up your chanter.

Then to his bags he flew wi' speed,
　About the drone he twisted ;
Meg up and wallop'd o'er the green,
　For brawly could she frisk it.
Weel done! quo' he—Play up! quo' she ;
　Weel bobb'd! quo' Rob the Ranter ;
'Tis worth my while to play indeed
　When I hae sic a dancer.

Weel hae you play'd your part, quo' Meg ;
　Your cheeks are like the crimson ;
There's nane in Scotland plays sae weel
　Since we lost Habbie Simpson.
I've lived in Fife, baith maid and wife,
　These ten years and a quarter ;
Gin' ye should come to Anster fair,
　Speir ye for Maggie Lauder.

"This old song," says Burns, "so pregnant with Scottish *naïveté* and energy, is much relished by all ranks. Its language is a precious model of imitation.—sly, sprightly, and forcibly expressive. Maggie's tongue wags out the nick-names of Rob the piper with all the careless lightsomeness of unrestrained gaiety."

KISSING'S NO SIN.

ANONYMOUS. Seventeenth or eighteenth century.

SOME say that kissing's a sin ;
　But I think it's nane ava,
For kissing has wonn'd in this warld
　Since ever that there was twa.

Oh, if it wasna lawfu',
　Lawyers wadna allow it ;
If it wasna holy,
　Ministers wadna do it.

If it wasna modest,
    Maidens wadna tak' it;
If it wasna plenty,
    Puir folk wadna get it.

We are indebted to Mr. Robert Chambers for the preservation of this characteristic fragment. It was recovered by him from the singing of a friend, and first printed in 1829 in his "Historical Essay on Scottish Song."

----♦----

FOR A' THAT AND A' THAT.

ROBERT BURNS.

Is there for honest poverty
    That hangs his head and a' that?
The coward-slave, we pass him by;
    We dare be puir for a' that.
For a' that and a' that,
    Our toils obscure and a' that;
The rank is but the guinea's stamp,
    The man's the gowd for a' that.

What though on hamely fare we dine,
    Wear hoddin' grey and a' that;
Gi'e fools their silks, an' knaves their wine,—
    A man's a man for a' that.
For a' that and a' that,
    Their tinsel show and a' that;
The honest man, though e'er sae poor,
    Is king o' men for a' that.

Ye see yon birkie ca'd a lord,
    Wha struts and stares and a' that;
Though hundreds worship at his word,
    He's but a coof for a' that.
For a' that and a' that,
    His riband, star, and a' that;
The man of independent mind,
    He looks and laughs at a' that.

A prince can mak' a belted knight,
   A marquis, duke, and a' that;
But an honest man's aboon his might—
   Guid faith, he mauna fa' that!
For a' that and a' that;
   Their dignities and a' that;
The pith o' sense and pride o' worth
   Are higher ranks than a' that.

Then let us pray that come it may,
   As come it will for a' that,
That sense and worth o'er a' the earth
   May bear the gree and a' that.
     For a' that and a' that,
   It's comin' yet for a' that,
That man to man, the warld o'er,
   Shall brothers be for a' that.

In reference to this immortal song, founded on a more ancient and very inferior one, with the same burden, or "overlay," Burns wrote to Mr. Thomson:—"A great critic (Aikin) on songs says that love and wine are the exclusive themes for song-writing. The following is on neither subject, and consequently is no song; but will be allowed, I think, to contain two or three pretty good prose thoughts inverted into rhyme."

SIC A WIFE AS WILLIE HAD.

. BURNS.   Air—"Tibbie Fowler in the glen."

WILLIE Wastle dwalt on Tweed,
   The spot they ca'd it Linkumdoddie;
Willie was a wabster guid,
   Cou'd stown a clue wi' ony bodie;
He had a wife was dour and din,
   Oh, Tinkler Madgie was her mither.
     Sic a wife as Willie had,
       I wadna gi'e a button for her.

She has an ee, she has but ane,
   The cat has twa the very colour;
Five rusty teeth forbye a stump,
   A clapper tongue wad deave a miller;
A whiskin beard about her mou',
   Her nose and chin they threaten ither.
     Sic a wife, &c.

She's bow-hough'd, she's hein-shinn'd,
　Ae limpin leg a hand-breed shorter ;
She's twisted right, she's twisted left,
　To balance fair in ilka quarter ;
She has a hump upon her breast,
　The twin o' that upon her shouther.
　　Sic a wife, &c.

Auld baudrans by the ingle sits,
　An' wi' her loof her face a-washin ;
But Willie's wife is nae sae trig,
　She dights her grunzie wi' a hushion ;
Her walie nieves like midden-creels,
　Her face wad fyle the Logan-water.
　　Sic a wife as Willie had,
　　　I wadna gi'e a button for her.

———◆———

·

MY SPOUSE NANCY.

Burns.　Air—" My jo Janet."

Husband, husband, cease your strife,
　Nor longer idly rave, sir ;
Though I am your wedded wife,
　Yet I am not your slave, sir.

" One of two must still obey,
　Nancy, Nancy ;
Is it man or woman, say,
　My spouse Nancy ?"

If 'tis still the lordly word,
　Service and obedience,
I'll desert my sovereign lord,
　And so, good bye, allegiance.

" Sad will I be so bereft,
　　Nancy, Nancy ;
Yet I'll try to make a shift,
　　My spouse Nancy."

My poor heart then break it must,
　　My last hour I'm near it ;
When you lay me in the dust,
　　Think, think, how you will bear it.

" I will hope and trust in heaven,
　　Nancy, Nancy ;
Strength to bear it will be given,
　　My spouse Nancy."

Well, sir, from the silent dead
　　Still I'll try to daunt you ;
Ever round your midnight bed,
　　Horrid sprites shall haunt you.

" I'll wed another like my dear
　　Nancy, Nancy ;
Then all hell will fly for fear,
　　My spouse Nancy."

" Your humorous English song to suit ' Jo Janet' is inimitable."—*Thomson, in a Letter to Burns.*

———◆———

WHISTLE O'ER THE LAVE O'T.

Burns.　Air—" Whistle o'er the lave o't."

FIRST when Maggie was my care,
Heaven I thought was in her air;
Now we're married—speir nae mair—
　　Whistle o'er the lave o't.
Meg was meek, and Meg was mild,
Bonnie Meg was Nature's child—
Wiser men than me's beguiled;
　　Whistle o'er the lave o't.

How we live, my Meg and me,
How we love and how we 'gree,
I carena by how few may see;
   Whistle o'er the lave o't.
Wha I wish were maggots' meat,
Dish'd up in her winding-sheet,
I could write—but Meg maun see't—
   Whistle o'er the lave o't.

TO DAUNTON ME.

Chiefly by Burns.

THE bluid-red rose at Yule may blaw,
The summer lilies bloom in snaw,
The frost may freeze the deepest sea;
But an old man shall never daunton me.
  To daunton me, and me sae young,
   Wi' his fause heart and flatterin' tongue,
   That is the thing ye ne'er shall see;
   For an auld man shall never daunton me.

For a' his meal, for a' his maut,
For a' his fresh beef and his saut,
For a' his gowd and white monie,
An auld man shall never daunton me.

His gear may buy him kye and yowes,
His gear may buy him glens and knowes;
But me he shall not buy nor fee;
For an auld man shall never daunton me.

He hirples twa-fauld, as he dow,
Wi' his teethless gab and auld bauld pow,
And the rain rins doun frae his red-blear'd ee:
That auld man shall never daunton me.

The original of this song will be found among "Hogg's Jacobite Relics." The subject is a favourite one with the early and later Scottish song-writers.

DUNCAN GRAY.

BURNS.

DUNCAN Gray cam' here to woo,
      Ha, ha, the wooing o't,
On blythe Yule night when we were fu',
      Ha, ha, the wooing o't.
Maggie coost her head fu' high,
Look'd asklent and unco skeigh
Gart poor Duncan stand abeigh
      Ha, ha, the wooing o't.

Duncan fleech'd, and Duncan pray'd,
      Ha, ha, the wooing o't;
Meg was deaf as Ailsa craig,
      Ha, ha, the wooing o't.
Duncan sigh'd baith out and in,
Grat his een baith bleer't and blin',
Spak o' lowpin o'er a linn,
      Ha, ha, the wooing o't.

Time and chance are but a tide,
      Ha, ha, the wooing o't;
Slighted love is sair to bide,
      Ha, ha, the wooing o't.
Shall I, like a fool, quoth he,
For a haughty hizzie dee?
She may gae to—France for me!
      Ha, ha, the wooing o't.

How it comes let doctors tell,
      Ha, ha, the wooing o't;
Meg grew sick as he grew well,
      Ha, ha, the wooing o't.
Something in her bosom wrings,
For relief a sigh she brings;
And, oh, her een they speak sic things!
      Ha, ha, the wooing o't.

Duncan was a lad o' grace,
                    Ha, ha, the wooing o't;
Maggie's was a piteous case,
                    Ha, ha, the wooing o't:
Duncan could na be her death,
Swelling pity smoor'd his wrath;
Now they're crouse and canty baith,
                    Ha, ha, the wooing o't.

Founded upon an old and licentious ballad of the same name, but having nothing in common with it but the chorus and the title. "Duncan Gray," says Burns to Thomson, "is that kind of light-horse gallop of an air which precludes sentiment. The ludicrous is its ruling feature." "Duncan," says Thomson in reply, "is a lad of grace, and his humour will endear him to every body." The Hon. A. Erskine, in a letter to the poet, says, "Duncan Gray possesses native genuine humour. 'Spak o' lowpin o'er a linn,' is a line that of itself should make you immortal."

CONTENTIT WI' LITTLE.

Burns.   Air—"Lumps o' pudding."

Contented wi' little and cantie wi' mair,
Whene'er I forgather wi' sorrow and care,
I gi'e them a skelp, as they're creeping alang,
Wi' a cog o' guid swats and an auld Scottish sang.

I whyles claw the elbow o' troublesome thought;
But man is a sodger, and life is a faught:
My mirth and good humour are coin in my pouch,
And my freedom's my lairdship nae monarch dare touch.

A towmond o' trouble, should that be my fa',
A night o' guid fellowship sowthers it a';
When at the blythe end of our journey at last,
Wha the deil ever thinks o' the road he has pass'd?

Blind Chance, let her snapper and stoyte on her way;
Be't to me, be't frae me, e'en let the jade gae;
Come ease or come travail, come pleasure or pain,
My warst word is, "Welcome, and welcome again!"

LAST MAY A BRAW WOOER.

Burns.   Air—" The Lothian lassie."

Last May a braw wooer came down the lang glen,
  And sair wi' his love he did deave me ;
I said there was naething I hated like men :
  The deuce gae wi'm to believe me, believe me;
  The deuce gae wi'm to believe me.

He spak o' the darts in my bonnie black een,
  And vow'd for my love he was dying ;
I said he might die when he liked for Jean
  The Lord forgi'e me for lying, for lying;
  The Lord forgi'e me for lying !

A weel-stockit mailin, himsel' for the laird,
  And marriage aff-hand, were his proffers :
I never loot on that I kend it or cared ;
  But thought I might hae waur offers, waur offers;
  But thought I might hae waur offers.

But what wad ye think? in a fortnight or less—
  The deil tak' his taste to gae near her !—
He up the lang loan to my black cousin Bess :
  Guess ye how, the jaud ! I could bear her, could bear her;
  Guess ye how, the jaud ! I could bear her !

But a' the neist week, as I fretted wi' care,
  I gaed to the tryste of Dalgarnock ;
And wha but my fine fickle lover was there !
  I glower'd as I'd seen a warlock, a warlock ;
  I glower'd as I'd seen a warlock.

But owre my left shouther I ga'e him a blink,
  Lest neebors might say I was saucy ;
My wooer he caper'd as he'd been in drink,
  And vow'd I was his dear lassie, dear lassie ;
  And vow'd I was his dear lassie.

I speir'd for my cousin fu' couthy and sweet,
  Gin she had recover'd her hearin',
And how my auld shoon fitted her shachlet feet;
  But heavens! how he fell a swearin', a swearin';
  But heavens! how he fell a swearin'!

He begg'd, for gudesake, I wad be his wife,
  Or else I would kill him wi' sorrow;
So, e'en to preserve the poor body in life,
  I think I maun wed him to-morrow, to-morrow;
  I think I maun wed him to-morrow.

GREEN GROW THE RASHES O!

BURNS.

GREEN grow the rashes O,
  Green grow the rashes O;
The sweetest hours that e'er I spent
  Were spent among the lasses O.

There's nought but care on ev'ry han',
  In every hour that passes O:
What signifies the life o' man,
  An' 'twere na for the lasses O?
            Green grow, &c.

The warly race may riches chase,
  And riches still may fly them O;
An' though at last they catch them fast,
  Their hearts can ne'er enjoy them O.
            Green grow, &c.

Gi'e me a canny hour at e'en,
  My arms about my dearie O;
An' warly cares an' warly men
  May a' gae tapsalteerie O.
            Green grow, &c.

For you sae douse, ye sneer at this,
  Ye're nought but senseless asses O ;
The wisest man the world e'er saw
  He dearly lo'ed the lasses O.
           Green grow, &c.

Auld Nature swears, the lovely dears
  Her noblest work she classes O ;
Her 'prentice han' she tried on man,
  And then she made the lasses O.
           Green grow, &c.

Founded on an old and licentious song with the same chorus.

----♦----

THE OLD MAN'S SONG.

Rev. John Skinner.   Air—"Dumbarton's drums."

Oh, why should old age so much wound us O ?
There is nothing in't all to confound us O ;
  For how happy am I,
  With my old wife sitting by,
And our bairns and our oes all around us O !

We began in the world wi' naething O,
And we've jogg'd on and toil'd for the ae thing O;
  We made use of what we had,
  And our thankful hearts were glad
When we got the bit meat and the claething O.

We have lived all our lifetime contented O,
Since the day we became first acquainted O ;
  It's true we've been but poor,
  And we are so to this hour,
Yet we never pined nor lamented O.

We ne'er thought of schemes to be wealthy O,
By ways that were cunning or stealthy O ;
  But we always had the bliss—
  And what further could we wiss ?—
To be pleased with ourselves and be healthy O.

What though we canna boast of our guineas O,
We have plenty of Jockies and Jeanies O ;
    And these I am certain are
    More desirable by far
Than a pock full of yellow steenies O.

We've seen many a wonder and ferly O,
Of changes that almost are yearly O,
    Among rich folk up and down,
    Both in country and in town,
Who now live but scrimply and barely O.

Then why should people brag of prosperity O ?
A straiten'd life we see is no rarity O ;
    Indeed, we've been in want,
    And our living been but scant,
Yet we never were reduced to need charity O.

In this house we first came thegither O,
Where we've long been a father and mither O ;
    And though not of stone and lime,
    It will last us a' our time,
And I hope we shall never need anither O.

* * *

JENNY'S BAWBEE.

Sir Alex. Boswell, Bart.

I met four chaps yon birks amang,
Wi' hinging lugs and faces lang ;
I speer'd at neebour Bauldy Strang,
    Wha's thae I see ?
Quo' he, Ilk cream-faced pawky chiel
Thought he was cunning as the deil,
And here they cam' awa to steal
    Jenny's bawbee.

The first, a captain to his trade,
Wi' skull ill-lined, but back weel-clad,
March'd round the barn and by the shed,
    And papp'd on his knee ;

Quo' he, " My goddess, nymph, and queen,
Your beauty's dazzled baith my een !"
But deil a beauty he had seen
    But—Jenny's bawbee.

A lawyer neist, wi' blatherin' gab,
Wha speeches wove like ony wab,
In ilk ane's corn aye took a dab,
    And a' for a fee.
Accounts he own'd through a' the town,
And tradesmen's tongues nae mair could drown,
But now he thought to clout his gown
    Wi' Jenny's bawbee.

A Norland laird neist trotted up,
Wi' bawsend nag and siller whup,
Cried, " There's my beast, lad, haud the grup,
    Or tie't till a tree :
What's gowd to me ? I've walth o' lan' ;
Bestow on ane o' worth your han'."
He thought to pay what he was awn
    Wi' Jenny's bawbee.

Drest up just like the knave o' clubs,
A thing came neist (but life has rubs),
Foul were the roads, and fu' the dubs,
    And jaupit a' was he :
He danced up squinting through a glass,
And grinn'd, " I' faith a bonnie lass !"
He thought to win wi' front o' brass
    Jenny's bawbee.

She bade the laird gae kame his wig,
The soger no to strut sae big,
The lawyer no to be a prig ;
    The fool he cried, " Tehee !
I kenn'd that I could never fail !"
But she prenn'd the dishclout to his tail,
And soused him in the water-pail,
    And kept her bawbee.

This song was contributed by its unfortunate author to Thomson's " Select
Melodies of Scotland." Sir Alexander was the son of James Boswell, whose in-

initable "Life of Dr. Johnson" has conferred a peculiar immortality upon his name. He was unfortunately killed in 1822, by Mr. James Stuart of Duncarn, in a duel arising out of a literary squabble in the "Sentinel," a Glasgow newspaper, to which Sir Alexander had contributed a "Whig song," supposed to be written by one of the *Jameses*, certainly not by King James the First or King James the Fifth, but probably by one of the house of *Stuart*." The song was very scurrilous, and reflected on the honour of Mr. Stuart. In after-life Mr. Stuart became editor of the London "Courier," and an Inspector of Mills and Factories.

JENNY'S BAWBIE.

Oldest version, upon which the preceding was founded by Sir Alexander Boswell.

An' a' that e'er my Jenny had,
My Jenny had, my Jenny had,
An' a' that e'er my Jenny had,
    Was ae bawbie.

There's your plack an' my plack,
An' your plack an' my plack,
An' my plack an' your plack,
    And Jenny's bawbie.

We'll put it a' in the pint-stoup,
The pint-stoup, the pint-stoup,
We'll put it in the pint-stoup,
    And boil it a' three.

JENNY DANG THE WEAVER.

Sir A. Boswell, Bart.

At Willie's wedding on the green,
    The lassies, bonnie witches,
Were a' dressed out in aprons clean,
    And braw white Sunday mutches:
Auld Maggie bad the lads tak' tent.
    But Jock would not believe her ;
But soon the fool his folly kent,
    For Jenny dang the weaver.

And Jenny dang, Jenny dang,
  Jenny dang the weaver;
But soon the fool his folly kent,
  For Jenny dang the weaver.

At ilka country-dance or reel
  Wi' her he would be babbing;
When she sat down, he sat down,
  And to her would be gabbing;
Where'er she gaed, baith but and ben,
  The coof would never leave her,
Aye kecklin' like a clacking hen;
  But Jenny dang the weaver.
    Jenny dang, Jenny dang,
      Jenny dang the weaver;
    But soon the fool his folly kent,
      For Jenny dang the weaver.

Quo' he, My lass, to speak my mind
  In troth I needna swither;
You've bonnie een; and if you're kind,
  I'll never seek anither.
He humm'd and haw'd; the lass cried, Peugh!
  And bade the coof no deave her;
Syne snapt her fingers, lap and leugh,
  And dang the silly weaver.
    And Jenny dang, Jenny dang,
      Jenny dang the weaver;
    But soon the fool his folly kent,
      For Jenny dang the weaver.

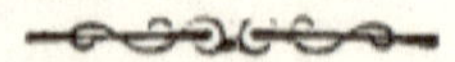

Convivial Songs.

—♦—

THERE'S CAULD KAIL IN ABERDEEN.

ANONYMOUS.   Air—" There's cauld kail in Aberdeen."

THERE'S cauld kail in Aberdeen,
And custocks in Stra'bogie,
And ilka lad maun hae his lass,
But I maun hae my cogie.
For I maun hae my cogie, sirs,
I canna want my cogie;
I wadna gi'e my three-gir'd cog
For a' the wives in Bogie.

Johnny Smith has got a wife
  Wha scrimps him o' his cogie;
But were she mine, upon my life
  I'd dook her in a bogie;
    For I maun hae my cogie, sirs,
      I canna want my cogie;
    I wadna gi'e my three-gir'd cog
      For a' the wives in Bogie.

'Twa three todlin' weans they hae,
  The pride o' a' Stra'bogie;
Whene'er the totums cry for meat,
  She curses aye his cogie,
    Crying, " Wae betide the three-gir'd cog!
      Oh, wae betide the cogie!
    It does mair skaith than a' the ills
      That happen in Stra'bogie."

She fand him ance at Willie Sharpe's;
  And, what the maist did laugh at,
She brak the bicker, spilt the drink,
  And tightly gouff'd his haffet,
    Crying, " Wae betide the three-gir'd cog!
      Oh, wae betide the cogie!
    It does mair skaith than a' the ills
      That happen in Stra'bogie."

Yet here's to ilka honest soul
  Wha'll drink wi' me a cogie;
And for ilk silly whinging fool,
  We'll dook him in the Bogie.
    For I maun hae my cogie, sirs,
      I canna want my cogie;
    I wadna gie my three-gir'd cog
      For a' the wives in Bogie.

This song was popular in Aberdeenshire in the middle of the eighteenth century.
There are at least half-a-dozen Scottish parodies upon, or emendations of it. One,
by Alexander fourth Duke of Gordon appears among the Miscellaneous Songs in
this volume; and a second was printed in Herd's Collection.

UP IN THE AIR.

ALLAN RAMSAY.

Now the sun's gane out o' sight,
Beet the ingle and snuff the light;
In glens the fairies skip and dance,
And witches wallop o'er to France.
    Up in the air
    On my bonny grey mare,
And I see her yet, and I see her yet.
    Up in, &c.

The wind's drifting hail and sna'
O'er frozen hags like a foot-ba';
Nae starns keek through the azure slit,
'Tis cauld and mirk as ony pit.
    The man i' the moon
    Is carousing aboon;
D'ye see, d'ye see, d'ye see him yet?
    The man, &c.

Tak' your glass to clear your een,
'Tis the elixir heals the spleen;
Baith wit and mirth it will inspire,
And gently puffs the lover's fire.
       Up in the air,
         It drives away care;
Hae wi' ye, hae wi' ye, and hae wi' ye, lads, yet!
       Up in, &c.

Steek the doors, keep out the frost,
Come, Willy, gi'e's about ye'r toast;
Till't, lads, and lilt it out,
And let us hae a blythsome bowt.
       Up wi't there, there;
         Dinna cheat, but drink fair.
Huzza, huzza, and huzza, lads, yet!
       Up wi't, &c.

This song is founded upon a very ancient ballad, of which some fragments only exist.

UP IN THE MORNING EARLY.

From a manuscript collection of Scottish songs by Peter Buchan.

Up in the morning, up in the morning,
   Up in the morning early;
Frae night till morn our squires they sat,
   An' drank the juice o' the barley.
Some they spent but ae hauf-crown,
   And some six crowns sae rarely;
In the alewife's pouch the siller did clink,
   She got in the morning early.
       Up in the morning early, &c.

I hae got fou, Beldornie cried;
   Wardess replied, I am fou tee;
Then said Darlicha, Beware o' a fa',
   An' haud by the wa' as I dee.
       Up in the morning early, &c.

Be wyllie, my boys, be wise, my boys,
  Lat sorrow gae through your thinking;
Gin ye haud on as ye hae begun,
  Your pouches will leave aff clinking.
    Up in the morning early, &c.

We will gae hame, said Lord Aboyne;
  Na, sit awhile, quo' Towie;
Oh, never a foot, said Lochnievar,
  As lang's there's beer in the bowie.
    Up in the morning early, &c.

There they sat the lee-lang night,
  Nor stirr'd till the sun shone clearly;
Then made an end as they began,
  And gaed hame in the morning early.
    Up in the morning early, &c.

The "boon companions" named in this song were all Aberdeenshire gentlemen.
The Lord Aboyne was afterwards Duke of Gordon, and author of one of the versions
of the song of "Cauld kail in Aberdeen."

THE ALE-WIFE AND HER BARREL.

From a manuscript collection of the songs of the north of Scotland by
Peter Buchan.

My mind is vex'd and sair perplex'd:
  I'll tell you a' that grieves me;
A drunken wife I hae at hame,
  Her noisome din aye deaves me.
    The ale-wife, the drunken wife,
      The ale-wife she grieves me;
    My wifie and her barrelie,
      They'll ruin me and deave me.

She takes her barrel on her back,
  Her pint-stoup in her hand,
And she is to the market gane
  For to set up a stand.
    The ale-wife. &c.

And whan she does come hame again,
　　She wides through girse and corn ;
Says, I maun hae anither pint,
　　Though I should beg the morn.
　　　　The ale-wife, &c.

She sets her barrel on the ground,
　　And travels but and ben ;
I canna get my wifie keepit
　　Out amo' the men.
　　　　The ale-wife, &c.

A COGIE O' YILL.

Andrew Sheriffs.　1787.

Air—"A cogie of yill," composed by Robert Macintosh, who died in London in 1807.

A cogie o' yill,
And a pickle aitmeal,
And a dainty wee drappie o' whisky,
　Was our forefathers' dose
　For to sweel down their brose,
And keep them aye cheery and frisky.
　　Then hey for the whisky, and hey for the meal,
　　And hey for the cogie, and hey for the yill ;
　　Gin ye steer a' thegither, they'll do unco weel
　　　To keep a chiel cheery and brisk aye.

When I see our Scots lads,
Wi' their kilts and cockauds,
That sae aften hae lounder'd our foes, man ;
　I think to mysel'
　On the meal and the yill,
And the fruits o' our Scottish kail-brose, man.
　　　Then hey, &c.

When our brave Highland blades,
Wi' their claymores and plaids,
In the field drive like sheep a' our foes, man ;
　Their courage and power
　Spring frae this to be sure,
They're the noble effects o' the brose, man.
　　　Then hey, &c.

But your spindle-shank'd sparks,
　Wha sae ill fill their sarks,
Your pale-visaged milk-sops and beaux, man;
　I think when I see them,
　'Twere kindness to gi'e them
A cogie o' yill or o' brose, man.
　　　Then hey, &c.

What John Bull despises,
　Our better sense prizes,
He denies eatin' blanter ava, man;
　But by eatin' o' blanter,
　His mare's grown, I'll warrant her,
The manliest brute o' the twa, man.
　　　Then hey, &c.

———◆———

THE DRUCKEN WIFE O' GALLOWAY.

From Herd's Collection.   Air—" Hooly and fairly."

Doun in yon meadow a couple did tarry:
The gudewife she drank naething but sack and canary;
The gudeman complain'd to her friends richt early—
Oh, gin my wife wad drink hooly and fairly!
　Hooly and fairly, hooly and fairly,
　　Oh, gin my wife wad drink hooly and fairly!

First she drank Crummie, and syne she drank Gairic,
And syne she drank my bonny grey marie,
That carried me through a' the dubs and the glairie—
Oh, gin my wife wad drink hooly and fairly!

She drank her hose, she drank her shoon,
And syne she drank her bonnie new goun;
She drank her sark that cover'd her rarely—
Oh, gin my wife wad drink hooly and fairly!

Wad she drink but her ain things I wadna care,
But she drinks my claes that I canna weel spare;
When I'm wi' my gossips it angers me sairly—
Oh, gin my wife wad drink hooly and fairly!

My Sunday's coat, she's laid it in wad,
And the best blue bonnet was e'er on my head ;
At kirk or at mercat I'm cover'd but barely—
Oh, gin my wife wad drink hooly and fairly !

My bonny white mittens I wore on my hands,
Wi' her neibour's wife she had laid them in pawns;
My bane-headed staff that I looed sae dearly—
Oh, gin my wife wad drink hooly and fairly !

I never was for wranglin' nor strife,
Nor did I deny her the comforts of life ;
For when there's a war I'm aye for a parly—
Oh, gin my wife wad drink hooly and fairly !

When there's ony money she maun keep the purse,
If I seek but a bawbee she'll scold and she'll curse ;
She lives like a queen, I but scrimpit and sparely—
Oh, gin my wife wad drink hooly and fairly !

A pint wi' her cummers I wad her allow ;
But when she sits down, oh, the jaud she gets fou,
And when she is fou she is unco camstarie—
Oh, gin my wife wad drink hooly and fairly !

When she comes to the street she roars and rants,
Has nae fear o' her neibours, nor minds the house-wants;
She rants up some fule-sang, like, Up your heart, Charlie !—
Oh, gin my wife wad drink hooly and fairly !

When she comes hame she lays on the lads,
The lasses she ca's baith bitches an' jauds,
An' ca's mysell an auld cuckol-carlie—
Oh, gin my wife wad drink hooly and fairly !

AULD LANG SYNE.

SHOULD auld acquaintance be forgot,
  And never brought to min' ?
Should auld acquaintance be forgot,
  And the days o' lang syne ?
    For auld lang syne, my dear,
      For auld lang syne,
    We'll tak' a cup of kindness yet
      For auld lang syne.

We twa hae run about the braes,
  And pu'd the gowans fine ;
But we've wander'd mony a weary foot
  Sin auld lang syne.
      For auld, &c.

We twa hae paidled i' the burn
  Frae morning sun till dine ;
But seas between us braid hae roar'd
  Sin auld lang syne.
      For auld, &c.

Q

And here's a hand, my trusty frien',
  And gie's a hand o' thine;
And we'll tak' a right guid-willie waught
  For auld lang syne.
      For auld, &c.

And surely ye'll be your pint-stoup,
  And surely I'll be mine;
And we'll tak' a cup o' kindness yet
  For auld lang syne.
      For auld, &c.

This world-renowned song is always included among the songs of Robert Burns. He did not himself claim the authorship of it. In a letter to Thomson, he says: "One song more, and I have done. 'Auld lang syne!' The air is but mediocre; but the following song, the old song of the olden times, and which has never been in print or even in manuscript, until I took it down from an old man's singing, is enough to recommend any air."—"Light be the turf," he says in another letter, "on the heaven-inspired poet who composed this glorious fragment!" The air to which the song is now universally sung is not the one which Burns thought so little of, but another, of which the author is quite unknown, but which appears to have belonged to the Roman Catholic Church, and to England quite as much as to Scotland. Several other cathedral chants, of which the authorship is claimed for English music, may be mentioned; more especially the air known as "John, come kiss me now," and "We're all noddin'," both of which are unmistakeably English. It is curious to reflect that the most popular song ever written in these islands, that of "Auld lang syne," is anonymous; and that we know no more of the author of the music than we do of the author of the words. It is equally curious to reflect that so much of Burns's great fame rests upon this song, in which his share amounts only to a few emendations.

OH, GUDE ALE COMES.

From "Johnson's Musical Museum," altered by Burns from an older song.
Air—"The bottom of the punch-bowl."

Oh, gude ale comes, and gude ale goes;
Gude ale gars me sell my hose,
Sell my hose, and pawn my shoon;
Gude ale keeps my heart aboon.

I had sax owsen in a pleuch,
And they drew teuch and weel eneuch:
I drank them a' just ane by ane;
Gude ale keeps my heart aboon.

Gude ale hauds me bare and busy,
Gars me moop wi' the servant hizzie,
Stand i' the stool when I hae done ;
Gude ale keeps my heart aboon.

Oh, gude ale comes, and gude ale goes ;
Gude ale gars me sell my hose,
Sell my hose, and pawn my shoon ;
Gude ale keeps my heart aboon.

GUDEWIFE, COUNT THE LAWIN.

Burns.

Gane is the day, and mirk's the night
But we'll ne'er stray for faut o' light ;
For ale and brandy's stars and moon,
And bluid-red wine's the rising sun.
   Then, gudewife, count the lawin,
   The lawin, the lawin ;
   Then, gudewife, count the lawin,
   And bring's a coggie mair.

There's wealth and ease for gentlemen,
And semple folk maun fecht and fen ;
But here we're a' in ae accord,
For ilka man that's drunk's a lord.
   Then, gudewife, count the lawin,
   The lawin, the lawin ;
   Then, gudewife, count the lawin,
   And bring's a coggie mair.

My coggie is a haly pool
That heals the wounds o' care and doul ;
And pleasure is a wanton trout—
An ye drink but deep ye'll find him out.
   Then, gudewife, count the lawin,
   The lawin, the lawin ;
   Then, gudewife, count the lawin,
   And bring's a coggie mair.

THE DEIL'S AWA' WI' THE EXCISEMAN.*

BURNS.

THE deil cam' fiddling through the town,
    Ard danced awa' wi' the exciseman ;
And ilka wife cried : Auld Mahoun,
    We wish you luck o' your prize, man.
We'll mak' our maut, and brew our drink ;
    We'll dance, and sing, and rejoice, man ;
And mony thanks to the muckle black deil
    That danced awa' wi' the exciseman.

* Mr. Lockhart, in his "Life of Burns," gives the following account of the composition of this poem :—" At that period (1792) a great deal of contraband traffic, chiefly from the Isle of Man, was going on along the coasts of Galloway and Ayrshire; and the whole of the revenue-officers from Gretna to Dumfries were placed under the orders of a superintendent residing in Annan, who exerted himself zealously in intercepting the descent of the smuggling-vessels. On the 27th of February, a suspicious looking brig was discovered in the Solway Frith, and Burns was one of the party whom the superintendent conducted to watch her motions. She got into shallow water the day afterwards, and the officers were enabled to discover that her crew were numerous, armed, and not likely to yield without a struggle. Lewars, a brother exciseman, an intimate friend of our poet, was accordingly sent to Dumfries for a guard of dragoons ; the superintendent, Mr. Crawford, proceeded himself on a similar errand to Ecclefechan ; and Burns was left, with some men under his orders, to watch the brig. and prevent landing or escape. From the private journal of one of the excisemen (now in my hands), it appears that Burns manifested considerable impatience while thus occupied, being left for many hours in a wet salt-marsh with a force which he knew to be inadequate for the purpose it was meant to fulfil. One of his friends hearing him abuse Lewars in particular for being slow about his journey, the man answered, that he also wished the devil had him for his pains, and that Burns, in the meantime, would do well to indite a song upon the sluggard. Burns said nothing ; but after taking a few strides by himself along the reeds and shingle, rejoined his party, and chanted them the well-known ditty, 'The deil's awa' wi' the exciseman.' Lewards arrived shortly after with the dragoons ; and Burns, putting himself at their head, waded, sword in hand, to the brig, and was the first to board her. The crew lost heart and submitted, though their numbers were greater than those of the assailing force. The vessel was condemned, and, with all her arms and stores, sold by auction next day at Dumfries ; upon which occasion Burns, whose behaviour had been highly commended, thought fit to purchase four carronades by way of trophy. But his glee," continues Mr. Lockhart, "went a step further ; he sent the guns, with a letter, to the French Convention, requesting that body to accept them as a mark of his admiration and respect. The present and its accompaniment were intercepted at the custom-house at Dover ; and here—there appears to be little room to doubt— was the principal circumstance that drew on Burns the notice of his jealous superiors. We were not, it is true, at war with France; but every one knew and felt that we were to be so ere long ; and nobody can pretend that Burns was not guilty on this occasion of a most absurd and presumptuous breach of decorum."

'There's threesome reels and foursome reels,
  'There's hornpipes and strathspeys, man ;
But the ae best dance e'er cam' to our lan'
  Was—the deil's awa' wi' the exciseman.
    We'll mak' our maut, &c.

WILLIE BREW'D A PECK O' MAUT.

Burns.

Oh, Willie brew'd a peck o' maut,
  And Rob and Allan cam' to see ;
Three blither hearts that leelang night
  Ye wadna find in Christendie.
    We are na fou, we're na that fou,
      But just a drappie in our ee ;
    The cock may craw, the day may daw',
      And aye we'll taste the barley bree.

Here are we met three merry boys,
  Three merry boys I trow are we;
And mony a night we've merry been,
  And mony mair we hope to be.
              We are na fou, &c.

It is the moon, I ken her horn,
  That's blinkin in the lift sae hie;
She shines sae bright to wyle us hame,
  But, by my troth, she'll wait a wee.
              We are na fou, &c.

Wha first shall rise to gang awa',
  A cuckold, coward loon is he;
Wha first beside his chair shall fa',
  He shall be king amang us three.
              We are na fou, &c.

"This air," says Burns, "is Masterton's; the song is mine. The occasion of it was this:—Mr. William Nicol, of the High School, Edinburgh, during the autumn vacation, being at Moffat, honest Allan, who was at that time on a visit to Dalswinton, and I, went to pay Nicol a visit. We had such a joyous meeting, that Masterton and I agreed, each in our own way, that we should celebrate the business." Dr. Currie, who mentions that Nicol's farm was that of Laggan, in Nithsdale, adds, that "these three honest fellows, all men of uncommon talents, were in 1798 all under the turf."

NEIL GOW'S FAREWELL TO WHISKY.

Mrs. AGNES LYON, born 1762, died 1840.—C.R.

YOU'VE surely heard o' famous Neil,
The man who play'd the fiddle weel;
He was a heartsome, merry chiel',
  And dearly lo'ed the whisky O.
For e'er since he wore the tartan hose,
He dearly liket Athol brose;
And wae was he, you may suppose,
  To play farewell to whisky O.

Alas! says Neil, I'm frail and auld,
And whiles my hame is unco cauld
I think 'twad make me blithe and bauld,
  A wee drap Highland whisky O.
Yet a' the doctors they do agree
That whisky's no the drink for me.
I'm fley'd they'll gar me tyne my glee
  By parting me and whisky O.

Though I can baith get wine and ale,
And find my head and fingers hale,
I'll be content, though legs should fail,
   To play farewell to whisky O.
But still I think on auld lang syne,
When Paradise our friends did tyne,
Because something ran in their min',
   Forbid like Highland whisky O.

Come, a' ye powers o' music, come;
I find my heart grows unco glum;
My fiddle-strings will no play bum,
   To say farewell to whisky O.
Yet I'll take my fiddle in my hand,
And screw the pegs up while they'll stand,
To make a lamentation grand
   For gude auld Highland whisky O.

As a performer on the violin Neil Gow was unequalled. "The livelier airs," says one of his biographers, "which belonged to the class of what are called strathspey and reel, and which have long been peculiar to the northern part of the island, assumed in his hand a style of spirit, fire, and beauty, which had never been heard before. There is perhaps no species whatever of music executed on the violin in which the characteristic expression depends more on his power of the bow, particularly in what is called the upward or returning stroke, than the Highland reel. Here accordingly was Gow's forte. His bow-hand, as a suitable instrument of his genius, was uncommonly powerful; and where the note produced by the up-bow was often feeble and indistinct in other hands, it was struck in his playing with a strength and certainty which never failed to surprise the skilful hearer. To this extraordinary power of the bow, in the hand of great original genius, must be ascribed the singular felicity of expression which he gave to all his music, and the native Highland *gout* of certain tunes, such as 'Tullochgorum,' in which his taste and style of bowing could never be exactly reached by any other performer. We may add the effect of the sudden shout with which he frequently accompanied his playing in the quick tunes, and which seemed instantly to electrify the dancers, inspiring them with new life and energy, and rousing the spirits of the most inanimate."

Neil Gow excelled also in the composition of Scottish melodies; and his sets of the older tunes and various of his own airs were prepared for publication by his son Nathaniel. In private life Neil Gow was distinguished by his unpretending manners, his homely humour, and strong good sense and knowledge of the world. His figure was vigorous and manly, and the expression of his countenance spirited and intelligent. His whole appearance exhibited so characteristic a model of a Scottish Highlander, that his portrait was to be found at one time in all parts of the country. Four admirable likenesses of him were painted by the late Sir Henry Raeburn; one for the county-hall at Perth, and the others for the Duke of Athol, Lord Gray, and Lord Panmure. His portrait was also introduced into the view of a "Highland Wedding" by the late Sir William Allan, along with that of Donald Gow, his brother, who usually accompanied him on the violoncello.—*Scottish Biography.*

GUDE NIGHT, AND JOY BE WI' YOU A'.

Sir Alexander Boswell.

Gude night, and joy be wi' you a';
  Your harmless mirth has cheer'd my heart:
May life's fell blasts out ower ye blaw;
  In sorrow may you never part!
My spirit lives, but strength is gone,
  The mountain fires now blaze in vain;
Remember, sons, the deeds I've done,
  And in your deeds I'll live again.

When on your muir a gallant clan
  Frae boasting foes their banners tore,
Wha show'd himself a better man,
  Or fiercer waved the red claymore?
But when in peace—then mark me there—
  When through the glen the wanderer came,
I gave him of our lordly fare,
  I gave him here a welcome hame.

The auld will speak, the young maun hear;
  Be cantie, but be guid and leal;
Your ain ills aye hae heart to bear,
  Another's aye hae heart to feel.
So, ere I set, I'll see you shine,
  I'll see your triumph ere I fa';
My parting breath shall boast you mine;—
  Gude night, and joy be wi' you a'!

Suggested evidently by Burns's song, " This night is my departing night."

AULD GUDEMAN, YE'RE A DRUNKEN CARLE!

Sir Alexander Boswell.

" Auld gudeman, ye're a drunken carle, drunken carle!
A' the lang day ye wink and drink, and gape and gaunt;
O' sottish loons ye're the pink and pearl, pink and pearl,
  Ill-far'd, doited ne'er-do-weel."

" Hech, gudewife ! ye're a flyting body, flyting body ;
Will ye hae; but, Guid be praised, the *wit* ye want.
The puttin' cow should be aye a doddy, aye a doddy ;
        Mak' na sic an awsome reel."

        " Ye're a sow, auld man ;
        Ye get fou, auld man ;
        Fie for shame, auld man,
        To your wame, auld man ;
    Pinch'd I win, wi' spinnin' tow,
    A plack to cleid your back and pow."

        " It's a lie, gudewife ;
        It's your tea, gudewife ;
        Na, na, gudewife,
        Ye spend a', gudewife.
    Dinna fa' on me pell-mell,
    Ye like the drap fu' weel yoursell."

" Ye's rue, auld gowk, your jest and frolic, jest and frolic ;
Dare ye say, goose, I ever liked to tak' a drappy ?
An' 'twerena just to cure the colic, cure the colic,
        Deil a drap wad weet my mou'."

" Troth, gudewife, an' ye wadna swither, wadna swither,
Soon to tak' a colic, when it brings a drap o' cappy ;
But twascore years we hae fought thegither, fought thegither ;
        Time it is to gree, I trow."

        " I'm wrang, auld John ;
        Ower lang, auld John,
        For nought, gude John,
        We hae fought, gude John ;
    Let's help to bear ilk ither's weight,
    We're far ower feckless now to fight."

        " Ye're richt, gude Kate ;
        The nicht, gude Kate,
        Our cup, gude Kate,
        We'll sup, gude Kate ;
    Thegither frae this hour we'll draw,
    And toom the stoop atween us twa."

THE YEAR THAT'S AWA'.

MRS. DUNLOP. Air—"It's good to be off wi' the old love.

HERE'S to the year that's awa' !
  We will drink it in strong and in sma';
And here's to ilk bonnie young lassie we lo'ed,
  While swift flew the year that's awa'.
    And here's to ilk, &c.

Here's to the sodger who bled,
  And the sailor who bravely did fa';
Their fame is alive, though their spirits are fled
  On the wings of the year that's awa'.
    Their fame is alive, &c.

Here's to the friends we can trust
  When the storms of adversity blaw;
May they live in our song, and be nearest our hearts,
  Nor depart like the year that's awa'.
    May they live, &c

LET VOTARIES O' BACCHUS.

ALEXANDER RODGER. Air—"Toddlin hame."
(From "Whistle Binkie," third series. Glasgow, 1841.)

LET votaries o' Bacchus o' wine make their boast,
And drink till it mak' them as dead's a bed-post;
A drap o' maut broe I wad far rather pree,
And a rosy-faced landlord's the Bacchus for me.
Then I'll toddle but and I'll toddle ben,
And let them drink at wine wha nae better do ken.

Your wine it may do for the bodies far south,
But a Scotsman likes something that bites i' the mouth,
And whisky's the thing that can do't to a tee,
Then Scotsmen and whisky will ever agree;
For wi' toddlin' but and toddlin' ben,
Sae lang we've been nursed on't we hardly can spean.

It's now thretty years since I first took the drap,
To moisten my carcase and keep it in sap;
And though what I've drunk might hae slacken'd the sun,
I find I'm as dry as when first I begun;
For wi' toddlin' but and toddlin' ben,
I'm nae sooner slacken'd than drouthy again

Your douse folk aft ca' me a tipplin' auld sot,
A worm to a still, a sand-bed, and what not;
They cry that my hand wad ne'er bide frae my mouth;
But, oddsake! they never consider my drouth;
Yet I'll toddle but an' I'll toddle ben,
An' laugh at their nonsense wha nae better ken.

Some hard-grippin' mortals wha deem themselves wise,
A glass o' gude whisky affect to despise;
Poor scurvy-soul'd wretches, they're no very blate,
Besides, let me tell them, they're foes to the state;
For wi' toddlin but and toddlin' ben,
Gin folk wadna drink, how could government fen'?

Yet wae on the tax that maks whisky sae dear,
An' wae on the gauger sae strict an' severe;
Had I but my will o't, I'd soon let you see,
That whisky, like water, to a' should be free;
For I'd toddle but an' I'd toddle ben,
And I'd mak' it rin like the burn after rain.

What signifies New'r day?—a mock at the best,
That tempts but poor bodies and leaves them unblest?
For ance-a-year fuddle I'd scarce gi'e a strae,
Unless that ilk year were as short as a day;
Then I'd toddle but an' I'd toddle ben,
Wi' the hearty het pint and the canty black hen.

I ne'er was inclined to lay-by ony cash,
Weel kennin' it only wad breed me more fash
But aye when I had it I let it gang free,
And wad toss for a gill wi' my hindmost bawbee;
For wi' toddlin' but an' toddlin' ben,
I ne'er kent the use o't but only to spen'.

Had siller been made in the kist to lock by,
It ne'er wad been rund, but square as a die;
Whereas by its shape ilka body may see,
It aye was design'd it should circulate free;
Then we'll toddle but an' we'll toddle ben,
An' aye when we get it, we'll part wi't again.

I ance was persuaded to " put in the pin,"
But foul fa' the bit o't ava wad bide in;
For whisky's a thing sae bewitchingly stout,
The first time I smelt it, the pin it lap out;
Then I toddled but an' I toddled ben,
And I vow'd I wad ne'er be advised sae again.

Oh, leeze me on whisky! it gi'es us new life,
It maks us aye cadgy to cuddle the wife;
It kindles a spark in the breast o' the cauld,
And it maks the rank coward courageously bauld;
Then we'll toddle but an' we'll toddle ben,
An' we'll coup aff our glasses, " Here's to you again!"

Jacobite Songs.

HERE'S TO THE KING, SIR!

ANONYMOUS. 1700.

HERE's to the king, sir!—
Ye ken wha I mean, sir—
And to every honest man
That will do't again!
Fill, fill your bumpers high;
Drain, drain your glasses dry
Out upon him, fie! oh, fie!
That winna do't again.

Here's to the chieftains
Of the gallant Highland clans!
They hae done it mair nor ance,
   And will do't again.
     Fill, fill, &c.

When you hear the trumpets sound
Tuttie taittie to the drums,
Up wi' swords and down wi' guns,
   And to the loons again!
     Fill, fill, &c.

Here's to the king o' Swede!
Fresh laurels crown his head :
Shame fa' every sneaking blade
   That winna do't again !
     Fill, fill, &c.

But to mak' a' things right now,
He that drinks maun fight too,
To show his heart's upright too,
   And that he'll do't again.
     Fill, fill, &c.

SUCH A PARCEL OF ROGUES IN A NATION!

ANONYMOUS. 1701.
Written on occasion of the Union between England and Scotland.

FAREWELL to a' our Scottish fame,
   Farewell our ancient glory ;
Farewell e'en to the Scottish name,
   Sae famed in ancient story !
Now Sark rins o'er the Solway sands,
   And Tweed rins to the ocean,
To mark where England's province stands:
   Such a parcel of rogues in a nation

What force or guile could not subdue
  Through many warlike ages,
Is wrought now by a coward few
  For hireling traitors' wages.
The English steel we could disdain,
  Secure in valour's station ;
But English gold has been our bane :
  Such a parcel of rogues in a nation !

I would, ere I had seen the day
  That treason thus could sell us,
My auld grey head had lain in clay
  Wi' Bruce and loyal Wallace !
But pith and power, to my last hour
  I'll make this declaration,—
We're bought and sold for English gold :
  Such a parcel of rogues in a nation !

----♦----

JOHNNIE COPE.

Adam Skirving, born 1719, died 1803.   Air—"Fye to the hills in the morning."

Cope sent a letter frae Dunbar,
Sayin', Charlie, meet me an ye daur,
And I'll learn you the art of war,
  If you'll meet me in the morning.
Hey, Johnnie Cope, are ye wauking yet?
Or are your drums a-beating yet?
If ye were waukin, I wad wait
  To gang to the coals in the morning.

When Charlie look'd the letter upon,
He drew his sword the scabbard from :
Come, follow me, my merry merry men,
  And we'll meet Johnnie Cope in the morning.
    Hey, Johnnie Cope, &c.

Now, Johnnie, be as good's your word ;
Come, let us try both fire and sword,
And dinna flee away like a frighted bird,
    That's chased frae its nest in the morning.
        Hey, Johnnie Cope, &c.

When Johnnie Cope he heard of this,
He thought it wadna be amiss
To have a horse in readiness
    To flee awa' in the morning.
        Hey, Johnnie Cope, &c.

Fie now, Johnnie, get up and rin,
The Highland bagpipes mak' a din ;
It is best to sleep in a hale skin,
    For 'twill be a bluidy morning.
        Hey, Johnnie Cope, &c.

When Johnnie Cope to Dunbar came,
They speer'd at him, Where's a' your men ?
The deil confound me gin I ken,
    For I left them a' in the morning.
        Hey, Johnnie Cope, &c.

Now, Johnnie, troth ye are na blate
To come wi' the news o' your ain defeat,
And leave your men in sic a strait
    Sae early in the morning.
        Hey, Johnnie Cope, &c.

Oh, faith! quo' Johnnie, I got sic flegs
Wi' their claymores and philabegs ;
If I face them again, deil break my legs
    So I wish you a gude morning.
        Hey, Johnnie Cope, &c.

This highly popular song was written when the Highlanders were in full and joyous excitement at the defeat of the king's forces at Prestonpans, by Prince Charles, on the 22d of September, 1745. The battle has been sometimes called the battle of Tranent Muir, and of Gladsmuir. Sir John Cope, it will be remembered, was tried by a court-martial for his sudden retreat on this occasion, and acquitted. The author of this song was a farmer in Haddingtonshire.

CARLE, AN THE KING COME.

ANONYMOUS. Air—"Carle, an the king come."

CARLE, an the king come,
Carle, an the king come,
Thou shalt dance and I will sing,
Carle, and the king come.

An somebody were come again,
Then somebody maun cross the main;
And every man shall hae his ain,
Carle, an the king come.

I trow we swappit for the worse,
We ga'e the boot and better horse;
And that we'll tell them at the corse,
Carle, an the king come.

When yellow corn grows on the rigs,
And gibbets stand to hang the Whigs,
Oh, then we'll a' dance Scottish jigs,
Carle, an the king come.

Nae mair wi' pinch and drouth we'll dine,
As we hae done—a dog's propine—
But quaff our draughts o' rosy wine,
Carle, an the king come.

Cogie, an the king come,
Cogie, an the king come,
I'se be fou, and thou'se be toom,
Cogie, an the king come.

The chorus of this song, known to have been sung in the time of Cromwell, has served on several occasions, not only in the Parliamentary struggles of Charles I., but in the rebellions of 1715 and 1745. Sir Walter Scott wrote a parody or imitation of it, entitled, "Carle, now the king's come," on occasion of the visit of George IV. to his Scottish dominions.

WAE'S ME FOR PRINCE CHARLIE.

WILLIAM GLEN.

A wee bird cam' to our ha' door,
  He warbled sweet and clearly;
And aye the o'ercome o' his sang
  Was "Wae's me for Prince Charlie."
Oh! when I heard the bonnie, bonnie bird,
  The tears came drappin' rarely;
I took my bonnet aff my head,
  For weel I lo'ed Prince Charlie.

Quoth I, "My bird, my bonnie, bonnie bird,
  Is that a tale ye borrow?
Or is't some words ye've learnt by rote,
  Or a lilt o' dool and sorrow?"
"Oh! no, no, no!" the wee bird sang,
  "I've flown since morning early;
But sic a day o' wind and rain!—
  Oh! wae's me for Prince Charlie.

"On hills, that are by right his ain,
  He roams a lonely stranger;
On ilka hand he's press'd by want,
  On ilka side by danger.
Yestreen I met him in a glen,
  My heart near bursted fairly;
For sadly changed indeed was he—
  Oh! wae's me for Prince Charlie.

" Dark night cam' on, the tempest howl'd
   Loud o'er the hills and valleys;
And where was't that your Prince lay down,
   Whase hame should be a palace?
He row'd him in a Highland plaid,
   Which cover'd him but sparely,
And slept beneath a bush o' broom—
   Oh! wae's me for Prince Charlie."

But now the bird saw some red coats,
   And he shook his wings wi' anger:
" O, this is no a land for me,
   I'll tarry here nae langer."
Awhile he hover'd on the wing,
   Ere he departed fairly;
But weel I mind the fareweel strain—
   'Twas "Wae's me for Prince Charlie."

LEWIE GORDON.

Dr. Alexander Geddes, born 1737, died 1802.
Air—"Oh, an' ye were deid, gudeman!"

Oh, send Lewie Gordon hame,
And the lad I daurna name;
Though his back be at the wa',
Here's to him that's far awa'!
   Ochon, my Highlandman!
   O my bonnie Highlandman!
   Weel would I my true-love ken
   Amang ten thousand Highlandmen.

Oh, to see his tartan trews,
Bonnet blue, and laigh-heel'd shoes,
Philabeg aboon his knee!
That's the lad that I'll gang wi'.
   Ochon, &c.

This lovely youth of whom I sing
Is fitted for to be a king ;
On his breast he wears a star,—
You'd tak' him for the god of war.
    Ochon, &c.

Oh, to see this princely one
Seated on a royal throne !
Disasters a' would disappear ;
Then begins the jub'lee year.
    Ochon, &c.

The " Lewis Gordon" of this song was a son of the Duke of Gordon.   He was im-
plicated in the affair of 1745, but fled to France after the defeat of Culloden.

--------◆--------

WHAT'S A' THE STEER, KIMMER?

ANONYMOUS. 1745.

WHAT's a' the steer, kimmer ?
    What's a' the steer ?
Charlie he is landed,
    An', haith, he'll soon be here.
The win' was at his back, carle,
    The win' was at his back ;
I carena, sin' he's come, carle,
    We were na worth a plack.

I'm right glad to hear't, kimmer,
    I'm right glad to hear't ;
I hae a gude braid claymore,
    And for his sake I'll wear't.
Sin' Charlie he is landed,
    We hae nae mair to fear ;
Sin' Charlie he is come, kimmer,
    We'll hae a jub'lee year.

I HAE NAE KITH, I HAE NAE KIN.

ANONYMOUS. 1745.

I HAE nae kith, I hae nae kin,
  Nor ane that's dear to me;
For the bonnie lad that I lo'e best,
  He's far ayont the sea.
He's gane wi' ane that was our ain,
  And we may rue the day
When our king's ae daughter came here
  To play sic foul play.

Oh, gin I were a bonnie bird
  Wi' wings, that I might flee!
Then would I travel o'er the main,
  My ae true-love to see.
Then I wad tell a joyfu' tale
  To ane that's dear to me,
And sit upon a king's window
  And sing my melody.

The adder lies i' the corbie's nest
  Aneath the corbie's wing,
And the blast that reaves the corbie's brood
  Will soon blaw hame our king.
Then blaw ye east, or blaw ye west,
  Or blaw ye o'er the faem,
Oh, bring the lad that I lo'e best,
  And ane I darena name.

WE'LL NEVER SEE PEACE SIN' CHARLIE'S AWA'

From Buchan's " Prince Charles and Flora Macdonald."

BY Carnousie's wa's, at the close of the day,
An auld man was singing, wi' locks thin and gray;
And the burden o' his sang, while the tears fast did fa',
Was, there'll never be peace sin' Charlie's awa'.

Our kirk's gaen either to ruin again,
Our state's in confusion, an' bravely we ken,
Though we darena weel tell, wha's to blame for it a';
But we'll never see peace sin' Charlie's awa'.

My sire and five brethren wi' Charlie they gaed,
On the muir o' Culloden now green grows their bed;
I ran wi' my life,—oh, how didna I fa'!
For nae pleasure I've seen sin' my prince was awa'.

Our auld honest master, the laird o' the lan',
He bauldly set aff at the head o' the clan;
But the knowes o' Carnousie again he ne'er saw,
An' a's gaen to wreck sin' Charlie's awa'.

Yon pale Lammas moon has come threescore times roun'
Sin' my laird tint his lan' and my prince miss'd his crown;
Threescore years I've wander'd without house or ha',
And I'll never see pleasure sin' Charlie's awa'.

This song, long supposed to have been lost, was recovered by Mr. Peter Buchan.
The song by Burns, which immediately follows, was founded upon it.

THERE'LL NEVER BE PEACE.

BURNS.

By yon castle-wa', at the close of the day,
I heard a man sing, though his head it was gray;
And as he was singing the tears down came—
There'll never be peace till Jamie comes hame.

The church is in ruins, the state is in jars,
Delusions, oppressions, and murderous wars;
We daurna weel say't, but we ken wha's to blame—
There'll never be peace till Jamie comes hame.

My seven braw sons for Jamie drew sword,
And now I greet round their green beds in the yaird:
It brak the sweet heart o' my faithfu' auld dame—
There'll never be peace till Jamie comes hame.

Now life is a burden that bows me down.
Since I tint my bairns and he tint his crown;
But till my last moments my words are the same,—
There'll never be peace till Jamie comes hame.

THE WHITE COCKADE.

From Herd's Collection, 1776.   Air—" The white cockade."

My love was born in Aberdeen,
The bonniest lad that e'er was seen;
But now he makes our hearts fu' sad—
He's ta'en the field wi' his white cockade.
　　Oh, he's a ranting, roving blade!
　　Oh, he's a brisk and a bonnie lad!
　　Betide what may, my heart is glad
　　To see my lad wi' his white cockade.

Oh, leeze me on the philabeg,
The hairy hough, and garter'd leg!
But aye the thing that glads my ee,
Is the white cockade aboon the bree.

I'll sell my rock, I'll sell my reel,
My rippling kame, and spinning-wheel,
To buy my lad a tartan plaid,
A braidsword, and a white cockade.

I'll sell my rokely and my tow,
My gude gray mare and hawket cow,
That ev'ry loyal Buchan lad
May tak' the field wi' his white cockade.

KILLIECRANKIE.

CLAVERS and his Highlandmen
  Came down upon the raw, man ;
Who, being stout, gave mony a shout ;
  The lads began to claw, then.
Wi' sword and targe into their hand,
  Wi' which they were na slaw, man ;
Wi' mony a fearfu' heavy sigh,
  The lads began to claw, then.

Ower bush, ower bank, ower ditch, ower stank,
  She flang amang them a', man ;
The butter-box gat mony knocks ;
  Their riggings paid for a', then.
They got their paiks wi' sudden straiks,
  Which, to their grief, they saw, man :
Wi' clinkum-clankum ower their crowns,
  The lads began to fa', then.

Her leap'd about, her skipp'd about,
  And flang amang them a', man;
The English blades got broken heads,
  Their crowns were cleaved in twa, then;
The durk and dour made their last hour,
  And proved their final fa', man;
They thocht the devil had been there,
  That play'd them sic a pa', man.

The Solemn League and Covenant
  Cam' whiggin up the hill, man;
Thocht Highland trews durst not refuse
  For to subscribe their bill, then:
In Willie's name, they thocht nae ane
  Durst stop their course at a', man;
But her-nain-sell, wi' mony a knock,
  Cried Furich, Whigs, awa', man.

Sir Evan Dhu and his men true
  Cam' linking up the brink, man;
The Hoggan Dutch, they fearèd such,
  They bred a horrid stink, then.
The true Maclean and his fierce men
  Cam' in amang them a', man:
Nane durst withstand his heavy hand;
  A' fled and ran awa', then.

Och on a righ! och on a righ!
  Why should she lose king Shames, man?
Och rig in di! och rig in di!
  She shall break a' her banes, then;
With furichinich, and stay awhile,
  And speak a word or twa, man,
She's gie ye a straik out ower the neck
  Before ye win awa', then.

Oh, fie for shame, ye're three for ane!
  Her-nain-sell's won the day, man;
King Shames' red coats should be hung up,
  Because they ran awa', then.

Had they bent their bows like Highland trews,
   And made as lang a stay, man,
They'd saved their king, that sacred thing,
   And Willie'd run awa', then.

Killiecrankie is celebrated as the place where General Hugh Mackay, the able general of King William III., was defeated by the gallant Viscount Dundee, the "Claverhouse" of popular tradition. Dundee lost his life in the battle.

WHA WADNA FECHT FOR CHARLIE?

ANONYMOUS.

Wha wadna fecht for Charlie?
   Wha wadna draw the sword?
Wha wadna up and rally
   At the royal Prince's word?
Think on Scotia's ancient heroes,
   Think on foreign foes repell'd,
Think on glorious Bruce and Wallace,
   Who the proud usurpers quell'd.

Rouse, rouse, ye kilted warriors!
   Rouse, ye heroes of the north!
Rouse, and join your chieftain's banners,
   'Tis your Prince that leads you forth!
     Wha wadna fecht, &c.

Shall we basely crouch to tyrants?
   Shall we own a foreign sway?
Shall a royal Stuart be banish'd,
   While a stranger rules the day?
     Wha wadna fecht, &c.

See the northern clans advancing!
   See Glengarry and Lochiel!
See the brandish'd broadswords glancing!
   Highland hearts are true as steel.
     Wha wadna fecht, &c.

Now our Prince has raised his banner,
   Now triumphant is our cause:
Now the Scottish lion rallies,
   Let us strike for Prince and laws!
     Wha wadna fecht, &c.

CHARLIE IS MY DARLING.

From "Johnson's Museum."

O CHARLIE is my darling,
  My darling, my darling;
O Charlie is my darling,
  The young Chevalier.
'Twas on a Monday morning,
  Richt early in the year,
That Charlie cam' to our town,
  The young Chevalier.
    O Charlie is my darling, &c.

As he was walking up the street,
  The city for to view,
Oh, there he spied a bonnie lass
  The window looking through.
    O Charlie is my darling, &c.

Sae licht's he jumped up the stair,
  And tirl'd at the pin;
And wha sae ready as hersel'
  To let the laddie in!
    O Charlie is my darling, &c.

He set his Jenny on his knee,
  All in his Highland dress;
For brawly weel he kenn'd the way
  To please a bonnie lass.
    O Charlie is my darling, &c.

It's up yon heathery mountain,
  And down yon scraggy glen,
We daurna gang a-milking
  For Charlie and his men.
    O Charlie is my darling, &c.

UP AND WAUR THEM A', WILLIE.

From " Hogg's Jacobite Relics,'" 1821.   Air—" Up and waur them a', Willie."

WHEN we went to the field o' war,
　　And to the weaponshaw, Willie,
Wi' true design to serve our king,
　　And chase our faes awa', Willie,
Lairds and lords came there bedeen,
　　And wow gin they were sma', Willie,
While pipers play'd frae right to left,
　　Fy, furich Whigs awa', Willie.
　　　Up and waur them a', Willie,
　　　　Up and waur them a', Willie;
　　　Up and sell your sour milk,
　　　　And dance, and ding them a', Willie.

And when our army was drawn up,
　　The bravest e'er I saw, Willie,
We did not doubt to rax the rout,
　　And win the day and a', Willie.
Out-owre the brae it was nae play,
　　To get sae hard a fa', Willie,
While pipers play'd frae right to left,
　　Fy, furich Whigs awa', Willie.
　　　　　　Up and waur, &c.

But when our standard was set up,
　　So fierce the wind did blaw, Willie,
The golden knop down from the top
　　Unto the ground did fa', Willie.
Then second-sighted Sandy said,
　　We'll do nae gude at a', Willie,
While pipers play'd frae right to left,
　　Fy, furich Whigs awa', Willie.
　　　　　　Up and waur, &c.

When brawly they attack'd our left,
　　Our front, and flank, and a', Willie,
Our bauld commander on the green
　　Our faes their left did ca', Willie.

And there the greatest slaughter made
  That e'er poor Tonald saw, Willie,
While pipers play'd frae right to left,
  Fy, furich Whigs awa', Willie.
                    Up and waur, &c.

First when they saw our Highland mob,
  They swore they'd slay us a', Willie,
And yet ane fyl'd his breeks for fear,
  And so did rin awa', Willie.
We drave them back to Bonnybrigs,
  Dragoons, and foot, and a', Willie,
While pipers play'd frae right to left,
  Fy, furich Whigs awa', Willie.
                    Up and waur, &c.

But when their general view'd our lines,
  And them in order saw, Willie,
He straight did march into the town,
  And back his left did draw, Willie.
Thus we taught them the better gate
  To get a better fa', Willie,
While pipers play'd frae right to left,
  Fy, furich Whigs awa', Willie.
                    Up and waur, &c.

And then we rallied on the hills,
  And bravely up did draw, Willie;
But gin ye speer wha wan the day,
  I'll tell ye what I saw, Willie:
We baith did fight, and baith were beat,
  And baith did rin awa', Willie;
So there's my canty Highland sang
  About the thing I saw, Willie.
                    Up and waur, &c.

O'ER THE WATER TO CHARLIE.

From " Hogg's Jacobite Relics," 1821.

COME, boat me ower, come, row me ower,
  Come boat me ower to Charlie;
I'll gie John Ross another bawbee
  To ferry me ower to Charlie.
    We'll over the water, and over the sea,
      We'll over the water to Charlie;
    Come weel, come woe, we'll gather and go,
      And live and die wi' Charlie.

It's weel I lo'e my Charlie's name,
  Though some there be that abhor him;
But, oh, to see Auld Nick gaun hame,
  And Charlie's faes before him!

I swear by moon and stars sae bricht,
  And the sun that glances early,
If I had twenty thousand lives,
  I'd gie them a' for Charlie.

I ance had sons, I now hae nane;
  I bred them, toiling sairly;
And I wad bear them a' again,
  And lose them a' for Charlie!

----♦----

THE WEE, WEE GERMAN LAIRDIE.

From " Hogg's Jacobite Relics."

WHA the deil hae we gotten for a king,
  But a wee, wee German lairdie?
And, when we gaed to bring him hame,
  He was delving in his kail-yardie:
Sheughing kail, and laying leeks,
But the hose, and but the breeks;
And up his beggar duds he cleeks,
  This wee, wee German lairdie.

And he's clapt down in our gudeman's chair,
   The wee, wee German lairdie;
And he's brought fouth o' foreign leeks,
   And dibbled them in his yardie.
He's pu'd the rose o' English loons,
And broken the harp o' Irish clowns;
But our thistle tap will jag his thumbs,
   This wee, wee German lairdie.

Come up amang our Highland hills,
   Thou wee, wee German lairdie;
And see the Stuarts' lang kail thrive,
   We dibbled in our yardie;
And if a stock ye dare to pu',
Or haud the yoking o' a plough,
We'll break your sceptre or your mou',
   Thou wee bit German lairdie.

Our hills are steep, our glens are deep,
   Nae fitting for a yardie;
And our Norland thistles winna pu',
   Thou wee bit German lairdie:
And we've the trenching blades o' weir,
Wad prune ye o' your German gear;
We'll pass ye 'neath the claymore's shear,
   Thou feckless German lairdie.

Auld Scotland, thou'rt ower cauld a hole
   For nursin' siccan vermin;
But the very dougs o' England's court
   They bark and howl in German.
Then keep thy dibble in thy ain hand,
Thy spade but and thy yardie;
For wha the deil hae we gotten for a king,
   But a wee, wee German lairdie?

PRINCE CHARLES AND FLORA MACDONALD'S WELCOME TO SKYE.

From "Hogg's Jacobite Relics."   Translated from the Gaelic.

THERE are twa bonny maidens and three bonny maidens
    Come o'er the minch and come o'er the main,
O'er the wind and the faem with the corrie for their hame,
    Let us welcome them bravely to Skye again.
Come along, come along, wi' your boatie and your song,
    Ye twa bonnie maidens and three bonnie maidens;
For the nicht it is dark, and the red-coat is gone,
    And you're bravely welcome to Skye again.

There is Flora my honey, sae dear and sae bonny,
    And one that is tall and comely withal;
But the one as my king, and the other as my queen,
    They're welcome, welcome to Skye again.
Come along, come along, with your boatie and your song,
    Ye twa bonnie maidens and three bonnie maidens.
For the lady of Maclain she lieth her lane,
    And you're bravely welcome to Skye again.

Her arm it is strong, and her petticoat is long,
    My one bonny maiden and twa bonnie maidens;
But their bed shall be clain 'mid the storm and the rain,
    And they're welcome, welcome to Skye again.
Come along, come along, with your boatie and your song,
    You one bonny maiden and twa bonnie maidens;
By the sea-moullit's nest I'll watch ye o'er the main,
    And you're dearly welcome to Skye again.

There's a wind on the tree and a ship on the sea,
    My twa bonnie maidens and three bonnie maidens;
On the lea of the rock shall your cradle be rock'd;
    And you're welcome, welcome to Skye again.
Come along, come along, wi' your boatie and your song,
    My twa bonnie maidens and three bonnie maidens;
More sound shall you sleep when you rock on the deep;
    And ye'se aye be welcome to Skye again.

AWA', WHIGS, AWA!

From " Hogg's Jacobite Relics."

OUR thistles flourish'd fresh and fair,
    And bonny bloom'd our roses;
But Whigs came like a frost in June,
    And wither'd a' our posies.
      Awa', Whigs, awa'!
      Awa', Whigs, awa'!
Ye're but a pack o' traitor loons;
    Ye'll ne'er do good at a'.

Our sad decay in church and state
    Surpasses my descriving;
The Whigs came o'er us for a curse,
    And we have done wi' thriving.

A foreign Whiggish loon bought seeds,
    In Scottish yaird to cover;
But we'll pu' a' his dibbled leeks,
    And pack him to Hanover.

Our ancient crown's fa'n i' the dust,
    Deil blind them wi' the stour o't!
And write their names in his black book
    Wha ga'e the Whigs the power o't.

Grim Vengeance lang has ta'en a nap,
    But we may see him wauken;
God help the day when royal heads
    Are hunted like a maukin!

The deil he heard the storm o' tongues,
    And ramping came amang us;
But he pitied us, sae cursed wi' Whigs,
    He turn'd and wadna wrang us.

Sae grim he sat amang the reek,
    Thrang bundling brunstane matches;
And croon'd 'mang the beuk-taking Whigs,
    Scraps of auld Calvin's catches.
      Awa', Whigs, awa'!
      Awa', Whigs, awa'!
Ye'll rin me out o' brunstane spunks,
    And ne'er do good at a'.

THE HIGHLAND WIDOW'S LAMENT.

ANONYMOUS.

OH, was not I a weary wight?
    Oh, ono chri, oh! oh, ono chri, oh!
Maid, wife, and widow in one night!
    Oh, ono chri, oh! &c.
When in my soft and yielding arms,
    Oh, ono chri, oh! &c.
When most I thought him free from harms,
    Oh, ono chri, oh! &c.

Even at the dead time of the night,
    Oh, ono chri, oh! &c.
They broke my bower, and slew my knight,
    Oh, ono chri, oh! &c.
With ae lock of his jet-black hair,
    Oh, ono chri, oh! &c.
I'll tie my heart for evermair;
    Oh, ono chri, oh! &c.

Nae sly-tongued youth or flattering swain,
    Oh, ono chri, oh! &c.
Shall e'er untie this knot again:
    Oh, ono chri, oh! &c.

Thine still, dear youth, that heart shall be,
  Oh, ono chri, oh! &c.
Nor pant for aught save heaven and thee,
  Oh, ono chri, oh! &c.

THE AULD STUARTS BACK AGAIN.

ANONYMOUS. 1745.

THE auld Stuarts back again!
The auld Stuarts back again!
Let howlet Whigs do what they can,
  The Stuarts will be back again.
Wha cares for a' their creeshie duds,
And a' Kilmarnock's sowan suds?
We'll wauk their hides and fyle their fuds,
  And bring the Stuarts back again.

There's Ayr and Irvine, wi' the rest,
And a' the cronies o' the west;
Lord, sic a scaw'd and scabbit nest,
  And they'll set up their crack again!
But wad they come, or daur they come,
Afore the bagpipe and the drum,
We'll either gar them a' sing dumb,
  Or, " Auld Stuarts back again."

Give ear unto this loyal sang,
A' ye that ken the richt frae wrang,
An' a' that look and think it lang,
  For auld Stuarts back again:
Were ye wi' me to chase the rae,
Out owre the hills an' far away,
And saw the lords come there that day,
  To bring the Stuarts back again.

There might ye see the noble Mar,
Wi' Athole, Huntly, and Traquair,
Seaforth, Kilsyth, and Auldublair,
  And mony mae, what reck, again.
Then what are a' their westlin' crews?
  We'll gar the tailors tack again:
Can they forstand the tartan trews,
  And " Auld Stuarts back again!"

THE DUKE OF CUMBERLAND.

From " The Wanderings of Prince Charles and Flora Macdonald,'
by PETER BUCHAN.

THAT mushrom thing call'd Cumberland
  Has lately pass'd the Forth, sir;
But he's commencèd plunderland
  Since he gaed to the north, sir;
    Sing audlie ilti, audlie ilti, audlie ilti, lara, lara;
    Sing audlie ilti, audlie ilti, audlie ilti, lara, lara.

He is the first of all the line
  Call'd Protestant, I swear, sir,
That ever kiss'd our ladies fine,
  Or breathed in Scottish air, sir.
          Sing audlie ilti, &c.

Our priest he has incarcerate,
  And burn'd our altars down, sir;
The godless Whigs rejoice at that,
  And bless the firebrand loon, sir.
          Sing audlie ilti, &c.

But when our tartan lads come back,
  And messieurs land at Dover,
We'll singe the lousy German pack,
  And drive them to Hanover.
          Sing audlie ilti, &c.

Then all the brood o'erwhelm'd with dool,
  I'll pledge my faith and troth, sir,
Instead of tarts and pies at yule,
  They'll slab their turnip-broth, sir.
          Sing audlie ilti, &c.

———◆———

OH, HE'S BEEN LANG O' COMING!

From PETER BUCHAN'S " Prince Charles and Flora Macdonald."

THE youth that should hae been our king
Was dress'd in yellow, red, and green;
A braver lad ye wadna seen
  Nor our brave royal Charlie.

Oh, he's been lang o' coming,
Lang, lang, lang o' coming;
Oh, he's been lang o' coming:
   Welcome, royal Charlie !

At Falkirk and at Prestonpans,
Supported by the Highland clans,
They broke the Hanoverian bands,
   For our brave royal Charlie.
               Oh, he's been lang, &c.

The valiant chief, the brave Lochiel,
He met Prince Charlie on the dale;
Then, oh, what kindness did prevail
   Between the chief and Charlie !
               Oh, he's been lang, &c.

Oh, come and quaff along wi' me,
And drink a bumper three times three
To him that's come to set us free.
   Huzza ! rejoice for Charlie.
               Oh, he's been lang, &c.

We daurna brew a peck o' maut,
But Geordie says it is a faut;
And to our kail cannot get saut
   For want o' royal Charlie.
               Oh, he's been lang, &c.

Now our good king abroad is gone,
A German whelp now fills the throne,
Whelps that are denied by none,
   They're brutes compared to Charlie.
               Oh, he's been lang, &c.

Now our good king is turn'd awa',
A German whelp now rules us a' ;
And though we're forced against our law
   The right belongs to Charlie.
               Oh, he's been lang, &c.

If we had but our Charlie back,
We wadna fear the German's crack,
Wi' a' his thieving hungry pack ;
   The right belongs to Charlie.
               Oh, he's been lang, &c.

O Charlie, come and lead our way,
No German whelp shall bear the sway;
Though ilka dog maun hae his day,
  The right belongs to Charlie.
                    Oh, he's been lang, &c.

FLORA AND CHARLIE.

From PETER BUCHAN's " Prince Charles and Flora Macdonald."

OWER yon muir and yon lofty mountains,
  Where the trees are clad with snow;
And down by yon murmuring crystal fountain,
  Where the silver streams do flow;
There fair Flora sat complaining
  For the absence of our king,
Crying, Charlie, lovely Charlie,
  When shall we two meet again?

Fair Flora's love it was surprising,
  Like to diadems in array;
And her dress of the tartan plaidie
  Was like a rainbow in the sky.
And each minute she tuned her spinnet,
  And royal Jamie was the tune,
Crying, Charlie, royal Charlie,
  When shalt thou enjoy thy own?

When all these storms are quite blown o'er,
  Then the skies will rent and tear;
Then Charlie he'll return to Britain,
  To enjoy the grand affair.
The frisking lambs will skip over,
  And larks and linnets shall sweetly sing,
Singing, Charlie, royal Charlie,
  You're welcome home to be our king.

THOUGH GEORDIE REIGNS IN JAMES'S STEAD.

From "Prince Charles and Flora Macdonald," by PETER BUCHAN.

THOUGH Geordie reigns in James's stead,
   I'm grieved, yet scorn to show that;
I'll ne'er look down, nor hang my head,
   On rebel Whigs for a' that;
But still I'll trust in Providence,
   And still I'll laugh at a' that;
And sing, He's ower the hills this night
   That I love weel for a' that.

He's far ayont Killebrae this night
   That I love weel for a' that;
He wears a pistol on his side,
   Which makes me blythe for a' that.
The Highland coat, the philabeg,
   The tartan trews, and a' that,
He wears that's o'er the hills this night,
   And he'll be here for a' that.

He wears a broadsword on his side,
   He kens weel how to draw that;
The target and the Highland plaid,
   And shoulder-belt, and a' that;
A bonnet bound wi' ribbons blue,
   A white cockade, and a' that,
He wears that's o'er the hills this night,
   And will be here for a' that.

The Whigs think a' that Willie's mine,
   But yet they mauna fa' that;
They think our hearts will be cast down,
   But we'll be blythe for a' that:
For a' that and a' that,
   And thrice as meikle's a' that;
He's bonny that's o'er the hills this night,
   And will be here for a' that.

But, oh, what will the Whigs say syne,
   When they're mista'en and a' that;
When Geordie maun fling by the crown,
   The hat and wig, and a' that?

The flames will get baith hat and wig,
  As ofttimes they've got a' that;
Our Highland lad will wear the crown,
  And aye be blythe for a' that.

And then our brave militia lads
  Will be rewarded duly,
When they fling by their black cockades,
  That hellish colour truly.
As night is banish'd by the day,
  The white will drive awa' that;
The sun will then his beams display,
  And we'll be blythe for a' that.

BONNIE LADDIE, HIGHLAND LADDIE.

Anonymous.

Where hae ye been a' the day,
  Bonnie laddie, Highland laddie?
Saw ye him that's far away,
  Bonnie laddie, Highland laddie
On his head a bonnet blue,
  Bonnie laddie, Highland laddie;
Tartan plaid and Highland trews,
  Bonnie laddie, Highland laddie.

When he drew his gude braidsword,
  Bonnie laddie, Highland laddie,
Then he gave his royal word,
  Bonnie laddie, Highland laddie,
That frae the field he ne'er wad flee,
  Bonnie laddie, Highland laddie,
But wi' his friends wad live and dee,
  Bonnie laddie, Highland laddie.

Weary fa' the Lawland loon,
  Bonnie laddie, Highland laddie,
Wha took frae him the British croun,
  Bonnie laddie, Highland laddie;

But blessings on the kilted clans,
  Bonnie laddie, Highland laddie,
That fought for him at Prestonpans,
  Bonnie laddie, Highland laddie.

Geordie sits in Charlie's chair,
  Bonnie laddie, Highland laddie;
Deil tak him gin he bide there,
  Bonnie laddie, Highland laddie.
Charlie yet shall mount the throne,
  Bonnie laddie, Highland laddie;
Weel ye ken it is his own,
  Bonnie laddie, Highland laddie.

Ken ye the news I hae to tell,
  Bonnie laddie, Highland laddie?
Cumberland's awa' to hell,
  Bonnie laddie, Highland laddie.
When he came to the Stygian shore,
  Bonnie laddie, Highland laddie,
The deil himsel' wi' fright did roar,
  Bonnie laddie, Highland laddie.

Charon grim cam' out to him,
  Bonnie laddie, Highland laddie;
Ye're welcome here, ye deevil's limb!
  Bonnie laddie, Highland laddie.
He tow'd him o'er wi' curse and ban,
  Bonnie laddie, Highland laddie,
Whiles he sank and whiles he swam,
  Bonnie laddie, Highland laddie.

On him they pat a philabeg,
  Bonnie laddie, Highland laddie,
An' in his lug they ramm'd a peg,
  Bonnie laddie, Highland laddie.
How he did skip! how he did roar;
  Bonnie laddie, Highland laddie;
The deils ne'er saw sic fun before,
  Bonnie laddie, Highland laddie.

They took him neist to Satan's ha',
  Bonnie laddie, Highland laddie,
There to lilt wi' his grandpapa,
  Bonnie laddie, Highland laddie.
Says Cumberland, I'll no gang ben,
  Bonnie laddie, Highland laddie,
For fear I meet wi' Charlie's men,
  Bonnie laddie, Highland laddie.

Oh, nought o' that ye hae to fear,
  Bonnie laddie, Highland laddie,
For fient a ane o' them comes here,
  Bonnie laddie, Highland laddie.
The deil sat girnin in the neuk,
  Bonnie laddie, Highland laddie,
Ryving sticks to roast the Duke,
  Bonnie laddie, Highland laddie.

They clapp'd him in an arm-chair,
  Bonnie laddie, Highland laddie,
And fast in chains they bound him there,
  Bonnie laddie, Highland laddie;
And aye they kept it het below,
  Bonnie laddie, Highland laddie,
Wi' peats an' divots frae Glencoe,
  Bonnie laddie, Highland laddie.

They put him then upon a speet,
  Bonnie laddie, Highland laddie,
And roasted him baith head and feet,
  Bonnie laddie, Highland laddie;
Then ate him up baith stoop and roop,
  Bonnie laddie, Highland laddie;
And that's the gate they served the Duke,
  Bonnie laddie, Highland laddie.

This famous Jacobite song, the best known perhaps of any of the collection, was the last revenge of the Highlanders upon their conqueror, the Duke of Cumberland. —a name that is still as much hated in the Highlands as that of Cromwell is in Ireland.

HERE'S A HEALTH TO THEM THAT'S AWA'.

Partly by BURNS.

HERE's a health to them that's awa',
  Here's a health to them that's awa';
And wha winna wish guid luck to our cause,
  May never guid luck be their fa'!
It's guid to be merry and wise,
  It's guid to be honest and true,
It's guid to support Caledonia's cause,
  And bide by the buff and the blue.

Here's a health to them that's awa',
  Here's a health to them that's awa';
Here's a health to Charlie, the chief o' the clan,
  Although that his band be but sma'.
May liberty meet with success!
  May prudence protect her frae evil!
May tyrants and tyranny tine in the mist,
  And wander their way to the devil!

Here's a health to them that's awa',
  Here's a health to them that's awa';
Here's a health to Tammie, the Norland laddie,
  That lives at the lug o' the law!
Here's freedom to him that wad read,
  Here's freedom to him that wad write;
There's nane ever fear'd that the truth should be heard,
  But they wham the truth wad indite.

Here's a health to them that's awa',
  Here's a health to them that's awa';
Here's chieftain M'Leod, a chieftain worth gowd,
  Though bred amang mountains o' snaw!
Here's a health to them that's awa',
  Here's a health to them that's awa';
And wha winna wish guid luck to our cause,
  May never guid luck be their fa'!

Many modern imitations of this old genuine Jacobite song have been written and
published.

STRATHALLAN'S LAMENT.

BURNS.

THICKEST night o'erhangs my dwelling,
  Howling tempests o'er me rave;
Turbid torrents, wintry swelling,
  Still surround my lonely cave.
Crystal streamlets gently flowing,
  Busy haunts of base mankind,
Western breezes, softly blowing,
  Suit not my distracted mind.

In the cause of right engaged,
  Wrongs injurious to redress,
Honour's war we strongly waged,
  But the heavens deny'd success.

Ruin's wheel has driven o'er us,
  Not a hope that dare attend,
The wide world is all before us;
  But a world without a friend!

Supposed to refer to the story of James Drummond, Earl of Strathallan, who escaped to France after the '45. "The air," says Burns, "is the composition of one of the worthiest and best-hearted men living—Allan Masterton, schoolmaster in Edinburgh. As he and I were both sprouts of Jacobitism, we agreed to dedicate the words and air to that cause. To tell the matter of fact, except when my passions were heated by some accidental cause, my Jacobitism was merely by way of *vive la bagatelle*."

THE CHEVALIER'S LAMENT.

BURNS.

THE small birds rejoice in the green leaves returning,
  The murmuring streamlet runs clear through the vale;
The hawthorn-trees blow in the dews of the morning,
  And wild-scatter'd cowslips bedeck the green dale.

But what can give pleasure, or what can seem fair,
  While the lingering moments are number'd by care?
No flowers gaily springing, nor birds sweetly singing,
  Can soothe the sad bosom of joyless despair.

The deed that I dared could it merit their malice,
  A king and a father to place on his throne?
His right are these hills, and his right are these valleys,
  Where the wild beasts find shelter, but I can find none.

But 'tis not my sufferings, thus wretched, forlorn,
  My brave gallant friends, 'tis your ruin I mourn:
Your deeds proved so loyal in hot bloody trial,
  Alas! can I make you no sweeter return?

CAM' YE BY ATHOLE BRAES?

HOGG.

CAM' ye by Athole braes, lad wi' the philabeg,
  Down by the Tummel, or banks of the Garry?
Saw ye my lad with his bonnet and white cockade,
  Leaving his mountains to follow Prince Charlie?
Charlie, Charlie, wha wadna follow thee?
  Lang hast thou loved and trusted us fairly!
Charlie, Charlie, wha wadna follow thee?
  King of the Highland hearts, bonny Prince Charlie

I hae but ae son, my brave young Donald;
  But if I had ten, they should follow Glengarry:
Health to Macdonald and gallant Clanronald,
  For they are the men that wad die for their Charlie.
                    Charlie, Charlie, &c.

I'll to Lochiel and Appin, and kneel to them,
  Down by Lord Murray and Roy of Kildarlie;
Brave Macintosh, he shall fly to the field wi' them;
  They are the lads I can trust with my Charlie.
                    Charlie, Charlie, &c.

Down through the Lowlands, down wi' the Whigamore,
  Loyal true Highlanders, down wi' them rarely!
Ronald and Donald, drive on wi' the brave claymore
  Over the necks of the foes of Prince Charlie!
                    Charlie, Charlie, &c.

WHA'LL BE KING BUT CHARLIE?

ANONYMOUS.

The news frae Moidart cam' yestreen,
  Will soon gar mony ferlie;
For ships o' war hae just come in,
  And landed Royal Charlie.
Come through the heather, around him gather,
  Ye're a' the welcomer early;
Around him cling wi' a' your kin,
  For wha'll be king but Charlie?
Come through the heather, around him gather:
  Come Ronald, come Donald, come a' thegither,
And crown your rightfu', lawfu' king;
  For wha'll be king but Charlie?

The Highland clans wi' sword in hand,
  Frae John o' Groat's to Airlie,
Hae to a man declared to stand
  Or fa' wi' Royal Charlie.
      Come through, &c.

The Lowlands a' baith great and sma',
  Wi' mony a lord and laird, hae
Declared for Scotland's king and law,
  An' spier ye wha but Charlie?
      Come through, &c.

There's ne'er a lass in a' the land
  But vows, baith late and early,
To man she'll ne'er gie heart or hand
  Wha wadna fight for Charlie.
      Come through, &c.

Then here's a health to Charlie's cause,
  And be't complete and early;
His very name my heart's blood warms—
  To arms! for Royal Charlie!
      Come through, &c.

HE'S OWRE THE HILLS THAT I LO'E WEEL.

ANONYMOUS.

HE's owre the hills that I lo'e weel,
He's owre the hills we daurna name,
He's owre the hills ayont Dunblane,
Wha soon will get his welcome hame.
My faither's gane to fight for him,
My brithers winna bide at hame,
My mither greets and prays for them,
And 'deed she thinks they're no to blame.

The whigs may scoff, the whigs may jeer,
But ah! that love maun be sincere
Which still keeps true whate'er betide,
An' for his sake leaves a' beside.
    He's owre the hills, &c.

His right these hills, his right these plains,
O'er Highland hearts secure he reigns;
What lads e'er did our lads will do,
Were I a lad I'd follow him too.
    He's owre the hills, &c.

Sae noble a look, sae princely an air,
Sae gallant and bold, sae young and sae fair;
Oh! did ye but see him, ye'd do as we've done,
Hear him but ance, to his standard you'll run.
    He's owre the hills, &c.

Then draw the claymore for Charlie, then fight
For your country, religion, and a' that is right;
Were ten thousand lives now given to me,
I'd die as aft for ane o' the three!
    He's owre the hills, &c.

BEN LOMOND AND LOCH LOMOND.

Miscellaneous Songs.

TULLOCHGORUM.

The REV. JOHN SKINNER, episcopal minister of Longside, near Peterhead, Aberdeenshire, born 1721, died 1807.

COME, gi'e's a sang, Montgomery cried,
And lay your disputes all aside,
What signifies't for folks to chide
   For what's been done before them?
Let Whig and Tory all agree,
Whig and Tory, Whig and Tory,
Let Whig and Tory all agree,
   To drop their Whig-mig-morum;
Let Whig and Tory all agree
To spend the night in mirth and glee,
And cheerfu' sing alang wi' me
   The reel of Tullochgorum.

T

Oh, Tullochgorum's my delight,
It gars us a' in ane unite,
And ony sumph that keeps up spite,
 In conscience I abhor him.
Blythe and merry we's be a',
Blythe and merry, blythe and merry,
Blythe and merry we's be a',
 And mak' a cheerfu' quorum.
Blythe and merry we's be a',
As lang as we hae breath to draw,
And dance, till we be like to fa',
 The reel of Tullochgorum.

There needs na' be sae great a phraise,
Wi' dringing dull Italian lays,
I wadna gi'e our ain strathspeys
 For half a hundred score o' 'em.
They're douff and dowie at the best,
Douff and dowie, douff and dowie,
They're douff and dowie at the best,
 Wi' a' their variorum.
They're douff and dowie at the best,
Their allegros, and a' the rest,
They canna please a Highland taste,
 Compared wi' Tullochgorum.

Let warldly minds themselves oppress
Wi' fears of want and double cess,
And sullen sots themselves distress
 Wi' keeping up decorum.
Shall we sae sour and sulky sit,
Sour and sulky, sour and sulky,
Shall we sae sour and sulky sit,
 Like auld Philosophorum?
Shall we sae sour and sulky sit,
Wi' neither sense, nor mirth, nor wit,
Nor ever rise to shake a fit
 At the reel of Tullochgorum?

May choicest blessings still attend
Each honest open-hearted friend,
And calm and quiet be his end,
 And a' that's good watch o'er him!

May peace and plenty be his lot,
Peace and plenty, peace and plenty,
May peace and plenty be his lot,
    And dainties a great store o' 'em!
May peace and plenty be his lot,
Unstain'd by any vicious blot!
And may he never want a groat
    That's fond of Tullochgorum.

But for the dirty, fawning fool,
Who wants to be oppression's tool,
May envy gnaw his rotten soul,
    And discontent devour him!
May dool and sorrow be his chance,
Dool and sorrow, dool and sorrow,
May dool and sorrow be his chance,
    And nane say, Wae's me for 'im!
May dool and sorrow be his chance,
And a' the ills that come frae France,
Whae'er he be, that winna dance
    The reel of Tullochgorum!

It is related that the author of this song was at dinner at the house of a lady named Montgomery, that the guests became excited on a political dispute, and that Mrs. Montgomery asked Mr. Skinner for a song, to put an end to it; expressing at the same time her surprise that so capital a tune as the " Reel of Tullochgorum " had no words to which it could be sung. Mr. Skinner afterwards produced this celebrated effusion, which, in Burns's opinion, was entitled to rank " as the first of songs."

The Rev. John Skinner, being asked by Mr. Fergusson, of Pitfour, what he could do to make him comfortable, gave the following answer:

" Lodged in a canty cell of nine feet square,
    Bare bread and sowans and milk my belly's fare;
Shoes for my feet, soft clothing for my back—
If warm, no matter whether blue or black:
In such a sober, low, contented state,
What comfort now need I from rich or great!

Now in my eightieth year, my thread near spun,
My race through poverty and labour run,
Wishing to be by all my flock beloved,
And for long service by my Judge approved;
Death at my door and heaven in my eye,
From rich or great what comfort now need I?

Let but our sacred edifice go on
With cheerfulness until the work be done;
Let but my flock be faithfully supplied,
My friends all with their lot well satisfied:

Then, oh, with joy and comfort from on high
Let me in Christian quiet calmly die,
And lay my ashes in my Grizel's grave,
'Tis all I wish upon the earth to have !

Thus lifted up above all vain desire,
And quench'd each foolish spark of passion's fire,
Deprived of her I justly held so dear,
Nor plagued with idle hope or idle fear,
The smiles or frowns of fortune I defy;
From rich or great what comfort now need I ?"

THE EWIE WI' THE CROOKIT HORN.

REV. JOHN SKINNER.

OH, were I able to rehearse
My ewie's praise in proper verse,
I'd sound it out as loud and fierce
   As ever piper's drone could blaw !
   A' that kenn'd her would hae sworn
   Sic a ewie ne'er was born
      Thereabouts, nor far awa'.

She neither needed tar nor keel
To mark her upon hip or heel,
Her crookit hornie did as weel
   To ken her by amang them a'.

She never threaten'd scab nor rot,
But keepit aye her ain jog-trot;
Both to the fauld and to the cot,
   Was never sweir to lead nor ca'.

A better nor a thriftier beast
Nae honest man need e'er hae wish'd ;
For, silly thing, she never miss'd
   To hae ilk year a lamb or twa.

The first she had I gae to Jock,
To be to him a kind o' stock ;
And now the laddie has a flock
   Of mair than thretty head and twa.

The neist I gae to Jean, and now
The bairn sae braw has fauls sae fu',
That lads sae thick come her to woo,
   They're fain to sleep on hay or straw.

Cauld nor hunger never dang her,
Wind or rain could never wrang her;
Ance she lay an ouk and langer
   Forth aneath a wreath o' snaw.

When other ewies lap the dyke,
And ate the kail for a' the tyke,
My ewie never play'd the like,
   But teesed about the barn wa'.

I lookit aye at even for her,
Lest mishanter should come ower her,
Or the fumart micht devour her,
   Gin the beastie bade awa'.

Yet, last ouk, for a' my keeping,
(Wha can tell o't without greeting ?)
A villain cam', when I was sleeping,
   Stow my ewie, horn and a'.

I socht her sair upon the morn,
And down aneath a bush o' thorn,
There I found her crookit horn,
   But my ewie was awa'.

But gin I had the loon that did it,
I hae sworn as weel as said it,
Although the laird himsel' forbid it,
   I sall gie his neck a thraw.

I never met wi' sic a turn,
At e'en I had baith ewe and horn,
Safe steekit up; but gin the morn
   Baith ewe and horn were stown awa'.

A' the claes that we hae worn
Frae her and hers sae aft was shorn ;
The loss o' her we could hae borne
   Had fair-strae death ta'en her awa'.

Oh, had she died o' croup or cauld,
As ewies die when they grow auld,
It hadna been by mony fauld
  Sae sair a heart to ane o' us a'.

But thus, puir thing, to lose her life
Beneath a bluidy villain's knife,—
In troth I fear that our gudewife
  Will never get abune't ava.

Oh, a' ye bards benorth Kinghorn,
Call up your Muses, let them mourn,
Our ewie wi' the crookit horn
  Frae us stown, and fell'd and a'.

THE AULD MINISTER'S SONG.

Rev. John Skinner. Air—" Auld lang syne."

Should auld acquaintance be forgot,
  Or friendship e'er grow cauld?
Should we nae tighter draw the knot,
  Aye as we're growing auld?
How comes it then, my worthy frien',
  Who used to be sae kin',
We dinna for each ither speer,
  As we did langsyne?

What though I am some aulder grown,
  An' ablins nae sae gay;
What though these locks, ance hazel brown,
  Are now well mix'd wi' gray:
I'm sure my heart nae caulder grows,
  But as my years decline,
Still friendship's flame as warmly glows
  As it did langsyne.

Sae well's I min' upo' the days
  That we in youthfu' pride
Had used to ramble up the braes
  On bonny Boggie's side.

Nae fairies on the haunted green,
　　Where moonbeams twinkling shine,
Mair blythely frisk aroun' their queen,
　　Than we did langsyne. .

Sae well's I min' ilk bonny spring
　　Ye on your harp did play ;
An' how we used to dance and sing
　　The livelang simmer's day.
If ye hae not forgot the art
　　To strike that harp divine,
Ye'll fin' I still can play my part,
　　An' sing as auld langsyne.

Though ye live on the banks o' Doun,
　　And me besooth the Tay,
Ye well might ride to Faukland town
　　Some bonny simmer's day.
And at that place where Scotland's king
　　Aft birl'd the beer and wine,
Let's drink an' dance, an' laugh an' sing,
　　An' crack o' auld langsyne.

JOHN OF BADENYON.

REV. JOHN SKINNER.

WHEN first I came to be a man of twenty years or so,
I thought myself a handsome youth, and fain the world would know.
In best attire I stept abroad, with spirits brisk and gay ;
And here, and there, and every where, was like a morn in May.
No care I had, no fear of want, but rambled up and down,
And for a beau I might have pass'd in country or in town ;
I still was pleased where'er I went ; and when I was alone,
I tuned my pipe, and pleased myself wi' John o' Badenyon.

Now in the days of youthful prime, a mistress I must find ;
For love, they say, gives one an air, and e'en improves the mind.
On Phillis fair above the rest kind fortune fix'd mine eyes ;
Her piercing beauty struck my heart, and she became my choice.
To Cupid now, with hearty prayer, I offer'd many a vow,
And danced and sung, and sigh'd and swore, as other lovers do ;

But when at last I breathed my flame, I found her cold as stone—
I left the girl, and tuned my pipe to John o' Badenyon.

When love had thus my heart beguiled with foolish hopes and vain,
To friendship's port I steer'd my course, and laugh'd at lovers' pain;
A friend I got by lucky chance—'twas something like divine;
An honest friend's a precious gift, and such a gift was mine.
And now, whatever may betide, a happy man was I,
In any strait I knew to whom I freely might apply.
A strait soon came; my friend I tried—he laugh'd, and spurn'd
          my moan;
I hied me home, and tuned my pipe to John o' Badenyon.

I thought I should be wiser next, and would a patriot turn,
Began to doat on Johnie Wilkes, and cry'd up Parson Horne;
Their noble spirit I admired, and praised their noble zeal,
Who had, with flaming tongue and pen, maintain'd the public weal.
But ere a month or two had pass'd, I found myself betray'd;
'Twas Self and Party, after all, for all the stir they made.
At last I saw these factious knaves insult the very throne;
I cursed them all, and tuned my pipe to John o' Badenyon.

What next to do I mused a while, still hoping to succeed;
I pitch'd on books for company, and gravely tried to read;
I bought and borrow'd every where, and studied night and day,
Nor miss'd what dean or doctor wrote that happen'd in my way.
Philosophy I now esteem'd the ornament of youth,
And carefully, through many a page, I hunted after truth;
A thousand various schemes I tried, and yet was pleased with none;
I threw them by, and tuned my pipe to John o' Badenyon.

And now, ye youngsters every where, who wish to make a show,
Take heed in time, nor vainly hope for happiness below;
What you may fancy pleasure here is but an empty name;
And girls, and friends, and books also, you'll find them all the same.
Then be advised, and warning take from such a man as me;
I'm neither pope nor cardinal, nor one of high degree;
You'll meet displeasure every where; then do as I have done—
E'en tune your pipe, and please yourself with John o' Badenyon.

WHEN I BEGAN THE WORLD.

Rev. John Skinner.   From a manuscript collection of songs of the North of
Scotland, by Peter Buchan.
Air—"The broom o' the Cowden Knowes."

When I began the world first, it was not then as now,
For all was plain and simple then, and friends were kind and true;
Oh, the times! the weary times! the times that I now see,—
I think the world is all gone wrong from what it used to be.

There was not then high-cap'ring heads prick'd up from ear to ear,
And cloaks and caps were rarities for gentle folks to wear;
Oh, the times! the weary times! the times that I now see,—
I think the world is all gone wrong from what it used to be.

There's not an upstart mushroom but what pretends to taste,
And not a lass in a' the land but must be lady-dress'd;
Oh, the times! the weary times! the times that I now see,—
I think the world is all gone wrong from what it used to be.

Our young men married then for love, so did our lassies too,
And children loved their parents dear, as children ought to do;
Oh, the times! the weary times! the times that I now see,—
I think the world is all gone wrong from what it used to be.

For, oh, the times are sadly changed, a heavy change indeed,
For love and friendship are no more, and honesty is fleed;
Oh, the times! the weary times! the times that I now see,—
I think the world is all gone wrong from what it used to be.

There's nothing now prevails but pride among the high and low,
And strife and greed and vanity is all that's minded now;
Oh, the times! the weary times! the times that I now see,—
I think the world is all gone wrong from what it used to be.

THE REEL O' BOGIE.

ALEXANDER fourth DUKE OF GORDON, born 1743, died 1827.
Air—"There's cauld kail in Aberdeen."

THERE's cauld kail in Aberdeen,
  And custocks in Stra'bogie,
Gin I hae but a bonnie lass,
  Ye're welcome to your cogie.
And ye may sit up a' the night,
And drink till it be braid daylight:
Gi'e me a lass baith clean and tight,
  To dance the reel o' Bogie.

In cotillions the French excel,
  John Bull loves country-dances ;
The Spaniards dance fandangoes well,
  Mynheer an allemande prances :
In foursome reels the Scots delight,
At threesomes they dance wondrous light,
But twasomes ding a' out o' sight,
  Danced to the reel o' Bogie.

Come, lads, and view your partners weel,
  Wale each a blythesome cogie :
I'll tak' this lassie to mysel',
  She looks sae keen and vogie :
Now, piper lad, bang up the spring ;
The country fashion is the thing,
To prie their mou's ere we begin
  To dance the reel o' Bogie.

Now ilka lad has got a lass,
  Save yon auld doited fogie,
And ta'en a fling upon the grass,
  As they do in Stra'bogie ;
But a' the lassies look sae fain
We canna think oursel's to hain,
For they maun hae their come-again
  To dance the reel o' Bogie.

Now a' the lads hae done their best,
  Like true men o' Stra'bogie,
We'll stop a while and tak' a rest,
  And tipple out a cogie.
Come now, my lads, and tak' your glass,
And try ilk other to surpass,
In wishing health to ev'ry lass
  To dance the reel o' Bogie.

This song, founded upon the popular bacchanalian ditty, the " Three gir'd cog," was first published in " Johnson's Musical Museum," 1790.

----•----

THE BONNY BREAST-KNOTS.

From " The Ancient Minstrelsy of the North of Scotland," collected by
Peter Buchan.

THERE was a bridal in this town,
And till't the lasses a' were boun',
Wi' mauky facings on their gown,
  And some o' them had breast-knots.
    O the bonny, O the bonny,
      Bonny, bonny, breast-knots!
    Tight an' bonny were they a',
      When they had on their breast-knots.

At eight o' clock the lads convene,
Some clad in blue and some in green,
Wi' shining buckles on their sheen,
  And flowers upon their waistcoats.
                  O the bonny, &c.

And there were mony lusty lad,
That ever handled graip or gaud,
I wot their manhood well they show'd
  At rifling o' their breast-knots.
                  O the bonny, &c.

The wives came ben wi' a great fraise,
An' wish'd the lassie happy days,
An' muckle thought they o' her claise,
  Especially her breast-knots.
                  O the bonny, &c.

The bride was drest in claes fu' braw
Frae head to feet without a flaw,
An' something mair she had to shaw,
  I maist forgot the breast-knots.
                O the bonny, &c.

In came her brither wi' a stend,
An' sware that he had seen the send,
Then cock'd his pistol to the bend,
  The fire, I wat, he mist not.
                O the bonny, &c.

Out spake her mither when she saw
The bride an' maidens a' sae braw,
 Wi' giggling clouts, black be your fa',
  Ye've made a bonny feast o't.
                O the bonny, &c.

Her mither took her by the cluck,
An' led her three times roun' the cruck,
Syne said: Gudewife, well mat ye bruik,
  While some great count their kiest not.
                O the bonny, &c.

The bridal breakfast down was set,
Some buirly kippards o' milk meat;
It scalded them, it was sae het,
  As soon as they did taste o't.
                O the bonny, &c.

The bree was het, did scauld their mou',
An' some into their cutties blew,
While some frae them their speens they threw,
  But yet their will they miss'd not.
                O the bonny, &c.

When ilka ane had claw'd their plate,
The piper lad he lookèd blate,
The folks a' said that he should ate,
  But he had lost the best o't.
                O the bonny, &c.

Ower stools and dales the chiels did loup,
An' a' the chains they gar'd them coup;
The piper said, Wi' them, deil scoup,
   He'd made a hungry feast o't.
            O the bonny, &c.

Out they gat then wi' a fling,
Ilk lass into her lad did hing,
Ilk o' them chose a different spring,
   The bride she chose the breast-knots.
            O the bonny, &c.

Some sat on dales, an' some on planks,
And some they sat on heads o' banks,
The piper lad stood on his shanks,
   And birled up the breast-knots.
            O the bonny, &c.

MY HEART'S IN THE HIGHLANDS.

Burns. Air—"Portmore."

My heart's in the Highlands, my heart is not here;
My heart's in the Highlands a chasing the deer;
Chasing the wild deer, and following the roe;
My heart's in the Highlands, wherever I go.
Farewell to the Highlands, farewell to the north,
The birthplace of valour, the country of worth;
Wherever I wander, wherever I rove,
The hills of the Highlands for ever I love.

Farewell to the mountains high cover'd with snow;
Farewell to the straths and green valleys below;
Farewell to the forest and wild hanging woods;
Farewell to the torrents and loud-pouring floods.
My heart's in the Highlands, my heart is not here;
My heart's in the Highlands a chasing the deer;
Chasing the wild deer, and following the roe;
My heart's in the Highlands wherever I go.

PORTMORE.

Air—" Portmore."

O Donaldie, Donaldie, where hae ye been ?
A hawking and hunting, go make my bed seen ;
Gae make my bed seen and stir up the strae ;
My heart's in the Highlands wherever I gae.

Let's drink and gae hame, boys, let's drink and gae hame,
If we stay any langer we'll get a bad name ;
We'll get a bad name and fill ourselves fou,
And the lang woods o' Derry are ill to gae through.

My heart's in the Highlands, my heart is not here ;
My heart's in the Highlands a hunting the deer ;
A chasing the wild deer, and catching the roe ;
My heart's in the Highlands wherever I go.

O bonny Portmore, ye shine where you charm,
The more I think of you, the more my heart's warm ;
When I look from you, my heart it is sore,
When I mind upon Valiantny and on Portmore.

There are mony words, but few o' the best,
And he that speaks fewest lives langest at rest ;
My mind by experience teaches me so,—
My heart's in the Highlands wherever I go.

" Donald Cameron," says Peter Buchan, in his " Ancient Ballads and Songs of
the North of Scotland," 1828, vol. ii., " was the author of this very beautiful and very
old song. It is well known to most poetical readers with how little success Burns en-
deavoured to graft upon this stock a twig of his own rearing. Even Mr. Cunningham,
in his ' Songs of Scotland,' admits the fact, and regrets that he could give no more
than the first four lines of the original. The whole is now, for the first time, given
complete from the recitation of a very old person." This song does not merit the
praise Mr. Buchan gives it, and appears to be a heterogeneous jumble of lines from
various songs and ballads previously current. Burns's song, though not one of his
best, is certainly an emendation of " Portmore," and is at all events consistent with
itself.

THE BONNIE HOUSE O' AIRLY.

Air—"The house of Airly."

It fell on a day, and a bonnie summer day,
　When the corn grew green and rarely,
That there fell out a great dispute
　Between Argyle and Airly.

The Duke o' Montrose has written to Argyle
　To come in the morning early,
An' lead in his men, by the back of Dunkeld,
　To plunder the bonnie house o' Airly.

The lady look'd o'er her window sae hie,
　And, oh, but she look'd weary;
And there she espied the great Argyle
　Come to plunder the bonnie house o' Airly.

" Come down, come down, Lady Margaret," he says,
　" Come down and kiss me fairly,
Or before the morning clear daylight,
　I'll no leave a standing stane in Airly."

" I wadna kiss thee, great Argyle,
　I wadna kiss thee fairly ;
I wadna kiss thee, great Argyle,
　Gin you shouldna leave a standing stane in Airly."

He has ta'en her by the middle sae sma',
　Says, " Lady, where is your drury ?"
" It's up and down the bonnie burn-side,
　Amang the planting of Airly."

They sought it up, they sought it down,
　They sought it late and early,
And found it in the bonnie balm-tree
　That shines on the bowling-green o' Airly.

He has ta'en her by the left shoulder,
　And, oh, but she grat sairly,
And led her down to yon green bank
　Till he plunder'd the bonnie house o' Airly.

"Oh, it's I hae seven braw sons," she says,
  "And the youngest ne'er saw his daddie;
And although I had as mony mae,
  I wad gie them a' to Charlie.

But gin my good lord had been at hame,
  As this night he is wi' Charlie,
There durst na a Campbell in a' the west
  Hae plunder'd the bonnie house o' Airly."

This song was recovered from oral tradition, and first printed towards the close of
the last century. It narrates an episode of the civil wars of the Covenant, and the
destruction of the castle of Airly, in Forfarshire, the seat of the Ogilvies, Earls of
Airly, by the Earl of Argyle.

BANNOCKS O' BARLEY.

From "Johnson's Musical Museum."

BANNOCKS o' bear-meal, bannocks o' barley,
Here's to the Highlandman's bannocks o' barley!
Wha in a brulyie will first cry a parley?
Never the lads wi' the bannocks o' barley!
  Bannocks o' bear-meal, bannocks o' barley,
  Here's to the Highlandman's bannocks o' barley!

Wha in his wae days were loyal to Charlie?
Wha but the lads wi' the bannocks o' barley?
  Bannocks o' bear-meal, bannocks o' barley,
  Here's to the Highlandman's bannocks o' barley!

QUEEN MARY'S LAMENT.

BURNS.

Now Nature hangs her mantle green
  On ilka blooming tree,
And spreads her sheets o' daisies white
  Out ower the grassy lea.

Now Phœbus cheers the crystal streams,
  And glads the azure skies,
But nocht can glad the weary wicht
  That fast in durance lies.

Now blooms the lily by the bank,
  The primrose doun the brae;
The hawthorn's budding in the glen,
  And milk-white is the slae.

Now laverocks wake the merry morn
  Aloft on dewy wing,
The merle in his noontide bower
  Makes woodland echoes ring.

The mavis mild, wi' mony a note,
  Sings drowsy day to rest;
In love and freedom they rejoice,
  Wi' care nor thrall oppress'd.

The meanest hind in fair Scotland
  May rove these sweets amang;
But I, the queen o' a' Scotland,
  Maun lie in prison strang.

I was the queen o' bonnie France,
  Where happy I hae been;
Fu' lightly rase I in the morn,
  As blythe lay down at e'en.

And I'm the sovereign of Scotland,
  And mony a traitor there;
Yet here I lie in foreign bands
  And never-ending care.

But as for thee, thou false woman,
  My sister and my fae,
Grim vengeance yet shall whet a sword
  That through thy soul shall gae.

The weeping blood in woman's breast
  Was never known to thee,
Nor the balm that draps on wounds of woe
  From woman's pitying ee.

My son, my son, may kinder stars
  Upon thy fortune shine;
And may those pleasures gild thy reign
  That ne'er would blink on mine!

U

God keep thee frae thy mother's faes,
  Or turn their hearts to thee;
And where thou meet'st thy mother's friend,
  Remember him for me.

Oh, soon to me may summer sun
  Nae mair licht up the morn;
Nae mair to me the autumn winds
  Wave o'er the yellow corn!

And in the narrow house o' death
  Let winter round me rave,
And the next flowers that deck the spring
  Bloom on my peaceful grave.

LORD GREGORY.

Burns.

Oh, mirk, mirk is this midnight hour,
  And loud the tempest's roar!
A waefu' wanderer seeks thy tow'r,—
  Lord Gregory, ope thy door.

An exile frae her father's ha',
  And a' for loving thee;
At least some pity on me shaw,
  If love it mayna be.

Lord Gregory, mind'st thou not the grove,
  By bonnie Irwine side,
Where first I own'd that virgin-love
  I lang, lang had denied?

How aften didst thou pledge and vow
  Thou wad for aye be mine!
And my fond heart, itsel' sae true,
  It ne'er mistrusted thine.

Hard is thy heart, Lord Gregory,
  And flinty is thy breast:
Thou-dart of heaven that flashest by,
  Oh, wilt thou give me rest!

Ye mustering thunders from above,
  Your willing victim see ;
But spare and pardon my fause love
  His wrangs to heaven and me!

--------♦--------

BESSY AND HER SPINNING-WHEEL.

BURNS.   Air—" The bottom of the punch-bowl."

Oh, leeze me on my spinning-wheel!
Oh, leeze me on my rock and reel!
Frae tap to tae that cleeds me bien,
And haps me fiel and warm at e'en.
I'll set me down and sing and spin,
While laigh descends the simmer sun,
Blest wi' content and milk and meal—
Oh, leeze me on my spinning-wheel!

On ilka hand the burnies trot,
And meet below my theekit cot ;
The scented birk and hawthorn white
Across the pool their arms unite,
Alike to screen the birdie's nest
And little fishes' caller rest ;
The sun blinks kindly in the biel'
Where blythe I turn my spinning-wheel.

On lofty aiks the cushats wail,
And echo cons the doolfu' tale ;
The lintwhites in the hazel braes,
Delighted, rival ither's lays ;
The craik amang the claver hay,
The paitrick whirrin o'er the ley,
The swallow jinkin round my shiel,
Amuse me at my spinning-wheel.

Wi' sma' to sell, and less to buy,
Aboon distress, below envy,—
Oh, wha wad leave this humble state
For a' the pride of a' the great ?
Amid their flaring idle toys,
Amid their cumbrous dinsome joys,
Can they the peace and pleasure feel
Of Bessy at her spinning-wheel ?

CRADLE SONG.

RICHARD GALL.

BALOO, baloo, my wee wee thing,
    Oh, saftly close thy blinkin' ee!
Baloo, baloo, my wee wee thing,
    For thou art doubly dear to me.
Thy daddie now is far awa',
    A sailor laddie o'er the sea ;
But Hope aye hechts his safe return
    To you, my bonnie lamb, an' me.

Baloo, baloo, my wee wee thing,
  Oh, saftly close thy blinkin' ee!
Baloo, baloo, my wee wee thing,
  For thou art doubly dear to me.
Thy face is simple, sweet, an' mild,
  Like ony simmer e'ening fa';
Thy sparkling ee is bonnie black,
  Thy neck is like the mountain snaw.

Baloo, baloo, my wee wee thing,
  Oh, saftly close thy blinkin' ee!
Baloo, baloo, my wee wee thing,
  For thou art doubly dear to me.
Oh, but thy daddie's absence lang
  Might break my dowie heart in twa,
Wert thou na left a dawtit pledge,
  To steal the eerie hours awa'.

THE AULD MAN.

BURNS.

BUT lately seen in gladsome green,
  The woods rejoiced the day,
Through gentle showers the laughing flowers
  In double pride were gay;
But now our joys are fled
  On winter-blasts awa';
Yet maiden May, in rich array,
  Again shall bring them a'.

But my white pow nae kindly thowe
  Shall melt the snaws of age;
My trunk of eild, but buss or beild,
  Sinks in time's wintry rage.
Oh, age has weary days,
  And nights o' sleepless pain!
Thou golden time o' youthful prime,
  Why com'st thou not again?

THE LARK.

JAMES HOGG.

BIRD of the wilderness,
Blythesome and cumberless,
Sweet be thy matin o'er moorland and lea;
Emblem of happiness,
Bless'd is thy dwelling-place:
Oh, to abide in the desert with thee!

Wild is thy lay and loud,
Far in the downy cloud;
Loves gives it energy, love gave it birth!
Where on the dewy wing,
Where art thou journeying?
Thy lay is in heaven, thy love is on earth.

O'er fell and mountain sheen,
O'er moor and mountain green,
O'er the red streamer that heralds the day
Over the cloudlet dim,
Over the rainbow's rim,
Musical cherub, hie, hie thee away!

Then when the gloaming comes,
Low in the heather blooms,
Sweet will thy welcome and bed of love be;
Bird of the wilderness,
Bless'd is thy dwelling-place:
Oh, to abide in the desert with thee!

HAP AND ROW.

WILLIAM CREECH, born 1745, died 1815.

WE'LL hap and row, we'll hap and row,
We'll hap and row the feetie o't;
It is a wee bit weary thing:
I downa bide the greetie o't.

And we pat on the wee bit pan,
To boil the lick o' meatie o't;
A cinder fell and spoil'd the plan,
And burnt a' the feetie o't.

Fu' sair it grat, the puir wee brat,
And aye it kick'd the feetie o't,
Till, puir wee elf, it tired itself,
And then began the sleepie o't.

The skirling brat nae parritch gat,
When it gaed to the sleepie o't;
It's waesome true, instead o' 'ts mou',
They're round about the feetie o't.

THE MACGREGOR'S GATHERING.

SIR WALTER SCOTT. Written for "Albyn's Anthology," 1816.
Air—"Thain a' Grigalach."

THE moon's on the lake, and the mist's on the brae,
And the clan has a name that is nameless by day:
Then gather, gather, gather, Grigalach! &c.

Our signal for fight, which from monarchs we drew,
Must be heard but by night in our vengeful halloo:
  Then halloo, halloo, halloo, Grigalach!

Glenorchy's proud mountains, Coalchuirn and her towers,
Glenstrae, and Glenlyon, no longer are ours:
  We're landless, landless, landless, Grigalach!

But, doom'd and devoted by vassal and lord,
Macgregor has still both his heart and his sword:
  Then courage, courage, courage, Grigalach!

If they rob us of name, and pursue us with beagles,
Give their roof to the flames and their flesh to the eagles:
  Then vengeance, vengeance, vengeance, Grigalach!

While there's leaves on the forest, or foam on the river,
Macgregor, despite them, shall flourish for ever:
  Then gather, gather, gather, Grigalach!

Through the depths of Loch Katrine the steed shall career
O'er the peak of Ben Lomond the galley shall steer;
And the rocks of Craig Royston like icicles melt,
Ere our wrongs be forgot, or our vengeance unfelt:
  Then gather, gather, gather, Grigalach!

DONALD CAIRD'S COME AGAIN!

Sir Walter Scott.   From "Albyn's Anthology."
Air—"Malcolm Caird's come again."

Donald Caird's come again!
Donald Caird's come again!
Tell the news in brugh and glen,
Donald Caird's come again!

Donald Caird can lilt and sing,
Blythely dance the Highland fling;
Drink till the gudeman be blind,
Fleech till the gudewife be kind;
Hoop a leglan, clout a pan,
Or crack a pow wi' ony man:
Tell the news in brugh and glen,
Donald Caird's come again!

Donald Caird can wire a maukin,
Kens the wiles o' dun-deer staukin;
Leisters kipper, makes a shift
To shoot a muir-fowl i' the drift;
Water-bailiffs, rangers, keepers,
He can wauk when they are sleepers;
Not for bountith or reward
Daur they mell wi' Donald Caird.

Donald Caird can drink a gill
Fast as hostler-wife can fill;
Ilka ane that sells gude liquor
Kens how Donald bends a bicker.
When he's fou he's stout and saucy,
Keeps the cantle o' the causey;
Highland chief and Lawland laird
Maun gie way to Donald Caird.

Steek the awmrie, lock the kist,
Else some gear will sune be mist;
Donald Caird finds orra things
Where Allan Gregor fand the tings:
Dunts o' kebbuck, taits o' woo,
Whiles a hen and whiles a soo;
Webs or duds frae hedge or yard:
Ware the wuddie, Donald Caird!

On Donald Caird the doom was stern,
Craig to tether, legs to airn;
But Donald Caird, wi' muckle study,
Caught the gift to cheat the wuddie.
Rings o' airn and bolts o' steel
Fell like ice frae hand and heel:
Watch the sheep in fauld and glen,
Donald Caird's come again!

ALLEN-A-DALE.

Sir Walter Scott.　From "Rokeby."

Allen-a-Dale has no fagot for burning,
Allen-a-Dale has no furrow for turning,
Allen-a-Dale has no fleece for the spinning,
Yet Allen-a-Dale has red gold for the winning:
Come read me my riddle, come hearken my tale,
And tell me the craft of bold Allen-a-Dale.

The baron of Ravensworth prances in pride,
And he views his domains upon Arkindale side,
The mere for his net and the lamb for his game,
The chase for the wild and the park for the tame;
Yet the fish of the lake and the deer of the vale
Are less free to Lord Dacre than Allen-a-Dale.

Allen-a-Dale was ne'er belted a knight,
Though his spur be as sharp and his blade be as bright;
Allen-a-Dale is no baron or lord,
Yet twenty tall yeomen will draw at his word;
And the best of our nobles his bonnet will veil,
Who at Rerecross on Stanmore meets Allen-a-Dale.

Allen-a-Dale to his wooing is come,
The mother she ask'd of his household and home:
"Though the castle of Richmond stands fair on the hill,
My hall," quoth bold Allen, "shows gallanter still;
'Tis the blue vault of heaven, with its crescent so pale,
And with all its bright spangles!" said Allen-a-Dale.

The father was steel, and the mother was stone,
They lifted the latch and bade him be gone;
But loud on the morrow their wail and their cry—
He had laugh'd on the lass with his bonnie black eye;
And she fled to the forest to hear a love-tale,
And the youth it was told by was Allen-a-Dale.

ON THE DEATH OF BURNS.

RICHARD GALL.

THERE's waefu' news in yon town
   As e'er the warld heard ava ;
There's dolefu' news in yon town,
   For Robbie's gane and left them a'.

How blythe it was to see his face
   Come keeking by the hallan wa' ;
He ne'er was sweir to say the grace,
   'But now he's gane and left them a'.

He was the lad wha made them glad,
   Whanever he the reed did blaw :
The lasses there may drap a tear,
   Their funny friend is now awa'.

Nae daffin now in yon town ;
   The browster-wife gets leave to draw
An' drink hersel', in yon town,
   , Sin' Robbie gaed and left them a'.

The lawin's canny counted now,
   The bell that tinkled ne'er will draw ;
The king will never get his due,
   Sin' Robbie gaed and left them a'.

The squads o' chiels that lo'ed a splore
   On winter evenings never ca' ;
Their blythesome moments a' are o'er,
   Sin' Robbie's gane and left them a'.

Frae a' the een in yon town
   I see the tears o' sorrow fa' ;
An' weel they may ; in yon town
   Nae canty sang they hear ava.

Their e'ening sky begins to lour,
   The murky clouds thegither draw ;
'Twas but a blink afore a shower,
   Ere Robbie gaed and left them a'.

The landwart hizzy winna speak;
  Ye'll see her sitting like a craw
Amang the reek, while rattons squeak—
  Her dawtit bard is now awa'.

But could I lay my hand upon
  His whistle, keenly wad I blaw,
An' screw about the auld drone,
  An' lilt a lightsome spring or twa.

If it were sweetest aye when wat,
  Then wad I ripe my pouch, an' draw,
An' steep it weel amang the maut,
  As lang's I'd saxpence at my ca'.

For warld's gear I dinna care,
  My stock o' that is unco' sma':
Come, friend, we'll pree the barley-bree
  To his braid fame that's now awa'.

INDEX OF THE FIRST LINES.

GLOSSARY.

A', all.
Aback, away, aloof.
Abeigh, at a shy distance.
Aboon, above, up.
Abread, abroad, in sight.
Abreed, in breadth.
Ae, one.
Aff, off; *aff loof*, unpremeditated.
Afore, before.
Aft, oft.
Aften, often.
Agley, off the right line, wrong.
Aiblins, perhaps.
Ain, own.
Airl-penny, earnest-money.
Airn, iron.
Aith, an oath.
Aits, oats.
Aiver, an old horse.
Aizle, a hot cinder.
Alake, alas!
Alane, alone.
Akwart, awkward.
Amaist, almost.
Amang, among.
An', and, if.
Ance, once.
Ane, one.
Anent, over against.
Anither, another.
Ase, ashes.
Asklent, asquint, aslant.
Asteer, abroad, stirring.
Athort, athwart.
Aught, possession; as in *a' my aught*, in all my possession.
Auld lang syne, older time, days of other years.
Auld, old.
Auldfarran, or *auld farrant*, sagacious, cunning, prudent.
Ava, at all.
Awa', away.
Awfu', awful.
Awn, the beard of barley, oats, &c.
Awnie, bearded.
Ayont, beyond.

Ba', ball.
Backets, ash-boards.
Backlins, coming back, returning.
Bad, did bid.
Baide, endured, did stay.
Baggie, the belly.
Bainie, having large bones, stout.
Bairn, a child.
Bairntime, a family of children, a brood.
Baith, both.
Ban, to swear.
Bane, bone.
Bang, to beat, to strive.
Bannock, a kind of thick cake of bread, a small jannack, or loaf made of oatmeal.
Bardie, diminutive of bard.
Barefit, barefooted.
Barmie, of or like barm.
Batch, a crew, a gang.
Batts, botts.
Baudrons, a cat.
Bauld, bold.
Bawk, bank.
Baws'nt, having a white stripe down the face.
Be, to let be, to give over, to cease.
Bear, barley.
Beastie, dimin. of beast.
Beet, to add fuel to fire.
Beld, bald.
Belyve, by and by.
Ben, into the spence or parlour.
Ben Lomond, a noted mountain in Dumbartonshire.
Bethankit, grace after meat.
Beuk, a book.
Bicker, a kind of wooden dish, a short race.
Bie or *bield*, shelter.
Bien, wealthy, plentiful.
Big, to build.
Biggin, building, a house.
Biggit, built.
Bill, a bull.
Billie, a brother, a young fellow.
Bing, a heap of grain, potatoes, &c.

Birk, birch.
Birken-shaw, *Birchen-wood-shaw*, a small wood.
Birkie, a clever fellow.
Birring, the noise of partridges, &c. when they spring.
Bit, crisis, nick of time.
Bizz, a bustle, to buzz.
Blastie, a shrivelled dwarf, a term of contempt.
Blastit, blasted.
Blate, bashful, sheepish.
Blather, bladder.
Blaud, a flat piece of anything, to slap.
Blaw, to blow, to boast.
Bleerit, bleared, sore with rheum.
Bleert and blin, bleared and blind.
Bleezing, blazing.
Blellum, idle talking fellow.
Blether, to talk idly, nonsense.
Bleth'rin, talking idly.
Blink, a little while, a smiling look, to look kindly, to shine by fits.
Blinker, a term of contempt.
Blinkin, smirking.
Blue-gown, one of those beggars who get annually, on the king's birth-day, a blue cloak or gown, with a badge.
Bluid, blood.
Bluntie, snivelling.
Blype, a shred, a large piece.
Bock, to vomit, to gush intermittently.
Bocked, gushed, vomited.
Bodle, a small gold coin.
Bogles, spirits, hobgoblins.
Bonnie or *bonny*, handsome, beautiful.
Boord, a board.
Boortree, the shrub elder; planted much of old in hedges of barn-yards, &c.
Boost, behoved, must needs.
Bore, a hole in the wall.
Botch, an angry tumour.
Bouk, vomiting, gushing out.
Bousing, drinking.
Bow-kail, cabbage.
Bowt, bended, crooked.
Brachens, fern.
Brae, a declivity, a precipice, the slope of a hill.
Braid, broad.
Bragin't, reeled forward.
Braik, a kind of harrow.
Brainge, to run rashly forward.
Brake, broke, made insolvent.
Branks, a kind of wooden curb for horses.
Brash, a sudden illness.
Brats, coarse clothes, rags, &c.
Brattle, a short race, hurry, fury.
Braw, fine, handsome.
Brawlyt or *brawlie*, very well, finely, heartily.
Braxie, a morbid sheep.
Breastie, diminutive of breast.
Breastit, did spring up or forward.
Breckan, fern.
Breef, an invulnerable or irresistible spell.
Breeks, breeches.

Brent, smooth.
Brewin, brewing.
Brie, juice, liquid.
Brig, a bridge.
Brunstane, brimstone.
Brither, a brother.
Brock, a badger.
Brogue, a hum, a trick.
Broo, broth, liquid, water.
Brose, broth; a race at country weddings, who shall first reach the bridegroom's house on returning from church.
Brugh, a burgh.
Bruilzie, a broil, a combustion.
Brunt, did burn, burnt.
Brust, burst.
Buckskin, an inhabitant of Virginia.
Bught, a pen.
Bughtin-time, the time of collecting the sheep in the pens to be milked.
Buirdly, stout-made, broad-made.
Bum-clock, a humming beetle that flies in the summer evenings.
Bumming, humming as bees.
Bummle, to blunder.
Bummler, a blunderer.
Bunker, a window-seat.
Burdies, diminutive of birds.
Bure, did bare.
Burn, water, a rivulet.
Burnewin, i.e. *burn the wind*, a blacksmith.
Burnie, dimin. of burn.
Bushie, bushy.
Buskit, dressed.
Busks, dresses.
Bussle, a bustle, to bustle.
Buss, shelter.
But, bot, with.
But an' ben, the country kitchen and parlour.
By himself, lunatic, distracted.
Byke, a bee-hive.
Byre, a cow-stable, a sheep-pen.

Ca', to call, to name, to drive.
Ca't or *ca'd*, called, driven, calved.
Cadger, a carrier.
Cadie or *caddie*, a person, a young fellow.
Caff, chaff.
Caird, a tinker.
Cairn, a loose heap of stones.
Calf-ward, a small enclosure for calves.
Callan, a boy.
Caller, fresh, sound, refreshing.
Canie or *cannie*, gentle, mild, dexterous.
Cannilie, dexterously, gently.
Cantie or *canty*, cheerful, merry.
Cantraip, a charm, a spell.
Cap-stane, cope-stone, key-stone.
Carl, an old man.
Carlin, a stout old woman.
Cartes, cards.
Caudron, a caldron.
Cauk and keel, chalk and red clay.
Cauld, cold.
Caup, a wooden drinking vessel.

Cesses, taxes.
Chanter, a part of a bagpipe.
Chap, a person, a fellow, a blow.
Chaup, a stroke, a blow.
Cheekit, cheeked.
Cheep, a chirp, to chirp.
Chiel or *cheel*, a young fellow.
Chimla or *chimlie*, a fire-grate, a fire-place.
Chimla-lug, the fire-side.
Chittering, shivering, trembling.
Chockin, choking.
Chow, to chew; *cheek for chow*, side by side.
Chuffie, fat-faced.
Clachan, a small village about a church, a hamlet.
Claise or *claes*, clothes.
Claith, cloth.
Claithing, clothing.
Claivers, nonsense, not speaking sense.
Clap, clapper of a mill.
Clarkit, wrote.
Clash, an idle tale; the story of the day.
Clatter, to tell idle stories; an idle story.
Claught, snatched at, laid hold of.
Claut, to clean, to scrape.
Clauted, scraped.
Clavers, idle stories.
Claw, to scratch.
Cleed, to clothe.
Cleeds, clothes.
Cleekit, having caught.
Clinkin, jerking, clinking.
Clinkumbell, who rings the church-bell.
Clips, sheers.
Clishmaclaver, idle conversation.
Clock, to hatch; a beetle.
Clockin, hatching.
Cloot, the hoof of a cow, sheep, &c.
Clootie, an old name for the devil.
Clour, a bump or swelling after a blow.
Cluds, clouds.
Coaxin, wheedling.
Coble, a fishing-boat.
Cockernony, a lock of hair tied upon a girl's head; a cap.
Coft, bought.
Cog, a wooden dish.
Coggie, dimin. of cog.
Coila, from *Kyle*, a district of Ayrshire; so called, saith tradition, from Coil, or Coilus, a Pictish monarch.
Collie, a general, and sometimes a particular, name for country curs.
Collieshangie, quarrelling.
Commaun, command.
Cood, the cud.
Coof, a blockhead, a ninny.
Cookit, appeared and disappeared by fits.
Coost, did cast.
Coot, the ancle or foot.
Cootie, a wooden kitchen dish; *also those fowls whose legs are clad with feathers are said to be cootie.*
Corbies, a species of the crow.
Core, corps, party, clan.
Corn't, fed with oats.

Cotter, the inhabitant of a *cothouse*, or cottage.
Couthie, kind, loving.
Cove, a cove.
Cowe, to terrify, to keep under, to lop; a fright, a branch of furze, broom, &c.
Cowp, to barter, to tumble over; a gang.
Cowpit, tumbled.
Cowrin, cowering.
Cowte, a colt.
Cozie, snug.
Cozily, snugly.
Crabbit, crabbed, fretful.
Crack, conversation, to converse.
Crackin, conversing.
Craft or *craft*, a field near a house (in *old husbandry*).
Craiks, cries or calls incessantly: a bird.
Crambo clink or *crambo jingle*, rhymes, doggrel verses.
Crank, the noise of an ungreased wheel.
Crankous, fretful, captious.
Cranreuch, the hoar-frost.
Crap, a crop, to crop.
Craw, a crow of a cock, a rook.
Creel, a basket; *to have one's wits in a creel*, to be craz'd, to be fascinated.
Creeshie, greasy.
Croud or *croud*, to coo as a dove.
Croon, a hollow and continued moan; to make a noise like the continued roar of a bull, to hum a tune.
Crooning, humming.
Crouchie, crook-backed.
Crouse, cheerful, courageous.
Crousely, cheerfully, courageously.
Crowdie, a composition of oatmeal and boiled water, sometimes from the broth of beef, mutton, &c.
Crowdie-time, breakfast-time.
Crowlin, crawling.
Crummock, a cow with crooked horns.
Crump, hard and brittle; *spoken of bread*.
Crunt, a blow on the head with a cudgel.
Cuif, a blockhead, a ninny.
Cummock, a short staff with a crooked head.
Curchie, a courtsey.
Curler, a player at a game on the ice, practised in Scotland, called *curling*.
Curlie, curled, whose hair falls naturally in ringlets.
Curling, a well-known game on the ice.
Curmurring, murmuring, a slight rumbling noise.
Curpin, the crupper.
Cushat, the dove or wood-pigeon.
Cutty, short, a spoon broken in the middle.

Daddie, a father.
Daffin, merriment, foolishness.
Daft, merry, giddy, foolish.
Daimen, rare, now and then; *daimen-icker*, an ear of corn now and then.
Dainty, pleasant, good-humoured, agreeable.
Dales, plains, valleys.

Darklins, darklin.
Daud, to thrash, to abuse.
Daur, to dare.
Daur't, dared.
Daurg or *daurk*, a day's labour.
Davock, David.
Dawd, a large piece.
Dawtit or *dawtet*, fondled, caressed.
Dearies, dimin. of tears.
Dearthfu', dear.
Deave, to deafen.
Deil-ma-care! no matter for all that.
Deleerit, delirious.
Descrive, to describe.
Dight, to wipe, to clean corn from chaff.
Dight, cleaned from chaff.
Dights, cleans.
Ding, to worst, to push.
Dinna, do not.
Dirl, a slight tremulous stroke or pain.
Dizzen or *diz'n*, a dozen.
Doited, stupified, hebetated.
Dolt, stupified, crazied.
Donsie, unlucky.
Dool, sorrow; *to sing dool*, to lament, to mourn.
Doos, doves.
Dorty, saucy, nice.
Douce or *douse*, sober, wise, prudent.
Doucely, soberly, prudently.
Dought, was or were able.
Doup-skelper, one that strikes the tail.
Doure and din, sullen, sallow.
Doure, stout, durable, sullen, stubborn.
Dow, am or are able, can.
Doucff, pithless, wanting force.
Dowie, worn with grief, fatigue, &c.; half asleep.
Downa, am or are not able, cannot.
Doylt, stupid.
Drap, a drop, to drop.
Drapping, dropping.
Dreep, to ooze, to drop.
Dreigh, tedious, long about it.
Dribble, drizzling, slaver.
Drift, a drove.
Droddum, the breach.
Drone, part of a bagpipe.
Droop, *rumpl't*, that droops at the crupper.
Droukit, wet.
Drounting, drawling.
Drouth, thirst, drought.
Drucken, drunken.
Drumly, muddy.
Drummock, meal and water mixed; raw.
Drunt, pet, sour humour.
Dub, a small pond.
Duds, rags, clothes.
Duddie, ragged.
Dung, worsted; pushed, driven.
Dunted, beaten, boxed.
Dush, to push as a ram, &c.
Dusht, pushed by a ram, ox, &c.

Ee, the eye.
Een, the eyes.
E'enin, evening.
Eerie, frightened, dreading spirits.

Eild, old age.
Elbuck, the elbow.
Eldritch, ghastly, frightful.
En', end.
Enbrugh, Edinburgh.
Eneugh, enough.
Especial, especially.
Ettle, to try, attempt.
Eydent, diligent.

Fa', fall, lot; to fall.
Fa's, does fall; waterfalls.
Faddom't, fathomed.
Fae, a foe.
Faem, foam.
Faiket, unknown.
Fairin, a fairing, a present.
Fallow, fellow.
Faud, did find.
Farl, a cake of bread.
Fash, trouble, care; to trouble, to care for.
Fasht, troubled.
Fasteren-een, Fasten's even.
Fauld, a fold, to fold.
Faulding, folding.
Faut, fault.
Fawsont, decent, seemly.
Feal, a field, smooth.
Feartu', frightful.
Fear't, frightened.
Feat, neat, spruce.
Fecht, to fight.
Fechtin, fighting.
Feck, many, plenty.
Fecket, waistcoat.
Feckfu', large, brawny, stout.
Feckless, puny, weak, silly.
Feckly, weakly.
Feg, a fig.
Fride, feud, enmity.
Feil, keen, biting; the flesh immediately under the skin; a field pretty level, on the side or top of a hill.
Fen, mud, filth.
Fend, to live comfortably.
Ferlie or *ferley*, to wonder; a wonder, a term of contempt.
Fetch, to pull by fits.
Fetch't, pulled intermittently.
Fidge, to fidget.
Fiel, soft, smooth.
Fient, fiend, a petty oath.
Fier, sound, healthy; a brother, a friend.
Fisle, to make a rustling noise; a fidget, a bustle.
Fit, a foot.
Fittie-lan, the nearer horse of the hindmost pair in the plough.
Flainen, flannel.
Fleech, to supplicate in a flattering manner.
Fleech'd, supplicated.
Fleechin, supplicating.
Fleesh, a fleece.
Fleg, a kick, a random blow.
Flether, to decoy by fair words.
Fletherin, flattering.
Fley, to scare, to frighten.

Flichter, to flutter as young nestlings when their dam approaches.
Flickering, to meet, to encounter with.
Flinders, shreds, broken pieces.
Flingin-tree, a piece of timber hung by way of partition between two horses In a stable, a flail.
Flisk, to fret at the yoke.
Fliskit, fretted.
Flitter, to vibrate like the wings of small birds.
Flittering, fluttering, vibrating.
Flunkie, a servant in livery.
Foord, a ford.
Forbears, forefathers.
Forbye, besides.
Forfairn, distressed, worn out, jaded.
Forfoughten, fatigued.
Forgather, to meet, to encounter with.
Forgie, to forgive.
Forjesket, jaded with fatigue.
Fother, fodder.
Fou, full, drunk.
Foughten, troubled, harassed.
Fouth, plenty, enough, or more than enough.
Fow, a bushel, &c.; also a pitchfork.
Frae, from.
Freath, froth.
Frien', friend.
Fu', full.
Fud, the scut, or tail of the hare, cony, &c.
Fuff, to blow intermittently.
Fufft, did blow.
Fur, a furrow.
Furm, a form, bench.
Fyke, trifling cares; to piddle; to be in a fuss about trifles.
Fyle, to soil, to dirty.
Fyl't, soiled, dirtied.

Gab, the mouth; to speak boldly or pertly.
Gaberlunzie, a pedlar.
Gadsman, a ploughboy, the boy that rides the horses in the plough.
Gae, to go; *gaed*, went; *gaen*, gone; *gaun*, going.
Gaet or *gate*, way, manner, road.
Gang, to go, to walk.
Gar, to make, to force to.
Gar't, forced to.
Garten, a garter.
Gash, wise, sagacious, talkative; to converse.
Gashin, conversing.
Gaucy, jolly, large.
Gawky, half-witted, foolish, romping.
Gear, riches, goods of any kind.
Geck, to toss the head in wantonness or scorn.
Ged, a pike.
Gentles, great folks.
Geordie, a guinea.
Get, a child, a young one.
Ghaist, a ghost.
Gie, to give; *gied*, gave; *gien*, given.
Giftie, dimin. of gift.

Giglets, playful girls.
Gillie, a boy, servant.
Gilpey, a half-grown, half-informed boy or girl; a romping lad, a hoyden.
Gimmer, an ewe from one to two years old.
Gin, if, against.
Gipsey, a young girl.
Girn, to grin, to twist the features in rage.
Girning, grinning.
Gizz, a periwig.
Glaikit, inattentive, foolish.
Glaive, a sword.
Glaizie, glittering, smooth like glass.
Glaund, aimed, snatched.
Gleck, sharp, ready.
Gled, a hawk.
Gleg, sharp, ready.
Gleib, glebe.
Gley, a squint, to squint; *agley*, off at a side, wrong.
Glib-gabbet, that speaks smoothly and readily.
Glint, to peep.
Glinted, peeped.
Glintin, peeping.
Gloamin, the twilight.
Glowr, to stare, to look; a stare, a look.
Glowr'd, looked, stared.
Gowan, the flower of the daisy, dandelion, hawk-weed, &c.
Gowany; *gowany-glens*, daisied dales.
Gowd, gold.
Gowff, the game of golf; to strike as the bat does the ball at golf.
Gowff'd, struck.
Gowk, a cuckoo, a term of contempt.
Grane or *grain*, a groan, to groan.
Gowl, to howl.
Grain'd and gaunted, groaned and grunted.
Graining, groaning.
Graip, a pronged instrument for cleaning stables.
Graith, accoutrements, furniture, dress, gear.
Grannie, grandmother.
Grape, to grope.
Grapit, groped.
Grat, wept, shed tears.
Great, intimate, familiar.
Gree, to agree; *to bear the gree*, to be decidedly victor.
Gree't, agreed.
Greet, to shed tears, to weep.
Greetin, crying, weeping.
Grippet, catched, seized.
Groat, *to get the whistle of one's groat*, to play a losing game.
Gronsome, loathsomely, grim.
Grozet, a gooseberry.
Grumph, a grunt, to grunt.
Grumphie, a sow.
Grun', the ground.
Grunstane, a grindstone.
Gruntle, the phiz, a grunting noise.
Grunzie, mouth.
Grushie, thick, of thriving growth.

Gude, the Supreme Being; good.
Guid, good.
Guid-morning, good morrow.
Guid-e'en, good evening.
Guidman and guidwife, the master and mistress of the house; *young guidman*, a man newly married.
Gully or *gullie*, a large knife.
Guidfather, *guidmother*, father-in-law and mother-in-law.
Gumlie, muddy.
Gusty, tasteful.

Ha', hall.
Ha'-bible, the great bible that lies in the hall.
Hae, to have.
Haen, had, *the participle*.
Haet, *fient haet*, a petty oath of negation; nothing.
Haffet, the temple, the side of the head.
Hafflins, nearly half, partly.
Hag, a gulf in mosses and moors.
Haggis, a kind of pudding boiled in the stomach of a cow or sheep.
Hain, to spare, to save.
Hain'd, spared.
Hairst, harvest.
Haith, a petty oath.
Haivers, nonsense, speaking without thought.
Hal' or *hald*, an abiding place.
Hale, whole, tight, healthy.
Haly, holy.
Hame, home.
Hallan, a particular partition-wall in a cottage, or more properly, a seat of turf at the outside.
Hallowmas, Hallow-eve, 31st of October.
Hamely, homely, affable.
Han or *haun*, hand.
Hap, an outer garment, mantle, plaid, &c.; to wrap, to cover, to hap.
Happer, a hopper.
Happing, hopping.
Hap, step, an' loup, hop, skip, and leap.
Harkit, hearkened.
Harn, very coarse linen.
Hash, a fellow that neither knows how to dress nor act with propriety.
Hastit, hastened.
Haud, to hold.
Haughs, low-lying rich lands, valleys.
Haurl, to drag, to peel.
Haurlin, peeling.
Haverel, a half-witted person; half-witted.
Havins, good manners, decorum, good sense.
Hawkie, a cow with a white face.
Heapit, heaped.
Healsome, healthful, wholesome.
Hearse, hoarse.
Hear't, hear it.
Heather, heath.
Hech! oh! strange!
Hecht, promised to foretell something that is to be got or given; foretold; the thing foretold; offered.

Heckle, a board, in which are fixed a number of sharp pins, used in dressing hemp, flax, &c.
Heeze, to elevate, to raise.
Helm, the rudder or helm.
Herd, to tend flocks, one who tends flocks.
Herrin, herring.
Herry, to plunder; most properly, to plunder birds' nests.
Herryment, plundering, devastation.
Hersel, herself; also a herd of cattle of any sort.
Het, hot.
Heugh, a crag, a coal-pit.
Hilch, a hobble, to halt.
Hilchin, halting.
Himsel, himself.
Hiney, honey.
Hing, to hang.
Hirple, to walk crazily, to creep.
Hirsle, so many cattle as one person can attend.
Histie, dry, chapt, barren.
Hitcht, a loop, a knot.
Hizzie, huzzy, a young girl.
Hoddin, the motion of a sage countryman while riding on a cart-horse; humble.
Hog-score, a kind of distance line, in curling, drawn across the *rink*.
Hog-shouther, a kind of horse-play, by jostling with the shoulder; to jostle.
Hool, outer skin or case, a nut-shell, pease-swade.
Hoolie, slowly, leisurely.
Hoolie! take leisure, stop.
Hoord, a hoard, to hoard.
Hoordit, hoarded.
Horn, a spoon made of horn.
Hornie, one of the many names of the devil.
Host or *hoast*, to cough.
Hostin, coughing.
Hotch'd, turned topsy-turvy, blended, mixed.
Hosts, coughs.
Houghmagandie, fornication.
Houlet, an owl.
Housie, dimin. of house.
Hove, to heave, to swell.
Hov'd, heaved, swelled.
Howdie, a midwife.
Howe, hollow, a hollow or dell.
Howebackit, sunk in the back (spoken of a horse, &c.)
Houff, a landlady, a house of resort.
Howk, to dig.
Howkit, digged.
Howkin, digging.
Howlet, an owl.
Hoy, to urge.
Hoy't, urged.
Hoyse, a pull upwards.
Hoyte, to amble crazily.
Hughoc, dimin. of hugh.
Hurchron, a hedgehog.
Hurdies, the loins.
Hushion, cushion.

I', in.
Icker, an ear of corn.
Ier-oe, a great grandchild.
Ilk or *ilka*, each, every.
Ill-willie, ill-natured, malicious, niggardly.
Ingine, genius, ingenuity.
Ingle, fire, fire-place.
I'se, I shall or will.
Ither, other, one another.

Jad, jade; also a familiar term among country folks for a giddy young girl.
Jauk, to dally, to trifle.
Jaukin, trifling, dallying.
Jaup, a jerk of water; to jerk as agitated water.
Jaw, coarse raillery; to pour out, to shut, to jerk as water.
Jillet, a jilt; a giddy girl.
Jimp, to jump, slender in the waist, handsome.
Jink, to dodge, to turn a corner; a sudden turning, a corner.
Jinker, that turns quickly; a gay sprightly girl, a wag.
Jinkin, dodging.
Jirk, a jerk.
Jocteleg, a kind of knife.
Jouk, to stoop, to bow the head.
Jow, *to jow*, a verb which includes both the swinging motion and pealing sound of a large bell.
Jundie, to jostle.

Kae, a daw.
Kail, colewort; a kind of broth.
Kail-runt, the stem of the colewort.
Kain, fowls, &c. paid as rent by a farmer.
Kebbuck, a cheese.
Keek, a peep, to peep.
Kelpies, a sort of mischievous spirits, said to haunt fords and ferries at night, especially in storms.
Ken, to know; *kend* or *ken't*, knew.
Kennin, a small matter.
Kenspeckle, well known.
Ket, matted, hairy; a fleece of wool.
Kiaugh, carking, anxiety.
Kilt, to truss up the clothes.
Kimmer, a young girl, a gossip.
Kin, kindred.
Kin', kind.
Kintra-cooser, country stallion.
King's-hood, a certain part of the entrails of an ox, &c.
Kintra, country.
Kirn, the harvest-supper, a churn.
Kirsen, to christen, or baptise.
Kist, chest, a shop-counter.
Kitchen, anything that eats with bread, to serve for soup, gravy, &c.
Kith, kindred.
Kittle, to tickle; ticklish, difficult.
Kittlin, a young cat.
Kittle, to cuddle.
Kittlin, cuddling.
Knaggie, like *knags*, or points of rocks.

Knappin, a hammer, a hammer for breaking stones.
Knowe, a smal' round hillock.
Knurl, dwarf.
Kye, cows.
Kyle, a district in Ayrshire.
Kyles, a narrow sea-passage between two islands, or between an island and the mainland.
Kyte, the belly.
Kythe, to discover, to show one's self.

Laddie, diminutive of lad.
Laggen, the angle between the side and bottom of a wooden dish.
Laigh, low.
Lairing, wading and sinking in snow, mud, &c.
Laith, loth.
Laithfu', bashful, sheepish.
Lallans, Scottish dialect.
Lambie, diminutive of lamb.
Lampit, a kind of shell-fish.
Lan', land, estate.
Lane, lone; *my lane, thy lane*, &c., myself alone, &c.
Lanely, lonely.
Lang, long; *to think lang*, to long, to weary.
Lap, did leap.
Lave, the rest, the remainder, the others.
Laverock, the lark.
Lawin, shot, reckoning, bill.
Lawlan, lowland.
Lea'e, to leave.
Leal, loyal, true, faithful.
Lea-rig, grassy ridge.
Lear, (pronoun, *lare*), learning.
Lee-lang, live-long.
Leesome, pleasant.
Leeze-me, a phrase of congratulatory endearment; I am happy in thee, or proud of thee.
Leister, a three-pronged dart for striking fish.
Leugh, did laugh.
Leuk, a look, to look.
Libbet, gelded.
Lift, sky.
Lightly, sneeringly; to sneer at
Lilt, a ballad, a tune; to sing.
Limmer, a kept mistress, a strumpet.
Limp't, limped, hobbled.
Link, to trip along.
Linkin, tripping.
Linn, a waterfall, precipice.
Lint, flax; *lint i' the bell*, flax in flower.
Lintwhite, a linnet.
Loan or *loanin*, the place of milking.
Loof, the palm of the hand.
Loot, did let.
Looves, *plural of* loaf.
Loun, a fellow, a ragamuffin, a woman of easy virtue.
Loup, jump, leap.
Lowe, a flame.
Lowin, flaming.
Lowrie, abbreviation of Lawrence.

Lowse, to loose.
Lows'd, loosed.
Lug, the ear, a handle.
Lugget, having a handle.
Luggie, a small wooden dish with a handle.
Lum, the chimney.
Lunch, a large piece of cheese, flesh, &c.
Lunt, a column of smoke; to smoke.
Luntin, smoking.
Lyart, of a mixed colour, grey.

Mae, more.
Mair, more.
Maist, most, almost.
Maistly, mostly.
Mak, to make.
Makin, making.
Mailen, farm.
Mallie, Molly.
Mang, among.
Manse, the parsonage-house where the minister lives.
Manteele, a mantle.
Mar's year, the year 1715.
Mashlum, *meslin*, mixed corn.
Mask, to mash, as malt, &c.
Maskin-pat, a tea-pot.
Maukin, a hare.
Maun, must.
Mavis, the thrush.
Maw, to mow.
Mawin, mowing.
Meere, a mare.
Meikle, much.
Melder, corn, or grain of any kind, sent to the mill to be ground.
Mell, to meddle; also a mallet for pounding barley in a stone trough.
Melvie, to soil with meal.
Men', to mend.
Mense, good manners, decorum.
Menseless, ill-bred, rude, impudent.
Messin, a small dog.
Midden, a dunghill.
Midden-hole, a gutter at the bottom of a dunghill.
Mim, prim, affectedly meek.
Min', mind, resemblance.
Mind't, mind it, resolved, intending.
Minnie, mother, dam.
Mirk, *mirkest*, dark, darkest.
Misca', to abuse, to call names.
Misca'd, abused.
Mislear'd, mischievous, unmannerly.
Misteuk, mistook.
Mither, a mother.
Mony or *monie*, many.
Moop, to nibble as a sheep.
Moorlan', of or belonging to moors.
Morn, the next day, to-morrow.
Mou, the mouth.
Moudiwort, a mole.
Mousie, dimin. of mouse.
Muckle or *mickle*, great, big, much.
Musie, dimin. of muse.
Muslin-kail, broth, composed simply of water, shelled barley, and greens.
Mutchkin, an English pint.

Mysel, myself.

Na, no, not, nor.
Nae, no, not any.
Naething or *naithing*, nothing.
Naig, a horse.
Nane, none.
Nappy, ale; to be tipsy.
Negl-ckit, neglected.
Neebor, neighbour.
Neuk, nook.
Niest, next.
Nieve, the fist.
Nievefu', handful.
Niffer, an exchange; to exchange, to barter.
Niger, a negro.
Nine-tailed-cat, a hangman's whip.
Nit, a nut.
Norland, of or belonging to the north.
Notic't, noticed.
Nowte, black cattle.

O', of.
O haith! O faith! an oath.
Ony or *onie*, any.
Or, is often used for *ere*, before.
O't, of it.
Ourie, shivering, drooping.
Oursel or *oursels*, ourselves.
Outlers, cattle not housed.
Owre, over, too.
Owrehip, a way of fetching a blow with the hammer over the arm.

Pack, intimate, familiar; twelve stone of wool.
Painch, paunch.
Paitrick, a partridge.
Pang, to cram.
Parle, speech.
Parritch, oatmeal pudding, a well-known Scotch dish.
Pat, did put; a pot.
Pattle or *pettle*, a plough-staff.
Paughty, proud, haughty.
Pauky or *pawkie*, cunning, sly.
Pay't, paid, beat.
Pech, to fetch the breath short, as in an asthma.
Pechan, the crop, the stomach.
Peelin, peeling.
Pet, a domesticated sheep, &c.
Pettle, to cherish; a plough-staff.
Philibegs, short petticoats worn by the Highlandmen.
Phraise, fair speeches, flattery; to flatter.
Phraisin, flattery.
Pibroch, a Highland war-song adapted to the bagpipe.
Pickle, a small quantity.
Pine, pain, uneasiness.
Pit, to put.
Placad, a public proclamation.
Plack, an old Scotch coin, the third part of a Scotch penny.
Plackless, penniless, without money.
Platie, dimin. of plate.
Plew or *pleugh*, a plough.

Pliskie, a trick.
Poind, to seize on cattle, or take the goods, as the laws of Scotland allow, for rent.
Poortith, poverty.
Pou, to pull.
Pouk, to pluck.
Poussie, a hare, a cat.
Pout, a poult, a chick.
Pou't, did pull.
Pouthery, like powder.
Pow, the head, the skull.
Pownie, a little horse.
Powther or *pouther*, powder.
Preen, pin.
Prent, print.
Prie, to taste.
Prie'd, tasted.
Prief, proof.
Prig, to cheapen, to dispute.
Priggin, cheapening.
Primsie, demure, precise.
Propone, to lay down, to propose
Provoses, provosts.
Pund, pound, pounds.
Pyle, *a pyle o' caff*, a single grain of chaff.

Quat, to quit.
Quak, to quake.
Quey, a cow from one to two years old.

Raible, to rattle nonsense.
Rair, to roar.
Raize, to madden, to inflame.
Ramfeezl'd, fatigued, overspread.
Ram-stam, thoughtless, forward.
Raploch, *properly* a coarse cloth, *but used as an adnoun for* coarse.
Rash, a rush; *rash-buss*, a bush of rushes.
Ratton, a rat.
Raucle, rash, stout, fearless.
Raught, reached.
Raw, a row.
Rax, to stretch.
Ream, cream; to cream.
Reamin, brimful, frothing.
Reave, rove.
Reck, to heed.
Rede, counsel, to counsel.
Red-wat-shod, walking in blood over the shoe-tops.
Red-wud, stark-mad.
Ree, half-drunk, fuddled.
Reek, smoke.
Reekin, smoking.
Reekit, smoked, smoky.
Remead, remedy.
Requite, requited.
Rest, to stand restive.
Restit, stood restive; stunted, withered.
Restricked, restricted.
Rew, repent.
Rief, *reef*, plenty.
Rief randies, sturdy beggars.
Rig, a ridge.
Rin, to run, to melt; *rinnin*, running.

Rink, the course of the stones, a term in curling on ice.
Rip, a handful of unthrashed corn.
Riskit, made a noise like the tearing of roots.
Rockin, spinning on the *rock* or *distaff*.
Rood, stands likewise for the plural *roods*.
Roon, a shred.
Roose, to praise, to commend.
Roun', round, in the circle of neighbourhood.
Roupet, hoarse, as with a cold.
Routhei, plentiful.
Row, to roll, to wrap.
Row't, rolled, wrapped.
Rowte, to low, to bellow.
Rowth or *routh*, plenty.
Rowtin, lowing.
Rozet, rosin.
Rung, a cudgel.
Runkled, wrinkled.
Runt, the stem of colewort or cabbage.
Ruth, a woman's name; the book so called; sorrow.

Sae, so.
Saft, soft.
Sair, to serve; a sore.
Sairly or *sairlie*, sorely.
Sair't, served.
Sark, a shirt.
Sarkit, provided with shirts.
Saugh, the willow.
Saul, soul.
Saumont, salmon.
Saunt, a saint.
Saut, salt.
Saw, to sow.
Sawin, sowing.
Sax, six.
Scaith, to damage, to injure; injury.
Scar, to scar, a scar.
Scaud, to scald.
Scauld, to scold.
Scaur, apt to be scared.
Scawl, a scold.
Scon, a kind of bread.
Sconner, a loathing, to loathe.
Scraich, to scream as a hen partridge
Screed, to tear, a rent.
Scrieve, to glide swiftly along.
Scrievin, gleesomely, swiftly.
Scrimp, to scant.
Scrimpet, did scant, scanty.
See'd, did see.
Seizin, seizing.
Sel, self; *a body's sel*, one's self alone.
Sell't, did sell.
Sen', to send.
Sen't, I, he, or she sent, or did send it.
Servan', servant
Settlin, settling; *to get a settlin*, to be frightened into quietness.
Sets, *sets off*, goes away.
Shaird, a shred, shard.
Shangan, a stick cleft at one end for putting the tail of a dog, &c. into by way of mischief, or to frighten him away.

Shaver, a humorous wag, a barber.
Shaw, to show; a small wood in a hollow place.
Sheen, bright, shining.
Sheep-shank; *to think one's self nae sheep-shank*, to be conceited.
Sherra-moor, Sheriff-moor, the famous battle fought in the rebellion, A.D. 1715.
Sheugh, a ditch, a trench, a sluice.
Shiel, a shed.
Shill, shrill.
Shog, a shock, a push off at one side.
Shool, a shovel.
Shoon, shoes.
Shore, to offer, to threaten.
Shor'd, offered.
Shouther, the shoulder.
Sic, such.
Sicker, sure, steady.
Sidelins, sidelong, slanting.
Siller, silver, money.
Simmer, summer.
Sin, a son.
Sin', since.
Skaith, see *scaith*.
Skellum, a worthless fellow.
Skelp, to strike, to slap; to walk with a smart tripping step; a smart stroke.
Skelpi-limmer, a technical term in female scolding.
Skelpin, *stapping*, walking.
Skiegh or *skeigh*, proud, nice, high-mettled.
Skinklin, a small portion.
Skirl, to shriek, to cry shrilly.
Skirling, shrieking, crying.
Skirl't, shrieked.
Sklent, slant; to run aslant, to deviate from truth.
Sklented, ran, or hit, in an oblique direction.
Skriegh, a scream, to scream.
Slae, sloe.
Slade, did slide.
Slap, a gate, a breach in a fence.
Slaw, slow.
Slee, sly; *sleest*, slyest.
Sleekit, sleek, sly.
Sliddery, slippery.
Slype, to fall over, as a wet furrow from the plough.
Slypet, fell.
Sma', small.
Smeddum, dust, powder, mettle, sense.
Smiddy, a smithy.
Smoor, to smother.
Smoor'd, smothered.
Smoutie, smutty, obscene, ugly.
Smytrie, a numerous collection of small individuals.
Snapper, stumble.
Snash, abuse, Billingsgate.
Snaw, snow, to snow.
Snaw-broo, melted snow
Sneck, latch of a door.
Sned, to lop, to cut off.
Sneeshin, snuff.
Sneeshin-mill, a snuff-box.

Snell, bitter, biting.
Snick-drawing, trick, contriving.
Snick, the latch of a door.
Snool, one whose spirit is broken with oppressive slavery; to submit tamely, to sneak.
Snoove, to go smoothly and constantly, to sneak.
Snowk, to scent or snuff, as a dog, horse, &c.
Snowkit, scented, snuffed.
Sonsie, having sweet engaging looks; lucky, jolly.
Soom, to swim.
Sooth, truth; a petty oath.
Sough, a sigh, a sound dying on the ear.
Souple, flexible, swift.
Souter, a shoemaker.
Sowens, a dish made of oatmeal; the seeds of the oatmeal, soured, &c., boiled up till they make an agreeable pudding.
Sowp, a spoonful, a small quantity of any thing liquid.
Sowth, to try over a tune with a low whistle.
Sowther, solder; to solder, to cement.
Spae, to prophesy, to divine.
Spairge, to dash, to soil, as with mire.
Spaul, a limb.
Spaviet, having the spavin.
Speat or *spate*, a sweeping torrent after rain or thaw.
Speel, to climb.
Spence, the country parlour.
Spier, to ask, to inquire.
Spier't, inquired.
Splatter, a splutter, to splutter.
Spleughan, a tobacco-pouch.
Splore, a frolic, noise, riot.
Sprattle, to scramble.
Spreckled, spotted, speckled.
Spring, a quick air in music, a Scottish reel.
Sprit, a tough-rooted plant, something like rushes.
Sprittie, full of spirits.
Spunk, fire, mettle, wit.
Spunkie, mettlesome, fiery; will-o'-wisp, or ignis fatuus.
Spurtle, a stick used in making oatmeal porridge.
Squatter, to flutter in water, as a wild duck, &c.
Squattle, to sprawl.
Squeel, a scream, a screech; to scream.
Stacher, to stagger.
Staek, a rick of corn, hay, &c.
Staggie, the diminutive of stag.
Stalwart, strong, stout.
Stan', to stand; *stan't*, did stand.
Stane, a stone.
Stank, did stink; a pool of standing water.
Stap, stop.
Stark, stout.
Startle, to run as cattle stung by the gadfly.
Staumrel, a blockhead, half-witted.

Staw, did steal; to surfeit.
Stech, to cram the belly.
Stechin, cramming.
Steek, to shut; a stitch.
Steer, to molest, to stir.
Steeve, firm, compacted.
Stell, a still.
Sten, to rear as a horse.
Sten't, reared.
Stents, tribute, dues of any kind.
Stey, steep; *steyest*, steepest.
Stibble, stubble; *stibble rig*, the reaper in harvest who takes the lead.
Stick an stow, totally, altogether.
Stile, a crutch; to halt, to limp.
Stimpart, the eighth **part of a Win**chester bushel.
Stirk, a cow or bullock a year old.
Stock, a plant or root of colewort, cabbage, &c.
Stooked, made up in shocks, as corn.
Stoor, sounding hollow, strong, and hoarse.
Stot, an ox.
Stoup or *stowp*, a kind of jug or dish with a handle.
Stoure, dust, more particularly dust in motion.
Stown, stolen.
Stownlins, by stealth.
Stoyte, stumble.
Strack, did strike.
Strae, straw; *to die a fair strae death*, to die in bed.
Straik, did strike.
Straikit, stroked.
Strappan, tall and handsome.
Straught, straight.
Streck, stretched, to stretch.
Striddle, to straddle.
Stroan, to spout.
Studdie, an anvil.
Stumpie, diminutive of stump.
Strunt, spirituous liquor of any kind; to walk sturdily.
Stuff, corn or pulse of any kind.
Sturt, trouble; to molest.
Sturtin, frightened.
Sucker, sugar.
Sud, should.
Sugh, the continued rushing noise of wind or water.
Suthren, southern; an old name for the English nation.
Swaird, sward.
Swall'd, swelled.
Swank, stately, jolly.
Swankie or *swanker*, a tight strapping young fellow, or girl.
Swap, an exchange; to barter.
Swarf, swoon.
Swat, did sweat.
Swatch, a sample.
Swats, drink, good ale.
Sweaten, sweating.
Sweer, lazy, averse; *dead-sweer*, extremely averse.
Swoor, swore, did swear.
Swinge, to beat, to whip

Swirl, a curve, an eddying blast, a pool, knot in wood.
Swirlie, knaggy, full of knots.
Swith, to get away.
Swither, to hesitate in choice; an irresolute wavering in choice.
Syne, since, ago, then.

Tackets, a kind of nails for driving into the heels of shoes.
Tae, a toe; *three-tae'd*, having three prongs.
Tairge, target.
Tak, to take; *takin*, taking.
Tamtallan, Tantallon, the name of a castle.
Tangle, a seaweed.
Tap, the top.
Tapetless, heedless, foolish.
Tarrow, to murmur at one's allowance.
Tarrow't, murmured.
Tarry-breeks, a sailor.
Tauld or *tald*, told.
Taupie, a foolish thoughtless young girl.
Tauted or *tautie*, matted together; spoken of hair or wool.
Tawie, that allows itself peaceably to be handled; spoken of a horse, cow, &c.
Teat, a small quantity.
Tedding, spreading after the mower.
Tent, a field-pulpit, heed, caution; take heed.
Tentie, heedful, cautious.
Tentless, heedless.
Teugh, tough.
Thack, thatch; *thack an rape*, clothing necessaries.
Thae, those.
Thairms, small guts, fiddle-strings.
Thankit, thanked.
Theekit, thatched.
Thegither, together.
Themsel, themselves.
Thick, intimate, familiar.
Thieveless, cold, dry, spited; spoken of a person's demeanour.
Thir, these.
Thirl, to thrill.
Thirled, thrilled, vibrated.
Thole, to suffer, to endure.
Thowe, a thaw, to thaw.
Thowless, slack, lazy.
Thrang, throng, a crowd.
Thrapple, throat, windpipe.
Thraw, to sprain, to twist, to contradict.
Thrawin, twisting, &c.
Thrawn, sprained, twisted, contradicted, contradiction.
Threap, to maintain by dint of assertion.
Threshin, thrashing.
Threteen, thirteen.
Thrissle, thistle.
Through, to go on with, to make out.
Throuther, pell-mell, confusedly.
Thud, to make a loud intermittent noise.
Thumpit, thumped.
Thysel, thyself.
Till't to it.

Timmer, timber.
Tine, to lose; *tint*, lost.
Tinkler, a tinker.
Tint the gate, lost the way.
Tippence, twopence.
Tirl, to make a slight noise, to uncover.
Tirlin, uncovering.
Tither, the other.
Tittle, to whisper.
Tittlin, whispering.
Tocher, marriage-portion.
Tod, a fox.
Toddle, to totter like the walk of a child.
Toddlin, tottering.
Toom, empty.
Toop, a ram.
Toun, a hamlet, a farm-house.
Tout, the blast of a horn or trumpet; to blow a horn, &c.
Tow, a rope.
Towmond, a twelvemonth.
Towzie, rough, shaggy.
Toy, a very old fashion of female head-dress.
Toyte, to totter like old age.
Trashtrie, trash.
Trews, trousers.
Trickie, full of tricks.
Trig, spruce, neat.
Trimly, excellently.
Trow, to believe.
Trowth, truth; a petty oath.
Trysted, appointed; *to tryste*, to make an appointment.
Try't, tried.
Tug, raw hide, of which, in old times, plough-traces were frequently made.
Tulzie, a quarrel; to quarrel, to fight.
Twa, two.
Twa-three, a few.
'Twad, it would.
Twal, twelve.
Twin, to part.
Tyke, a dog.

Unco, strange, uncouth, very, very great, prodigious.
Uncos, news.
Unkenn'd, unknown.
Unsicker, unsure, unsteady.
Unskaith'd, undamaged, unhurt.
Unweeting, unwotting, unknowingly.
Upo', upon.
Urchin, a hedgehog.

Vap'rin, vapouring.
Vera, very.
Virl, a ring round a column, &c.

Wa', wall; *wa's*, walls.
Wabster, a weaver.
Wad, would; to bet; a bet, a pledge.
Wadna, would not.
Wae, woe, sorrowful.
Waefu', sorrowful.
Waesucks! or *waes me!* alas! O the pity!
Waft, the cross thread that goes from the shuttle through the web; woof.

Wair, to lay out, to expend.
Wale, choice, to choose.
Wal'd, chose, chosen.
Walie, ample, large, jolly; also an interjection of distress.
Wame, the belly.
Wamefu', a belly-full.
Wanchancie, unlucky
Wanrestfu', restless.
Wark, work.
Wark-lume, a tool to work with.
Warl or *warld*, world.
Warlock, a wizard.
Warly, worldly, eager on amassing wealth.
Warran, a warrant, to warrant.
Warst, worst.
Warstl'd or *warsl'd*, wrestled.
Wastrie, prodigality.
Wat, wet; *I wat, I wot*, I know.
Water-brose, brose made of meal and water simply, without the additions of milk, butter, &c.
Wauble, to swing, to reel.
Waught, draught.
Waukit, thickened, as fullers do cloth.
Waukrife, not apt to sleep.
Waur, worse, to worst.
Waur't, worsted.
Wean or *weanie*, a child.
Wearie or *weary*, feeble; *mony a wearie body*, many a different person.
Weason, weasand.
Wee, little; *wee things*, little ones; *wee bit*, a small matter.
Weel, well; *weelfare*, welfare.
Weet, rain, wetness.
Weird, fate.
We'se, we shall.
Wha, who.
Whaizle, to wheeze.
Whang, a leathern string, a piece of cheese, bread, &c.; to give the strappado.
Whare, where; *whare'er*, wherever.
Wheep, to fly nimbly, to jerk; *penny-wheep*, small beer.
Whase, whose.
Whatreck, nevertheless.
Whid, the motion of a hare running, but not frightened; a lie.
Whidden, running as a hare or cony.
Whigmeleeries, whims, fancies, crotchets.
Whingen, crying, complaining, fretting.
Whirligigums, useless ornaments, trifling appendages.
Whissle, a whistle, to whistle.
Whisht, silence; *to hold one's whist*, to be silent.
Whisk, to sweep, to lash.
Whiskit, lashed.
Whitter, a hearty draught of liquor.
Whun-stane, a whin-stone.
Whyles, whiles, sometimes.
Wi', with.
Wick, to strike a stone in an oblique direction, a term in curling.
Wicker, willow (the smaller sort).
Wiel, a small whirlpool.

Wifie, a diminutive, or endearing term for wife.
Wimple, to meander.
Wimpl't, meandered.
Wimplin, waving, meandered.
Win, to win, to winnow.
Win't, winded, as a bottom of yarn.
Win', wind; *win's*, winds.
Winna, will not.
Winnock, a window.
Winsome, hearty, pleasing, winning, gay.
Wintle, a staggering motion; to stagger, to reel.
Winze, an oath.
Wiss, to wish.
Withoutten, without.
Wizen'd, hide-bound, dried, shrunk.
Wonner, a wonder; a contemptuous appellation.
Wons, dwells.
Woo', wool.
Woo, to court, to make love to.
Woodie, a rope; more properly, one made of withs or willows.
Wooer-bab, the garter knotted below the knee with a couple of loops.
Wordy, worthy.
Worset, worsted.
Wow! an exclamation of pleasure or wonder.

Wrack, to tease, to vex.
Wraith, a spirit, a ghost; an apparition.
Wrang, wrong, to wrong.
Wreeth, a drifted heap of snow.
Wud, mad, distracted.
Wumble, a wimble.
Wyle, beguile.
Wyliecoat, a flannel vest.
Wyte, blame, to blame.

Ye: this pronoun is frequently used for thou.
Yearlings, born in the same year, coevals.
Year, is used for both singular and plural years.
Yell, barren, that gives no milk.
Yerk, to lash, to jerk.
Yerkit, jerked, lashed.
Yestreen, yesternight.
Yett, a gate, such as is usually at the entrance into a farm-yard or field.
Yill, ale.
Yird, earth.
Yokin, yoking, a bout.
Yont, beyond.
Yoursel, yourself.
Yowe, a ewe.
Yule, Christmas.

J. & W. RIDER, Printers, 14, Bartholomew Close, London, E.C.